you might be

BAD
FOR ME

xoxo

YOU MIGHT BE BAD FOR ME

From best selling author Willow Winters, comes a collection dark romance readers have been begging for...

He'll burn the world for me.

He's shown me that truth more than once. His dark gaze holds a secret that filled with turmoil and regret. And his lips on mine, his hands on my body... There's nothing I want more. Even if he is bad for me.

The standalone novels included are:

It's Our Secret, Possessive and A Kiss to Tell.

These three dark romance novels gently pull you into the merciless world most know as All He'll Ever Be. It is dark, seductive and addictive.

Enjoy this bingeable collection.

Sebastian was bad news and Chloe was the sad girl who didn't belong.
Then one night changed everything.

Possessive (a standalone novel)
It was never love with **Daniel Cross** and she never thought it would be. It was only lust from a distance. Unrequited love maybe.
He's a man Addison could never have, for so many reasons.

Merciless Saga
Merciless
Heartless
Breathless
Endless

Ruthless, crime family leader **Carter Cross** should've known Aria would ruin him the moment he saw her. Given to Carter to start a war; he was too eager to accept. But what he didn't know was what Aria would do to him. He didn't know that she would change everything.

All He'll Ever Be (Merciless Series Collection of all 4 novels)

Irresistible Attraction Trilogy
A Single Glance
A Single Kiss
A Single Touch

Bethany is looking for answers and to find them she needs one of the brothers of an infamous crime family, **Jase Cross**.
Even a sizzling love affair won't stop her from getting what she needs.
But Bethany soon comes to realise Jase will be her downfall, and

she's determined to be his just the same.

Irresistible Attraction (A Single Glance Trilogy Collection)

Hard to Love Series
Hard to Love
Desperate to Touch
Tempted to Kiss
Easy to Fall

Eight years ago she ran from him.
Laura should have known he'd come for her. Men like **Seth King**
always get what they want.
Laura knows what Seth wants from her, and she knows it comes
with a steep price.
However it's a risk both of them will take.

Not My Heart to Break (Hard to Love Series Collection)

Tease Me Once
Tease me once... I'll kiss you twice.
Declan Cross' story from the Merciless World.

Spin off of the Merciless World

Love the Way Series
Kiss Me
Hold Me
Love Me

With everything I've been through, and the unfortunate way we
met, the last thing I thought I'd be focused on is the fact that I love
the way you kiss me.

Extended epilogues to the Merciless World Novels
A Kiss To Keep (more of Sebastian and Chloe)
Seductive (more of Daniel and Addison)
Effortless (more of Carter and Aria)
Never to End (more of Seth and Laura)

Sexy, thrilling with a touch of dark Standalone Novels

Broken (Standalone)
Kade is ruthless and cold hearted in the criminal world.
They gave Olivia to him. To break. To do as he'd like.
All because she was in the wrong place at the wrong time. But
there are secrets that change everything. And once he has her, he's
never letting her go.

Forget Me Not (Standalone novel)
She loved a boy a long time ago. He helped her escape and she left
him behind. Regret followed her every day after.
Jay, the boy she used to know, came back, a man. With a grip
strong enough to keep her close and a look in his eyes that warned
her to never dare leave him again.
It's dark and twisted.
But that doesn't make it any less of what it is.
A love story. Our love story.

It's Our Secret (Standalone novel)
It was only a little lie. That's how stories like these get started.
But with every lie Allison tells, **Dean** sees through it.
She didn't know what would happen. But with all the secrets and
lies, she never thought she'd fall for him.

You Are Mine World

You Are My Reason (You Are Mine Duet book 1)

You Are My Hope (You Are Mine Duet book 2)
Mason and Jules emotionally gripping romantic suspense duet.
One look and Jules was tempted; one taste, addicted.
No one is perfect, but that's how it felt to be in Mason's arms.
But will the sins of his past tear them apart?

You Know I Love You
You Know I Need You
Kat says goodbye to the one man she ever loved even though **Evan**
begs her to trust him.
With secrets she couldn't have possibly imagined, Kat is torn
between what's right and what was right for them.

Tell Me You Want Me
A sexy office romance with a brooding hero, **Adrian Bradford**,
who you can't help but fall head over heels for... in and out of the
boardroom.

Small Town Romance

Tequila Rose Book 1
Autumn Night Whiskey Book 2
He tasted like tequila and the fake name I gave him was Rose.
Four years ago, I decided to get over one man, by getting under
another. A single night and nothing more.
Now, with a three-year-old in tow, the man I still dream about is
staring at me from across the street in the town I grew up in. I
don't miss the flash of recognition, or the heat in his gaze.
The chemistry is still there, even after all these years.
I just hope the secrets and regrets don't destroy our second chance
before it's even begun.

A Little Bit Dirty

Contemporary Romance Standalones

Knocking Boots (A Novel)
They were never meant to be together.
Charlie is a bartender with noncommittal tendencies.
Grace is looking for the opposite. Commitment. Marriage. A baby.

Promise Me (A Novel)
She gave him her heart. Back when she thought they'd always be together.
Now **Hunter** is home and he wants Violet back.

Tell Me To Stay (A Novella)
He devoured her, and she did the same to him.
Until it all fell apart and Sophie ran as far away from **Madox** as she could.
After all, the two of them were never meant to be together?

Second Chance (A Novella)
No one knows what happened the night that forced them apart.
No one can ever know.
But the moment **Nathan** locks his light blue eyes on Harlow again, she is ruined.
She never stood a chance.

Burned Promises (A Novella)
Derek made her a promise. And then he broke it. That's what happens with your first love.
But Emma didn't expect for Derek to fall back into her life and for her to fall back into his bed.

Valetti Crime Family Series:
A HOT mafia series to sink your teeth into.

Dirty Dom
Becca came to pay off a debt, but **Dominic Valetti** wanted more.
So he did what he's always done, and took what he wanted.

His Hostage
Elle finds herself in the wrong place at the wrong time. The mafia
doesn't let witnesses simply walk away.
Regret has a name, and it's **Vincent Valetti**.

Rough Touch
Ava is looking for revenge at any cost so long as she can remember
the girl she used to be.
But she doesn't expect **Kane** to show up and show her kindness
that will break her.

Cuffed Kiss
Tommy Valetti is a thug, a mistake, and everything Tonya needs;
the answers to numb the pain of her past.

Bad Boy
Anthony is the hitman for the Valetti familia, and damn good at
what he does. They want men to talk, he makes them talk. They
want men gone, bang - it's done. It's as simple as that.
Until Catherine.

Those Boys Are Trouble (Valetti Crime Family Collection)

To Be Claimed Saga
A hot tempting series of fated love, lust-filled secrets and the
beginnings of an epic war.

Wounded Kiss
Gentle Scars

Collections of shorts and novellas

Don't Let Go
A collection of stories including:
Infatuation
Desires in the Night and Keeping Secrets
Bad Boy Next Door

Kisses and Wishes
A collection of holiday stories including:
One Holiday Wish
Collared for Christmas
Stolen Mistletoe Kisses

All I Want is a Kiss (A Holiday short)
Olivia thought fleeting weekends would be enough and it always
was, until the distance threatened to tear her and **Nicholas** apart
for good.

Highest Bidder Series:

Bought
Sold
Owned
Given
From USA Today best selling authors, Willow Winters and Lauren
Landish, comes a sexy and forbidden series of standalone
romances.

Highest Bidder Collection (All four Highest Bidder Novels)

Bad Boy Standalones, cowritten with Lauren Landish:

Inked

Tempted
Mr. CEO
Three novels featuring sexy powerful heroes.
Three romances that are just as swoon-worthy as they are
tempting.

Simply Irresistible (A Bad Boy Collection)

Forsaken, (A Dark Romance cowritten with B. B. Hamel)
Grace is stolen and gifted to him; Geo a dominating, brutal and a
cold hearted killer.
However, with each gentle touch and act of kindness that lures her
closer to him, Grace is finding it impossible to remember why she
should fight him.

View Willow's entire collection and full reading order at
willowwinterswrites.com/reading-order

Happy reading and best wishes,
Willow xx

IT'S OUR SECRET

AUTHOR'S COPYRIGHT

It's Our Secret was previously published as She Asked for It.

PROLOGUE

Allison

Say you're sorry.
As if the words mean something.

Say you won't do it again.
And pretend like you mean it.

You know you hurt me.
But that's what you wanted.

And you'll do it again ...
And that's fine.
Because it's what I'm after.

There are moments that define you. As I stand outside of the house I've rented two blocks from the university's dorms, one night in particular keeps coming back to me.

That one night, six years ago, is what brought me here.

It's the night that made me who I am.

DEAN

SIX YEARS AGO

"'Suck my dick?'" Principal Talbot asks as she stares at me with a serious expression. "Did you really tell Mrs. Pearson to *suck your dick?*" She's pissed, and that makes her question all the more comical.

Not that I wanted to cause more problems with my teachers, but come on, is it really that serious? They're just words.

She slams the window in her office shut, hushing the sounds of the students walking just outside the room. The bell rang only a minute ago, but everyone's already running from class and eager to get the hell away from Stewart High, a private school on the east side of town. That's the real problem. This place is full of uptight a-holes.

My fingers itch to be out there too, so I can sneak in a smoke before I have to go home. Everyone says it's so damn bad for you, but it's one of the only things keeping me sane. If I have to keep going through the motions and playing along, I'd rather do it stoned.

My lips twitch with the threat of a smirk but I make sure I keep a passive look on my face. I shrug and lean back in my chair as I glance over my shoulder toward her office door. "I said I was sorry."

"Do you think this is funny?" she asks me, her nostrils flaring as she stands up from her chair. She slams both hands down on her desk and leans over it to glare at me. "Do you think this is some sort of game?" With every word, her voice gets louder.

My spine stiffens, and I feel the familiar anger rising. It's not for her. Or Mrs. Pearson, for that matter. It's just that I'm so used to being screamed at. My body's ready for what's next.

I scratch my shoulder blade and try not to show anything other than a relaxed posture. I won't let any of them get to me.

"It's school, Miss Talbot. School is certainly not a game," I answer her with a solemn tone and square my shoulders, folding my hands in my lap although my foot taps anxiously on the floor. Maybe I'm baiting her but then again, maybe I don't give a fuck. I don't want to be here any more than they want me here.

It's only a matter of time until my mother or stepfather comes through the door. I anticipate it swinging open but at the same time, I'm not sure if they'll even bother to show.

"Three schools this year, Dean. You've already been kicked out of two and now you're on your way to being kicked out of your third. Are you looking to set a record?" the principal asks me.

I don't answer her. It's rhetorical anyway.

I'm sure she has a speech prepared and I'd just hate to interrupt her.

I like being quiet. Pops used to say if you're quiet long enough, the words you finally say have more impact. Sometimes I think he only told me that so I'd shut up.

She takes her seat again and angrily clicks on her mouse as she reads through the offenses on her monitor. "Aggravated assault and drug possession, resulting in expulsion from Hamilton."

It was just pot and that fucker, Darrell, knew he was going to get his ass beat. That's what happens when you try to steal from someone. Even if it was only fifty bucks for some weed. He had it coming but then he decided to be a little bitch and rat.

Darrell can go fuck himself, Hamilton too.

She pauses to glance at me for my reaction before scrolling down what must be my school record.

I don't react and just wait for the rest of the list. It doesn't matter. None of it matters and the fact they think it does just shows how little they know.

"Destruction of public property and public indecency," she says and then purses her lips.

The last one makes me crack a smile and I have to hide it with my hand, covering my mouth, but it doesn't fool her.

"I'll ask you again. Do you think this is funny?" She has a pinched brow now.

"I was just showing my ass," I tell her even though I know it's going to tick her off. It doesn't matter what I say right now anyway. The end result will be the same.

"And was it funny when you told Mrs. Pearson to suck your dick?" she asks and then slips off her wire-rimmed glasses, folding them and calmly setting them down on the desk. Her blond hair remains perfectly straight.

I rest my elbow on the chair and prop up my chin to look at her. "I didn't think she'd hear it," I say. That's the truth.

One eyebrow shoots up slightly. "So it'd be okay if she hadn't heard it?"

"Not really," I say, feeling my defenses rise. "But it's not okay to call someone a failure and a waste of space either," I add, and my words are pushed through clenched teeth as I try to remember what else my algebra teacher said. I know she said "failure" at least. I know for a fact she did. All because I couldn't remember a stupid formula. If you can look it up on Google, you shouldn't be required to memorize it.

"This is about your repeated offenses, Dean. There's a clear pattern of behavior you need to address," the principal says, ignoring my statement, but there's a hint of hesitation in her response. She takes her glasses and gently puts them back on.

"You're only a freshman and your options for both public and private schools are dwindling. Do you think acting like this is going to help you deal with your issues?"

My body goes rigid at her last word. The air between us tenses and I see her expression change. It morphs to one of victory; she's finally found something that gets to me.

Principal Talbot shakes her head, the look of disappointment clearly forced. "You have no idea how much you're hurting yourself," she tells me as if she really cares.

I scoff at her and look back to the closed door.

None of them care. They just want me gone so I'm not their problem to deal with anymore.

"I can't have this type of behavior here and quite frankly, this was a favor to your mother." She looks me in the eye as she adds, "Who, I'm sure, is going to be very disappointed in you."

Her voice is stern, but that's not what gets to me. It's not what makes me rip my gaze away from hers and pick at the fuzz on the red upholstery fabric covering the armrests of my chair. It's the fact that my mother won't give a damn. Maybe she'll say she does. Maybe she'll even stand there next to that prick she married while he cusses me out for wasting his time. But does she really care? Not about me, she doesn't. She only cares about the steady supply of Xanax and the allowance he gives her.

"So, what now?" I ask, staring at Principal Talbot.

"We wait for your parents to get here—"

"Parent," I correct her and hold her gaze as she narrows her eyes at me. "I only have one parent." My voice almost catches. I almost let my true feelings show. But thankfully, they're mostly hidden, still buried where they belong.

"Your mother and stepfather then," she says.

I huff and focus on the lint gathered at the edge of the chair cushion, picking up the tiny pieces between my thumb and forefinger.

She'd better get comfortable. The last time this happened they never even bothered to show up.

ALLISON

"*Y*ou know you look like a ho," Sam tells me, cocking her brow like it's a question.

"Shut up," I respond dismissively, although I can't hide my smile or the laughter in my voice. It's a blip of happiness that's quickly dimmed by my rising anxiety.

After applying another coat of caramel apple lip gloss, I step back and try to pull the hem of my jean skirt down. It doesn't budge much.

"Is it too much?" I ask her the legitimate question, feeling an overwhelming need to hide and not go out tonight. My heart races as my gaze sweeps from my short skirt to the clock on the wall of my bedroom. It's one thing to think about sneaking out to meet a boy. It's another to actually do it.

Samantha rolls her eyes as she slips on a white blazer over her short red dress. It's skintight, showing off her curves and barely covering her breasts, but Sam's always flaunting her boobs.

She hit puberty first and it was damn good to her. Not so much to me.

"It's perfect," she answers with a wink.

"My mom would kill me," I mutter as I take one last look in the mirror.

"Well, your mom's not here, so there's nothing to worry about," Sam says like this is no big deal.

"I don't know," I say softly. Sam's my friend. My *best* friend. I've never kept anything from her. She already knows my stomach's acting up and I'm getting cold feet. She devoured half the pizza we ordered with the twenty bucks my mom left us for dinner. Almost all of my half is still untouched in the kitchen. I'm leaving the box on the counter. I know it'll tick my mother off to see I left it out, but I do forget to put it away every time Sam stays over, and I don't want her to think we were up to anything.

Like sneaking out.

My heart flutters with anxiousness, warning me, yet again, that this is stupid. That *I'm* stupid.

Sam's face falls slightly and she leans against my dresser as she asks, "Is it because you think Mike's going to want some?"

I huff out a sarcastic laugh and shake my head no as I stare at the ceiling to avoid her prying eyes. *Yes. Yes it is.*

"I thought you wanted to lose your V-card?" she asks me with genuine interest.

"I do," I answer immediately. "I've been thinking about how I want to do it."

"There's nothing wrong with being a virgin," Sam says, and there's a look on her face I can't quite place. Not even a trace of a smile is there. "If you want to wait, then wait."

"It's not that, I just really like him and what if he's not into it?" I swallow thickly and pick at my nail polish. Dammit. Now it's ruined. "Or what if that's not what he expects?" I say and shrug as if it doesn't matter, even though my tone doesn't match the movement.

"But you want it too, don't you?" she says. Samantha straightens her back and I can see her swallow as she looks directly ahead. "I want to know what it's like," she admits to me.

"I know. I want to know too," I tell her as if that's not obvious. "I just really like him, but if we do it tonight, is Mike going to think that I'm like … easy or something?"

"Oh please," Samantha says and rolls her eyes. "You're thinking about this too much. If you want to do it, then do it. If you don't, then don't." She's already back to facing the mirror and fixing her necklace. "It's literally that easy," she tells me as if she's done this before when I know she hasn't, then turns toward the dresser, the tension from just a moment ago apparently all but forgotten.

"We're finally in high school, Allie," Sam says and I nod my head, although I keep my eyes on my reflection. I wish I looked like I was old enough for high school. It's clear Sam's more mature, but it's the confidence she has that I truly lack.

"Sneaking out is a rite of passage," she tells me. "I get that you like Mike and all, but just have fun tonight."

"But there's so much pressure," I say, feeling anxiety running through me again.

Sam shrugs, putting away her lip gloss and striding toward the bed for her shoes. "So what?" she asks me. "It's just a party and it's going to be a blast, and everything's going to be fine."

"Are you going to drink?" I ask her and then feel like I'm my mother.

She laughs and her eyes go wide as she says, "Duh!" While she ties up the laces to her shoes around her ankles she adds, "Are you even sure his brother got the beer?"

"He said he was getting all sorts of things." Mike's brother is a few years older and technically it's his party. Mike invited me and Sam. I was so excited when he told me, but right now I'm feeling something completely different from excitement.

"And what'd you tell him?" she asks me.

"That I like vodka," I say softly, feeling my cheeks heat with a blush and she laughs again.

"Have you ever even had vodka?" she teases me.

"Shut up," I say then push her shoulder slightly and she just laughs some more, throwing her head back. "It's not like you've had it before either."

"Yeah, yeah. Hey, check this out," Sam says in a singsong voice as she reaches into her tote bag. It's all smooth black leather and I think she stole it from her mom's closet.

"Holy shit," I say under my breath with my eyes focused on the bottle.

"It's like a party present or something," Sam says as I pick up the bottle of red blend wine. "Hostess favor," she says, although she sounds a little uncertain. "Is that what it's called when you bring a gift to a party?" she asks me.

I set the heavy bottle back down in her bag. "I don't know," I tell her, still feeling uneasy.

"Hey, relax," Sam says and then sits in the center of my bed. It creaks under her weight. "As far as your mom knows, we're having a sleepover and tomorrow morning when she comes home, we'll be right here." She pats the bed and then grips my shoulders. "Tonight, we're going to go to Mike's house," she says and tilts her head as she emphasizes my crush's name with her broad, pearly white grin. "And we're going to be chill and cool and he's going to get to know you better."

"Maybe we can use the wine to play spin the bottle?" I say as the idea of sitting in Mike's basement and flirting makes me feel giddier than anything else has tonight.

Her smile widens and her eyes brighten. "Fucking fantastic idea," she squeals. "This is why I love you," she adds and then jumps off the bed.

"It's not because we've been friends forever?" I joke back with her.

"Best friends for life!" she answers and then twirls her long, dark brown hair around her finger. "Seriously, tonight is going to be amazing," she says with so much excitement and happiness, it's contagious.

"Can I ask you something?" I blurt out, cutting through the happiness yet again.

"Anything," Sam says instantly, looking right at me and giving me her full attention.

"Does it make me a whore if I want to have sex?" I say. "Like, even if I don't really want to be with Mike, but I just want to know what it's like?"

"Pretty sure that's normal, babe," she says with a smile. "If not, I'm fucked."

DEAN

$\mathcal{M}$y uncle's truck rumbles to a stop in front of my stepfather's house. It's the corner lot on the street, a two-story colonial with blue shutters and a porch swing right out front.

It only took my dad's death for my mother to have the house of her dreams. She even got her white picket fence.

"I don't see the point," I say to my uncle as I stare at the front door and then the driveway. "Both their cars are here." I turn to look at Uncle Rob as I speak. "If they don't want me, what's the point of even going in there?"

"You need to face the music, kid." He says it like that's why I don't want to go in there. My eyes narrow and I feel my forehead pinch.

"You don't get it. It's not just about today or yesterday. It's every day. Every single day I have to live in a house where I'm hated."

"Knock it off, Dean," my uncle says as though what I'm saying has no weight to it.

It's quiet for a long time, but my heart's pounding and all I can hear is the blood rushing in my ears. I want to get it all out. Uncle

Rob's the only one who listens to me. He's the only one who gives a shit.

"Ever since Dad died," I say, and it hurts to say the words out loud as I continue, "she doesn't want me anymore."

"That's not true—" he starts to say but I raise my voice and cut him off.

"It is true!" My eyes sting and I hate it. I hate everything. I hate her the most.

"You're just angry," Uncle Rob says although he twists his hands on the leather steering wheel and looks out the window like he's judging my words. "Why can't you just be like Jack's kid?" he asks me. Jack is his friend who has two sons; one's a kid my age. "Go out and have fun. Sneak a beer, kiss a girl. Why do you have to run your mouth and make a scene?"

"It's easy for you to say," I mumble under my breath. I was going to go out with *Jack's kid* to a party tonight. I was actually looking forward to meeting Mike and a few of the guys he knows. It's been lonely since Dad died. I'm desperate enough to admit that and I finally said yeah, I'd go out. No fucking way that's happening now.

Maybe my uncle's right and that's where I should be tonight. Instead this is what I've got to look forward to.

"She didn't even cry at his funeral." My words come out hollow, matching how my chest feels. "She was already with *him*." I look him in the eye. "He slept over when Dad was in the hospital."

Uncle Rob is my mother's brother. I know he'd never say a bad word about her, but he can't deny the truth. The minute my dad got sick, my mother started counting how much she'd get from the insurance policy. Richard came next. Just like that, she moved on and didn't look back. Leaving me behind and alone when my dad died. She wasn't there with me in the hospital room and she sure as hell wasn't there after. I can't forgive her.

Uncle Rob looks uncomfortable as he runs his hand through his thinning hair and sighs.

"Why can't I just come live with you?" I practically beg him. I would give anything to get away from them. I would do anything. "You at least cared that Dad died."

"It's not that she didn't care." He doesn't say anything after that. I wait for more. For some sort of explanation that would make any of this all right, but nothing comes.

"She was happy he was going to die. All they did was fight." Although it hurts to admit the truth, there's relief in saying it out loud. Even more so because Uncle Rob doesn't deny it.

"Look, Dean, different people cope with things differently. It's hard when someone's dying and you have to handle everything."

"It was so hard that she went on smiling every day," I tell him. I don't want pretty little lies. I'm tired of living this fake-ass life my mother created. "Why can't I just live with you?" I ask him again. He's all I have. If not him, then I have no one.

"You just can't," he says like that's final and my blood chills. A sense of unease rocks through me, followed by hopelessness.

"All right then," I say and open the door to the truck, sick of arguing over pointless shit.

"It's life, kid," Uncle Rob calls after me.

"Life can go fuck itself," I tell him as I get out, making the truck rock forward and then I slam the shiny red door shut.

A sickness churns in my stomach with each step I take closer to the house.

Day in and day out. I can't do this anymore. I can't be reminded every day of how easily someone else replaced Pops. That asshole my mother cheated on my dad with expects me to listen to him? No fucking way.

I push the door open and then slam it shut from pure adrenaline, but I regret it the second the loud bang reverberates through the house.

Do I regret what I said in school? Yeah, I do. I say stupid shit, I pick fights. Maybe I am angry. Maybe I'm filled with hate.

But when I get in here, it changes.

19

I'm just fucking sad. I'm sad that this is my life.

The kitchen is in the center of the house and my mother's right there on a barstool, a glass of wine in her hand and the half-empty bottle on the granite countertop.

"Mom," is all I say to greet her then slip my bookbag off my shoulder, leaving it by the door. I grit my teeth when she looks up at me with daggers. She's quick to change her expression. Like she wants to hide how she really feels about me. She doesn't have to, though. I know I ruined her chance at a perfect life with Richard. The son who was an accident, forcing her to marry my father. If only I'd died with him. Then we'd all be happier.

"I can't believe you," my mother says with tears in her eyes. Or maybe they're just glossy because she's drunk. Her lips look even thinner with her mouth like that, set in a straight line.

I don't say anything; I can hear Rick getting up from the recliner in the living room.

"There you are," he says as if I'm at fault for not being here on time.

"They wouldn't let me leave till someone picked me up," I answer him with my words drenched in spite, looking him square in the eye as he storms over to me. My body tenses with the need to run or at least hold up my arms in defense.

"Is that what you got to say?" he yells at me. Rick's a former marine and he acts like it. Only angrier and usually drunk. That's one thing he and my mom have in common. His face turns red as he shouts at the top of his lungs.

The backhand comes quick, but I'm expecting it. The pain rips through my jaw, sending me backward as I hit the front door.

"You want to act like a little punk, I'll treat you like one," he spits at me. I can vaguely hear my mother screaming in between Richard's threats and the ringing in my ears.

I expected the first blow but as I stand up, I don't expect the next.

Or the one after that.

I really should have. Richard doesn't stop until I'm crying. It's not like I'm big enough to fight him, so I don't know why I try to hold back the tears. I should've just come in here looking how I feel, defeated and hopeless. Maybe then it wouldn't have lasted so long.

* * *

METAL IS ALL I can taste when I wake up. My lips are bruised and swollen. My body's stiff from sleeping in a weird position since it hurt my face to lay on my side.

The side of my face still stings and I'm sure it looks like shit too.

I'm not going to school. Not looking like this. It would make Richard all too happy to know I had to go out with the proof that he beat the shit out of me so easily seen.

Even better for him because those asshole teachers think I deserve it. Everyone does. I'm just the piece of shit kid from her first marriage who's acting out and needs his ass beat.

That's what the last principal told my mom. That I needed my ass beat.

Maybe I do. I don't need to be sneaking out and going to parties. I just need my ass beat day in and day out until I don't feel this way anymore.

I swallow thickly and sit up in bed to crack my neck.

There's only a dresser and my bed in this room. I don't have much since we moved after Dad died. Most of my stuff I left behind. My gaze moves toward the closet, where I have two duffle bags.

My uncle doesn't want me, but that doesn't mean I can't leave. I can go somewhere. I have a little bit of cash saved up from working with Uncle Rob this past summer. I can buy a cheap car and live in it.

I might be kicked out of school; I don't know, and I don't care. I can still get a job with Nick up the street, doing landscaping. He'd hire me. He knew my dad and I've met him a few times.

I force myself off the bed quietly. The only question on my mind is whether or not I should even bother telling my mother goodbye. A sharp pain shoots from my jaw to the back of my skull, radiating there when I bend down to the bottom dresser drawer to pack up my jeans.

I don't think she'd give a fuck either way. But maybe it'd be easier for her if I don't tell her. Then she won't have to pretend like she feels a certain way. She can just be happy with Rick and her new life.

I'm not a piece of shit like he calls me. I'm not a waste of life.

I close my eyes and refuse to cry. I'll never cry because of what they think of me.

They can both go fuck themselves.

ALLISON

*M*y heart pounds in my chest. It's way too loud and I can't hear anything else for a moment, but as the front door to Mike's place opens wide, the music overwhelms me. With each beat, it thumps and stirs the anxiety in my stomach.

I'm really doing it.

"I'm here for Mike," I say abruptly the second the guy opens his mouth. He's tall, so tall I have to crane my neck. I don't recognize him. He's a skinny guy with long hair, and pimples line his jaw. His face is red too. It takes me a moment to realize the color in his cheeks is from drinking.

"We brought booze," Sam says, shoving the bottle of wine into the guy's chest and then walks right in like she belongs here, brushing past his shoulder.

The guy just laughs, a half-drunken sound, holding out the bottle and pointing to the back room with it. He smells like skunk and whiskey. It's what Sam's mom's boyfriend smells like all the time.

I follow Sam's lead and avoid looking around the house too obviously. But I chance a peek here and there as I move inside and slip off my coat. Every time I look around, I see someone kissing or rubbing someone else. I would feel underdressed without the protection of my jacket, but given what the other girls here are wearing, I think I fit right in. *Thank God.*

There's a lot of laughter coming from the kitchen and I'm happy Sam's steering me in that direction. Where there are people other than couples trying to dry hump in the dark corners of the living room.

I'm still looking around and taking in the place when Sam shrieks, "Mike!"

She yells over the music and makes a show of running over and hugging him. One heel kicks up in the air as she pulls Mike closer, wrapping her arm around his neck and then pointing at me. Her enthusiasm always makes me laugh. "Look what I brought you," she says playfully while I stand there tucking a stray blond lock behind my ear. The nerves settle some though when Mike smiles, and Sam lets go of him.

"Hey," I say, and it doesn't quite come out loud enough over the music, but that doesn't stop Mike from coming closer and practically yelling in my face, "I'm so glad you came."

He leans in and all I smell is beer. Probably some cheap beer that he spilled on his shirt hours ago.

"You want something to drink?" Mike asks me as he takes a half step forward, his sneaker landing on my foot. I try to play it off, but he sees me wince and backs away.

"Oh shit," he says with his forehead pinched. "You okay?" he asks and I wave him off. With my heart hammering, all the anxiousness comes right back.

It hurt like hell but with all the nerves running through me, I don't care. "I'm fine," I tell him and again, I should have spoken louder.

"Yo, Mike," the guy who answered the door yells out across the countertop and beckons Mike over. It might be his older brother; I can see a similarity with their noses beyond them both being red.

"Here," Sam says loudly, stepping into the space between the two of us and I'm grateful for her as always. She pushes a red Solo cup into my chest and I take it with both of my hands like it'll save me.

"Be right back," Mike says and I half think he slurred the last word, but the music's so loud, I could be wrong.

"We've got to catch up," Sam says as she takes a sip and then scrunches her nose and makes a god-awful face. "This tastes like piss," she says.

"Isn't it supposed to?" I ask her genuinely, but she laughs like it's a joke.

"Okay, so, let's do a round, scope the place out and find a spot to get comfy." She lays out the plan and I nod my head, eager to do whatever she thinks is best. We decided tonight would be chill. If we're feeling it, good. If not ... we'll figure something out.

"What about Mike?" I ask her, and she gives me this look. It's a look that says I'm being stupid.

"Girl, he wants you. He'll find you, you don't have to worry about a thing." She talks as she takes my hand and leads me away from the crowded kitchen, back through the dark living room with the grinding couples having makeout sessions. We pass a set of speakers sitting on the floor and it's no wonder the bass is pounding through me. They're gigantic.

We don't stop, though. Sam leads me straight through another room that's mostly empty apart from a couple of guys smoking, then down the stairs to the basement. I follow her gratefully. Sam knows what she's doing. Or at least she looks like she does.

The door's cracked open and the lights are on. The music fades and in its place, a horde of loud and drunk voices ricochet up the skinny staircase.

"Maybe I should tell Mike we're down here?" I ask Sam as we sit on an empty sofa in the back corner of the large basement. The room itself isn't finished. It's just cinder blocks. But there's a pool table and a dartboard, plus a bar with a ton of liquor bottles lining it. Right across from the sofa is a ping-pong table with cups arranged on it.

"Babe, quit stressing," Sam tells me, draining her cup and getting up to pull her dress down. She's confident as she walks to the table and puts her cup in line with the rest. "He's going to come looking for you. Make him chase you," she says and I nod my head, although the doubt is still there. I can still barely breathe.

"I've never given you bad advice, have I?" she asks me and I know she hasn't, but she's not exactly the person I'm looking to take relationship advice from. Sam says she doesn't want a boyfriend. She just wants to kiss and that's it. But I think she's in denial. I think she lies to herself because of the shit her mom's gone through. Everyone wants to be loved. Whether they admit it to themselves or not.

That being said, she gets to kiss any boy she wants. So maybe she is right. Maybe I should make him chase me.

It only takes a couple of minutes of whispering about which nearby guy Sam likes most, before the door to the basement opens.

I'd be jealous of the attention she's getting if I didn't have my sights set on Mike. I smile into my cup as he comes down the stairs, spotting me on the couch and grinning.

"This is my cousin," Mike says while the guy behind him taps his shoulder and yells out, "We need more beer, I'll be right back." I don't pay him any attention as I scoot to my right, squishing Sam and making a spot on the sofa for Mike to my left.

He takes it and leans in close, wrapping his arm around my shoulders and making me blush. "So, what do you guys want to do?" he asks. His voice is still loud as hell like he hasn't realized it's quieter down here.

Sam laughs and shrugs. "You want to play spin the bottle?" she says like it's a joke but I know damn well she's being serious.

"You want to?" Mike asks and looks around as if there'd be a bottle magically waiting on the coffee table. Guess we dropped the ball there.

"Why the hell not?" is Sam's answer.

"We brought a bottle to play with." I have to roll my eyes before sheepishly adding, "You know, or to drink or whatever." I hide my embarrassment by taking another sip.

"Where is it?"

"I gave it to the guy who opened the door," Sam cuts in with her hands up in an apology. "My bad," she says with a giant grin on her face. "I freaked and just handed it over." She laughs into her cup again and chugs it, emptying it and biting the rim.

"Solo cups don't work quite as well," I joke but I'm not sure Mike heard.

"So, you want to do stuff?" Mike asks and I glance at Sam, who humorlessly raises her brow.

"Getting right to it, aren't you?" she asks him flippantly, and I smack her.

"Like what kind of stuff?" I say. I know what he means. And yes, I do. I've watched porn before. A few times with Sam, although it got a little weird, so we quickly turned that shit off. It's how she knows I like things a little different, though. "I could do stuff," I say casually as my body heats.

"Drinks!" Mike's cousin interrupts us, stomping down the stairs holding two red Solo cups and spilling beer all over the floor as he makes his way over. Sam jumps back, laughing and raising her arms in surprise and Mike's cousin shoves one of the cups into her open hand.

"Drinks," Mike bellows and clinks the plastic cups which only results in more beer being spilled and our conversation getting lost.

"Drinks," Sam mocks them, widening her eyes and imitating their excitement, but she's smiling the entire time and both the guys laugh, clinking their plastic cups with hers.

I take another sip and much to my dismay, it still tastes like piss.

* * *

HOURS PASS, I think. My sense of time is fuzzy.

Everything tilts when I lean against Mike. It's quieter too. Only for a moment and then it's all louder. Is this what being drunk is like?

"I just need to lie down for a sec," Sam says, gripping my arm and before I can say anything, she's already headed up the stairs.

"You want me to come with you?" I call up after her but the music is so loud that she doesn't hear me. The bass blasts through the house and makes my chest feel tight then hollow with each beat as I follow her.

"Need help?" I think I hear Mike say but when I look back, he's talking to one of the guys who's now playing beer pong.

I feel dizzy and it's all so much. "Water," I say softly and force myself to go back to the kitchen. Sam needs water. Hell, I need water too.

The smell of beer and pot hits me the second I round the corner.

Holy shit. I want to throw up.

Sam keeps moving, climbing the stairs to the second floor with both of her hands over her ears. "I'm coming, Sam," I mumble as I run to the kitchen faucet and fill two cups. One for me and one for her.

Exhaustion and a thick cloudy haze greet me as I turn the corner to go up the stairs. It takes me a moment; while I stand there, a few guys pass by me and go upstairs. Mike's cousin is one of them. The other two wait in line for the bathroom.

I watch as Mike's cousin goes into a bedroom. The door was open, but he closes it behind him.

"Hey, you going up there?" A guy's voice startles me just as I start to call out Sam's name and I swear my heart almost leaps out of my chest. My ass hits the railing as I whip around to him and spill both cups.

"Me?" I say, fear clearly evident.

"You okay?" he asks me again with a broad smile like this is funny.

But it isn't. The cups fall from my hands like I'm watching in slow motion.

"Whoa," the guy says. Some part of me dimly notices he's tall as he catches me when I tip forward. I know that I'm falling. I'm aware of it, but then it all goes black. I can hear him for a moment, asking if I'm all right and calling for help.

I guess that makes it okay, so I give in to sleep. Help is coming.

IN ONE DAY

In one day, a life can change. Or more than one.
Sometimes it's a single moment that alters everything in existence.
Sometimes it's the chain reaction of falling dominoes, lined up in pretty
little rows and designed so that each one will cause more and more pain
as it topples.
In a single day, everything changed, and there's no way to go back.

ALLISON

SIX YEARS LATER

From the moment I laid eyes on Dean, I knew he'd be trouble.

I didn't anticipate *this*, though.

I didn't expect to let it get this far.

I didn't want him to be a casualty of my obsession.

Someone to my right clears their throat and I look down the row of people. A woman looks back at me; she's older with graying hair, wearing a thick sweater with a cowl neck that's practically swallowing the frail woman. She holds my gaze, narrowing her eyes and pressing her lips together into a flat line.

I know what she's thinking. What they're all thinking, and it makes me want to throw up.

She asked for it.

They have no idea.

No one does.

Not even Dean, as he awaits his fate.

They can judge me because I deserve it.

If I could go back, I would.

I close my eyes and try to hold back the tears, the pain. Every moment that led us here is another flaw in my armor. Picking away at my defenses as the events flash before my eyes.

When I open them, through the veil of tears scattered on my lashes, I see Dean looking back at me.

I'm so fucking selfish, and that's what pushed me over the edge.

I knew Dean would be trouble. A crimp in my plans perhaps, but I didn't think I'd fall in love.

I justified using him. I craved his touch so much that I pulled him into my web.

"I'm sorry," I mouth and Dean's expression slips.

They're right when they say I asked for it.

I didn't just ask for it, though.

No, no.

I fucking prayed for it.

* * *

Two months earlier

FOURTEEN BOXES.

Packing and unpacking fourteen boxes takes a toll on the body. My shoulders are sore; my core feels like it's on fire.

But I'm here.

I actually went through with it and applied to this school, got in, rented a house and now I'm here.

I hear them first as I round the building that houses all the equipment for the fields. The bleachers come into sight first, followed by the men I came to see.

My hips sway a little more than before, my lips tilting up into a half smile even though my heart races. I'm so much different from the girl I was back then. Unrecognizable.

I glance at each one, taking them in as sweat glistens on their backs and chests. Most of the rugby players only have on a pair of gym shorts, ranging from blue to black to red. Their laughter drifts across the field as they huddle around the small area where all their gear is laid out.

Some of the guys play on the field of perfectly trimmed grass. Seven of them, to be exact. The field is nestled between two old brick buildings that can house hundreds of students, if not more.

Is this what college life feels like? The smell of a late summer breeze paired with jittery nerves clamber up my throat. Well, maybe the second part is just because it's me and I'm here, scoping out the intramural rugby team for the university.

Most of these guys don't take it seriously. Which is why there's no one here, no scouts or fans. A couple students sit in the grass off to the right of the bleachers, but they aren't paying attention. This rugby team isn't for show. It's just a reason to get out some aggression; judging by each of the guys' history, there's a lot of aggression here.

I knew they'd be here, practicing and putting all their goods on display.

A small hum slips from me into the late August heat as I spear my hand through my hair and let the wind push it out of my face and off my shoulders.

It doesn't take long for one of them to notice me walking a little closer than I should.

The field backs up to woods behind the buildings and the only reason I'd be walking out here on this side of the field is for them. And now they know it.

The guy closest to me tilts up his chin as he asks, "What's going on?"

The rest of them quiet down when I walk up to the bleachers and take a seat, letting my bag fall into the grass as I rest against the metal. I'm in jeans, so I spread my legs just a bit as I lean forward, my body language suggestive. Yeah, nothing like the girl I used to be.

"I just came to see the game," I say sweetly and let my eyes drift from the tall blond with broad shoulders, to the darker brunette with a full sleeve tattoo down his left arm.

"No game today, sweetheart," a man at the far end of the group tells me, but I don't turn to look that way.

"There's always a game," I say. "I'm Allison," I add, flirtation evident in my voice.

"Well, hello," the closest guy—the dark blond, or dirty blond as I like to call it—says and strides closer to me, taking a seat to my left but far enough away that I'm still comfortable. "I'm Daniel," he tells me.

"I know," I say and then bite down on my lower lip. "Daniel, the one with the Irish temper," I add, quoting his bio from the website for the frat that sponsors the team. I look at the remaining six men on the field. Daniel isn't a student, just a guy listed as "occasional manager" on the website. I imagine it's an inside joke. It took hours to look them all up and Daniel definitely caught my eye. I'm not into blonds normally, but I certainly noticed him.

"James has the beard," I say to the man with the neatly trimmed facial hair and then add, "Don't shave it or I might forget who you are." That gets a laugh from them. He's classically handsome, but only slightly above average looking.

I finally take a look at the guys on the fringe. I expect to feel a certain way, but what's a complete surprise is how my gaze is caught, trapped by a beast of a man. His eyes pierce through me, pinning me in place. It takes a moment for me to even register any other defining feature. I can practically feel his sharp jawline covered in stubble that would be rough to the touch. His hair is nearly black and just long enough to grip at the top, but shorter on the sides.

His shoulders ... broad enough to trap me under him. *Thud.* One beat is all my heart gives me. Then the poor thing plays dead.

"I don't know yours," I say, feeling my pulse pump a little harder. My body heats with the way he looks at me. Like he's

35

looking me up and down, trying to undress me with that sharp hazel gaze of his.

There's something different about him. The air around him is tense. And I'm grateful for the distraction.

"Dean," he tells me and his expression stays hard. I'd almost say it's cold but that's so wrong. Plenty of heat is there, a heat of defiance. And something else, something dangerous.

He's the type of man who gives you chills even as he heats up everything else.

The kind of man you know you're supposed to stay away from because he'll ruin you without thinking twice ... The kind my dreams are made of.

A small smirk lifts up Dean's lips as if he can read my mind. As if the dirty thoughts in my head are what his dreams are made of too.

"We're just finishing up a workout," Daniel says and I nod as he adds, "We're getting ready to party." His voice is deep, but Dean's is deeper.

"Damn, I was really looking forward to your practice," I answer him with a pout, finally ripping my eyes away from Dean. Back to the entire point of being here.

"You want to come?" Daniel asks, inviting me to whatever party they're having, and I shake my head before peeking at Dean. He's still watching me with that hunger in his eyes. "Come on, I know you do," he teases and the playfulness in his voice makes me smile. He's cute in a charming way.

"Not today," I say, my voice coming out a little smaller than I'd like.

"Suit yourself," Daniel says and stands up, walking to where he's laid his bag on the ground. "If you change your mind, come on down to Broom Street." He smiles with a warmth that's inviting. "It's going to be fun," he adds.

A few guys let out a rough laugh, deep and low. "You'll know which house is us," one of them says.

I keep finding my gaze drifting toward Dean's and each time I do, his intense stare is on me. I didn't come here for him. A little flirtation here and there is all I was aiming for, but the way he looks at me is doing something to me that I can't deny.

He's bad for me. But I can't help what I want.

DEAN

I like how she's acting like she doesn't recognize me. The way she twirls the pen in her brunette curls, looking up at the professor then slipping the tip of that pen between her teeth.

Fucking tease.

Her name's Allison. I love the way it slips off my tongue.

I didn't look at her twice the first day we sat in this room. But I noticed when we crossed paths in the building next door, the one with the cafeteria. And I noticed when she started walking away from campus and toward the houses down Connell Street, only two blocks down from Broom Street.

The tiny glances and the subtle way she shifts her thighs each time she sees me … that got my attention even more.

Maybe it's the curve of her waist or the way her lips are almost always just slightly parted. But something drew me to her and now the idea of her on her knees in front of me as her lips open wider to take the head of my dick is all I can think about.

And then she can treat me to the same sucking she's doing to that pen right now.

Maybe she's got my attention because Chem 201 is boring as hell.

Or maybe it's because Little Miss Allison looks as though she'd be down for a dirty fuck, but she's avoiding me at all costs.

Like right now. She's got to know I want her. Maybe she likes the chase.

All she's doing is skimming that pen across her bottom lip, making my dick twitch with need.

"And you?" the professor asks, his voice directed this way. I'm one row behind and two seats to the left of her.

"I'm sorry?" she questions Professor Grant, caught off guard. My lips curl up into a smile, although I hide it behind my fist as I brace my elbow against the desk. Yeah, I know I'm getting to this broad. Whether she wants to let on that I am or not.

"What's the constitution of the nucleus of an atom?" he repeats his question, and my brow raises slightly. We're only five days into the semester and this class meets Mondays, Wednesdays, and Fridays. Week one is too fucking early for this shit.

"Electrons and neutrons," she answers hesitantly.

"Wrong," the professor's voice rings out and Allison purses her lips. The pen in her hand taps on the textbook in front of her as the class know-it-all pipes up, not even waiting to be called on.

The answer is protons and neutrons, not that I give a shit. My major's undecided for now but there's zero chance of me going into chemistry for a career.

I lean over, feeling the metal bar separating our rows pushing into my ribs.

"Maybe you should pay attention." I whisper my first words to Allison, and she finally looks at me.

She gives me a side-eye paired with an asymmetric grin and I give her a charming smile back before relaxing into my seat.

After the professor turns his back to us, ranting about something he's scribbled on the chalkboard, she looks over her shoulder toward me.

Her teeth sink into her bottom lip and she blushes, peeking at me and then once again pretending to pay attention to him and not me.

That only makes me want her more. I know she's thinking about me. I want to know exactly what she's daydreaming about. That way I can make it come true.

I know she didn't recognize me yesterday on the field, but I recognized her. She's fucking gorgeous, assertive. Doesn't know what's in an atom, though. I smirk and act like I give a shit about what's on the board when Professor Grant turns around and looks right at me. I even nod for his benefit.

The desk groans as I readjust in my seat and get another glance from Allison when the lecture continues and his voice drones on.

Not a lot of women approach a group of men with confidence. There's a shyness but also a sense of playfulness in this one that I like. It's something I want to explore and judging by the way she acted yesterday, compared to how she's been in class the last two times, quiet and reserved, I'm guessing she'd like to explore some shit too.

The large clock above the door ticks by so damn slowly as I wait for class to end. *Tick, tick, tick.* Every time Allison puts that pen into her mouth, my dick gets a little harder. She lets it roll down her bottom lip and she'd be lying if she said she wasn't doing it on purpose.

By the time two o'clock hits, I'm hard as fucking steel.

I stay in my seat as everyone around me packs up, my eyes still on my prey.

As she closes her book, she deliberately avoids my gaze again.

"I thought you'd be shy," I say as the person to my right leaves, blocking my view of Allison for only a fraction of a second. She sets the heavy textbook into her backpack and zips it up, all the while looking at me with an expression that tells me she doesn't know how to answer.

"When I saw you the last two classes," I tell her and then close my book, "you seemed shy and not at all like you were yesterday."

"Is that right?" she asks, tucking her hair behind her ear and setting her bag back down on the floor. She turns in her seat to face me and says, "I didn't know we had a class together. I guess it was just nerves."

"You didn't look too nervous yesterday."

"Why do you say that?" she asks me, but there's a spark of mischievousness in her eyes. It makes my smile widen.

"It seemed like you wanted something particular."

"And what would that be?" she says. I notice how her chest rises and falls with her shallow breathing.

I lean forward and lower my voice. "Can I tell you something?"

"What?" Her lips stay parted just slightly and she stares at me with curiosity.

"I called dibs when you left," I tell her. It's not true. After she left, her hips swaying and a small bit of that shyness returning when she saw me watching her fine ass walk away, all that the guys were talking about was how much ass they're going to get in college.

Her ass, any ass. It doesn't matter to them. But this one I'd noticed before. This one is obviously in need. So when she left the field, the vision of her soft lips stayed in my mind.

"Did you really call dibs?" she asks me and then shakes her head like I'm ridiculous.

They don't get *this* ass. Not until I get my fill first.

"Yeah," I tell her and look around the now empty room. "Where's your next class?"

"I don't have anything else after this," she says.

"Me neither," I tell her and she throws her head back, laughing.

"You're such a liar," she says, calling me out with a voice full of humor. Her genuine smile grows and a beautiful shade of pink colors her cheeks. "You want to get into my pants badly enough that you'd miss your next class?"

My adrenaline spikes. "How'd you know?" I ask her.

"Your schedule's right there," she says and rolls her eyes. She grabs the paper off my desk and verifies that she's right before tossing it back to me.

"It's right next door but you're going to be late if you wait any longer," she says confidently and stands up, swinging her backpack over one shoulder.

"It can wait if you want to get out of here," I offer her.

"You're shameless," she says and then she grips the strap of her bookbag and asks me softly, "You think I'm that easy?"

"I think you want it. You might be afraid to get it, though."

Her expression slips just slightly, so quickly I almost don't see it and I second-guess my approach. "I think you know what you want." I speak clearly and wait for her light green eyes to reach mine. "I fucking love that."

"Oh yeah?" she says, her confidence returning and the air between us heating again. The tension between us thickens as I stand up, closing the small space that separates us. She stays still, letting me get close enough to touch her. I don't, though. I can make her want the chase too.

"Yeah, and I know what I want too," I tell her and lean forward, so fucking close, but she turns her shoulder to me, brushing against my chest and arm as she walks away, leaving my heart beating hard.

"Well right now, I want to go home, Dean," she says over her shoulder.

"Love the way you say my name too," I tell her and she pauses in the doorway. "I can make it sound even better when you scream it."

She lets her head fall back with a feminine peal of laughter. "You really are shameless."

"We have a game tonight," I say quickly before she can leave. It grabs her attention and she looks back at me. "On the field. Nothing big, but you should come."

"You're inviting me to your game?" she asks me with a hint of a smile. It makes her happy, I can tell.

"I am and I'm going to win you over," I say, picking up my bag and following her out of the room. "I know you want me," I tell her, cocky as fuck.

"We'll see," she says softly, letting her gaze roam down my chest to my cock, then back up to my eyes. "Not today, though. Get to class," she commands, and her voice hardens.

"Bossy," I tease her as she turns left. I debate following her. But now's not the time. She's just the right mix of shy and curious, but also confident and sexy as hell. I watch her disappear before turning right to go to my next class. "All right, Allie Cat, round one goes to you," I say lowly.

My dick's still hard and there's a trace of a smile left on my lips.

College just got that much better.

ALLISON

I shouldn't be thinking about Dean Warren.

I definitely shouldn't be going to this game for him.

And the smile on my lips when he does a double take over his shoulder, as I sit on the uncomfortable metal bleachers, that really shouldn't be showing.

He's a mistake waiting to happen.

The cockiness and arrogance mixed with the hard edge in his eyes are what tell me that much. As if a simple look wasn't enough to warn me off.

He's the type of guy who will force you against a hard wall, lift your skirt and tear off the thin fabric beneath it with a forceful tug. The type of guy who will hold you there while you scream as he takes you harder and harder.

He's the type of guy my mother told me I should stay away from.

Good thing I stopped listening to my mother years ago.

He's a mistake I've made before. Not just once or twice, and you'd think I'd have learned my lesson by now. Maybe I can blame it on insta-lust.

My heart slams against my rib cage, hating that I'm in such denial.

He's a distraction. Dean is a distraction who could ruin everything. And maybe that's why I can't resist him. *Do I really want to do this?* I clear my throat and square my shoulders as my shoes sink into the grass. The urge to turn around without looking back is strong.

I was headed this way anyway.

The thought makes me smile. It almost makes me think that it's even okay. That everything was meant to work out like this.

It's a little late for me to be starting college but hey, being thrown to the wolves when you're legally allowed to drink isn't the worst thing in the world. I'm only a year behind and I have plenty of catching up to do. I'm shocked at how easy it is to get back into the student life. I graduated high school, went to community college for a year, then dropped out when Grandmom got sick only. One year later and I'm picking up the pieces, but blending in has been easier than I thought it would be.

"Go State!" I yell out and clap after setting my bag down on the ground.

There are maybe a dozen people scattered throughout the stands.

The field is small, as is the university. No one comes here because of their athletics program, that's for damn sure.

It's just an intramural team and there's not even a real game today. It's basically some guys fucking around. Shirts versus skin and lucky for me, Dean happens to be one of the shirtless players.

Just as I let my eyes admire his body, he jolts forward and tackles the shit out of another guy—Daniel, I think. It's only when the guy stands up that I confirm it's Daniel. Oh my. I'm not going to lie; this isn't as bad as I thought it would be.

Rugby's a violent sport.

The violence is what attracts me. It's like playing with fire … and that's what I came to do.

The men crash together, and I keep staring at one in particular. They slam into each other, brutalizing one another, all in the name of a good game.

It's not a game to me. There's too much at stake to call it that.

I can't watch, but I also can't rip my eyes away.

Thud. Thud. My heart pounds harder and harder as the memories slowly come back to me, and I need to shove them away. Hide them, bury them deep down inside.

Deep breaths. Calming breaths.

It only takes a glance in the wrong direction at the wrong time and it all comes flooding back.

I force a small smile to my lips, unclenching my fists and only just now realizing how my nails dug into my skin. As I reach for the water bottle in my bag, I lift my gaze back to the field, only to find Dean staring at me. The grim look proves he was watching me and knowing that, I can't breathe.

It's like he can see right through me. I'm saved by the loud clap of someone else sitting in the bleachers behind me. Our connection is broken and only then is my body willing to play it off. To relax and pretend like it's all right.

Dean is like a drug to a recovering addict.

He makes me question everything. All the things I have planned.

He makes me want to run but at the same time, he paralyzes me.

Five more minutes and I'll leave, I promise myself.

I'm waiting for them to break up their huddle and keep playing, but that's not what happens.

The bottle nearly slips from my grasp as Dean strides over to me and the other guys line up on the field without him.

Dean takes a seat next to me and I'm instantly hit with his warmth and masculine scent. His sweat smells sweet and addictive.

"What are you doing?" he asks me.

"I was watching this hot guy who has a crush on me play this dumb sport," I say and fail to hide my smile as I add, "He gave up, though."

He chuckles and that gorgeous smile flickers onto his face. "I wasn't sure you were going to stay, and I wanted to make sure I let you know before you left that we're having a party tomorrow night at James's place," he tells me.

"First a game and now a party?" I ask him, taking another swig from the bottle and fiddling with the plastic cap in my left hand. "You like asking me on dates, don't you?"

He shrugs and glances at the guys on the field, but I keep my eyes on him. "I think you'll like the party better. I'll be able to give you a little more attention."

I roll my eyes and almost turn back to the field, but I stop myself. I don't want to look that way right now.

"You think if you get a little alcohol in me, you'll have a better chance?" I ask him, although I keep glancing behind him to the right side of the field to see if any of the guys are watching us.

Dean makes a show of looking over his shoulder in the direction I keep checking out before shifting to block my view and standing a little closer. His broad shoulders tower over me. This is the second time he's been this close to me, and it only makes me want to be closer.

I can smell his unique, sexy scent and feel the heat in his eyes when I meet his gaze. It's a heady combination. To have someone you're innately drawn to so close. To know they want something you also want. But to also know with complete certainty it's the last thing you should do. The temptation heats the air around us and turns everything to a blur of white noise.

"I don't need a better chance," he finally answers me, his eyes narrowing. "I already told you, I want you and I'm not going to stop until you're screaming my name just how I want to hear it."

"So confident," I say, although it comes out differently than I'd planned. It was supposed to be sarcastic but instead, there's a hint of reverence.

"Come to the party," he tells me like it's a command and ignores the voices on the field. The ones calling out for him to head back. I use that as my excuse to leave.

"You go play, and I'll see you this weekend," I answer him without thinking.

"You're leaving already?" he asks me and I nod.

"I've got shit to do now that I have plans for tomorrow." He likes that; I can tell by the way he smiles, and it does something to me. Something it shouldn't.

"Twenty sixteen Broom Street," he tells me, but I already know the address.

DEAN

"So, what do you think about college?" Dr. Robinson asks me. He lowers his thick, horn-rimmed glasses and sets them down on the notepad in his lap. "Is it a good change?"

My right ankle rests on my left knee as I sit back, running both my hands through my hair. "Yeah, it's different. It's good."

"Talk to me about it," he says, prodding me for more. He's good at that.

"I don't want to disappoint Jack, and I'm grateful. I still don't know what I want to do, though."

"Well, it's only been a week and I'm sure Mr. Henderson wouldn't have sponsored you if he thought you'd disappoint him."

"We all know it was a favor to my uncle. I live off favors," I say flatly, although I don't look him in the eye. My gaze is on the ceiling fan in the center of the room. When I close my eyes, I can just barely feel the soft breeze. I wonder if anyone else in college feels as lost as I do. Like this is their last chance. I've been on my last chance for years now, so maybe this is my version of normal.

"Do you think you don't deserve it?" he asks me and I lower my gaze so I can meet his eyes. His expression is one of curiosity.

"A free ride to college isn't something I ever thought I'd get."

"And anger management? How about that?" he says, shifting in the seat of his dark brown leather chair. "Is that something you thought you'd get?"

A low chuckle makes my shoulders shake. "Yeah, that makes sense to me," I say with a grin.

"How do you think this is working for you?"

"I feel good," I answer him and hope the gratitude comes through. "It's nice to just say the shit I'm thinking."

"Have you thought more about my last suggestion?" he asks me and I shake my head.

"Well, yeah, I've thought about it," I say, correcting myself, realizing I was answering no to the wrong question. "I'm not doing it, though."

I left my mother's house six years ago. From there I survived by hopping from friend to friend. Crashing at my uncle's when he'd let me. I haven't gone back to that hellhole my mother calls home and I don't plan on it.

She doesn't want me there, so why would I?

"You don't think your mother would be interested in seeing your progress?" he asks.

"I don't see it as progress," I say.

"Why's that?"

The answer is obvious. College isn't a job. There's no worth to it. No value in it.

I don't know what the hell I'm doing with my life. I'm not offering anything to anyone. I'm just ... here. How is that progress? It's better for me, don't get me wrong. It's not better for anyone else, though.

"I don't see the point to it." I pause and swallow thickly, bending forward and repositioning so my elbows are on my knees. I can feel the stretch through my back, loosening my tight shoulders and coiled muscles. "I like the team, I like the gym."

"The physical release?" he asks me, and I can't help but think of Allison.

My fingers interlace as I nod. "Yeah, the physical release," I say and look up at him to keep from thinking about what I'd do to her if I got the chance.

"And you think you need this physical release?"

"I need something," I answer quickly. I don't tell him the truth. About how all that shit puts me on edge. How it makes me need more. How that alone will never be enough. Deep inside I know it, but I don't admit it.

"Anything else?" he asks as if he read my mind.

"Nothing yet," I tell him and falter, but decide to talk about her. Why the hell not? It's better than talking about my emotions. How easily the hate comes out. How I can't control the shit I say and the shit I do sometimes.

Well, maybe not so much that I can't, but that I don't want to.

"There's this girl," I start telling him while I pick up a fidget block from the glass coffee table. It's pointless. A block of buttons and switches that do nothing, but it keeps my hands busy.

"She's real flirtatious and cute. We have chemistry together." After seeing his brow raise, I add to clarify, "The class." It's quiet as he scribbles on the notepad.

"I keep running into her," I tell him. "I guess she's on my mind because of that."

"You're seeing her?"

I shake my head. "Nah, I wouldn't say that."

"Have you been physical?" he asks me.

I tell him the truth, but in my head? Fuck yeah. Imagining getting her under me has been a good distraction.

That second day of class, she was dressed in a tight shirt and a short little skirt.

The shirt wasn't see-through like I was fantasizing about, but with the blue plaid skirt, she was working that schoolgirl look. She did a damn fine job of it too.

All during class, all I did was think about everything I could do to her. How I could bend this shy girl over the desk so easily.

Every time she readjusted in her seat, I imagined being behind her, lifting her ass up and positioning her just how I wanted. I could hear how the desk would scrape across the floor as I pounded into her.

It only took a few minutes before I was rock hard and eager to see just what I'd have to do to get under that skirt.

The second class was over, Little Miss Brunette, my personal tease, was gone before I even shoved my notebook into my bag.

"Why do you think you're drawn to her?" he asks me, pulling me from the explicit thoughts running through my head.

"She's got a mouth on her," I reply and think I should elaborate on how it's what she says, more than her body, that gets me going. Hell, either way you look at it is accurate.

"So, you're going to pursue her?" he asks me, picking up the notebook again to jot something down.

If by pursue her, he means fuck her until my cock is spent, then yes, that's what I'm planning.

I don't tell him that though, I just nod my head once when he looks up.

"So, you have your workout sessions, your rugby team, you have a love interest," he lists then pauses as I snort, but I clear my throat and gesture for him to continue.

"Have you thought about changing your major?" he asks me then adds, "It's just something to keep in mind. I know it's still early, but undecided is not exactly what you want from this experience, is it?"

"No, I definitely want to figure shit out," I say and toss the fidget block back on the table. "I feel wound tight, like I just need something."

"What do you need?" he asks me.

"I don't know," I tell him honestly. "I want to know, though." I nod my head, swallowing back the disappointment, the fear that

I'll never know what I need to get over this anger. Or worse, that it's just too late.

I have a good idea why I'm like this. It doesn't take a genius to figure it out. But I don't know how to change and even worse, I don't know what I'll be like when I do change. And that scares the shit out of me.

According to the good doctor, college is where you go to find out who you are. So far, I've learned I'm a man who has a vivid imagination when a sexy piece of ass wears a short plaid skirt to class. There's a shocker.

ALLISON

"Your flowers are dying," I say out loud although there's no one else here. My fingertips brush against the soft petals on a single bloom that's still alive. "This one will be dead soon too," I say and pause, letting my hand fall. "This window will be good for you, though," I add as I water the first plant and then the next in the large bay window. It faces east and there's plenty of sun.

This was my grandmother's therapy. Plants need to be talked to, she used to tell me. I thought she was crazy, but I did it anyway.

And when she gave me a violet of my own, I took her advice. Shame the thing's dying. Maybe I should talk more.

My throat feels dry and itchy when I stand back, no longer busying myself.

"Miss you," I whisper. "You wouldn't be so proud of me if you were here, though," I say. I spent most of my first year out of high school with my grandmother. She needed someone and I did too. She'd have liked this house, I think. I'm happy I was able to rent it. The price is good, but the location is everything. It's exactly where I need it to be.

For the longest time, Grandmom was the only one I talked to. I'd work at the bakery, take care of Grandmom and then go home to sleep. It kept me busy and somehow my grandmother rubbed off on me. Over time, it became easier to refuse to let anyone in.

Maybe it's because she's a hard woman too. Or was. She knew how hard it is to give even a little piece to anyone. Opening up a little inevitably means breaking down.

She was tough and she showed me how to survive being this way.

But now she's gone and I'm here all alone.

The click of the air conditioner is met with the curtains swaying. They're bright white with bluebirds scattered across them. This is the only area in the entire house that's decorated; it's supposedly the dining room, but the table that came with the sparsely furnished place is strangely small for such a large room. And I don't have any desire to put in any effort anywhere else. I can't stand to be here any longer than I need to be.

At that thought, I head to the kitchen for a cup of tea.

The electric kettle is Grandmom's too. Another reminder.

The plants, the tea … well, maybe that's it.

Standing at the laminate countertop, I look around the mostly empty kitchen. I don't even have cutlery. But that's okay, I don't think I'll be staying here long. "I brought your plants, though," I say out loud like a fucking lunatic. Does it make it any better if I know I'm unwell? I tell myself it's for the plants. Talking out loud to my dead grandmother is so the plants can grow. Yeah … okay.

The kettle beeps and the light goes off, so I go about my business. Tea and then research. I pause after pouring the hot water into the porcelain cup, remembering Dean.

He's definitely a man who leaves an impression. I smile into the tea, drinking it unsweetened and loving the warmth as it flows through my chest. Dean's also a wanted distraction.

"You'd hate him, Grandmom," I say with my eyes closed. "Or maybe not," I say then shrug and remember how she gave me the advice to get over one man by getting under another. It was only a joke to her but I think she was onto something.

With each sip of tea, I think about Dean. His large, strong hands. The way he likes to pretend he's not wound tightly when it's obvious he is. The hot tea is a soothing balm, but getting rid of this wound called Dean requires more than a mere hot drink. I should know.

Just as I'm starting to relax, just as I feel a bit sane, my phone rings in the living room. My pace is slow, and all the good feelings are replaced with ice.

There's only one person who calls me and I don't want to talk to her. I will, but all she'll get are the pieces of me that remain. The remnants of who I used to be. She made her choice, and now we both have to deal with it.

I take my time tossing the used tea bag into the trash, where it hits an empty box of hair dye. I absently twist the brunette curl dangling in my face around my finger as I walk to my phone. I don't want to look like the girl I once was. I don't want to be her anymore. Dyeing my hair helps.

"Hello," I answer the phone, setting the cup down on the floor and sitting cross-legged to look out the sliding doors at the back of the house.

"You answered." My mother sounds surprised, and maybe she should be. It's been a long time since I've heard her voice.

"What's going on, Mom?" I ask her, feeling a sense of loneliness I haven't felt in a while. Maybe it's not the anger that keeps me at a distance from her. Maybe it's just because she's a reminder of what happened.

"I wanted to let you know I bought you a sofa." Her voice has a feigned sense of happiness to it. Like she can pretend we're okay and one day we'll be back to normal. "I need your address so I can send it. And a TV stand too. And if you need anything else ..."

"Mom, you didn't have to do that," I tell her simply. It hurts when I talk to her. Physically hurts. Because I still love her, but I hate her too. I can't forgive myself and she's the one who led me down that path. I'd rather hate her than hate myself.

"I wanted to, and I know that you quit working when … she passed away four months ago, so money must be tight. If you need any …" my mother falters then continues, "I don't know what you have saved, but I can send you—"

"I'm fine." I hated that job at the bakery anyway. It was just killing time and numbing the truth of what I needed to do. It's not like I was going anywhere running the register.

"Will you let me send them to you?" she asks me and it's the anguish in her voice that makes me cave.

It's not that I want to hurt my mother. I know she's in pain like I am. I just don't want to be around her. I don't want to forgive her because then it would be like what happened was okay.

And it never will be. Never.

"Sure, I'll text my address to you," I agree mostly out of guilt.

"Thank you," she says, and I think she's crying on the other end of the phone.

"Are you okay?" I ask her.

"I just miss you; I miss your grandmother too."

"I miss her too … She's in a better place now." I say the words, but I don't mean them. They're only for my mother's benefit. If it wasn't for my grandmother's death, I'm not sure my mother and I would even have a relationship. It's been six years of hardly saying a word to each other. For most of them, I lived under her roof. Both of us keeping busy and ignoring each other.

I remember when I started sneaking out how she pretended I wasn't.

I kept pushing and she let me get away with murder. She didn't want to fight me. She didn't want a reason for us to argue. It's the guilt that does that. Either that or the shame.

"I have to go, Mom," I tell her as I watch the leaves on the trees behind my house gently sway with the wind. It wasn't until I moved in with my grandmother that my mom admitted our relationship was strained. She likes to pretend, but I don't have the strength for that. Or maybe it's the other way around.

"Well, call me," she tells me hurriedly before I can hang up. "If you need anything."

"I will," I answer, although that's not going to happen. I already know that and I'm sure she does too. "Thank you for the furniture," I add. "I really appreciate it."

"You don't already have anything, do you?" she asks me. "It didn't seem like you packed much."

"No, I didn't. Thank you."

I end the call as fast as I can. I know Mom wants to talk. But she's saying all the wrong things.

Then again, I am too.

I'm holding back; I know that much is true.

I know what I need to do, but it hurts to think about it. It's going to change everything, and I don't know who I'll be after it happens.

And that's what scares me the most. When this is over, I don't know what will be left.

DEAN

*F*oam spills over the rim of the red Solo cup as I fill it. It falls into the bucket with the rest of the spilled beer.

The last time I had a drink from a keg was at a party for my uncle's company. He's in construction and so was I until I got set up with Jack Henderson, Kev's uncle and my uncle's friend. That beer was in celebration of hard work. This beer is just because we can drink all night and not give a shit.

And it's the first of many to come. Cheers to that.

I down the cold beer and put my cup back under the spigot to fill it up again.

A pretty little thing sidles up next to me, letting out a small laugh when she bumps her ass on my thigh. Like it was an accident and she was just reaching for the corkscrew on the countertop in front of us.

"My bad," she says with a smile and throws her hair over her shoulder as she grabs the corkscrew. She looks back at me one more time as she walks away in her tight faded jeans and tank top that rides up, showing off the tramp stamp on the small of her back. It's a tribal design around a rosebud. Probably something she picked off the wall of the tattoo shop.

"No problem," I tell her and take another sip as she walks off. She's cute but the one girl I want to see hasn't come through the front door. I've been sitting here all night long, the beer right next to me. My back's against the counter as I face the front door watching everyone shuffle in and out, with the night sky getting darker, the music louder and everyone in here drinking more and more.

James's family house is the perfect location for these parties. Right off campus and it's within walking distance to the dorms but also the frat and sorority housing. All you have to do is follow the train tracks up the block and it leads you right here. Walking on the railroad tracks isn't the best thing to do when you're drunk, but at least you can't take a turn down the wrong street.

Just as I down the rest of the beer and think about heading to the pool room in the back, the front door opens and in walks Allison. Her pouty lips are pulled into a curious smile as she tucks her clutch under her arm and closes the door. I like how she leans against the door, taking in the place before pushing off and heading this way.

My eyes follow her, waiting for the moment when she sees me. Her hips sway in the most tempting rhythm as she glances over her shoulder, moving the hair behind her ear and exposing more of her neck. With her black dress and red lips, she's elegantly beautiful, but it's tainted.

By the way she walks.

By the expression on her face.

By the way she halts, sinking her teeth into her bottom lip and looking me up and down. I smirk as she lets her eyes roam and then stalks toward me.

"You're late," I tell her and that only makes her laugh.

"I come when I'm ready," she says in a sultry voice. She eyes the keg and then where I'm standing, which is right in the fucking way.

I'm only an observer as she takes a cup off the counter and then slips between me and the keg, settling her ass right against my dick. She takes her time, bending over as much as she can while she fills her cup.

My dick stiffens and the second it does, she winks over her shoulder at me.

Taking a sip of beer, she scoots out from between me and the keg and then turns to face me. I wouldn't have been surprised if she'd walked right out of the kitchen, leaving me hanging again.

"Oh, and I always come first too," she says, holding up her cup and arching her brow. "That's one of my rules."

"You're a tease," I tell her as my pulse quickens. She holds my gaze and those pale green eyes flicker with heat.

More people filter into the room, a horde of girls all stumbling in their heels and spilling their drinks, laughing as they crowd the kitchen.

Allison doesn't object when I grab her hand and pull her out of there, heading to the living room on the right.

"It's loud," she says, raising her voice and tugging on my hand, stopping me from taking her to the back.

"There's a rec room this way," I tell her and move my hand around her waist to keep her moving. I love how she doesn't protest.

She walks with me through the living room, past the speakers, through the back hall and straight out to the pool room. There are a few arcade games too in the back and there are more people waiting around them than there are playing pool.

I tilt my chin up at Daniel as he stands up, holding the pool cue in his hands and watching the six ball sink straight into a back pocket. He's an all right guy. Out of all the guys, he's the one I've clicked with most since I moved here. He's an outsider in a lot of ways. Like me. And I know he only hangs around because of some dealings he's got going on under the table. It's not my business and I stay out of it. It's as simple as that.

The second he sees my Allie Cat, he smiles wider. It's a triumphant grin and it matches the one on my face when he gives me a nod.

"Aw," Allison says as she walks toward the side wall where the barstools are set up, "I thought it was going to be empty." She smirks after saying it and her eyes light up with mischief.

"Like I said, you're a fucking tease."

"And you like it," she says back then lifts the cup to her lips. She doesn't take her eyes off me, though.

I have to readjust my dick in my pants before I can sit down and watch the pool game.

"Admit it," she says, her voice a bit stronger than I expected.

"Admit what?" I ask her.

"That you like it."

"Yeah, so what if I do?" I tell her with confidence. "You already know that."

"I just like hearing you say it," she says and shrugs her small shoulders, making the dip in her collarbone that much more pronounced. The second she turns away from me, her cheeks color a beautiful shade and her legs sway. Like she's shy all of a sudden, just hearing that I like her. I'll keep that in mind, how easy it is to make her look like that. I like seeing this timid side of her.

"What else do you like to hear?" I ask her, and she just smiles slightly into her cup, tilting it back and taking a larger gulp. "I'll tell you whatever you want." My offer goes with the rest unspoken. I'll give you what you want, you give me what I want. It seems fair as fuck to me.

"Is this the room?" she asks me curiously and tilts her head.

"The room?" I ask her to clarify and she slips her hand up my shirt. Her fingers tickle along my skin as she leans forward. "You know," she says then licks her lower lip and adds, "the room where everything happens. Or is there an empty bedroom?" As she leans back, she takes her touch with her, leaving me wanting more and wishing there was a room to take her fine ass.

"I'm in the dorms, I don't stay at the frat house." She seems surprised by that, so I fill her in. "Kev's uncle is paying my ride here to keep me out of trouble and Kev thought I'd make a good addition, but this isn't really my style."

"Then what is your style, Dean Warren?"

"Doing whatever I have to, so I can hear you say my name just how I've been dreaming."

Her delicate simper widens, and I take a chance, setting my hand on her thigh.

"Oh, the first move has been made," Allison says sarcastically but leaves my hand right where it is. She shifts on the barstool and it makes the thin fabric on her already short dress ride a little higher. My fingers are so fucking close to the hem, and just beneath that, the apex of her thighs.

"You like it," I say and then pinch the hem of her dress and pull it down as much as I can before taking the cup from her hand.

"Hey, I wasn't done," she says and sulks but I ignore her, walking to the bar and grabbing the vodka and a can of Sprite. I hold it up for her to see and her eyes light up.

"I guess that'll do," she says with a devilish glint in her eyes.

I grab the whiskey for me and pour my own drink in a glass.

"No ice?" she asks when I hand her the drink I've fixed her and stand in front of her, effectively caging her in.

"You want ice in yours?" I ask her.

"I mean in yours," she says softly, her voice a bit huskier than it was a moment ago. She says the words quickly as well. As though she's afraid I'd mistake her questioning my drink for being unhappy with her own.

"No ice in mine. You like it?" I ask her, nodding to the drink in her hand and she nods back, biting down on her lip.

"Good."

I watch as her breathing comes in harder. I let my left hand fall to her thigh and then slip slowly down, trailing my fingers across her soft skin before gripping the edge of the barstool she's sitting on. Even with her up this high, I still tower over her. She's a petite little thing.

"You come on strong," she says, peeking up at me through her thick lashes. "Do you know that?"

I nod my head once and search her face for her reaction. "I don't do small talk," I tell her, thinking that's what she wants to hear.

"What if I want small talk?" she asks me without any trace of humor in her voice.

I make a show of taking an exaggerated look out the back window and tell her with a smile, "The weather's nice tonight."

She laughs at my stupid joke and the tension eases. Taking a step back, I pull out the barstool next to her further and take a seat.

"It's hard to get a read on you," I tell her and take another sip of the whiskey. It warms my chest as it goes down. It's the good stuff, not that cheap shit I have back at my place.

"Mm-hmm, I'm such a puzzle," she says flatly although I think it's meant to be taken with humor. There's something else there, some hint of truth that keeps me from laughing.

"Where are you from?" I ask her, keeping that small talk suggestion of hers in mind. I thought she'd be a bit easier than this. I know she wants it. And she knows I do too.

"Brunswick," she says, holding my gaze.

"Small world; I've got family in Brunswick," I tell her and start to think about my mother and the last time I was there. I regret referring to her as family the moment the word is out of my mouth. With both hands on my drink, I try to think of something else to talk about. The beer's already hitting me though, clouding my mind with memories I don't want to relive. Thankfully, she changes the subject.

"So, whose place is this?" she asks me and I tilt my head in James's direction, back by the arcade games. "His father's." Spoiled rich kid is a term I'd use to describe James. I don't really like him. Then again, I don't much like anyone.

"Lot of alumni here," she says beneath her breath, glancing at the row of photographs on the walls rather than at James.

"Your family go here?" I ask her and she shakes her head. The only people I know who are here because it's their family's college are Kev and James. My family sure as shit didn't go to college.

"You're good at small talk," she says sweetly. "Maybe you should lead with that next time."

"Next time?" I ask her, cocking a brow and leaning forward.

"Yeah, next time, with the next girl you try to pick up," she says, and her legs swing slightly from side to side like she's getting a kick out of teasing me.

"You should know better than that," I tell her.

"Oh? Is this your last time?" She leans forward slightly. "You're done with your old ways and I'm the only one for you?" she says, mocking me.

"As in, you should know better than to think I'm giving up on chasing you until I get what I want," I correct her and hold her gaze. She breaks it though, easing back against the wall and crossing her ankles as she watches the pool game. The hard spheres crashing against one another and the crowd's reaction when one sinks makes me turn around for a moment.

"I like the chase," she says and then reaches out to brush her knuckles against my arm. "I bet you could catch me fast if I let you."

I huff a laugh and smirk at her. "If you let me?"

"Yeah," she says with a note of temptation in her voice like she's baiting me, then takes another drink.

"Allie Cat, you don't fool me. You love this little cat and mouse game."

"If I'm the cat, that means you're the mouse?" she asks me and it's only then that I realize what I said and how I said it. Maybe the whiskey's already getting to me.

"No, no, you got that wrong. You're my Allie Cat, but this game we're playing, I'm the one who's doing the chasing."

"Are you now?" she says in a seductive voice as she raises the cup to her lips. I don't know if it's the alcohol buzzing through my veins or the way she says it that makes me second-guess myself. She lets out a feminine chuckle into her cup and smiles at me with the hint of a blush creeping up her cheeks.

"I'm just playing with you, Dean," she says sweetly and slides off the barstool. I widen my legs as she stands between them and pops up on her tiptoes to plant a small kiss on the side of my jaw. I close my eyes, enjoying the soft touch. My fingers slide down the curve of her waist. But she pulls away before I can get more of what I want.

Just as she does, I see Kev and Brant make their way into the room. Allie brushes her fingers along my knuckles and then takes a step back, rocking on her heels.

"You're cute, but I have to go," she says and tugs her hands away.

"Already?" I say. She hasn't even been here for an hour.

"I got shit to do," she tells me and I immediately bite back, "Yeah, me."

She gets a laugh out of that, spearing her fingers through her hair and the floral fragrance of her shampoo drifts toward me as she turns on her heels. "I'll see you on Monday," she murmurs innocently like I'm just going to watch her go.

"I can at least walk you out," I offer and stand up, reaching forward to snatch her by her waist.

She lets out a yelp that gets the attention of a few of the guys.

"I think I'm fine," she tells me and grabs my wrist, moving my hand off her waist.

A crease settles deep in my forehead and I can feel it when I say, "You don't want me to even walk you out?" I ask the question, but already I'm talking to her back.

She turns around to walk backward, teasing me some more. As

she shakes her head, her hair falls over her shoulders, covering up that soft skin of hers. "Not tonight, Dean," she says.

"I don't know if this is a test, but that's bullshit if it is," I call after her, my feet planted firmly on the floor. Her sweet laugh follows her out of the room and I stay put.

I'll chase her if she wants, but fuck if I know what's going through that girl's mind.

Craziest thing though is that watching her leave only makes me want her more.

ALLISON

*M*y pen scribbles over the numbers, morphing them from identifiable figures to squares of black. I can't pay attention to the lecture, not when I can feel Dean's eyes on me.

I can hardly breathe as I close my eyes. I'm so close to the edge, to losing it and falling into a bottomless pit with no way to return. I can feel it now, how liberating it would be to just let go. Years of holding it in, years of doing nothing.

My eyes slowly open to the droning white noise of the professor's lecture. It's only then that I see I've broken the tip of the pen, the ink seeping into the pages and staining them.

Not just a few sheets but nearly all of them, maybe thirty or forty pages in this notepad. Have I been sitting here that long?

"You okay?" the girl to my right asks. I recognize her face. She has a certain look about her, like someone you could easily trust. Her voice is gentle too. She glances straight ahead and then back at me when I don't answer, merely staring at her and trying to snap out of it.

"Fine." I manage to push out the single word.

"I'm Angie, by the way," the girl whispers as she brushes her curly blond hair away from her face. Then she asks, "Do you need another pen?" She practically mouths the words so she doesn't disrupt the lecture.

"Oh, no," I say and wave her off, pushing away all the thoughts. "I'm fine, thanks."

We share an easy smile like nothing's happened. I suppose outwardly, nothing has. Just a broken pen and spilled ink on a notebook.

I hear a desk somewhere to the left of and behind me scratch across the floor. *Dean.* My body begs me to look back, but I don't.

God, I want to. It's different with him. A good different in some ways, but so bad in others.

He's a distraction.

With clammy hands, I reach into my bag and pull out another pen. I rip off a single piece of paper and wrap up the ruined pen, setting it to the side of the desk to toss on the way out.

That scraping sound catches my attention again, but this time Angie's as well. She looks over her shoulder and then back to the front of the room.

My neck is refuses to budge, all because I can feel his gaze. I know he's watching and he's going to want an answer. Or an explanation. Or maybe neither. Maybe if I just ignore him, he'll leave me alone.

That's what I should want, but it hurts to think of that possibility. Inexplicably so.

It's funny how time passed so slowly before I came here. Every day was agonizingly painful. Now that I'm so very aware I need to make a decision, the class is over before I can let out a breath.

I need to force my body to relax and move normally so I'll look just like everyone else. The moment I do, I look behind me, arching my neck and succumbing to temptation.

Dean's dark eyes stare back at me.

I don't know how I thought for even one second he'd have looked away.

Maybe he has an obsession like I do.

All that anxiety, that fear, it all slips away as the clock ticks and our gazes meet. As though I'm his reflection, his lips lift into a slow smile and mine follow.

Dean could be my personal heroin. And I want a hit. I want it hard and fast.

It terrifies me. But I want that distraction more than ever now. I want him to take me away from this. However he can. I know it'd be simple too. As effortless as jotting down on paper that I want him and exactly where to find me. It would be all too easy.

Time resumes as I wrap my hand around the leaking pen and toss it into the wastebasket at the front of the room. I don't look up as everyone walks past me heading for the exit, including Angie and her friendly smile. Trying to keep my composure, I head back to my seat, only to peek up and see Dean waiting for me.

I fucking love it. I love how he makes his intentions clear and that he's willing to give chase, to put himself out there. *I love that he wants me.*

"What's on your mind?" he asks me. My first instinct is to joke, to flirt, to keep things light.

If only he knew the truth.

He's already too close. And I'm too invested.

I should have stopped this before it got this far. A dark and deadly voice in the back of my mind whispers, coaxing in its cadence, *It has to happen. It's meant to be this way.*

"Nothing," I answer him immediately, ignoring the voice and reaching down for my bag.

"I knew it," he says with a cocky grin. "I knew there was literally nothing going on in there."

"Fucking asshole," I mutter as my smile broadens. I feel naturally at ease around him … happy even. And that's dangerous. His rough chuckle makes my entire body heat. Some places more than others.

"I can tell you what I was thinking," he says as he leans closer, so close that I get a hint of his cologne. It's clean and crisp, but with a hint of woodsy musk that makes me lean in too.

"I bet I already know exactly what you were thinking," I immediately retort, which only makes him scratch the stubble on his jaw, his smile ever present.

"What do you think?" he asks me, and I arch a brow to admonish him.

"Thoughts like that don't belong in the classroom."

"Where else are we going to find a desk?" he asks me, and I can't help how my thighs clench and my chest and cheeks warm with a slow, heated blush.

I always have a comeback but not this time.

"So, you want to go out?"

"No." I laugh off his suggestion. "Do *you* want to go out?"

"I could go out," he answers effortlessly. Like it doesn't bother him in the least.

"I don't know," I tell him, feeling that unease from earlier crawling back into my skin. I forget why I'm really here when I'm with him and I can't let that happen.

"You want a boyfriend or something?" Dean asks me, and I scoff. "What?" he says. "I don't know what the hell you want."

"Neither do I." I answer him with the most honesty I've spoken since I laid eyes on him and turn my back to leave.

"The hell you don't. You said you wanted me," he persists. There's a certain tone in his voice and a flicker of something in his eyes that I recognize. It's a pain I know all too well. I hate it. I want to take it away and with Dean it'd be easy. He wants me, and I want him. There's so much more at stake, though.

A slow prickle of ice settles along my skin as I think about what's going to happen. I shouldn't lead him on like this. It's wrong.

But I've been fucked up for a while now, and he's just so tempting.

"You know I do," I tell him, turning around to face him after zipping up my bookbag. My lower back grazes it as my ass hits the desk. "I'd love for you to fuck me raw. Right here on this desk." I reach behind me to grip it and then nod my head to the side and add, "Or against the wall maybe."

His expression darkens with lust. I watch as his eyes widen with amusement at first, but even so, his pupils dilate with desire. Every second of silence is another degree of heat added between us.

I lean closer to him, feeling the tension rise as he adjusts his cock in his pants. His eyes don't move from my lips as I whisper, "I imagine it all the time." My fingertips play at the buttons on his shirt. Seeking consent, all the while luring him in.

"I bet you do too," I tell him, staring into his dark eyes and willing him to picture exactly what I've been dreaming about. "It would be bad for me, though. You'll fuck me then leave." At the last thought, my hands fall to my side. That's not the reason why, but I'm not above using the logic to keep him away.

It takes him a moment to process my confession. Like he's paralyzed from what I've done to him, and that gives me a thrill I can't put into words.

"So you do want a boyfriend?" he manages to say, and I'm equal parts amused and exasperated. The lies make the hole I'm digging for myself that much deeper.

"Look, Dean." I start to tell him it's not going to happen. I swear I had every intention of cutting him off. But there's a look in his eyes that makes my heart still just a beat too long. A look that heats the small space between us. A look that I'm addicted to.

"Yeah? I'm listening," Dean says as he takes a half step closer, decreasing the distance between us. He towers over me, his broad shoulders blocking out everything else. I'm caught in his gaze, caught in the moment.

I'll blame it all on that.

"If you want to fuck me, you should just show up at my house," I tell him and slip the ripped piece of paper in his hand.

The paper I've been scribbling on all class long.

The paper with my address on it.

DEAN

I don't know how I wound up outside of Allie's house with that scrap of paper in my pocket. It's part of a cute little row of houses off the edge of campus with white picket fences and a one-way street.

The only excuse I've got for showing up the moment my last class was over, is that I didn't have any blood my brain could use. It's all in my dick and that's the reason I ended up here, pushing the doorbell and acting like a damn puppy.

She said jump and I fucking jumped. But it's for pussy, so I can't beat myself up too much.

I shrug my shoulders to readjust my jacket as the sound of her walking through the house greets me from the other side of the door. There's a sheer curtain on the window and Allie pulls it back to look at me.

I only get a glimpse, but the look of surprise is something that makes me rethink what the hell I'm doing.

Until the door unlocks with a loud click and Allie opens it wide.

Any thoughts of turning around vanish. Her blouse hangs low

and nearly covers up the cutoff jean shorts. It's thin and almost transparent, a button-down white number that would look professional with slacks.

But in those shorts and a burgundy bra, it's downright sinful.

"Dean," she says my name and then leans into the door, showing off the curve of her waist as she juts out her hip. "I wasn't expecting you, to be honest."

"I wasn't sure I was going to come either, but I thought you might want some company," I tell her and readjust my dick in my jeans. She knows what I want, and I have no intention of hiding it.

I love how she blushes just slightly, moving a finger to her lower lip as she gives me this shy smile that doesn't seem right on my Allie Cat.

"I guess I could use some," she says and moves aside to let me in, although the way she eyes me is more like a hunter and not the prey. Like she's the one in control here.

She needs a little lesson.

"I want your mouth first," I tell her as she closes the door. She's quiet as she turns around, not answering me as I let my jacket slide off my shoulders and lay it on the back of a dining room chair.

The first floor of her place is small; a set of stairs to my left, an eat-in kitchen on the right and a cozy living room with a sofa. Right in front of us are a love seat and a TV stand. The sunshine filtering through the open blinds of her sliding doors is the only light in the place. I take a quick look around, wondering what she was up to before I came in, but she distracts me, letting out a small hum of appreciation.

"Is that so?" she asks, and I don't answer her. There's a teasing lilt in her voice that drives me crazy. It's a hint that she can take more. It suggests I'm not a man who can handle her.

What's more? She's letting me get away with pushing her. And I fucking love it. It only makes me want to push her harder.

She follows me in and her eyes roam down my body as I take off my shirt, tossing it on top of my jacket. I keep walking, moving to the window to shut the blinds and darkening the small living room. I want the lights on, though. I need to see this. Every. Fucking. Bit of it.

"Yeah, mouth and then your cunt," I tell her confidently, flicking on a light switch and watching how she stalks toward me, those wide hips rocking back and forth and taunting me. My dick gets harder just watching her.

"You going to keep teasing me, Allie Cat?" I love how her breathing is coming out harder. A smirk kicks up my lips and then I lick them, slowly. Her eyes follow my movement and a shiver runs down her body. "I know you will. You love teasing me," I tell her with confidence and her gaze meets mine, narrowing as she decides what she wants to admit.

"Is that so?" she asks me in a flirtatious voice and takes a step back as I take one forward. The half smile widens.

"No more," I say and keep my tone stern. "You can tease me again tomorrow, but right now I'm done playing." My heart hammers hard in my chest, knowing how aggressive I'm being. But Allie's a woman who wants to be pushed.

"Tell me you don't want me right now," I offer her. "Tell me you don't want me to sink deep into you and fuck you how you deserve to be fucked, and I'll leave."

My heart spasms, hating that I've given her an out. But getting her enthusiastic consent first is key. I'm not really worried that she'll make me leave, though. I know Allie; I know what she wants, and I can give it to her better than any other man.

"I'm not a liar, Dean," she says quietly, and I watch as she catches her bottom lip between her teeth. "Yeah, I do."

"Say it."

"I want you. I want every inch of you."

"Good," I say and start to lean forward, to kiss those plump lips of hers, but she surprises me, dropping to her knees.

She doesn't say anything as she unzips my pants and I let her lead for now.

A little give, and a little take.

Her small hands pull my jeans down in a single tug and my thick cock juts out right in front of her face. A small gasp slips from her lips and I love how her eyes widen. I stroke my dick once, rubbing the precum already leaking out over the head.

Before I can take away my hand, she gives the head a quick lick, her tongue slipping along the slit and making me hiss.

Her eyes flash to mine as she wraps her lips around the head of my cock and sucks.

I don't hold back the groan from deep in the back of my throat. She deserves to know just how good she makes me feel. My hands fist her hair as she sucks me down, hollowing her cheeks and working my dick like a pro.

It's mesmerizing to watch her worshipping my cock with that sassy mouth of hers. I've thought about it every fucking night since I first saw her.

About time I have her right where I want her. I try to ignore the thoughts running through my head. The ones telling me this is a one-time thing. I already know I want more, and I refuse to let her deny me when this is through.

She moans around my cock and it sends a tingle up my spine. Fuck, she's even better than I thought she'd be.

I let her have her fun for a minute and then I shove myself to the back of her throat. Again, and again, and again. "Fuck," I groan. My blunt nails dig into the back of her head as my toes curl and my eyes shut tight. She feels too fucking good. "I'm going to cum just from your mouth," I barely get out through my clenched teeth.

She continues like she didn't hear me, swallowing me down and trying to take more of my length. I have to pull out before I lose it. I'm not ready to be done just yet. My breath leaves me as she pants, quickly trying to catch her breath. I stare down at her and I'm in awe of her eagerness for more. Her lips are swollen and her eyes wide and glassy.

She's fucking perfect. A greedy little slut just for me.

She opens her mouth wider and leans forward as I stroke my cock once, running my palm over the head. The air is chilly compared to her hot mouth, but I can't let her suck me off anymore. If I do, it'll all be over too soon. I didn't come here for a blowjob. I want more from her.

"Get up," I tell her sternly as if she doesn't have me on the edge of coming undone. She reacts immediately, desperate to please me and I can't help but notice how her upper thighs clench and she whimpers softly.

I'm not careful as I rip open her shirt, forcing a button to pop off and fall to the floor. Her gasp reminds me to keep a straight face. *I'm in control*, I tell myself as I unclasp her bra. It dangles in front of her, laying across her torso as the straps are caught in her sleeves. But her full breasts stand at attention, her pale pink nipples pebbling and making my mouth water. She stands like a mannequin, letting me almost violently undress her.

My dick twitches when I run the back of my hands across her hardened peaks. My tongue grazes across my lower lip before I dip down and take her left breast into my mouth. Sucking and swirling my tongue around her sensitive bud.

She reacts exactly how I want, spearing her hands through my hair and arching her back. Her soft, strangled moans of pleasure are music to my ears.

I release her nipple from my mouth with a loud pop and take my time playing with the other one, pinching it between my thumb and forefinger before sucking it into my mouth. I bite down just slightly, and she hisses. Not holding back my smile with my teeth still clamped, I pull back again and watch her face as I do. Her eyes are wide, and her mouth forms a perfect O. The same mouth that just sucked me off like that's what it was made to do.

When I release her, I take a step back and I miss her instantly. Her breathing is shallow as her hands move to the button on her shorts but she hesitates, waiting for me to give her permission.

I let her stand there, looking at me and dying for her own

release as I stroke myself. The sight of her is everything to me. I want a fucking photograph so I can remember this moment forever.

Her hair already looks like she's just been fucked. Her green eyes are dark with desire, and with a torn shirt and her gorgeous breasts bared, she's everything I've ever wanted.

"I don't know if I want the shirt on while I fuck you or not," I say out loud although it's more of a thought and not a question. More of a tease for her than anything else.

She shifts her weight and stands there patiently, waiting for my decision. I stroke my dick again and her eyes instantly dart down to watch. Still, she's quiet. Good girl.

"Take it off, all of it, and bend over," I tell her and nod to the armrest of the sofa. She obeys but undresses slowly, letting each garment fall to the floor as I step out of my jeans.

The second I slip inside of her, I know I'm fucked.

I'll need more than tonight. *More of her.* She feels too fucking good.

I'm not gentle with her. I love how her face presses into the cushion. How she doesn't hold back the screams as I pound into her all the way to the hilt on the first stroke.

The sounds of wet flesh smacking together mixed with her cries of want make me fuck her harder. My balls slam against her clit over and over as I push into her as deep as I can with each thrust.

Her nails scratch on the fabric as she screams out my name and it's all I can take.

Her pussy spasms and I empty myself inside of her.

I can't breathe as I collapse on top of her, bracing my weight with my forearms and kissing her upper back and shoulders with soft, open-mouth kisses that make her shudder again.

I let the tip of my nose glide along her back, smelling her sweet scent as I give her one last kiss.

After I catch my breath, still buried inside of her I say, "I told you that you wanted me."

She tosses her hair over her shoulder to look back at me, her ass still up and my cum leaking from her pretty pink pussy. A soft moan leaves her, making her chest rise and fall before she replies, "Pretty sure you're the one who was dying for this, Dean."

ALLISON

One-night stands are easy.

I come, and I go. I smirk at the thought. They make me feel better for a while and then when I want more, I find someone else. I'm safe and always use protection; everything always happens on my terms too. It's always easy that way.

But *he* isn't a one-night stand. He's not one of the guys I'd go pick up at the back of O'Malley's. A man whose face I'd never see again. I've had my share. I've wasted so many nights waiting to be taken back to a shitty motel or fucked against the side of a car.

I loved each and every one. Because they made me feel better in some fucked-up way.

I always knew I could leave them behind me and walk away like nothing had happened.

Dean will be right in my path after tonight. I can't get away from him. I can't say goodbye and never see him again. Worse, I let it happen.

I should have known better than to have Dean come here. It's a rule: never at my place. I don't break my rules. Never. My back teeth grind as I remember my slipup. Well, two of them. I didn't even make him wear a rubber. The thought should anger me but instead it makes me feel deliciously dirty. I let myself get carried away. I should have thought it out more. I shouldn't be so damn reckless.

The bathroom light switches off and he appears in all his glory in the doorway. Stark naked with chiseled abs and his thick cock still at half-mast.

I can see why he's so fucking conceited now.

He lazily scratches the back of his head as he stalks toward me, not at all trying to cover up any part of his body. I've slipped my shorts back on already and I'm busy pulling up a bra strap when he asks, "What are you doing?"

"What's it look like?" I answer him with a side-eye and bend down to pick up my shirt. Which is torn beyond any hope of repair. The memory makes my pussy clench and the sweet ache only makes me want Dean again. "Well, I guess this is trash now," I say although it comes out light and humorous more than anything else.

I can feel how my body reacts to his. It's innate. It's clear from the way I peek at him through my lashes, the way the heat creeps up into my cheeks and even how my breathing is attuned to his.

Like prey to a hunter ... or vice versa.

With him, it's dangerous because I desperately want to be the prey.

His face scrunches in sympathy. "Sorry about that," he says, taking the shirt from my hands and letting his strong fingers brush against mine. They're rough to the touch and send sparks of want through me, even as the soreness between my thighs intensifies by the second. Dean's damn good at what he does. I'll give him that.

"You want me to get you a new one?" he asks me.

"Why? So you can rip that one up too?"

"What else am I good for?" he jokes as I shake my head and stare at the ruined fabric in my hands.

"I knew you were bad news," I say and again it's meant as a tease, to come out playfully and add to the banter between us.

"You don't know my story," he says and his voice comes out hard. No humor, only defensiveness.

I'm caught off guard as I watch him bend down for his shirt. Still completely naked, but he reaches for the shirt first, of all things.

"Really?" I tease him, pretending the tension doesn't exist. I wait for him to look up at me and that guarded expression still clouds his handsome face. It calls to me differently than before. My fingers itch to touch his jaw. To calm the sadness, but I resist. "Your shirt is what you go for first?" I keep my voice light and he huffs out a breath but lets a smile grow on his face.

"It's for you," he tells me as he balls it up and hands it to me. "Since you're so hell-bent on having me rip another shirt off you."

The laughter that erupts from me at his response is genuine, as is the warmth that flows through me. He's bad news *for me*. He doesn't get that. It's all bad news waiting to happen.

"It's been a while since I've smiled this hard," I confess and then bite back the happiness and honesty in that statement.

"That's a shame," Dean says and takes the shirt back before I can accept it. "You've got a beautiful smile." He leaves it hanging there in the air, and I take the bait, reaching out and trying to snatch it from him. A rough chuckle fills the air between us when I miss.

"You want it?" he asks me with a smirk on his face.

Do I want his shirt? I'm in my own damn house. I could go upstairs and put on whatever I want. But do I want his? The one he's taunting me with? Not to mention the only shirt he has here.

I nod once, feeling my hair tickle my back. The stare between us grows hotter as he takes a half step back, but holds out the shirt. My heart races faster with each passing second and the tips of my fingers glide against one another as he shakes it, as if to say, "Here, it's all yours."

83

I act as fast as I can, reaching for it and tearing it from him, but it's in vain.

He lets me have it without a fight in the least.

The cotton shirt is bunched in my hands as he drops his to his side and scratches his abs.

"Aw, you're even prettier when you pout," he mocks me and I roll my eyes, tossing his shirt carelessly behind him.

"You're no fun," I tell him. He takes a large stride toward me, wrapping his arms around my waist and pulling me against his hard chest before I can blink.

"Allie Cat, all you have to do is tell me you want it," he says as I gasp and reach both my hands up to his bare chest. My blood heats as he lowers his lips to the shell of my ear. "Sometimes it's fun to take, but we both know how that would end between us," he whispers, and it sends a chill across my skin.

He nips at my neck and runs the tip of his nose along my jaw. My eyes close slowly as I lift my lips to his. The first kiss is gradual, teasing even; I'm still reeling from his comment. The second is deeper but the moment his tongue slips across the seam of my lips, I have to laugh. His dick is hard again and poking me in my stomach.

I pull away from him, but just with my upper half, seeing as how he still has a firm grip on my waist.

"Already wanting more?" I tease him. He groans deep and presses another kiss to my lips. This time I open my mouth, greeting his hot tongue with swift, deep strokes of my own.

I moan into his mouth as he slowly unbuttons my shorts and yanks them down, shoving his hands between my legs and cupping between my thighs like he owns what's there. My neck arches and my strangled cry of pleasure is muted when Dean covers my mouth with his. He devours me forcefully and unapologetically.

And I can't bring myself to regret it.

Not this time or the next. Not even when I wake up early the next morning to find he's already gone but left his shirt behind with a note telling me it's mine to keep until he replaces the other.

At least he left a note. I'll give him that.

DEAN

*M*y muscles ache, and the burn feels so fucking good. My heart's racing and I can faintly taste the blood from the cut on my lip.

I live for this shit.

My pops used to watch rugby. I don't have many fond memories of him since he was sick for so long but as I stand in my position, cracking each knuckle one by one and waiting for the signal, I remember how I used to sit cross-legged only inches from the screen when we'd watch television together. I can still smell the beer Pops always had next to him during a game. I can still hear him cheering them on. And the second I can, I rush forward, crashing my skull into Kev's shoulder and digging my hands between his chest and the ball.

My teeth are clenched; my heart isn't fucking moving. Nothing is.

All that matters is that I get possession. My shoulder knocks hard against Kev's and he's thrown backward. As I fall forward, I rip the ball out of his hands and quickly throw it to Daniel. Fast possession, fast plays.

I tumble downward and don't even try to brace myself. My shoulder cracks as it meets the ground and the wind is knocked from me.

Before I can even get up, Kev's shoving me back down to the ground, nearly trampling me to get to the action. Fucker steps on my hand, grinding it into the dirt. Fuck!

My eyes narrow as my breath comes back to me. I almost grab his ankle and yank it toward me, just to see his scrawny ass bust his mouth on the way down. But I bite back the anger. It's not what I need. It's not good for me.

A whistle goes off and Brant, the third player on our side, pats my back as I stand up, brushing the soil from a scratch on my arm. His hand thumps my back as he says something I can't make out over the ringing in my ears. I focus on counting in my head.

Counting all the times I've lost control. All the times I've let my anger get the better of me.

All the shit it's brought me. Several broken noses, although I've only had one myself. It's one thing to pop off and pick fights because I'm bored, or because I'm angry, or even because I'm fucking lost. It's another thing entirely to let it control me. To fall back on it. I know this, I've been over this shit with Dr. Robinson, but I'll be damned if it helps me as much as getting locked up did.

I can hear the guys rallying up again as the white noise and ringing slowly fades.

All I'm concentrating on is my rage, taming it. Keeping it in. After all, it's Kev's uncle who helped me out. He's friends with the judge who agreed to the terms of my probation and beating the shit out of his nephew isn't the best way to pay him back.

"Fuck yeah, man!" I hear Daniel yell in a deep voice before throwing the ball down on the ground in front of me and jumping on my side, wrapping his arms around my neck and thrusting his hips once before jumping off.

"Whoo!" he calls out, clearly pleased with himself and the team.

The smile stretches slowly across my face as I watch as him celebrate with Brant.

"Go, team!" I hear her soft feminine voice shouting and cheering before I see her.

Hard to believe that sweet voice could come from such a sinful mouth. I can't help but to look over at her; Allie's in the back of the bleachers this time, clapping her hands and blending in with the small crowd. Well she's trying to, but a woman like that wasn't meant to blend in. It's not even so much a crowd as it is a group of kids killing time before class. It doesn't look like any of them are paying attention.

She smiles brightly when I catch her gaze. I wasn't sure if I'd see her today or not. Everything I did yesterday morning was deliberate.

Leaving my shirt—it was an excuse to seek her out in case she doesn't come back to me.

Not leaving my number—so she can't snub me and leave me hanging. I got her number from her phone before leaving, though. I didn't say I play fair.

And taking off before she woke up—to make her want the chase this time.

Yesterday came and went easily enough. I thought about her ass and almost texted her. I'd feel pathetic about how she's got me wrapped around her little finger if she wasn't sitting in the bleachers right now.

She came because she wants to see me. Plain and simple.

And I fucking love that.

My little Allie Cat may think that was a one-time thing, but I'm not even close to having my fill yet. She's a girl I can play with and I can already feel the excitement in my blood at what I'm going to do to her.

"Lookee, lookee," I hear Kevin say as we huddle up. When I look to my left at him, his eyes are on her. "You got yourself a fan, bro," he tells me and wraps his arm around me. Today we're on opposite sides, mixing it up for fun.

"Let's run some more fast plays," James starts saying, hands on his knees and far too into practice. As if anyone really cares about this game.

"You tap that?" Kev asks and it irritates James, but only for a second, until he looks behind my shoulder and catches sight of her.

Daniel peeks up at her too.

"What the fuck?" I snap at them.

"I was just looking," Daniel says defensively and tilts up his chin and adds, "Didn't take long, huh?"

"Longer than I wanted," I tell them and it makes Kev's brows knit together. "She likes to be chased," I explain and then feel uncomfortable talking about her to these guys. I barely fucking know them and it's none of their business.

They don't need to know that she's a challenge. Because she's for me. Not them.

"Let's just call it," Brant says. "Sun's going down and I'm fucking beat."

"Nah, one more," James argues. "We're getting lazy as fuck."

I crack my neck to one side and then the other.

"So, what's she like?" Kev asks, nudging me and yet again pulling the topic back to Allie.

"Fucking worth it," I tell him without hesitation. I knew she'd feel like that. Tight in all the right places, gripping my dick and working it like it belonged to her. There's more to come. I can already taste it. There's something in her that's just like me. Something easy to recognize. I can feel it. And I know it's going to make it that much better when I have her next.

"She likes it rough, doesn't she?" Kev asks and James elbows him as he adds, "Rough and dirty."

I catch Daniel glancing between the two of us. He doesn't say anything, but I don't like the look on his face or the shit they're saying.

"We going in again or not?" Kev asks. I couldn't give two shits.

"Once more," Daniel finally speaks up. Then he asks, "You want the goal this time? Chicks fucking love it when you score." I snort at his suggestion.

"Yeah they do," Brant agrees with him and again he looks back to check her out.

I shrug like I don't give a damn but then say, "Yeah, I want it this time."

"Yeah you want it," James says like a jackass. He humps the air like a jackass too. I rub the back of my head, feeling my ears burn.

"Fucking embarrassing," Daniel says, pushing James over so he falls on his ass. As the other guys laugh, I look behind me, just a quick glance to see if she saw.

But I don't know if she did or not, because she's already gone.

ALLISON

*H*e keeps looking over at the bleachers like I'm going to magically appear, and I can't help that it makes me smile. But the tug upward on my lips falters as quickly as it forms.

I know this story. And the sweet bubbly feelings in my chest, well, they don't mean shit compared to the growing sense of dread in the pit in my stomach.

I'm smarter than this.

But I want him.

The smile widens, and I kick up my foot to hit the brick wall behind me when the guys walk this way. Straight to the locker room I just happen to be standing in front of.

It gives me a sick sense of pleasure when Dean nearly trips as he catches sight of me.

He notices my smile too, which makes him narrow his eyes. I love this game. More than anything else, I love the way it makes me feel.

Even if it is temporary.

"Stay right there," Dean tells me, not slowing his pace as he walks right past me to go through the doors. "Just need to grab something."

He doesn't even wait for me to nod. Doesn't wait for any sign at all I heard him.

My jaw hangs open. Fucking dick.

I grin slightly as I realize he won that round. I can hear a bell ding in my head and see him getting a point on a scoreboard. "Touché," I mutter as the rest of the guys file in. He knows I came for him.

Why do I love that he's such an asshole?

I'm left pondering that very question and kicking the dirt when I hear another voice.

"Well, hello again. Did you enjoy the game?" Kevin Henderson asks me as the hairs on the back of my neck stand up. He stops only a foot in front of me, watching as some of the other guys walk past him. I have to remind myself we're not alone. Not really. The field is right behind us. The study group that was on the bleachers is still there. Still within earshot.

My shoulders move involuntarily into a shrug as I try to act casual and keep it light, but flirtatious. It takes me a moment to look Kevin in the eyes and when I do, I make sure to flash him a dazzling smile.

"Looked like a practice to me," I tell him while my heart thuds once, then twice. *It's not a game.*

He manages a half smirk and moves his thumb to the corner of his mouth before replying, "I thought you said it's always a game?"

The pounding of my heart gets louder and my blood turns to ice in my veins. I can picture how it would happen right now, how he'd pin me here against the brick wall, how it would scrape against my back. But it would have to be late. The skies would be black and my scream, when I finally did scream, would echo for miles.

"Didn't you?" he asks me, his voice bringing me back to the present and I have to manage my composure, making sure I add a touch of shyness as I take the strand of hair in front of my face and tuck it behind my ear.

My eyelashes flutter as I tell him, "You have a good memory."

"You dye your hair?" he asks and my stomach clenches. As if he knows who I used to be. "Why? Blondes have more fun, don't they?" he says in jest before flashing me a smile and I struggle to respond. *He's just making random conversation. It doesn't mean anything.*

"Yo," Kevin says as he rips his eyes off me and the sound of footsteps slowly coming to a stop greet me.

"Everything good?" I hear Dean ask, but I still don't look in his direction. I can't right now. Not after this little encounter.

It's odd to feel as if I've betrayed him. As if I should feel guilty, and maybe that's what this twisting in my gut is.

"Yeah, yeah," Kevin says and tells me, "Catch you later," before half jogging into the locker room.

"He giving you a hard time?" Dean asks me and when I hear Kevin's sneakers skid across the cement pad in front of the doorway, I finally look up at Dean. Right into a possessive stare.

One that sees right through me.

His hard gaze makes me feel like my hand has been played. Like I can't trust the words in my mouth.

"You want to tell me something?" he asks me and my bottom lip wobbles slightly. I want to tell him everything. *I'm desperate to tell someone.*

"Did you see him score?" Daniel's voice interjects. When I look at him, Dean takes a step back, narrowing his eyes and focusing them on Daniel. "He said it was for you," Daniel adds as he slips his arm around Dean's shoulders and flashes me a charming smile, but I see right through it.

He's a good liar. From what I've heard in the last few weeks from whispers on campus, it's a family trait of his. Apparently all the Cross' have a reputation. I don't know what the hell Daniel

Cross is doing here or with men like Kev and I don't care. Consequences be damned, I'm going to get what I want.

"I saw a bit of the action," I finally answer Daniel and then meet Dean's stare to add, "I like watching him score."

A flicker of humor touches his eyes but he doesn't smile until I say, "I'm glad you guys are done, though. I don't like waiting for what I want."

I shouldn't have said it really. But I wanted to see him smile. I wanted it so bad that I lost control again. He makes me reckless.

"You heard her," Dean says with a lopsided grin and slaps Daniel's arm away.

"You made her wait long enough I guess," Daniel says before walking off and nodding a farewell.

A short moment passes and I don't know what Dean's next move will be. It makes me nervous.

"So, you ready to go?" Dean asks me, and I gawk at him.

"Go where?"

The muscles on his broad shoulders ripple as he moves the strap of his duffle bag over his shoulder and across his body.

"I just came to give you your shirt back."

"That's nice of you," he says then looks at my purse and my cheeks burn. I don't actually have it with me. I just said that to make it difficult for him.

"So?" he asks and another breeze goes by, sending goosebumps up my arm. It's colder in the evening and especially in the shadows.

"So what?"

"The shirt?" he asks then adds, "Really, it's for you to hold on to until I can get you a new one."

I shrug off the chill. "You don't have to do that."

"I want to, though. You all right with that?" he asks like it's a dare and my heart skips a beat as I'm caught in his heated gaze. He traps me so easily.

Luckily, I'm saved by his next comment.

"I like being with you for some reason." It's a backhanded compliment. He's such an asshole. But such a good-looking, playful one.

"Yeah, well, you're an asshole jock and jocks aren't my thing," I tell him back just as dismissively. Both of us are smiling, though. This is what I like about him.

"I'm not a jock."

I wait for him to comment on the asshole part and when he doesn't, I let out a small laugh.

Rolling my eyes, I wrap my arms around my chest as a gust blows my hair off my shoulder. Dean looks up and it's as if that's the cue for the sky to visibly darken.

"So, where do you want to go?" he asks.

"I'm not sure that's smart."

"It's just a date."

"I don't think we should date. I don't really do dating." My gaze falls to his chest, moves to his shoes then continues to the ground as I feel the truth of why I even bothered to go against my gut and show up to the field today. I push the hair back from my face as the breeze picks up and wish I'd worn a thicker coat.

The sound of Dean rustling in his duffle bag gets my attention, and he pulls out a jacket then hands it out to me. "Put it on," he tells me and it's clearly a command. Like a good girl, I reach out for it, but then feel ridiculous and pathetic and drop my hand before I grab it.

"Dean, I'm not good for you." I push out the words even though they hurt, even though they make me feel worse than just playing along.

"You're cute, Allie Cat, but that 'it's not you, it's me' bullshit isn't going to work on me. I'm too used to being pushed away," he tells me, and I watch his expression shift as he realizes what he's said. He's used to being pushed away. I'd just be one more asshole doing the same.

"Come on, take it," he urges, shaking the jacket and the memory of last night forces me to take it.

I'm silent as I put it on. Fuck. Shit. Dammit. I hate this. I hate that I started this.

"So, date," Dean says as he grips the strap with both of his hands and watches me slip on his jacket. It's oddly warm for being so thin. "Where are we going?" he asks.

I roll my eyes and tell him, "I don't date."

"Just fucking then," he says, nodding his head. "Your place or mine?" he asks with a cocky grin.

"I'm not here just so you can get in my pants," I say, trying desperately to clear my head and figure out what the hell I'm doing.

"Then why'd you come?" he asks me.

"I told you I just wanted to give you your shirt back," I tell him, but I can already see the spark of mischievousness in his eyes.

"I was talking about the other night, and it's because you fucking loved it."

I can't help the smile that comes with his joke or the way his dirty words make me feel like it's all okay. Belting his chest, I turn away from him. "You're awful," is all I can say, the smile still there. When he slides up behind me, pulling my body close to his, I relax into his heat. I hear the wind blow behind us but with my back to his chest, and my body facing the wall, not a bit of it touches my skin. Instead of a chill, I'm greeted with warmth as he gently nips my jaw and then releases me.

"You look good in my clothes," he tells me when I turn to face him. His eyes roam freely down my body and the heat intensifies in my cheeks.

"Thanks for the jacket." It's only a quiet whisper but I mean it. I'm grateful for him.

Both of us are silent as we watch a few more guys leave the locker room. I cross my arms over my chest and peek up at him.

"I like you, Allison," Dean says, taking a step forward. "I'm not going to let you get away so easily."

My lungs still for a moment as his fingers brush along my face and he tucks a strand of hair behind my ear.

"Maybe I'd like that," I say, admitting the sentiment out loud. The moment I do, I'm certain I shouldn't have said them.

"We're going to fuck, but I need to eat first," he tells me. "And you're coming with me because you need to eat too."

"You're taking me out to dinner?" I ask incredulously, although I'm not blind to the fact that it makes me happy. Truly. That should bother me more than it does. All of this should bother me much more than it does.

"Just feeding you, Allie Cat. Don't read too much into it."

"I thought we were just fucking?" I say.

"A man's got to eat."

I huff a response, although the smile lingers on my lips. But only for a moment.

DEAN

The corner diner on campus isn't classy or fancy. The booths are covered in red vinyl that matches the stools at the narrow bar in front of the kitchen. The black and white checkered floors, vinyl records on the wall and jukebox in the far corner give it a retro feel. It's not really what I'd consider a good date place but they make a damn good burger.

Allie takes the lead the second we walk in, heading for a booth at the back and I follow her. She's been quiet since we left the field, and I don't like it.

I don't like the way she was looking at Kev even more.

A waitress carrying two baskets of fries calls out, "Be right with you," as I take my seat in the booth Allie picked.

"You been here yet?" I ask Allie, still trying to figure out what's going on in her pretty little head.

She lifts a brow at me as she slips the jacket off her shoulders. *My* jacket. "You learn quick," she tells me, and I feel my forehead crease.

"How's that?"

"Small talk, you do well when you lead with it."

There's a hum of pleasure running through me when she smiles. "I try," I say and then glance over my shoulder as the waitress heads back to the kitchen rather than toward us.

When I look back at Allie, she's quiet again, a contemplative look on her face.

I can't help but wonder if it's because of Kevin. Maybe he's the one she really wanted.

My muscles coil at the thought and I can feel anger rising at the thought of her with him. *She's mine.* That little prick isn't good enough for her.

I pick at the napkin on the table out of habit, my mind going back to the sight of her batting her lashes at him and giving him that sweet look that belongs to me. Doesn't she know better than that? I'll treat her good. I have what it takes to keep her.

"So, you don't like jocks?" I ask, preparing to bring it up. To make sure she knows her ass is mine right now. Even in kindergarten, everyone knew it—I don't share well with others.

"Not really," she answers me, but that playfulness in her voice is gone. She squirms in her seat like she's uncomfortable.

"They're just not your type?" I ask with my eyes narrowing, each second bringing me closer to the place I was when I came out of the locker room and saw her with him.

She meets my gaze head-on. "I've fucked a lot of them, but I guess I just prefer other types of guys."

"You like being thought of like that, don't you?"

"Like what?" she says, egging me on.

"Like a slut," I say, not missing a beat.

"I like it when people call me that to my face. I like them to know it doesn't bother me. I fucking own it." Her breathing picks up, her body tensing. Like she's ready for a fight and to defend her position. I don't want a fight, though. I fucking love how she knows what she wants.

"Then what type do you like? Since you're so good at owning it."

"I have lots of types, I guess."

"But no one type in particular?" I ask her. "Not like, I don't know, my height, my eye color?" She barely looks at me and then I add, "Tall, dark, and handsome?" I expect her to laugh or give me something back. But I get nothing.

Something happened between the time I walked into the locker and the time I came out. I'm damn sure of it because I've never seen her like this.

She presses her lips together in a thin line and looks past me when a loud bang and clatter comes from the kitchen. The couple at the other end of the restaurant is looking too.

It's only when I look back to the piece of napkin in my hands that I realize it's shredded.

"No. No type in particular," Allie says flatly.

"You're being moody as fuck."

"I'm just moody in general," she says with a smile that doesn't reach her eyes. Those beautiful eyes are narrowed at me and I know she's warring with something, but I don't know what. I just want her to tell me.

"Give me something." The words may come out as a command but I'm fucking begging. I'm practically on my knees wanting this girl to trust me.

"Something?" That resolute look in her eyes flickers, like she didn't expect that. *Like she didn't expect me.*

"You don't have to hide from me," I start to say but before I can finish, she's already shaking her head.

"I didn't ask for this," she bites back.

"Then leave," I tell her because I'm irritated. Because the fact that she's giving me attitude and pushing me away is doing nothing but pissing me off.

It takes all of half a second for her to stand up, leaving my jacket where it is, and make a beeline for the back exit.

"What the hell is wrong with you?" I call after her.

"A lot," she answers, and I should let her walk away. I should watch her do it and order myself something to eat. Forget about her.

I'm sure there's a lot of shit I should do, but logic and reasoning aren't really my strong suit.

And I fucking want her.

More than anything else right now. I. Want. Her.

I shove the table away as I stand, and it squeaks across the floor. "Allison," I call after her as the door shuts, but she doesn't look back.

I'm quick. Quicker than her as I round the back exit to the deserted parking lot.

My hand slams on the brick wall as I catch up to her, boxing her in and stopping her in her tracks.

"You're in my way," she says through gritted teeth.

"I don't like games."

"I told you, Dean," she says sarcastically, although her expression is riddled with pain. "It's always a game."

"What's going on with you? You're making me crazy with this shit."

"You think I don't care about myself, huh? That I don't have any self-worth?"

"Where the fuck is that coming from?"

"From you asking me if I'm a slut."

"That's not what I said, I said you like being thought of like that. There's a difference."

Her expression softens slightly but she continues this bullshit. "It's the same for you."

"It's not. And I didn't say shit about your *self-worth.*" I mock the way she said it and feel like an ass, but it pisses me off she'd even say that. "I only want you because you are worth it. How can you not see that?"

She flinches at my question.

"Just let me go," she whispers and pushes at my arm, but I hold firm.

"No, you're not leaving like this." I've never met someone like her. She needs someone. It's so fucking obvious.

"You don't get to tell me what to do," she says but even as she does, I can see her fight is gone.

We're in the back lot, with dumpsters right behind us and there are only two cars back here. We have plenty of privacy and at the realization, I step even closer to her. Upping the ante.

"You're not leaving like this. Not until you give me an explanation."

"Fuck you," she tells me.

"That's right, Allie Cat, that's exactly what you're about to do. You're finally getting fucked against the wall like the dirty whore you are."

"I already crossed that off my wish list."

"Not with me and not like this. And it's not your wish list, Allison, it's your to-do list."

"You're such a cocky bastard. You think because you tell me to fuck you, I will."

"No, it's because you want to. It's because you love it when my dick's deep inside of you. And I may be cocky, but you're the one who's pushy. You want control, you want to pull me this way and that and the moment I follow, you want to push me away. Not. Fucking. Happening."

"You think you're so good, don't you?" she taunts me.

"Tell me I'm not, and I'll leave."

My heart's a fucking battering ram, trying to crash out of my chest, but she doesn't answer me. She bites tongue for once.

I know one thing about Allie. She'll stay with me if I'm loving on her. I can do that. I can keep her coming back.

"Now, getting back to your to-do list. You're going to take my cock into your tight cunt that's already wet for me. Then you're going back inside and you're going to sit down next to me while my cum leaks out of your cunt like the dirty girl you are."

"Just because I liked it once, doesn't mean I'll like it again," she tells me and shoves against my chest. The look on her face tells me everything I need to know.

She wants to hurt me. To push me away. I won't let it happen. I can't.

"I let a lot of people push me out of their lives. None of them wanted me. But you do. I know you do," I tell her, and I'm shocked by the admission. The look on her face shows she's surprised too.

"What are you doing to me?" I ask her although there's no way in hell she could answer.

The air changes in an instant and I feel weak. Like I've lost her, all because I can't control my mouth.

I pull my arm away, my palm stinging from being against the hard brick for so long. *What the fuck is she doing to me?*

"Can I tell you something, Dean?" she says and lowers her voice, her features softening. Half of me expects her to kiss me, the other half thinks she's going to slam her head into my nose. I never know what to expect from her.

"Tell me whatever you want, Allie."

"You scare me."

"I don't mean to," I tell her apologetically. My face falls. "Fuck, that's the last thing I want."

"No, no, not like that," she's quick to respond and this time she actually comes to me.

"Like what, then? I can fix it." Damn, I sound like a little bitch. Even hearing it in my own voice, I don't care. Because she cups my jaw and leans in to say, "I feel like I'm safe when I'm with you, and that scares the fuck out of me." Her whisper gently caresses my jaw and a chill runs down my neck.

"Let's pretend that's a good thing," I tell her, and she gives me a sad smile.

"I don't do well with pretending."

"I don't believe that for a second. I bet you have lots of fantasies."

"That's not the same."

"Yeah it is," I say and cup her cheek in my hand. I press a kiss to her forehead and whisper, "I bet you'd like to pretend with me."

Her body shivers beneath me. A shiver that makes me feel like I've won.

"I like the idea of you ..." she trails off, closes her eyes and whispers, "pushing me against the wall." When she opens her eyes, it looks like she's not breathing. Her green eyes stare back at me with an unspoken question. Asking if I understand what she's saying.

"And then what?" I ask her as my mouth goes dry. The need to taste her, to shove her back and take from her is riding me hard. I have her right now, but I need to give her every reason to stay. My hands clench into fists at my side and my body goes rigid. One piece of my anatomy is noticeably harder than the rest.

"I'd like it," she barely speaks the words before visibly swallowing. "I'd like it if you were rough. If you ..." she trails off while her gaze falls away from mine and she takes an unsteady breath.

"You want me to fuck you like I own you. Like your cunt belongs to me and I'll take what I want from you?" I ask her and finally trust myself enough to take her small hand in mine. My touch is gentle as I rub the rough pad of my thumb along her knuckles.

"Yes," she answers me quickly and I take a half step back, so I can look her in the eyes, searching them and trying to decide if she knows what she's asking for.

"If I did what I wanted to you," I start to say and then want to take it back. I can already see this going the wrong way. Back to her leaving me.

"What?" she asks.

I look at the empty parking lot and then back at her. *Give and take.* I gave some; I can take it now.

"What if I punished you?" I suggest as I run the back of my pointer finger down the side of her face. "For flirting with another man." I almost say one of my friends. *Kevin.* I almost single him out. But I have a feeling Allie likes to flirt a lot. And with whomever the fuck she wants.

I'd admire that if her ass wasn't already claimed by me.

She glares at me.

It's full of defiance and even a touch of hate. I can't take her hate. That's not what I want from her.

I almost take it back. I'm so close to apologizing but then she opens that mouth of hers.

"I can do what I want," she finally says. Her eyes dare me to contradict her.

"You already told me you wanted me, and that comes with a price," I tell her. "You know better than that, Allie."

"If I want attention, I'm going to get it," she speaks softly, staring past my shoulder and out across the parking lot. I can give that to her. Anything she needs, I can give to her.

"You just need to be fucked, don't you? You'd fall on anyone's dick to please this greedy little cunt."

Her lips part, but she hesitates.

"Fuck you," she finally says but it's half-hearted and she's breathing heavier. And that's just what I need. A sign that she still wants me. Or at least will give me a chance.

"That's exactly what I want," I tell her and she scoffs, but doesn't break the heated gaze between us.

I take a step forward and she takes one back, but it's shorter than mine, stopped by the hard brick wall behind her.

"Don't you know this is mine until I've had my fill?" I say beneath my breath as I reach between her thighs and cup her pussy.

Her mouth parts slightly, even as her back arches and she pushes her cunt against my hand.

"You're bad for me," she tells me in a heated whisper and then her eyes close with a small moan as I rock my palm against her clit.

I might not be the best thing for her, but that doesn't mean I'm letting her go.

I pull away right before those soft moans can turn into something more than just foreplay.

"Tell me what you want." I give her the command, but it comes out as desperate. One half step back gives her the exit she was after when I walked out here. "Just tell me, Allie."

I don't care that I'm weak for her. I just want her weak for me.

"I want you," she says in a rushed breath and before the last word is spoken, I'm already on her. Shoving my hands up her skirt and ripping my thumb through the thin lace. I hear it tear as she moans my name into the hot air. I shove the ripped panties into my pocket and look to my right and left before pulling out my dick.

"This has to be quick," I tell her and then kiss her neck ravenously. As though I'm starved for her. Her slender fingers grip into my shoulders as I wrap her legs around me and tease the head of my dick against her heat. I'm easing it in, sliding back and forth and she's already soaking wet.

The deep, gruff sound at the back of my throat is all for her as I push myself all the way in to the hilt in one swift stroke.

She cries out, slamming her head back, but it's muffled as she bites down into her lip.

I thrust upward as hard as I can, burying myself in her tight cunt. Fuck, she feels so damn good. She claws at my back as I slam into her, her back pushing against the wall each time.

My pace is steady, relentless and each pump of my hips has her climbing higher and higher.

Before I even feel the need to cum, she's already clamping down on my dick and whimpering her release.

It's the sweetest fucking sound I've ever heard. I want to hear it every damn day. I want her to cling to me like she needs me.

And to trust that I'll give it to her. I'll give her everything.

I pick up my pace, racing for my own release and riding through hers.

"So fucking good," I moan into the curve of her neck. Nipping and kissing as I take her like I want her.

I meant for it to be quick, but I hold back just enough so I can make it last a little longer. I want to hold on to her. She needs to know that.

She's limp when I'm done with her. Her legs are trembling and I have to lean her against the wall so I can pull my pants back up. Her eyes are closed when I look up at her, and I don't think I've ever seen someone look so damn beautiful.

She doesn't fight me when I grip her chin between my thumb and forefinger, getting her attention so I can look her in the eyes and tell her, "Stop pushing me away. I don't like it."

Her chest is still heaving, but her shallow breath is starting to come back to her.

I wait a second for her to search my gaze, and I hope she finds what she's looking for because I mean it.

"I can give you everything you want, Allie. All you have to do is let me."

ALLISON

"You know I'm no good, right?" I can't help but ask him as we sit next to each other in the diner. In the back of my head, I can hear myself saying he's no good for me too. But it's so quiet. The hum of something else has taken over. He gives me a fuzzy feeling. One I haven't felt in a long time. *One that makes me want more than what I'd planned.*

The food's half-gone on my plate. Just chicken tenders and fries. You can't go wrong with that. Dean's finished his burger and is working through the pile of fries left on his plate. A pair of Cokes top off the meal.

He huffs like it's a joke and doesn't answer me, reaching for his drink instead. I find it fascinating watching him. He's different. A kind of different I like.

He makes me feel safe and wanted. It's foolish, but I want that. *I want him.* All of him. And that's something I've never wanted before.

"I think this weekend I'm going away. I don't have to worry about you running off, do I?" he asks me.

"You probably should," I say as a joke. Judging by the expression on his face, he doesn't like my answer. "Where are you going?" I ask to change the subject. I like his smile the best. My skin pricks at the realization. Knowing that my own happiness is somehow attached to someone else's. I don't care for it because people come and go. They leave you, disappoint you. They die.

And then you're left all alone.

"To Brunswick. I think," he says.

"You think?" I ask him playfully, but my heart hurts. My mother's in Brunswick. All of it happened in Brunswick. I hate Brunswick.

"I haven't decided if I'm going yet."

I let out a small chuckle; it's more a breath of a laugh. "I swear I won't run off, so you can go," I tell him.

"I just wanted to hear you say it. Right now, you're mine. We don't need labels, but I'll be damned if I'll let you think I'm fine with you fucking someone else." His words are hard and brutish. Almost like a slap in my face.

"What if I want to?" I ask him, and he looks me square in the eyes.

"Do you?"

No, I don't. I hesitate, and my heart seems to struggle with each second. I can't do this to him.

"I guess not. You fuck well enough," I say and stuff a fry into my mouth, hating how much it hurts me to play it off.

"I'm serious, Allie," he says and his voice is hard, with no room for negotiation. "I don't want to think about you just up and leaving."

"I don't even know you," I answer in jest, but all humor leaves me when I see the look in his eyes. They're dark, piercing. *Possessive.*

"Yeah, you do. You know enough." He lets out a heavy breath, pushing his plate away. "I'm telling you I want you and I don't want you running around on me. That's all I'm asking."

"I think I like that," I say, mesmerized by how easily he

admitted that. How easily he made himself vulnerable. I really like it. "I want that too."

"You want me?" he asks with the hint of a smile and I nod, then say, "Yeah, I want you."

"Only me?" he asks, cocking a brow.

"Sure, for now," I answer him with a flirtation I think he likes.

The smile on my face only grows, as does his. That's the thing about him that's addictive. The pain vanishes when he smiles.

It's quiet for a minute. A long minute and I don't like the tension, but I'm the one who caused it to begin with. A dull ache pulses between my legs as I lean closer to him and cross them.

"You did a number on me," I whisper and brush my cheek against his arm. My fingers play around his large wrist for a moment, just to feel him.

He's so close, only inches away since we're sitting on the same side of the booth. I guess he wanted to make sure I wasn't going to take off again. Smart of him.

"Is that right?" he says, putting down his drink so he can rest his hand on my thigh. We both watch as he rubs it with his thumb in slow, soothing circles. "How's your shoulder?" he asks me, and it takes a second to register.

Reaching up with my hand to push the fabric aside, I take a look and let out a small laugh. "I match you now," I tell him.

He brushes my hand away and gently soothes the scrape. I can hardly feel it; I barely feel anything but exhaustion at the moment.

"It's nothing," I tell him and he glances at me, but then back at my shoulder.

"Beds are better," he says with a small smile, but it doesn't reach his eyes. "Did you like it?" he asks me.

"Dean, you have no idea what I'd let you do to me." I shake my head and feel embarrassed by how quickly and honestly I responded. I should know better.

"Is that why you think you're no good? Because you like it hard?"

"Not just hard."

"Brutal, anal, gangbang, rape fantasy, what?" He says the words like they're no big deal. Maybe to him, they aren't. Some people, though … some people use them to hurt others. "How fucking bad do you go, Allie Cat?" he asks me and I hesitate. So much is threatening to spill out. My heart's racing and my hands are feeling clammy.

"It's not as easy as me just picking a fantasy and you deliver," I tell him, watching my hands as I pick at my fingernails.

"Sure it is. Unless it's a gangbang situation you're after. It's going to be hard for me to fill that order by my lonesome."

I snicker and slowly shake my head, finally peeking up at him.

"I like to fuck," he says as he leans in closer to me. "And I'll tell you a little secret," he whispers as he lowers his lips to my ear. "I've done dirtier shit and loved it."

"Like what?" I ask him instantly, desperate to know.

"I've used rope before," he finally answers before reaching for his soda and taking a drink. My eyes lift to his, willing him to continue. "I like having control. So long as I have that, I can push the boundaries. I can chase you down, pin you beneath me. You need to tell me what you want, but if you think you're oh so bad, little kitten, I can assure you that you're not."

He has no idea that he's the one playing with fire, not me.

"I just like …" I pause but force myself to look him in the eyes as I continue, "to fight back." It's a secret I haven't told anyone else. I want to play. I want to push my limits. I haven't met someone I could do it with. Not until Dean.

"You didn't fight me much out there," he responds, and a spark of desire ignites within me.

"Did you want me to?" I ask him and he shrugs in response, picking at the fries on his plate.

"I don't care how I fuck you so long as I get to," he answers me with a slowly growing smirk on his face.

I find it hard to focus. To eat. To do anything other than think about how much Dean could push me, and how I could push him right back.

DEAN

She's a little kitten, my Allie Cat. She thinks she's so dirty and bad, but really she just likes rough and hard sex. It's cute. Well, as long as she listens it's cute. As long as she stays where she belongs.

The first step after dinner was to take a look at the kind of porn she's into. She can get all quiet and shy talking about it, but her search history doesn't hide a damn thing.

Brutal fuck.

Hard rough fuck.

Choked, slapped, punished.

I huff a small laugh when I see her phone on the nightstand. She brought up a picture of a girl all tied up with rope.

Fuck that. My answer: *I don't have time for that shit.* She got a kick out of my reaction. Maybe I'll tie her ass up for Christmas or something if we're still together then, but right now, I just need her ass to sit pretty.

Yeah, she's a little kitten. And she deserves to be fucked however she wants it. Just thinking about it is getting my dick hard again. Even with the knowledge she's passed out and her cunt's sore and swollen from the hard fuck I just gave her.

Her sweet smell drifts toward me as she cuddles in close. She's only got a twin bed and her bedroom looks like she just moved in. There's just a bed and a dresser full of clothes.

It reminds me of my room after my father died and we moved.

I clear my throat and wrap my arm around her small form, pressing her soft body into mine. Her little murmur of satisfaction stops the thoughts of my father in their tracks.

Thank fuck for that, but I still can't sleep.

It's almost 3:00 a.m. and I'm wide awake, although I don't know why. I should've exhausted myself into a coma, but I can't turn off thinking about everything that's happened this week. It's been fast and furious with Allie. I'm not the type that gets attached. This girl is getting to me, and I don't know why. I can't explain it.

A low groan rumbles in the back of my throat as I remember how I made her get down on all fours with her ass in the air, all so I could watch my cum leak out of her pretty little pussy.

Another groan, another memory. My dick twitches and hardens with need. The last straw is when she throws her leg over my thigh and her bare pussy rubs against me.

"You doing that on purpose?" I ask her and the little minx smiles. Guess I'm not the only one who can't sleep.

I push her onto her back and nuzzle her neck to wake her up.

"I want you," I tell her and nip her ear. Her palms push weakly against my chest until I rock my hard dick against her pussy. My lips drop to the crook of her neck as I moan, "You're so fucking wet."

She mewls an incoherent response.

Getting on my knees, I try to push her onto her stomach, but she protests. "What if I want you like this?" she asks me. Her eyes are half-lidded, and her hair's a messy halo scattered across the pillow.

She digs her heels into my ass as she spreads her thighs for me. "Just like this."

My heart beats harder. "Just on top?" I tease her, letting my fingers trail up her thigh to the dip in her waist. The shiver that runs through her body makes me smile.

She gives me a simple nod and props herself up on her elbows so I can wrap my arms around her back. Nestling my hips against hers, I line up my dick and slide in gently.

"Nice and slow," she says softly, sleep evident in her voice. Her head falls back the second I push inside of her.

I'm gentle at first, letting the bed rock with us in slow motions. It hits the wall every time. I thought we'd managed to put a hole in the drywall with the last round.

The smell of sex fills the air as I keep up a steady pace. I'm deliberately holding back. Forcing her to writhe under me and dig her heels into my ass harder.

She cries out a strangled plea for more. I can feel her cunt tighten, but she'll never get off like this. Not for a while at least.

She's breathless when she looks up at me. "Harder," she begs me.

And I give her just what she wants, feeling her heart race against mine.

I lift her up on her side first, straddling her leg so I can push all the way into her without her hips hitting mine. The second I slide into her, still gentle with my thrust, her plump lips part with a gasp and she grips the comforter as she screams out.

"Dean!" she cries out my name as I slam into her again. A deep, rough noise is forced from me when I feel the head of my dick bump against her cervix.

Fuck yes.

I pound into her again and again, gripping onto her thigh with a bruising force to keep her right where I want her. Even as she tries to move away from me.

She pushes against me, struggling and writhing with the intensity of what I'm what doing to her. It's almost too much. Her nails scratch at my chest and dig into my skin. Her face scrunches with a mixture of pain and pleasure, but I don't hold back. Bending down, I kiss her jaw and she's eager to meet my lips with hers. It's hot and heavy and different. Different between us and electric.

I can feel she's close from the way her pussy tightens and from the sweet sounds she's making. I fucking love it. I love what I can do to her.

"Dean, fuck!" she yells out as her neck arches and her head digs into the pillow. I lean closer to her so I can bite down on her neck, sucking and nipping as I push her higher and higher. A small whimper is followed by a sibilant sound on her lips. I can hear the word *stop* on the tip of her tongue. It's the smallest hint of this being too much for her, making me pull back slightly. Only slightly, and I keep up my pace.

My heart beats hard and fast, desperate for more but knowing she's on the edge of it hurting her, of being too much. It's for her. I can hardly breathe as I wait in that short moment where I know I've pushed too hard.

She doesn't miss a beat though, completely oblivious to the fact that I'm taking it easy on her. She's a tight fit and feels too damn good to stop.

The bed slams into the wall and her fingers cling to my shoulders, urging me on but still fighting me.

SHE PUSHES against me and writhes with the need to get away; it's so fucking intense, but I don't stop. I need more. More of this. *More of her.*

"Dean!" she screams out my name as her cunt spasms on my cock and her body goes rigid, paralyzed from pleasure.

"Thank fuck," I whisper against her neck, feeling her heat surround me as I hammer into her over and over, ruthlessly fucking her deeper and deeper as her arousal leaks between us.

I ride through her orgasm and take what's mine until I feel the telltale signs of my own release.

Her blunt nails scratch into my shoulder as I thrust deeply one last time and feel thick hot streams leave me in waves.

"Allie." It's all I can manage to say as my body rocks with the thrill of my release.

When I finally come back down, Allie's legs are shaking and she's still trembling beneath me with her own pleasure.

My mouth is dry and my heart racing as I slip out of her, letting our combined cum drip down her thigh.

"Oh my God," Allie murmurs as she turns on her side and curls up.

All I feel is pride as I pull the covers over her. She's still shaking.

"You all right?" I question and she nods her head, but keeps her eyes tightly shut. "You're on the pill, right?" I ask her as I stand up and grab my shirt to wipe myself off and then go back to clean her up.

I finally feel spent, but I should've asked about the pill days ago.

She shakes her head, and I stand there dumbfounded for a moment.

It's quiet. Allie's still in the same position.

"You need me to go get you some Plan B or something?" I say and try to figure out how many days or hours that shit works for.

She laughs into her pillow and then winces as she rolls onto her back and pulls the covers up tighter around her. "On the shot, dummy," she says and it's only then I let out a breath.

"Well shit, you could have led with that."

The sweet cadence of her joyful laugh fills the night air.

"You think you're funny," I tell her and she's quick to respond with, "You're the one who jokes so much."

"Yeah well, sad people like to rely on humor," I say without thinking. A chill flows over my skin, hating that I just said that. I don't know what Allie does to me, but goddamn does she bring out a side of me no one else gets to see.

"That's funny, because I never joke," she says without missing a beat, parting her legs for me when I slip the shirt between her thighs.

"You sad, Allie Cat?" I ask, wiping her up and then tossing the shirt into the hamper in the bathroom. She doesn't answer me. Maybe she says shit to me she shouldn't too. That'd only be fair.

"You know I'm going to break down your walls," I whisper against her lips and then slide beneath the covers with her on this tiny bed. I can feel the weight of exhaustion already pulling me under.

"I wish you wouldn't," she says but presses her body against mine, nuzzling next to me and wrapping her arm around my abs.

"Maybe that's why I want to so bad."

ALLISON

I feel so deliciously used.

My nipples harden every time I feel that deep ache between my thighs, which is practically every time I move.

Even now, as I slide into my chair on the right side of the classroom. I'm early for once in my life. And I'm grateful the only other person here to see me and my sit of shame is Angie.

"Ooh," she says, making a perfect *O* with her mouth and then snickers as she slips the bookbag off her shoulders. "Looks like you're having a good time, huh?"

I haven't spoken to her since that first time, even though she's been friendly.

I just don't make friends. Or have them. I don't want them, and I wouldn't make a good friend in return either. So, there's no point.

But I've never been too good to brag.

"You could say that," I respond with an expression of pure content and a Cheshire cat smile.

"So ..." she says, "who is he?" She talks while opening her textbook followed by her notebook, filled with what looks like an actual outline and highlighted words.

It's obvious she actually gives a fuck about chemistry or at least about passing the class. Good for her.

Before I can even open my mouth, I catch a glimpse of Dean from the corner of my eye. With his height and broad shoulders, he takes up the whole doorframe before walking in. I can feel my body react to his. The way my heart skips, my thighs tighten. I'm more than acutely aware of his presence.

I bite down on my lip, raise a brow and nod my head in his direction although I keep my eyes on Angie's.

I can hear him stride across the room and take the seat next to mine, but all the while Angie's expression drops. Her back stiffens and she forces a smile that's not genuine.

"Just be careful," she mutters without looking me in the eye and then goes back to her notes.

That's not the reaction I was expecting, and my gaze lingers on her longer than it should.

I don't like it. Not in the least.

During the entire class, I can't help but to glance at her. I'm still trying to make sense of her reaction but she ignores me entirely.

Even when Dean puts his hand on my thigh. Even when he leans over and covertly whispers dirty little promises in my ear. My focus is on Angie, who looks more and more uncomfortable even though she's not looking at us.

Before we're even halfway through class I pass him a note and feel like I'm back in fucking high school. This ... whatever this is between us, is stupid. All of it. But I guess I'm the stupid one really because I keep falling for this shit with Dean.

THE QUESTION IS SIMPLE; *did you fuck her?*

I get a what-the-fuck expression in return from him, paired

with a furious headshake and then a cocky smirk. The note he sends back pisses me off. He likes that I'm jealous.

I'm not fucking jealous.

This right here, this is why I don't have friends. Or boyfriends or fuck buddies or *anyone* in my life. I don't need the spiked lump in my throat that makes me wish I had more water in the bottle in my bag so I could take a large gulp. Or maybe vodka in the bottle. I could use a shot to get rid of this tension.

I have to force myself to relax and the moment I do, finally listening to the professor, Angie gives me a friendly smile. Genuine. Maybe I'm just crazy.

I'm irritated, all because of one look from a girl I don't even know. That's not me. Just as I'm shaking it off, Dean's heavy hand lands on my desk holding a scrap of paper meant only for my eyes.

You want a list of the girls I've fucked?

"Oh my God, shut up." I don't hide my irritation as I mumble the response.

Professor Grant glances our way as Dean chuckles. At least he's having a good time with it all.

He lowers his hand to my thigh again, scooting his desk closer to mine as quietly as he can. He's a big brute in that tiny desk and can't do a damn thing quietly. I don't know why it makes me smile like it does. He plays it off, mouthing he's sorry to the professor and I find myself trying to bite back the humor.

But I instantly realize why he moved closer when he slips his hand onto my thigh.

I should look to see if the professor sees, or maybe even Angie. My dirty mind looks to see what time it is and quickly calculates how many minutes are left before class will be over.

When I peek at him, knowing there are only ten minutes or so remaining, he's sinking his teeth into his lower lip, giving me a sexy grin as he squeezes my upper thigh and then lets his fingers drift closer and closer to where they want to be.

I'm in jeans so there's no way he's going to be doing anything too scandalous. I like his ownership of me. I like that he likes me and doesn't mind showing people.

I like that I like him too.

Even if Angie has a stick up her ass about it. Or not ... what do I know?

And so I part my thighs just a bit, enough for him to slip his fingertips all the way up, pressing the seam of the jeans against my clit.

My breath hitches and I look straight ahead as if my body isn't igniting under his touch.

He doesn't try to get me off, and he's gentle more than anything else. Petting me and pausing when my eyes close.

It's over before it really gets started, though.

The sound of everyone packing up is the cue he needs to pull back his hand. I'm riding a high from the forbidden foreplay and I don't acknowledge her when Angie says goodbye. I hear her, but I pretend I don't. Maybe that makes me callous or catty or something else. It doesn't matter. I didn't come here to make friends.

Although I didn't come here for Dean either.

We're the last two remaining. It's becoming a habit. One I'm starting to grow fond of.

"What's going on tonight?" he asks me, and I don't answer.

He's a tornado. Destructive and all-consuming. And just like a natural disaster, I'm not quite sure how to handle Dean or if I can use this situation to my advantage.

One thing is certain, there's going to be a path of wreckage left in his wake.

"I'm staying home this weekend I think," I answer him honestly. I'll be alone in the house, planning and considering all my options.

"Like at your parents' place?" he asks me.

"No, just here." The thought of going home to my mother's is one I don't give the time of day.

"Got it," he says, moving his bookbag he didn't even touch to the top of his desk.

"Well, I'm heading out early tomorrow morning. You want to hang out tonight?" he asks me and then winks. *He's not going to be here this weekend.* My heart slams hard against my rib cage, although on the surface I keep my body relaxed. I had plans. Plans that were easy because he'd be at the frat party. But maybe this means I can save him from all this. Maybe it's meant to be this way.

"Come on, don't make me go to bed all alone," Dean says and pouts when I don't answer fast enough for him.

I can't help but laugh.

"You want to fuck me but not bring me home to your mother, that it?" I tease him back.

"You want to come? I'll bring you."

"You're fucking crazy." My laugh is joined by the zip of my bag as I close it.

"I'm not staying there long; you want to come with?"

"I don't think I'm the type of girl you bring home to your parents." *And I have things planned.* I don't tell him that part. He can't know.

"First, you're blind and delusional. Second, I hate my mother."

"So, bringing me home would be to spite her?" Suddenly feeling lightened by the situation, a smirk graces my face. "Like to piss her off?" It's another game.

"You're something else, you know that?" he says, not answering my question.

If only he knew.

"What about rugby? Don't you guys have a game or something?" I ask him, feeling a stir of anxiety deep in my stomach. It radiates outward as he answers.

"It's not important, and the guys know I'm leaving. I'm not an official member anyway. It was just Kevin's idea that I join."

"You close to Kevin?" I ask him.

"His uncle really. He's paying my ride here."

"Why?" Shifting my backpack to rebalance the weight of the

heavy books, I wait for an answer. I didn't know that. It's not something I would have been able to look up online, but damn I don't like it.

"I got into some stuff, beat a guy pretty fucking bad and Jack's friends with both my uncle and the judge. He said he'd watch me and offered to 'set me straight.'" He huffs a laugh but it's obvious that Dean's grateful for it.

"He sounds like a good guy." I breathe out the words although I feel empty saying them.

"It's a favor to my uncle. Not that I don't appreciate it."

He runs his fingers along his stubble as he looks up at the clock. He's got another class to attend and we're already taking too long in this empty room, but I have to ask. "Why'd you get into a fight with that other guy?"

"He was just getting a little too handsy."

"With you?" I joke, but he doesn't even smile.

There's a hardness about Dean, just beneath his cocky and facetious exterior. "With this chick. I was drunk and so were they. Turns out she was his wife."

"He was just flirting with his wife and you beat the shit out of him?" I say but again he doesn't laugh.

"If flirting means grabbing her by the hair to pull her out of the bar, then yeah. Sure."

"Why the hell did you get locked up then?" I ask him, feeling my heart drop at the image of what he's describing playing in my head.

"She lied. She didn't want her husband to go to jail."

Sickness coils in my stomach. "I'm sorry."

"Yo," I hear someone call out and turn to see Daniel in the doorway.

He nods at Dean, his face cleanly shaven and his hair pushed back. "You got a minute?" he asks Dean and my heart hammers hard and fast, like I've just been caught in a lie.

Daniel doesn't even look at me. It makes me wonder if he

knows something he shouldn't. Or if I'm maybe missing a piece to the puzzle.

"One sec," Dean says quietly and then plants a kiss on my jaw before leaving me behind. It's odd what one little kiss will do.

Knowing before he left, he had to leave me with one little kiss.

I just hope it's not my last.

DEAN

*P*issed off is something I'm used to.

Enraged, irate, resentful.

But none of them compare to how I feel right now.

"You can't even really tell it's her," Daniel says and I don't trust myself to answer just yet. I can't even take my eyes away from the picture on the phone.

"You think she'll be upset?" he asks me.

Do I think Allison is going to be upset that a picture of her riding my dick by the dumpsters at the diner is on the university's social media accounts and it's circulating like wildfire? Yes. Yes, I fucking do. You can't identify me in the picture, but her? Clear as day. At least to me.

I grit my teeth and flex my jaw, looking over my shoulder and back at Allie.

"Yeah," I answer him with one word as my heated blood pumps harder. "I fucked up," I tell him, wiping a hand down my face. The anger is nothing compared to the feeling of knowing something I did is going to hurt her.

I fucking loved what I did to her in that moment.

And I know she loved it too.

"Don't read the comments. It's just going to set you off." I glance up at him before scrolling and reading through the messages. "I know how you are," Daniel adds. "Just ignore them," he tells me and reaches for the phone, but I push him back. Just one shove, just enough to tell him to back off.

What a slut.

She's getting fucked by the dumpsters like the trash she is.

That bitch is dirty.

I wonder if there's a line for that whore out there now.

Every comment makes my anger feel closer to spiraling out of control.

"Seriously, people talk shit. It's what they do. It's not like they can even tell it's her." Daniel keeps rambling, trying to calm me down but all I can see is red.

"They're not going to know it's her. She's fine."

"I don't want to show her this," I admit to Daniel, my throat tight and my muscles even tighter.

"I mean … you might want to give her a heads-up. Just in case?" he suggests and I know he's right, but fuck that.

"A heads-up about what?" Allison's voice is happy but reserved as she walks up to the two of us right outside the classroom door.

My back stiffens.

She shifts the strap of her backpack as a few people walk past us, heading out of their classes and toward the stairs. "Everything okay?" she asks, looking up at me.

Fuck. "You know you're late now, right?" she questions but the wary look on her beautiful face tells me she knows being late doesn't mean shit right now.

When I don't answer, Daniel chimes in. "What's going on?" he asks her.

She shrugs. "Not much. What's going on with you?"

"Same," he says and then it's awkward. "Not much." Real fucking awkward as she looks between the two of us.

"Some shit happened," I tell her, forcing out the words. I try to keep my words even, although my chest feels tight and I don't know if I'm breathing. I only just got her ass to settle down. And now this?

"I'm sorry," I tell her and Allie's smooth forehead pinches with a deep crease. Again she shifts the strap, holding on to it with both her hands.

"What is it?" she asks me in a hollow voice.

Daniel and I exchange a look before I hand Allie his phone.

It takes her a moment to register what she's looking at, a long moment but then her eyes go wide, and she covers her mouth with her hand.

"Oh my God!" she breathes through her hand and then uncovers it to reveal a bit of a smile. "I look so fat," she says comically as if it's a holiday portrait of her.

"You can always go back and I'll take a different one," Daniel jokes and I want to smack the fucker upside his head.

"These people are assholes," Allie says as she scrolls through the comments like it's no big deal.

I'm surprised she isn't shaken in the least. Not pissed off at all like I am. She's a strong girl, I know that, but still. The comments are brutal. She hasn't even read them all. Her smile dims but she isn't pissed, she isn't angry, she isn't hurt. If she is, she's good at hiding it.

Daniel's smiling like a fool. "Well if it makes you feel any better, the picture doesn't make me think about you any differently than I did before." His comment makes Allie laugh but not me.

"Fuck off," I tell him.

Daniel puts both hands up. "Just trying to lighten the mood," he says although his eyes darken slightly. He's good at joking, but it's only a facade. I know one when I see one.

"It's fine," Allie says easily, handing Daniel his phone back. "Seriously, I don't care. You can't even tell it's me, can you?"

"Nope. That's what I told the Hulk over here," Daniel says, and I glare at him.

"The Hulk?" Allie smiles. "Is that what they call you?" she asks me.

"It's a stupid fucking nickname."

"It's because he gets pissed so often," Daniel says to Allie, sliding his phone into his back pocket and then looking up at me, but someone else catches his eye.

"Anyway, I'm going to head out," he says to both of us although he's watching some chick. I get a quick look at her walking down the stairs and when I look back at him, his gaze is fixated on her. I don't think I've seen her before.

"Hey, thanks," I tell him before he heads off chasing whomever she is.

"Yeah, no problem," he says and then finally looks back at me. "Seriously, it's not a big deal. Just thought you'd want a heads-up."

"Thanks, Daniel," Allie calls after him as he stalks away in the opposite direction of that chick. "Delete that from your spank bank, please." I love her smile and humor, but not right now. Not when I know a piece of her has to be hurting.

If only she'd admit it.

"You sure you're all right?" I ask her.

"Yeah, I don't care."

I lean against the wall as I consider her. "Not even a little?"

"Nope," she says, really emphasizing the word and her mouth lets out a little *pop* as she does. "It is a little dirty and it's not like voyeurism isn't trending right now ... but I know who I am and they don't. They just want to feel better about themselves. That's the only reason for saying those things. I'll admit I'm happy you can't really see my face," she says, lowering her voice as she walks closer to me, letting her hands settle against my chest. "And you kind of look hot from that view. It's not one I get to see."

I let out a hint of a chuckle and give her the response she wants.

"If you want, I'll track down the asshole who shared it," I offer her. I don't add that I'll be breaking his fucking phone over his little prick head.

"Seriously, Dean. It's not that big of a deal."

She leans against the brick wall, her bookbag squished behind her. "It's nothing I haven't heard before. Pretty sure most women hear it at some point." Letting out a short laugh, she adds, "Maybe not for fucking where people can see ..." She gets up on her tiptoes and plants a small kiss on my lips as if to end the conversation.

I don't like it.

I don't like it at all.

"Your ass is coming with me this weekend," I tell her, and her mouth opens in surprise. It's the possessiveness in me that made up my mind. If I'm going, she's going.

"I'm coming with you?" She repeats my statement like it's a question although her brow raises like it's a challenge.

"Yes," I say sternly, wrapping my hand around her waist and crushing her into my chest. "I want you to come with me." My skin tingles with the heat of anxiety.

I anticipate a fight, but I get a sweet, "Okay," and a quick peck on the lips.

I guess I'm really going now.

ALLISON

There's an uneasiness in the pit of my stomach.

That's what makes me so aware that everything is wrong and off-kilter.

I know it when I get into Dean's car. I'm conscious of it in every fiber of my body as I click the seat belt into place. This unsettled feeling won't leave. I know something bad is going to happen.

But he keeps smiling at me.

So, I swallow it down and try to breathe.

It's partly because I'm so fucking aware that I want more of him. That I'm on the verge of giving him whatever he'd want, just to keep him. That's the crux of it. I want him. And more than that, I want him to want me.

The car engine clicks over and the radio booms to life. I keep telling myself that I can pretend. I lie and tell myself I'll like pretending.

I think I've lied so much up to this point that I'm not even sure what's real anymore.

"This song blows," I say, reaching for the stereo just to fuck with him and distract myself, but Dean smacks my hand away. It stings for a moment and I feign a pained expression.

"My car, my radio," he says, completely deadpan.

"Seriously," I tell him, giving up on switching the dial since he keeps thwacking me with the back of his hand. "I'm not listening to this for two hours." My brow is raised and the most serious of expressions is on my face.

"You have to be kidding." Dean stares at me with a look of despair in his eyes and I finally break my composure, settling back into the seat and kicking off my flip-flops so I can sit cross-legged.

"Yeah, I am. This is the only station I actually like up here." I can't hold back my smile as that familiar warm feeling flows through me. The one where I give a damn about how my words will be taken. If he gets me.

I've heard Dean laugh a few times and usually it's this sexy, deep and rough chuckle that seems to vibrate up his chest, but this laugh, this is different. It's easy as he throws his head back and gives me a handsome smile.

It's a dangerous look because it makes me smile too.

"Thank fuck," he says and then he turns the radio down before putting the car into reverse. It's at that volume level where you know the other person wants to talk. Right now, I don't like that level. I'd rather blare music the whole way down.

"Hey, I like that song," I tease him but he ignores me. The car moves easily out of the spot in the parking garage and for the first time since this trip came up, I start questioning it.

Dean clears his throat and puts the car into drive.

"You all right?" I ask him, feeling a sense of wariness grow in my chest.

"My mom's kind of a bitch," he tells me and as much as that sucks, I'm happy to hear that's what's making his face look all uncomfortable.

"I think that's normal maybe?" I say and take another look around the car. The bags are in the back seat, but he doesn't want to stay long and assured me we're *absolutely not* staying at his mother's. Which is nice, because fuck staying over at someone's mother's house. That's a given.

Next to my duffle bag, there's a white plastic shopping bag.

"What's in the bag?" I ask Dean.

He glances at me and then blows out a short huff of a laugh. "I picked up a shirt. For you." He examines my expression, watching to see how I react.

"From where?" I ask him as I reach into the back seat, taking the bag and reading the drugstore label on the bag.

"From the mall, it's just in that bag because it was laying around."

The wide and joyful smile on my face won't budge. I lift the fabric out of the bag. It's simple white cotton, but high quality. It's not quite like the one he ruined, but it's pretty and soft. I'm sure I could make it look dirty, though.

Even as my playful banter and perverted thoughts try to shove it all down, this little feeling pricks up, making me hot and uncomfortable. A feeling I want to reject. Immediately. Or at least I would have before.

"I didn't know your size but—" he says and I cut him off before he can continue.

"I love it." I wait for his gaze to meet mine before I lean across the small car and plant a chaste kiss on his lips. "You didn't have to, you know?" I say, slipping the shirt back into the bag and setting it down in the back seat again.

"Well, I'm happy it made you smile."

The comfortable silence between us comes and then goes. Whatever's eating him makes the air tense in this small car. "So, your mom?" I prod him for more information.

"She's just," he says then pauses and the sound of the turn signal, the steady clicking, fills the cabin. We slow to a stop at a crosswalk and he looks at me. "We haven't gotten along in a long time, but my," he says as his eyes flicker to mine and then back to the road before the car moves again and he continues, "my anger management therapist ..." he trails off after saying the words slowly.

"Your shrink?" I say and when he quirks a brow and gauges my expression I give him a comforting smile. "What's your shrink say about her?"

"Not much. He thinks I should go see her, though."

I pick at my nails and peek up at Dean. Freshly shaven. I hadn't noticed that before. "Has it been a while since you've seen her?" I ask him and suddenly feel way too uncomfortable.

We're not even ten miles from his place. We have hours to drive. This conversation is a little too heavy for comfort.

But ... I'm curious. I can't deny that. What the hell did she do to him?

"Yeah, it's been a while," he says and his answer's short. Maybe it's heavy for him too, but that only makes me want to push him more.

"How long's a while?" I ask him.

"I left home when I was sixteen."

"Sixteen is a good age for change," I mumble, looking out of the window as he turns onto the highway and finally picks up speed. The trees blur by and I keep talking before Dean can comment. "When was the last time you saw her?"

He doesn't look at me as he switches lanes and answers, "When I was sixteen."

"Damn."

"Yeah," he says and then adds, "I probably should've told you."

"I mean ... I'd have thought it would have come up in conversation, maybe?" I say jokingly but really, what the fuck?

"I wasn't going to go, but then I wanted to get away after that picture. And I wanted to take you with me."

"So you just figured it'd be fine to drop it all on me once I was securely fastened in your car?"

He shrugs, making the shirt that's already tight across his

shoulders look that much tighter. "It seemed like a sign, I guess." His words come out soft and they're nearly drowned out by the faint music and the sound of the air conditioner, but I heard them.

"Anyway, I just wanted to apologize since it may be a little weird. But you asked for this," he adds, lightening his tone and trying to be playful.

My heart thuds and feels like it's flipping. Like it's trying to move inside my chest. It takes a moment for me to realize it's because I'm not breathing. "Yeah, I did."

"So, it's normal for moms to be bitches?" Dean asks me, and I glance at him in my periphery, picking at my nails. That's all he's getting right now. He doesn't let up though, eager to push the conversation. "I'm guessing mine's going to be worse than yours."

"I was just trying to make you feel better," I respond half-heartedly, and he gets a chuckle out of it that makes me smile.

"Well, shit," he answers and then glances up at the large green sign on the side of the road.

"So?" I say, drawing out the word.

"What?"

"What'd she do that made her a bitch?"

"Oh," he says and his tone drops again. "She just is." I nod once, thinking he's going to leave it there. But as I pull a book out of my bag to read, committed to sitting in silence the entire trip, Dean proves me wrong.

"I didn't think she was when I was younger."

"Most kids love their moms." I think about how my mom was my hero. She was the one who was supposed to make it all better.

"She was bad with money; my parents were always fighting about it." He glances at me and then asks, "You really want to know?"

Placing my hand on the book in my lap, I tell him, "Consider me the in-car shrink. Tell me everything."

"There's not much to tell. My mom's a greedy bitch. My dad got sick and my mom cashed in on his insurance."

135

"Is he okay?" I ask hesitantly, and Dean shakes his head.

"He died a long time ago," he tells me and before I can even tell him I'm sorry, before I can share that my dad's gone too, he keeps talking. I recognize the nature of his voice, how it's like a story. Someone else's story he's telling. It's so he can pretend it doesn't affect him anymore. And that makes the wound that much deeper. "She couldn't wait for it to come. She married a guy more well-off than my father," he says and then lowers his voice to continue, "who was a fucking asshole."

I'd laugh at his tone and the way he said it, but he can't hide the pain in his eyes.

He keeps going. "And then he died, so now she's all alone."

"Your stepdad?"

"Yeah, his name was Rick."

"She has bad luck with men," I tell him in a monotone and then quickly add, "I'm sorry. "

"It's all right. Rick was an asshole and a drunk."

"Well, about your dad and everything. I'm really sorry." I mean every word and that unsettled feeling that bothered me when we first got in this car comes back, but I push it down.

It's not about me right now. That thought makes it feel better.

He tries to shrug it off but I feel compelled to at least reach out to him. Shifting in my seat so I'm leaning close enough to him, I rest my hand on his thigh. My fingers move rhythmically against the rough denim. "I really am sorry."

A warmth spreads through every inch of me when Dean covers my hand with his, his other twisting on the steering wheel. His touch on my hand starts at the very tips of my fingers but then spreads when he picks up my hand and kisses the tips of my fingers ever so gently. His gaze never strays from the road. He's a beast of a man. A brute. It makes the soft touches that much more meaningful.

He sets my hand back down and it's soothing. Deep inside of

me, something feels not so broken anymore. Like a kindled fire come back to life.

"I'm all right," he says like that's the end of it. But I want more now.

There's something about knowing other people's shit that comforts me. Like if they can go through all that and come out okay, then maybe I'll be all right. It's why I like to read thrillers and dark romances. No matter how bad it gets, when it ends, usually there's a happily ever after. That doesn't happen every time, though.

"Why does your anger management therapist," I say, repeating the words like he said them but it doesn't budge the stern expression on his face, "want you to go see her?"

"My uncle called and said I should see go her since Rick died. He said she's not handling it well."

"So, not awkward at all," I say then shrug and try to bring back the playfulness.

His rough chuckle eases the tension that's nearly suffocating me; the feeling that we're rapidly approaching being too close. "I told her I'd just stop by but that we also had other plans."

"What plans?" I ask him.

"Maybe we go to dinner and you tell me your story?" he suggests, taking a quick peek at me.

Shaking my head and ignoring my racing heart, I answer quickly, "So, you want to be bored to death?"

"I know there's something there," he says and I feel like a monster. Guilt and regret creep up my body in a slow wave.

"Nothing that's interesting."

"You don't always have to brush things off. It's okay to let someone in, you know?" As he talks, he periodically looks at me. Like he's gauging my reaction.

"I think I'm good."

"It took a lot for me to tell you about my mom. You could open up a little too."

"I did that once. Like I said, I think I'm good," I tell him as I pull my knees to my chest, stretching the seat belt over them and looking out of the window.

"I'm guessing it didn't end well?" he says.

"Nope." My answer is simple, my voice high pitched and peppy, but inside I'm screaming. Inside it hurts. All the pain is wound up and coiled into barbed wire, cutting me open and wishing I would spill it all. I told my mom. And it was supposed to get better. She was supposed to make it all better.

"Well, who was it you told?" He's keeping his voice light and acting like he's just making small talk, but I can see right through him.

"No one you know," I tell him and feel guilty for not confiding in him. I usually don't care if I disappoint someone, but Dean is different.

"You know how I just said it's okay to let people in?" he reminds me with a smirk and then rests his hand on my thigh when I don't respond. He rubs his fingers back and forth in soothing strokes. Like he's comforting me. It feels like a setup.

Silence greets me, backs me into a corner. Waiting for me to make the next move.

"It's not fair that you decided to make this trip a fucking therapy session."

His laugh is brief before he replies, "Life's a therapy session, Allie Cat." He doesn't move his hand, he just keeps it on my thigh and I find myself wanting to put my hand on top of his and run my thumb along his knuckles.

"Sam ... Sam is who I let in." I give him that small bit of information even though it's not quite what he asked. He asked who I told. I gave him who I let in. Big difference, but he doesn't need to know that. Hearing her name makes me feel like I've betrayed her. Has it been that long since I've said her name out loud?

"What'd he do?" Dean asks and I let out a genuine laugh, pretending the tears in the corners of my eyes are from humor.

"Sam as in Samantha."

"Oh, a chick?" Dean leans forward and then relaxes back in his seat, clearly not expecting that. "So, was this like, a thing?" he asks me, and the smile stays plastered on my lips.

"Sorry to disappoint you, but I'm only into dick."

"Got it," Dean says. "She was a friend?"

I just nod and look back out the window although I don't really see anything. Blurs of scenary as we make our way along the highway. I remember when Sam and I met in preschool. We were so young and stupid, fighting over some rainbow eraser until the teacher took it away and made us share a plain one. Back when everything was okay, and we were just kids. When "best friends for life" meant something special.

"What was she like?" he asks me. Dean isn't getting the hint but for some reason, I like it. Maybe it's the memories or the soothing sound of the engine rumbling and the wind passing by the car. Or maybe it's just been a while since I've thought of Sam back before the night that changed everything happened.

It takes me a moment to think of the best way to answer him. "A lot like me," I start, although it's not quite right. I'm just pretending to be a lot like her.

"Big boobs. She was gifted with them." I add that difference humorously and I think about stopping there, but I don't. "She had the most beautiful smile and laugh. She used to joke that she was going to be a dentist because everyone would pay big bucks for a smile like hers. And she laughed at everything and it was real." I remember how happy she always was. "She was just a very confident, happy person."

"Sounds like a good friend," he says after a moment.

"Keep your eyes on the road," I scold him when I notice he's spending more time looking at me than he is paying attention to driving.

"What happened?" he asks me.

"My mom didn't want us hanging out," I tell him and I'm

surprised how easily I said it. Like it doesn't feel like my heart is shattered by the memory. "We were just girls, fourteen and fifteen at the time."

"Why's that?"

"People said some things. Blamed some things that happened on Sam, and my mom said it was her fault." My voice cracks and I feel myself breaking down, so I reach for the volume on the stereo again. I turn it up, feeling guilty about so much and not wanting to deal with it.

Guilty about what happened back then.

Guilty about what's going to happen.

"Hey," Dean says softly, and I just barely hear him over the constant bass of whatever song this is. I don't recognize it. I glance at him, wishing I could hide, but he does that thing again, taking my hand and kissing the tips of my fingers. "You did good, Allie Cat."

If guilt could kill someone, I'd be dead.

DEAN

*T*his is a bad idea.

The shrink was wrong. Driving all the way to 24 Easton Avenue in Brunswick wasn't anything I needed. As I watch my mother, who's sitting on the steps of the porch taking another puff of her cigarette, I already know I'm not going to get anything from her. And that this was a bad idea.

Closure, mending fences—whatever the hell Dr. Robinson thought I'd get from this isn't here.

My mother looks the same in a lot of ways but also beaten down, as if the years haven't been kind to her, or maybe I just remember her differently. She's in loose-fitting clothes that make her seem even smaller than when I saw her last. She looks frail beneath them.

Dr. Robinson is just like everyone else, thinking I'm exaggerating or that my perception is skewed. But showing up out of nowhere to tell my mother I'm working on my anger and making progress was a fucking mistake.

Allie stretches in her seat, slowly waking up from the nap she took for the last thirty minutes of the drive.

She's so damn beautiful when she sleeps.

I wish she'd stayed asleep, so I could keep driving.

"We're here?" she asks sleepily and tries to hide her yawn. I watch her look up at the house we're parked in front of. The seat protests as she leans forward and takes in the porch, a red and blue wreath adorning the front door and two matching pots with baby's breath on either side of it. "It's cute," she says sweetly.

I gesture across the street to my mother's place with my hand as it rests on the steering wheel and then turn off the ignition. "That one."

She's quick to turn her head and say it's cute too. And maybe it's all right on the outside. No homey details and it looks just like it did six years ago when my mother bought it with that asshole. Only more weathered ... just like my mother.

"You can stay here if you want," I say. My anxiety is getting the best of me. I told Dr. Robinson I'd do it, so I will. I'm not a little bitch. But no one likes being pushed aside and dismissed. Especially by their own mother. And definitely not in front of the woman they're seeing.

"I'll come," she says as she unbuckles her seat belt. As she reaches for her purse on the floorboard, my mother's gaze finally finds its way over here.

A puff of smoke slowly billows from her mouth. Other than that, there's no reaction. I know she recognizes me though, because she doesn't look away. My chest tightens, making each breath more difficult. I focus on forcing air in and out. Just in and out.

The neighborhood is quiet when I step out, listening to the sound of Allie's door and then mine clunk close before I turn to look back at my mother. She's still seated, blowing out another puff before stubbing out her cigarette on the concrete step.

Allie waits for me before making her way across the street.

This was fucking stupid. It's all I can think as I make my way back to a house I hate, back to a woman I loathe. The anger is subdued, though. It's so messed up that even after all these years, I want something to change between the two of us.

That's the first mistake. Having hope.

"Dean?" my mother says and slowly stands up on the stoop. Her sweatpants hang loose on her body, as does the shirt she's wearing. I keep my shoulders square and look my mother in the eye.

"What are you here for?" she asks, setting her hands on her hips and narrowing her gaze.

I was right in my assumption from the car, she's lost weight. Could be the cigarettes or it could be the stress of losing Rick. Maybe she's been like this for years. I don't know.

"I heard about Rick," I tell her and as I do, I feel Allie's small hand brush against mine, so I take it. It's funny how that little touch makes my heart hammer harder but in a way, it's calming.

My mother breaks eye contact and looks past me as I tell her I'm sorry for her loss.

"I'm sorry too," Allie says politely but in a voice that's genuine and full of pain.

"Yeah ... well, thanks," my mother says coldly, dismissively.

"Mom," I say, and it feels odd calling her that, so I have to pause before continuing, "this is Allison. Allison, this is my mother."

I introduce them and Allie steps forward with her hand out to give my mother a handshake, even though she's still standing two steps higher than us.

True to form, my mom's a fucking bitch, leaving Allie hanging there with an empty hand held high. She looks at Allie good and hard before nodding her head and saying, "Hi."

The air turns frigid around me when I see Allie's face fall. Allie's innocent in all this. I shouldn't have brought her here.

Taking a large step forward, I shield Allie from my mother. "Just wanted to tell you that I'm doing fine, if you were wondering." My words come out hard and bitter. I don't know what the good doctor was thinking or what I was thinking when I decided to take his advice.

But there, I've told her, so we can get the fuck out of here.

"Fine? Is that what you call getting arrested?" My anger falters, even if just for a moment while my mother's face forms a twisted sneer. "I always knew you were no good."

I bite my tongue and hold back the explanation. She doesn't deserve one.

Just as I'm about to tell her goodbye forever, Allie steps around me, brushing against my leg as she shoves herself in front of me.

She's short, shorter than both me and my mom and she has to crane her neck to look in my mother's hard eyes as she tells her, "He was trying to do the right thing."

I haven't seen Allie angry really. I've seen her want to run, or pick a fight. But I've never seen her pissed like this. Her little hands fisted at her side. Her chin held high and her eyes narrowed. It's sweet of her, but I wish it weren't because of me.

"I'm sure," my mother says and then pulls out another cigarette. She lights it and adds, "If you're here for money, Rick didn't leave anything to you."

My body tightens and my heart feels like it's being squeezed. It fucking hurts. I can't deny it.

I don't know why what she said pains me even more. Not that Rick didn't give me anything, but that she'd think I'd come back here looking for a handout.

Then again, money's the only thing that ever mattered to her.

"He's not going to do anything with his life, so you should really consider your other options," my mother tells Allie. She nods her head condescendingly as she speaks to Allie and doesn't even bother to look at me.

"What a bitch," Allie says with a high-pitched voice, looking my mother directly in the eye. "You didn't tell me she was this much of an asshole." She turns her head to look at me with disbelief and then seems to check her anger when I don't respond.

"Your son's a good man and I have no clue how he got lucky enough to get away from you."

My mother laughs. "Aww, sweetheart, I hope you enjoy getting your heart broken."

Allie opens her mouth again, and her face is scrunched up as she bites her tongue. She's letting my mother get the best of her.

The difference between these women is simple. Allie cares; my mother doesn't.

I wrap one arm around Allie's waist and pull her in close to me, letting her ass press against my upper thigh and cut her off.

"Like I said, just wanted to give you my condolences."

Allie peeks up at me with a bewildered look. "Let's go," I tell her softly, not bothering to tell my mother goodbye.

ALLISON

"*A*re you angry with me?" I ask Dean and then try to swallow. But I can't. There's a spiked lump in the back of my throat that won't go away.

I know I'm a bitch. I'll be the first to admit it.

I like to hate people before they can hate me. I'll call them out, but I call myself out on my own shit. I know it doesn't make it right, though.

"I didn't mean to upset you when I called your mother a bitch... or an asshole. Whatever the hell I said to her." Even as I give him the apology, I feel awkward and like I've done him a disservice. He wanted to make things right with her and I think I just made things even worse. I don't even remember what all I said.

I fidget with my thumbs nervously as I wait for Dean to look at me. I feel awful. "I should have just been quiet," I tell him, and my voice cracks a little.

"You're fine," he says and lifts the turn signal lever, the ticks echoing in the hollow cabin of the car.

"What I said wasn't, though," I say. "I'm sorry, truly."

Dean softens. He's been tense and stiff ever since we left. My words have been caught in the back of my throat. It's weird feeling this overwhelming urge to be forgiven. I'm not used to it. At least not like this.

"I told you she's a bitch," he says as he straightens out the wheel and leans back, setting his hand on my thigh in that same spot as before. Moving his thumb in the way I like. I'm getting used to him doing that and even more, I'm growing to love the little touches. I cover his hand with mine and peek up at him.

"Next time, I'll be quiet."

He turns to look at me with a pinched expression. "There's not going to be a next time." My stomach sinks and I can't breathe until he adds, "I'm not going back there again."

"Well, if there's ever any other thing ..." I stumble over my words. "I won't—"

"I like that you stood up for me," Dean says, cutting me off.

"You like it, so you forgive me? Or you like it—"

"I like the way you handled yourself. I'm not mad at all. There's nothing to forgive."

"So we're okay?" I ask him desperately, my heart hurting more than it should and it's only just now that I realize what I really feel for Dean. This wasn't supposed to happen. Wiping under my eyes I close them and lean my head back against the seat, attempting to calm down.

Dean lets out a humorous breath which gets my attention, with a light in his eyes that eases me. "You're sweet, Allie Cat," he tells me and then gives me a soft smile.

"Where are we going?" I ask, finally relaxing back into the seat and sitting cross-legged. Again, pretending this is okay. He tries to take his hand away, but I put it right back on my thigh and he lets me. Right now I need him to keep from falling apart. I can figure out the rest tomorrow.

"The hotel around the corner has good room service," he says. "Or at least it used to."

"I like room service."

"And then you can tell me something to take my mind off the fact that I'm fucking stupid for coming down here at all."

"Why did you?" I ask him.

"Because my shrink said I should."

"Why?"

"My guess would be, so we could talk about our issues."

I let that sink in for a moment before I ask him, "Do you want to talk about them?"

He hesitates and takes his hand back, but only to steer into a parking lot. It's not until he puts the car in park and turns it off before he answers. "Sometimes I think I do." With the hum of the engine and the stereo off, it's quiet. Too quiet.

"I'm here if you want to talk," I offer him although my stomach twists and that unsettled feeling comes back to me.

"I'd like to talk about something else," he says.

"About what?" I ask him, straightening my shoulders and preparing myself to talk about whatever he wants.

"I don't know," he says and I let out a small laugh. "How about your major?"

"Undecided."

"No shit? Me too." He gives me a handsome grin that settles those nerves and I reply, "Great minds, huh?"

"My lack of direction and commitment in choosing a major is one of the reasons Dr. Robinson said I should talk to my mother." He keeps tapping his thumb on the wheel and I'm not sure why he's so nervous.

He looks out the front windshield and toward the street as he talks. "Shit, I don't want to talk about that."

"You have no direction or commitment? Oh God, I really should hightail it out of here," I joke to lighten up the mood.

He chuckles, that deep, rough chuckle I love to hear and grabs my hand, pulling it to his lips. I love his smiles but I hate that he's only doing this to make me feel better. If I weren't here, he wouldn't be smiling. I know that much. "I like you, Allie," he says softly and then adds, "I'm sorry I brought you and you had to see that."

In this moment, I'm drowning. I'm in over my head and the weight of everything pushes against my chest, forcing me farther down into an abyss that's sure to consume me.

But I want it to. Go ahead, swallow me whole.

When I look into Dean's eyes and see the emotion that stares back at me, I see myself and it hurts. It's a sweet, deep pain that I want to take from him. If that means drowning, so be it.

"Hey, you okay?" Dean asks me and it's only then I realize I wasn't breathing. That keeps happening around him.

"I'm just sorry," I croak out and Dean pulls me into his lap. It's odd with the wheel behind me but he's quick to push back his seat and I find myself tearing up. I haven't cried in years and I'm embarrassed.

"Shhh," Dean shushes me, and I hate myself. He's the one who has a right to be angry, to be upset, yet he's comforting me.

"I'm sorry," I say again, angrily wiping at my eyes and refusing to cry.

"It's okay," he whispers, petting my hair as the air hits my heated face.

"I don't know why I'm being like this." I wrap my arms around myself. It doesn't stop him from pulling me back against his chest and I instantly melt into his warmth.

"It doesn't matter, I'm here," he tells me and for the first time, it feels like those words carry weight. Like nothing else matters, as long as he's here.

I know it's not true but for a moment, it's nice to feel like it's real.

None of this was supposed to happen.

I wasn't supposed to fall for him.

DEAN

I knew she was breakable.

The moment I saw her, I fucking knew it.

She was hiding something and barely holding herself together, still is.

I could feel it in my bones.

After all this time, I still don't know what it is that's going to break her, though.

The door to the hotel room opens slowly with a creak and I have to glance over my shoulder to see if she's still with me. Her eyes are distant but she's there. She tucks a strand of her brunette hair behind her ear but it quickly falls back to where it was, and she doesn't bother with it again.

"Home sweet home," I say more to get her attention than anything else and push the door open wider. Her smile is weak but it's an offering I take.

"Thanks," she says as she walks in, hitching the strap of her duffle bag up her shoulder.

I grit my teeth. Even in this moment, with her little head

messed up and something dark slowly consuming her, even now she won't let me hold her bag.

I walk in behind her, listening to the sound of my heart beating in rhythm with her soft breathing. As the door closes with a loud click, the air conditioner turns on and the curtains stir, making Allie jump.

She reaches up to her collarbone with her hand and then lets out a small laugh.

"You all right, Allie?" I ask her for the third time since we got out of the car. I already know the answer, even as she swallows thickly and lowers herself to the bed, all the while nodding. "Fine."

"You seem a little shaken," I tell her. "Something's bothering you."

"I'm fine," she says again with a sharp defiance in her voice.

The corners of my lips kick up. "And I'm the pope." I turn my back to her, picking up my bag to put it on top of the small dresser and unzip it but leave it there untouched.

"You're not thinking about running, are you?" I ask her, partly joking, partly serious.

"I'm just sorry, okay?" she says to my back and I turn to look at her, but I don't say anything.

She clears her throat and the soft lines of her bare neck get my attention as she talks. My eyes travel to the dip in her throat, then back to her lips.

"Sorry for getting all worked up," she clarifies.

"You can do what you want," I say while pulling the shirt over my head. It's hot as fuck in here and as I ball up my shirt I look for the thermostat, finding it on the other side of the room. She talks as I walk past her.

"Sure." As I dial down the temperature, she flops down on the bed, her legs still over the edge but her back flat on the mattress. "It doesn't mean I should, though," she whispers.

"I'm happy you let me in a little," I say and my chest pangs with pent-up emotion at the admission. Maybe it's pain, maybe it's gratitude. It's hard to tell the difference.

"You don't look so happy," she says.

"Is that why you're all upset?" I ask her, stopping at the edge of the bed and towering over her. Upset's not quite the right word but I don't know how to say it. "All because I'm pissed off that my mom is … the same she's always been." Again the air clicks on and her shoulders shake slightly from the noise.

"I'm not upset," she says but the words come out sounding more like a question, her eyes searching mine.

"Ever since we walked in here, you look like you've seen a ghost," I tell her. "Like you're on edge and waiting for something bad to happen." I stand my ground and the faint light from the sole window in the room casts a shadow of my form over Allison.

"Bad things always happen," she says after a moment of consideration. "Whether you wait for them or not."

"You look scared, Allie, and I don't like it."

"I am scared," she confesses in a hoarse whisper.

"I know my mother looks like shit, but I promise she's not as scary as she looks," I joke and she finally breaks a smile although the second she does, she closes her eyes and her face crumples. Goddamn, it hurts. It hurts to see her like this. It's even worse because I don't know how to make it better.

The bed groans, protesting as I sit on the edge and pull her small body into my arms. I don't talk as her shoulders shake. I just kiss her hair and rub her back.

Her body molds to mine for a small moment. A tiny but significant moment where she lets it out.

I'd swear she was crying if she didn't peek up at me with glossy eyes but not a tear leaving her. "I'm okay." She mouths the words more than speaking them and pulls away from me.

My fingertips brush over her shoulders and she catches my hand in hers as she sits cross-legged on the bed. "I just …" She doesn't finish and shakes her head instead.

"Is it because of your mom?" I ask her. It's all I can think of. There wasn't a damn thing said that seemed to set her off. It was after the silence in the car and the time to think. Sometimes our inner thoughts are our worst demons.

"No," she says with a sad smile and sniffles. She gives me a smile and even though the light in her eyes is dimmed, she almost looks normal. Like she can bandage up her pain and hide it. I suppose that's what she's used to and my body tenses as I debate what to do. Push her for more, not let her hide? Or just try to ease the pain and go along with this facade. I don't know what the hell to do, but I'm terrified she's going to push me away.

Her thumb brushes along the knuckles of my hand.

"I think I do want to text her, though," she says and swallows. The nervousness in her voice reflects in her eyes. She chews on her lower lip and searches my eyes again.

It looks like she's lying.

That's exactly what it looks like.

I don't know why or what's gotten to her, but she's fucking lying to me.

"You should," I say absently and let her hand fall as I walk back to the dresser. "Unless she's like my mom, in which case, fuck it."

"It took a lot for you to go to her."

I only nod at Allie's words. I don't look behind me as I slip into sweatpants even though I can hear her crawling on the bed.

"I would say I'm proud of you, but who am I to say that?" she says sarcastically. That protective armor of hers is sneaking up again.

"It makes me feel good that you're proud," I tell her bluntly.

Her gaze catches mine for a moment before she rubs the exhaustion from her eyes.

"I only did it because the shrink said to," I tell her.

"You still did it," she says softly, so soft I almost didn't hear but then she raises her voice to add, "It's hard to go through with things sometimes."

"Like what things?" I ask but she doesn't answer.

I wait a while, looking through the pile of binders on the night-stand until I find the one with the menu in it. She still hasn't answered, so I drop it.

"You want to split something?" I ask and she nods weakly.

"I'm not too hungry, but if you order fries I'll probably eat some … or all of them." The small bit of humor forces the start of a smile on my face and I pick up the phone to place the order.

A burger with all the fixings and two orders of fries.

Hanging up the phone, I still don't feel right. I never thought bringing Allie out here would wind up like this. With me feeling A-fucking-okay and her looking like she's been beaten up.

"Thanks for coming with me," I tell her as she picks at some-thing on the pajama pants she slipped on while I was ordering food. She lies on the bed, stretching out and tells me it's been a blast, again making the tense air lighter. She's good at that. Good at playing things off like they don't matter. Even now while she's breaking down right in front of me.

"Can I ask you something, Allie?" I say and then turn around to see her texting something. She doesn't stop until she hits send and then looks up at me.

"Whatever you want." Before I can say another word, the screen of her phone lights up and pings. She tries to ignore it but on the second ping, she has to look down to silence her phone.

"I can wait," I say but she only shakes her head in response, tossing her phone onto the nightstand with a heavy breath and tired eyes.

Something is killing her inside. And it fucking hurts that she's hiding it from me still.

"What is it you wanted to ask?" she says with a soft and kind voice, one that begs for mercy. Our eyes lock and there's a shift between us. One of vulnerability. One seeking refuge in me.

"I just don't want you to ever lie to me." I don't know why that's what comes out. But it's all I've got for her. "You don't have to tell me shit," I begin but pause when her expression falls and she fails to hide the sadness there. "You don't have to tell me shit, but don't lie to me."

She nods once and then agrees in a small voice, "That's not really a question but … No lying. Can do."

"You all right?"

"Yeah," she says but doesn't look me in the eyes as she pulls the covers back.

"And that's the truth?" I ask her, reminding her of the assurance she just made.

"As all right as I can be," she says and then slowly raises her eyes to mine. "Just a lot of things happened when I was younger, and something reminded me of a promise I made but almost broke."

"What promise?"

"Can we just eat and go to sleep?" she asks in return and chances a quick glance at me, again picking at some nonexistent fuzz on her pants.

"It's not that late," I tell her out of impulse. It can't be any later than nine.

"How about we just cuddle and watch something funny?" she asks, and her voice is stronger, more hopeful.

"A comedy? I'm always down for that."

Crawling into bed beside her feels right. Like that's what I'm supposed to do right now. Before I even have a chance to wrap my arm around her waist and pull her into me, she's already nestling her ass into my crotch and getting comfortable.

She reaches behind her, looking back at me and takes the remote off the nightstand. Before getting back into position she gives me a quick peck and then picks up my hand in both of hers.

"Your hands are so small," I say absently as she traces the lines on my hand with the tip of her finger. It's soothing and gentle, but it stops when she kisses the tips of my fingers like I did with hers.

"I wish things were different," she whispers. There's a sincerity there, a fear too.

"Like what? My mom?"

She shakes her head and settles her back against me, letting my hand fall to her waist.

"Just circumstances," she says without looking back.

With the remote in hand, she searches the channels while I watch her. The light from the television brightens her face.

I see every detail. There are moments in time that don't seem like they mean anything at all when they happen. Moments that hold no significance at the time.

But later, those moments are burned into your memory.

The way the light hits her hair, the way she blinks away the tears that threaten to fall. The way she smiles up at me with the sound of some movie playing on the television in the background. Some moments are burned into your memory forever, and maybe it's because deep inside we wish it could stay like this. With her nestled in my arms, knowing she's safe and that nothing bad is going to happen tonight.

THERE ARE TIMES IN LIFE

There are times in life when you run toward something.
And there are times you run away.
Neither choice is shameful.
But either way, you're running.

ALLISON

"*S*am?" *I call out her name again and my voice echoes in the empty hallway.*

There's no one else around. The deserted halls of the school mock me as I move from room to room looking for her. "Sam," I barely whisper her name.

It feels odd as I open the doors. Almost like they're expecting me, since they open so easily. They creak open slowly though, making me wait as I hold my breath.

Each room gives me nothing. They're all empty and dark and every time it scares me to move beyond the doorframe. So, I just look in and whisper her name. Quietly, praying she'll hear me.

Door after door, I keep moving through the hall. Waiting to see her. I can picture how she used to sit on top of her desk, cross-legged with her book in her lap. I keep waiting to see her there smiling back at me. But there's nothing. Just empty rooms, each one darker than the next. The halls grow cold and I forget why I need her.

I thought I was following her. I swear I heard her call for me.

She needs my help. The reminder makes my body freeze as a chill flows over me and makes the hairs on the back of my neck stand up. I can feel it. Deep down in my gut, the pain twists and turns, writhing into a coil that crawls up my spine.

She needs me, and I'm failing her.

The last door opens before I touch the knob. The light flickers on and off and then settles dimly in the center of the room. On Sam. But she's not seated on the desk. She's slumped against the wall, sitting on the floor by the closed, dark window.

Her eyes are sad and her face hollowed.

The darkness around her makes her seem pale and colorless.

"I'm sorry," she whispers.

MY BODY JOLTS upright as the silent scream tears through me.

My heart races and sweat covers my body. I can hardly hear Dean as he grips me harder, staring at me and pushing the hair out of my face. I can't see or hear anything other than Sam.

It was like I was really there.

Like she was right there.

"Allison," Dean says, his voice piercing through the memory. "Are you okay?"

He's breathless, his fingers digging into my shoulder and his dark gaze pinning me in place. It takes me a long second before I realize he's here with me. He's here now. His palm brushes against my forehead again, pushing the loose strands of hair away from my face. He's so warm and my body's freezing.

I blink away the vision of the night terror and try desperately to calm my breathing as his hold loosens and I bring the covers up closer to my neck.

Her voice was so clear.

My breathing won't calm. My chest heaves violently as I wipe my eyes and pull away from him. She was right there. Sam was right there.

"Talk to me," Dean commands me but that's just not possible.

Slowly, my heart calms.

"You were having a nightmare," Dean tells me like I don't know what happened. "It was just a nightmare."

My head nods of its own accord as I slip back beneath the covers, seeking their warmth.

I can still feel the cold metal of the doorknob.

"Sometimes I have bad dreams," I tell Dean. To stop his questioning.

"About what?"

The words slip from me immediately. "I don't want to talk about it."

I haven't had a dream like that in a long damn time.

I haven't fallen asleep so easily in just as long.

"Are you okay?"

He's asked me that so many times in the last twelve hours.

"I'm fine," I say. "I'm sorry."

"Don't be sorry," he tells me and it's only then that his expression comes into focus.

My heart melts, slowly but with a heat that's undeniable. "I just want to make sure you're all right," he says as he brushes my hair from my face. In this moment, I'm weak with want for him and his touch.

I didn't know until this day what I'd do for him and how much he meant to me.

Maybe that's why she came back to remind me.

To remind me of the promise I made to her and why I'm here.

"I'm fine," I tell him. I know it's a lie when I say it. A lie and a broken promise I've only just made. I should feel guilty. But I don't. The other promise is more important.

I don't feel guilty while I cup his cheek in my hand and brush my lips against his.

Not while I let him hold me.

Not even as he whispers he loves me into my hair when he

thinks I've fallen asleep. And that's what it is. Love. I feel it too. I'm not blind to it. I even accept it although I can't have it. I can't have Dean. This has gone on for far too long.

It's not okay to be okay.

That would be the worst tragedy.

DEAN

"*B*ottoms up!" Kev says over the sound of the music echoing off the walls of the room. The bass pounds through my veins as I toss the shot back. Partially to let go, partially out of anger.

Allison fucking ghosted. Hasn't been to her classes, isn't returning my texts. The second we got back here, she left me high and dry.

My fist clenches around the empty shot glass as the whiskey burns down my throat.

I should have known better than to pretend she was fine.

I should have seen this shit coming.

"Ahh," James hisses as he shakes his head, slamming the glass down on the coffee table. His face is scrunched even as he yells out, "Whoo!" as if he's having the fucking time of his life.

And maybe the other assholes here are. As each glass hits the table, everyone around me seems lighter, happier, ready to party. That's what this is. A party.

The air from my lungs leaves me as Kev's hand pounds on my back.

"You my wingman tonight?" he asks me, lowering his face to mine as I hunch over the countertop. I follow his gaze to the set of brunettes across the room.

One with short hair and a bright pink tank top, while the other has her long hair pulled back and is wearing a short little black dress. They laugh as they spot Kev staring them down like they're prey. They're nothing like Allie. Kev can have them both. He nods and they blush, covering their faces with the red plastic cups of beer in their hands.

"Not tonight," I finally answer. I'm not feeling it. There's only one girl I want to see here, and I know for a fact she knows I'm here. She knows where to find me. She's not here because she doesn't want me. I'm not stupid and her hints aren't subtle.

I went to her place, but she didn't answer.

She's pissing me off more than anything. With the whiskey flowing through my veins, there's not much of anything keeping me from going back to her house right now.

"Why the fuck not?" he asks me, rearing his head back to look at me like I'm being unreasonable.

"Not tonight," I repeat and toss the plastic shot glass into the trash. That was the third or fourth shot I've had over the course of fifteen minutes. Maybe fifth. One after the other and I sway slightly, but the cup makes it into the bin.

"Is it that chick?" he asks. *That chick.* That's not her name.

"Yeah," I tell him and my body feels tight, even as my vision tilts. She's fucking with me and she knows it. Worst of all, I'm letting her.

"Suit yourself," he says as he fills a cup from the tap of the keg.

Anger rises in a slow billow as I watch the foam rise to the top of the rim.

"What the fuck does that mean?" The words slip from me without any deliberate intention. It's the anger taking over. Not at him. It's anger directed at her.

"Calm down," Kev tells me, scrunching his brow and looking over his drink at me. "I didn't mean shit."

James laughs and it pisses me off. The room tilts in the opposite direction when I look at him.

"You got something to say?" I ask him. Because the fucker looks like he has something to say. The second the question leaves me, the front door opens and there she is.

The short dress hits her upper thigh as she kicks the door shut, letting the thin fabric swirl around her. From head to toe, she has every detail in place. From her straightened hair to the high heels that complement the bracelets adorning her wrist.

That devilish smile isn't in sight as she turns toward the kitchen, toward us, and instantly catches my gaze. Like she could feel me watching her. I take her in slowly, feeling like an asshole for thinking she was avoiding me.

She wouldn't have come if she didn't want me. Right?

But then her eyes flash and she rips her gaze away.

She came to end it.

My heart slams once, then twice, as she stalks toward us. In my blurred periphery, I see James lean in closer and say quietly but with an arrogance I'm not in the mood for, "That's the type of girl who fucks you raw when you show up to her house. Lets you fuck her in public. Likes to flirt. Likes attention. And will do anything to get it. Or anyone." He nods his head as he talks, staring at something behind me. My knuckles turn white as the anger builds in response to his oblivious nature. "You really want to be tied up with that?" he asks me and my head turns slowly. So fucking slowly and against my will as Allison heads right for us.

"Watch your fucking mouth." My words come out sharp and as I turn toward him, everyone else takes a step back.

The heat rises and my shoulders feel tense.

James looks at me like a deer in fucking headlights. Like he didn't see it coming. Like those weren't fighting words that just came out of his mouth.

Before I can say a damn thing, I feel a strong arm push me back slightly, making me face Allison and not that asshole.

"Look who's in the house," Daniel says, wrapping his arm tighter around my shoulder and inserting himself between me and James. He keeps a strong grip on me and whispers for me to calm down. That she's here and everything's fine. That it's not worth it. And that last line is what repeats itself as Allie comes closer, looking between all of us like she wishes she hadn't come. *That it's not worth it.*

The fuck it isn't.

I struggle to know what to do. The whiskey and the anger swirl into a deadly concoction in the pit of my stomach.

I'm a fucking mess. Daniel's good-natured laugh seems at odds with what's flowing in my veins.

But he's different from me. Daniel has a way of smiling through the bullshit. Of acting like things don't bother him, when inside he's envisioning slitting your throat. It's how he was raised.

"What's up, sweetheart?" he asks Allie as she glances from James to him, then to me before setting her purse down on the counter.

The metal links of the strap clink as they hit one another, and I force myself to focus on that, rather than the sound of James leaving the kitchen.

My teeth and fists are still clenched, the skin pulled taut over my knuckles.

"You tell me, *sweetheart*," she says, mocking Daniel but her confidence is barely there, and her focus is split between us and watching James's back.

"Shot?" Daniel asks as the music plays the word over and over. *Another round of shots.*

Her eyes flicker from me to him and as she parts her lips to respond, I interject. "Come on," I tell her, grabbing her wrist and shrugging Daniel off of me.

He hovers for a moment as she stares back at me, ripping her arm away.

The tension grows and the air goes still and quiet; even the fucking music seems to dim as she considers whether or not to listen to me.

Shit, I guess it doesn't matter either way.

I can see it written on her face. She's running. From me and what we had. She only came here to tell me as much. Least she could do is to not say it in front of them.

"Lead the way, Neanderthal," she says sarcastically, avoiding Daniel's piercing gaze. Like he's her fucking protector. I can see it. He's watching the two of us like he knows shit's about to go down. Judging by the way everyone averts their gaze when I look at them, he's not the only one thinking that.

I ignore him as much as she does and lead her to the door, not really touching her, just staying close as we walk outside.

The music dies the second the door shuts and the sticky heat of the late summer air and faint sounds of crickets from the woods behind us surround us.

I could use a drag. It's been ages since I've had a smoke but right now, I'm hit hard with the need for a cigarette.

"What's wrong with you?" Allie asks me the moment she turns on her heels to face me.

"Where have you been?" I question her in return. "We came back Sunday. You missed two classes, texted me back with one-word answers and have been blowing me off." I pace on the small cement landing in front of the door. "I mean, I knew shit was off on the way home, but all I asked from you was for you to be honest."

"What wasn't honest?" Allie bites back with anger. Good. I hope she's pissed like I am.

"You don't have to lie to be dishonest," I say and even in my drunken stupor, I know that those words make more sense than any excuse she can come up with.

166

"Yeah, well, I wanted to tell you something anyway," she starts and I scoff at her.

"I gave you the fucking over you needed, huh?"

She shakes her head, that gorgeous hair of hers swirling around her shoulders as the heat climbs and I run a hand through my hair. No matter how put together she is, her eyes can't lie to me. She can look pissed or like she doesn't care. But her eyes have the same sad look in them they did at the hotel.

"What are you talking about?" Exasperation is clear in her voice.

"You want to be with me or not, Allie?" I ask her the only question I need an answer to and her plump lips part slightly, the immediate answer begging to slip from them, but she stops herself, slamming her mouth shut and swallowing the words.

"I knew it," I tell her and feel pathetic. I'm not the pathetic one, though. This is on her. She's the one running from this. She's the one who's scared.

"It's not you," she says with way too little emotion in her voice. Like it doesn't even matter.

"Oh, it's not me, it's you?" I ask with a bitter taste in my mouth. "Is that what you're going for? Really? You can be more creative than that." She flinches at the anger in my voice. "Come on Allie, I'll give you a minute to come up with something better," I sneer and lean into her. I'm pissed. I'm so fucking pissed.

It's easier than being hurt.

Everyone pushes me away because they don't want me. She wants me. I know she does. And still, I can't hold on to her.

"How about the fact that you were ready to get into a goddamn brawl when I walked in. How about that?"

"How about it?" I ask back. I don't remember quite what happened or what she knows. All I remember is that someone said something that they deserved to be punched for. I don't tell her that though, I stand there like an ass, waiting for her to fill me in on what the hell happened.

I shouldn't have drunk so much. If I'd known she was coming, I wouldn't have.

"I don't need you to stick up for me," she says and James's stupid fucking face flashes in my head.

"It's not about sticking up for you. You're *mine*." I thump my hand against my chest to emphasize my words.

"I'm not yours. I don't belong to anyone!" she screams at me and takes a step closer. The heat from the argument is at odds with the chill in the night air.

"Knock it off," I tell her. "You know what I mean."

"This is why I can't ..." she starts to say, but even she can't hold on to the thin excuse.

"Quit pushing people away—quit hiding," I beg her through clenched teeth.

"How am I the one who's hiding?"

"You just need a reminder of who you belong to, don't you?" I ask her and take a step forward, closing the space between us. She's so close. So small and all I want to do is pick her ass up and show her she's mine. I can remind her. She just needs my touch.

"You're drunk," Allie says in a harsh whisper and looks behind me at the door to the frat house. I watch the hollow of her throat as she swallows thickly, and something flashes in her eyes.

"Would that make it better or worse?" I ask her and imagine taking her right here, right now. "If I fucked you right there in the dirt," I offer her.

"Dean, don't," she whimpers and closes her eyes, wrapping her arms around her shoulders. Like it hurt her. "Please," she begs me and it's like a slap in the face.

"Please what?" I ask her calmly, trying to pull my shit together. "I didn't mean to ..." Hurt her. I didn't mean to put that look on her face.

"Allie Cat," I speak softly, reaching up to hold her shoulders and pull her in closer, but she takes a step back. Her heels clack on the landing.

"I don't want this," she finally says and it's then I see the tears. Real tears, flowing freely and she doesn't brush them away. It stuns me for a second.

"Please, you're drunk and this, what's between us, it's over."

"Why?" I expect anger, but this feeling in my chest isn't that. "Just tell me why. I'll fix it."

I swear I can fix it. I can change. For her, I will.

"You don't commit to a goddamn thing," she says out of nowhere. Like she finally remembered the made-up excuse she could use.

"I committed to you!" The words come out loud and leave me hollow and empty. "I love you!" I yell the words although I don't mean to. So loud, the words burn on their way up. I fucking love her. My heartbeat slows and the anger leaves in a slow wave at the realization. It's been a long damn time since I've felt loved by someone, but I know she loves me back. Whether she says it or not. Somewhere in there she does. But she doesn't want to and that's what's different about us.

"Well, that was your first mistake," she says and waits. I stand there, letting everything hit me. What I feel, what she feels. When she turns around and the rapid pace of her heels echoes through the air, I feel numb.

Not because of what she said, I knew it was coming.

It's because even feeling all this for her and knowing I love her, and that she loves me, it's not enough.

Even with all that being true, she won't stay with me. And I don't know why.

ALLISON

I don't know why I can't stop crying.

It's not just little hiccups and occasional outbursts when you least expect it. It's the violent sobs that refuse to leave. The kind of crying that hurts your chest to the point where you're in physical pain. The kind that makes you curl up and huddle in the middle of the floor with only a throw blanket as if it will save you.

But nothing can. Because the pain is from the inside.

This isn't me. Dean broke me. He flipped a switch somewhere deep within me and I can't find it. I can't flick the damn thing back to where it's supposed to be.

There's not a part left remaining of the girl I set out to be. This isn't what I planned.

Right now, all I want is him. I want to take it all back.

I want to be someone else. It's not fair that these are the cards I was dealt. Or maybe I'm just an idiot for how I played them.

I pull the blue plaid throw tighter around my shoulders as a shiver runs through me. There's a pile of used tissues next to me and I hate them. They're evidence that I'm losing myself. Or maybe I've just been hiding all along.

The thought makes my spine prickle with yet another freezing bite.

It's cold.

Loneliness is cold.

Regret is even colder.

As I sit in the empty house, eerily quiet and waiting for the next bout of bullshit tears to consume me, I try to think of which part of all this I regret the most. Or maybe, a more difficult question to answer: at what point did I start to feel regret?

My body jolts when the phone in my hand pings.

I have several messages from my mother to read still. I can't bring myself to look right now. I'm so weak I'd tell her everything.

I can feel the confession on the tip of my tongue. The last time I confessed to her, it ruined me and turned me hateful. I can't make that mistake again.

I need to tell someone.

The words are so close to escaping, I almost told Angie. A girl I don't even know. Simply because she was there to listen.

She spoiled it, though. I could feel the weight lifting off my shoulders before I even let the truth escape. Class was over, Dean never showed, and the emptiness inside me brewed to a boil. Even though it was perfect. *This is perfect.*

"I think it's best to stay away from guys like that," she told me.

And that's what made me keep quiet.

What kept the words deep down inside.

What if I didn't want to stay away?

What if I knew what I was doing?

She wouldn't understand and she'd be disgusted with me if I told her what I really wanted. More than anything else. But it's our secret. Our promise. They won't know why.

My phone pings again and my body shudders. I'm quick to

place it on silent but then the thought of missing a text from Dean makes me change it back.

Pathetic.

I'm so fucking pathetic. Clinging to the idea of what could be.

As if it would even be possible for someone like me.

Someone so consumed with destruction.

I glance at the texts from my mom.

The first line is from me to her.

Only an apology, and a vague one at that.

I'm sorry, I told her. I couldn't not say it. Not while I sat in that hotel room wishing she were with me. Wishing I could take it all back. If only it were so easy to pluck words from the air and tuck them into your back pocket.

The series of texts from my mother hasn't stopped since then.

I think she thought I'd killed myself until I told her I hadn't.

I'm sorry for running. I sent her that text to explain, but it's not much of an explanation at all. I can't tell her the truth though because I'm still running, and she'll stop me.

Just like Dean would.

They can't stop this from happening. My body stiffens when I see my mother's last text.

I'm coming to see you.

I start to respond, but what can I say? *No, don't.* It's not like she'll listen.

When I delete it without hitting send, another text from her comes through.

You won't talk to me and this has to stop.

What has to stop? I text back.

I know that will make her drop it. Because she can't admit what happened. She can't apologize to me for what she did. She can't speak the truth.

I miss you, she finally answers me.

I wonder which version of me she misses. Probably the younger version. The one that isn't so fucked in the head.

I miss the old me too. But she's long dead and has been for years.

DEAN

The beer is cold and the head of it foams just right. It looks like a picture for a beer ad as it sits on the walnut bar of the Iron Heart Brewery on Lincoln and Church.

My back's to the door as I sit at the far end of the bar, closest to the large glass window. More people walk into the already crowded place, but I don't pay any attention to the chatter. I only stare out the window at the parking lot across the street.

"You want something else?" the bartender asks me and when I look up at him, interrupting whatever thought was in my head, he nods to the untouched beer.

"Nah, I'm good," I tell him and take a swig. Maybe I should ask for something stronger. Maybe I shouldn't drink at all. I don't know. I don't know shit and that's all I know for sure.

"All the way out here?" a voice too close for comfort asks and I turn around to see Daniel sliding onto the barstool next to me.

"I'll have what he's having," he tells the bartender and then squares his shoulders forward and squints like he's looking up at the menu.

"Some funny names for beer," he says absently.

"All local drafts," I tell him.

"Is that why you came all the way out here?" he asks me and I turn my gaze back to my beer and then take another long pull. I'm here because it's right around the corner from Dr. Robinson's office. I'm here because it's easy. The beer's good, the vibe is right, and everyone here leaves me the hell alone.

"How'd you find me?" I ask him and he shrugs.

"Been barhopping," he says like it's a coincidence. I huff in disbelief but I don't push him. Daniel's background isn't exactly sparkling clean.

He slaps down a few five-dollar bills as his beer hits the bar and then he finally faces me.

"She really messed you up that bad?" *Going right in for the kill.*

"I don't want to talk about it," I answer him simply, returning my gaze to the cracked concrete sidewalk across the street. A few people walk by and no one seems to notice it.

"Fair enough," he says with a nod and then asks for a menu.

"You're making yourself right at home, aren't you?"

"I've got to eat."

I take a good hard look at him as he opens the menu and pretends like this is some casual meetup.

"You don't have anything better to do?" I ask him and his dark gaze meets mine. There's a challenge in his eyes but one he lets go of quickly.

"Nothing I feel like doing right now."

Another moment passes and he closes the menu and pushes it forward, glancing over his shoulder to check out the game.

"What would you do?" I finally ask him. "If you were me?"

"If I wanted a girl, but she didn't want me?" he asks like that's what happened.

"She wants me," I tell him confidently and he huffs a sarcastic laugh. "She's scared," I tell him in a raised voice I didn't intend.

"Scared of you?" he asks like it's a valid question and I can't believe he'd say that.

"You think I'd hurt her?" My hackles raise, my muscles coiling. "I'd never give her a reason to fear me. I wouldn't hurt a woman."

"You're the one who said she's scared," he answers me and I let the anger wane, listening to the murmur of talking around us and the sounds of the football game on the screen as I think about how to explain my Allie Cat.

"What's she afraid of then?" Daniel asks me before I can tell him anything and I just shrug.

"What are we all afraid of?" I shoot back and then snort like I'm some fucking philosopher.

"Getting hurt ... or maybe that we'll be the ones to do the hurting," Daniel answers with nothing but sincerity. My throat tightens and I struggle to release my breath as I take in the weight of what he said.

I nod and chug my beer, drinking it all down. It hits the bar with a loud ring from the empty glass and I signal for another.

"Sometimes people hurt the ones who get close to them."

"I didn't hurt her," I say without looking away from the bar. I watch the bartender fill the glass, the beer spilling over before he wipes it off.

"I wasn't talking about you doing the hurting. Seems like she's the one who's got you on a leash."

I smirk at him and grab the beer with both hands.

"Maybe I like the leash," I joke and he finally breaks into a smile, but it's gone when he opens his mouth next.

"You like her doing that, though?" he asks. "Leading you on like that?"

"It's not what it looks like," I tell him and he's quick to respond with, "That's what they all say."

"I'm telling you, Allie feels something for me. There's something real there."

"But she's scared?" he asks like I'm being ridiculous. Without waiting for me to try to explain more, he continues.

"You can't make someone commit to you." His voice turns

bitter as he adds, "You can't make them want you." I'm struck by his words and the force of them until I realize he's talking about something else. *Someone else.*

"If she'd just tell me what the hell got to her, I'd make it right."

"Did you ask?"

The world seems to still at his question. The obvious answer is yes. I didn't, though, not really. I backed off. I didn't push her like I thought about doing. I could have pushed. I should have. I was so close, and I didn't do it.

"I didn't want to scare her off," I say and the words are a murmur.

"Instead you lost her," he says back and I stare at him like he's the asshole here. He shrugs and takes another sip of his beer before telling me, "Sometimes they come back, and sometimes you just have to go get them."

ALLISON

*T*here's something about these pajamas.

They remind me of Sam. She always wore pajamas, even to school. Blue and flannel with a tank top underneath, the pants folded over at the waist. A small smile graces my lips as I grab the bottle of Cabernet from the fridge.

That's how I want to remember her.

It's been five years, and only recently have I started to remember her like that. Back when she was the Sam I knew and loved. Back when we were best friends for life.

She wore pajamas like this when she was happy.

Not me, though. My heart sinks as I glance at my phone, sitting on the countertop of the small kitchen.

I think that was the final straw. Dean will never want me again.

That should make me happy, considering what my only goal is. The one thing I've wanted for so long. This arrangement is the best scenario. Available. Vulnerable. And the reputation of a slut. *Easy.* It would be all too easy.

As I pour the mostly empty bottle into the glass, I wonder if I'm crazy. The plan was crazy from the beginning, certainly not something a sane person would do. I knew that.

Then again, not many people would remain sane after seeing what I saw and knowing what I know.

Tragedies happen, but usually there's justice. A villain you can blame and prosecute.

When the villain gets off scot-free and destroys your life forever, that does something to a person. When he walks away unscathed and blends into a crowd that looks back at you like you're the one who's in the wrong.

It's even worse when you played a part in the wreckage and the small pieces that were shattered turn to ashes in your hands. You'll make all sorts of promises then. Promises to make wrongs right. At any cost.

"Whatever it takes," I whisper and lift the wine to my lips, drinking it in large gulps.

I barely taste it although the sweetness turns bitter quickly as it sits on my tongue.

It's a good thing I pushed Dean away, I think. *He deserves so much better.*

The bottle clinks and the sound resonates in the kitchen as I set it down. There wasn't even enough left to fill the glass.

One hand holds the wine, while the other picks up my phone.

I will him to text me, but nothing happens.

Slipping onto the stool, I lay my cheek down on the cold granite and stare at my phone. I scroll through our messages; I even laugh once or twice, even though it's a sad sound. These texts are proof that at one point I was happy.

I'm sorry. I text him, unable to keep myself from doing it. I'm sorrier than he'll ever know.

I glance around this place and hate that I'm even here. The sickness that's been in the bottom of my gut for so long begins to creep up.

I don't want to be here anymore. I don't want to do this.

It all hurts too much. *But I'm so close to the edge.* If only I can just hold on.

I'm so close to keeping a promise I never thought I could.

I drown my self-pity in the wine, throwing it back and trying to block out the images that keep coming back to me, but I have to stop when I hear a loud knock at the door. My eyes fly to the screen of my phone, the message marked as read.

Dean.

My feet trip over one another and I nearly fall in my desperation to get to the door. I'll tell him. I'll confess and he'll save me. God help me please, because I don't know what to do anymore.

With a racing heart and nearly breathless, I whip open the front door, not bothering to check to see who it is.

It's not Dean and my heart slows, as does time.

I guess this was what he needed. It's what he was waiting for.

A weakness leading to a way in.

I knew I was close to the edge, but I wasn't ready to jump. I guess I would never have jumped, though; it was all about being pushed.

I swallow the lump growing in my throat. "Kevin." I say his name out loud. This is the second time I've talked to him. Other than that night six years ago at Mike's house. I thought it would have taken more to lure him in. I didn't even try yet. I was still setting up the dominoes.

"What are you doing here?" I ask him, trying to hide the swell of anger … and fear. My knuckles turn white as I grip the doorknob harder. "How did you know my address?" I ask him as it registers that I never told him. I'd planned on it, of course. My heart beats harder as I think about how this is exactly what I wanted. But not right now. Not like this.

I can barely breathe as he tells me, "I saw you walk home the other night from the frat house. It's not too far away."

It's not. I rented this place just for that reason. I didn't realize he'd noticed. I thought I'd have to tell him.

"I was just dropping by to check on you," he says and then looks to his right and left. "You alone?" he asks.

I don't want to tell him I am but I nod once regardless. That's what a good victim would do. The perfect victim for him.

This is what I came here for. The entire reason I came to this town, this university.

The sole reason for my existence for the last six months. As soon as Grandmom died and there was nothing left to live for anymore.

To make him pay for what he did to her.

Even if I set him up, if the justice served is for what he does to me right now, it'll be worth it. She deserves to have him pay for what he is.

"Do you want to come in?" I ask him and I let my body sway slightly, thinking of Sam and how she needed this. I have a glass of wine in me, only one but I play up the drunkenness. Maybe that will make this happen quicker.

He doesn't answer me but he looks over his shoulder before coming in and shutting the door.

"You drinking?" he asks me, looking pointedly at the glass still in my hand. The dark liquid swirls as I shrug and try to think of what to say.

To think of what's happening right now and not the night that he crept into the bedroom where Sam was. I try not to think of what he did to her and what he's about to do to me. I was right there. So close to saving her. So close to preventing all this.

But I can make it all better now. I can make it right.

I can be his next victim and make him pay. Because that's what I came here to do.

"Dean doesn't want me anymore, so I thought I'd celebrate being single again," I say to the ground, keeping my eyes half-shut. I think maybe he'll use that to convince me to talk to him. Or to somehow try to weasel his way into me sleeping with him for revenge or something.

Whatever it takes.

"Already a bottle in?" he says with a smirk, looking at the empty bottle on the dining room table as he reaches for the buckle on his belt.

"What are you doing?" I ask out of instinct. My hair stands on end and my blood slows, my heart stops.

"I know how to make you feel better," he says as he pulls the leather through the loops of his pants. *Say something.* Two different voices scream in my head. One to let him, to agree with him. One to tell him no.

My blood runs cold. *Say something.* The need to run almost overwhelms me but I stand still. It's only when he drops the belt on the ground and lets the buckle clang that I can't hold it back any longer.

I don't want to tell him no because I want him to hurt me. This is exactly what I planned but I can't do it. I can't keep my promise to her.

"You should—"

"Come here," he interrupts me before I can say go.

I try to push him off of me, hating how he grips my arm. His thick fingers dig into my skin, bruising me and holding me still.

I didn't expect this. She was on the bed. She could barely move. She told me. But this isn't like that.

A scream tears from my throat and I try to run but he trips me, grabbing my thigh and covering my mouth.

"We both know you wanted this," he grunts as he digs into the waistband of my pajama pants.

He has no idea.

This is all I've wanted for so long.

For justice, the only way I know how to get it.

Even so, when he pushes me back against the sofa, I continue to fight him. At first, I think it's instinct. But when he smiles and grips my hips, pushing me and pulling me down, the sick feeling of regret makes my skin go cold.

"Leave me alone," I yell, scorching my throat but he doesn't listen. My nails rake the back of his hand as he shoves me down with a bruising force.

I wish I could stop him.

"Stop!" I scream out, kicking him, but he covers my face. My heart beats wildly.

I changed my mind. I don't want this. I try to scream again but he yanks my arm behind my back and pins me in place, forcing me facedown on the sofa.

"I've always wanted to play with a girl like you."

* * *

I'LL NEVER FORGET the smell of the blood. The air was thick with it although I didn't know what it was until later.

The floor creaked as I stepped into Sam's bedroom. I called out her name, pushing the door open wider, but deep down I already knew something had happened. The house was quiet, save the click of the air conditioner turning on. Even that made me jump.

Sam! I called out louder when I didn't see her on her bed where she usually was. Her phone was there, though. Right in the center of the neatly made bed.

I can still see her now, sitting cross-legged and bobbing her head, making her ponytail swish back and forth as she listened to the music blaring from her earbuds. But that was the old Sam. The girl who knew who she was and loved herself.

That was before she was raped. Before she was told it was her fault. That she should have known better. Before everyone looked at her like she was the only one to blame.

Before she believed that she'd genuinely deserved it. That there was something innately wrong with her. That she really had it coming to her. That's what everyone told her, so why would she think any different? Even if she didn't want it, it was because of what she'd done that he hurt her. And she was the one who was the problem.

I tried to call out her name again but my voice was hoarse as I saw the light filtering through the crack of the open bathroom door. And the note on the floor.

I'M SORRY.

I'm sorry I ended it.
I'm sorry I went to the party.
I'm sorry I kissed those boys and led them on.
I'm sorry I drank. I'm sorry I ever talked to Kevin.
It hurt when he held me down.
I promise I tried to scream. I'm sorry you didn't hear me.
I'm sorry I didn't tell you sooner, Mom.
I'm sorry all of this happened.
I don't want to be this person.
I swear to you I'm sorry.

THE WORLD MADE HER BLIND. She wasn't supposed to be sorry. Victims aren't the ones who are supposed to be sorry. I walked away unscathed, but Sam wasn't so lucky. She didn't hear my voice telling her that she wasn't a bad person because everyone else spoke in unison. She asked for it. What did she think would happen?

What did they think would happen when she was gone and only I was left, knowing her truth?

THE PAPER CRINKLED in my hand. I'll never forget how neat her penmanship was. How even with her last words, she made sure they were pretty and that she'd written each letter as best as she could.

My thumb traced over the one spot on the sheet of paper that was crinkled and slightly discolored. Where she'd let her tears fall onto the paper.

I don't know how I forced myself to move. Every step to the bathroom made my fear more real, made my skin that much colder.

My hand shook as I pushed open the bathroom door wider, my heart refusing to continue beating when I saw her.

Sam never cried before that night.

And she never smiled after it either.

"Sam," I said, and my voice scratched my throat as I fell to my knees in the bathroom. The tile was cold and hard. She was in the tub with the drain open and the water barely running. It mixed with the blood and pooled around her body.

Her pajama pants were stuck to her legs, soaking wet and stained with the blood.

I covered my mouth as I cried, hating the sight before me. After she slit her throat, she must have lurched forward; blood was splattered on the wall and on her arms. Like maybe she tried to stop it. But the knife lay by her thigh and she was still.

"Sam." I could barely say her name as I inched forward.

I had to touch her, even with her eyes open and staring back at nothing, a stillness that only comes with death. Even then I still had to climb into the tub and hold her, begging her to wake up.

But she never would.

Even as a fifteen-year-old girl, I knew that.

She hated herself for what she'd done. She came to believe she deserved it because that's what everyone told her. She was confused and she forgot how to be happy. She must've thought she never would be again and maybe she was right.

Worst of all, I left her.

I listened to my mother and left her when she needed me most. It could have been me and I didn't even stand beside her.

I COULD NEVER TAKE THAT BACK. But I made her a promise that night.

DEAN

*T*here's an expression about seeing red.

They say when you're consumed with rage, you see red. Your sense of awareness is skewed. Your thoughts aren't logical. Your decisions aren't sane.

You're seeing red.

I've been angry before. I've let it get the best of me rather than accepting the pain that was always there.

I never knew the true meaning of seeing red until I heard Allie scream.

I could hear her behind the door.

I thought I heard her all the way from the sidewalk. It was a scream that made the hairs on my arm stand on end. A scream the neighbor heard as well and I caught her looking toward Allie's door with concern.

My heartbeat picked up and it was already pounding in my chest.

Every step I took before I heard her, I thought about the text I sent her. I was fixated on it.

I almost didn't send it. I almost acted like a coward and let her leave me.

If Daniel hadn't convinced me to get my sorry ass out of the bar, I might not be here now.

You need to stop pushing me away, *I texted her.* I don't know what the hell your problem is, but you've got to stop this shit. I'm coming over.

She didn't reply. I didn't expect her to, but I was still coming to get her.

I was thinking about what I was going to say and how I was going to say it. It felt like it was my last chance. The Hail Mary of getting her back but also keeping her. And then I heard her.

My boots slapped on her porch as I picked up my pace.

My fists slammed on the door as I called out her name.

But I could barely hear them over the sound of the chaotic pounding in my chest, the sound of my blood rushing in my ears.

The sound of her screaming out again. With fear.

My shoulder crashed into the door without thinking twice. The pain rippled up my neck and down my back.

"Allie!" I screamed her name as the wood cracked and I shoved myself into the room. She was right there but still so far away.

The sight will be burned into my memory forever.

The scratch on Kevin's arm, deep and bright in color, the redness in Allie's skin and clear fear written on her face, cheeks tearstained and her voice raw and hoarse as she screamed again. How he was hovering over her, shoving her down even as he looked up at me.

Red.

It's all red.

I don't know how my body moved, but it did. I don't think I breathed until I picked up the lamp.

I remember him getting up and I could see him thinking about how to play it off. I could see the look in his eyes. Like he wasn't actually hurting her. Like I'd just caught him playing around.

The lamp was so light in my grasp. As though it weighed nothing as I whacked him over the head with it. My body was tight and screaming. It took no energy at all. No thought. His head was the part of him closest to me as he stood. The easiest to strike.

The sound is something I don't think I'll ever forget either. The crack of the lamp, the crunch of his bones.

The blow was solid. Even though his wrist blocked the first swing, the next bash of the lamp struck him right where I aimed. The cord swung around, whipping him in the face and then back to my arm. I aimed again as he yelled at me to stop.

And I know I aimed. I can remember that.

Again and again, my arm lifted and slammed the lamp down. My throat burned with a scream I couldn't hear. I pushed my muscles harder and harder, feeling like I was on fire.

I just wanted her to stop screaming. I wanted all this to go away. To be a nightmare and nothing more.

For a moment, I questioned myself. As if my sudden lapse of sanity was over. As if I wasn't angry, and I was wondering what I was doing.

But the moment was quickly forgotten when I heard Allie scream again.

And that's when the hammering of the base of the lamp turned to a slash from the broken ceramic.

It's all a haze of red.

Like I wasn't seeing things clearly. Like it wasn't real.

It stayed that way as the blood spilled from his neck where a shard of the glass pierced his skin. It covered his shoulder and poured onto my leg and onto the sofa. I've never seen anything like it. And maybe the surprise of it is what stops me. I can't be sure.

His eyes stare through me. With every breath, I wait for him to blink but he doesn't. What the hell just happened? My heart pounds and my pulse is louder than anything I've ever heard. I'm dizzy as I imagine him reaching up to stop the steady flow of blood, but his body is still. *This isn't real. This didn't happen.*

I can barely hear Allie but I know her screams have stopped, and she's saying something else now as she hunches over, but not taking her eyes from me. Something laced with dread and guilt, but I can't hear her over the ringing in my ears. I can hardly focus my vision on her. My body's shaking and I can't move. I'm frozen. It feels that way as I drop what's left of the lamp to the floor. It thuds and then cracks, that's clear to me. But Allie's words are mixed with the memory of her scream.

I can hardly feel her tugging on me as I stare at her ripped pajamas, hanging from her chest.

It all stays red until the scream from behind me forces me to realize there's someone else here. Someone other than Allie. Allie's weeping on the ground, her hands covered in blood as she crouches on the ground and then looks up at me with fear and sorrow swirling in her eyes and it takes another scream before I turn around to face the front door and see who's screaming.

Someone who would bear witness to what I'd done.

Someone who heard the screaming and came in through the front door.

Someone who saw Kevin's dead body at my feet.

Allie's neighbor from earlier, is screaming in the doorway behind me.

ALLISON

No. I take it back.

I take it all back.

This wasn't supposed to happen.

"Dean, stop!" I try to scream at him but my voice is hoarse, the pain ripping my throat as I topple over. The bleeding won't stop. I keep pushing against Kevin's throat with my trembling hands as if I can stop the flow. But it won't.

It's too late.

I know it is but I can't stop trying.

I can barely breathe as my shaking hands move away from the limp body. He's still warm but blood isn't pumping from the wound anymore. It's hardly a trickle.

"Are you okay?" I hear Dean ask over the sound of a shrill scream.

It takes me a moment to realize he's trying to pick me up and move me, but I can't move. I can't be touched. I only catch a glimpse of a woman's back from the doorway.

My heart races and my body chills.

"Dean," I say. *What did I do?*

It happened so fast. Too fast to control. Too many moving parts to see what would come next.

I didn't mean for this to happen. I try to blink away the vision. The memory. As the feeling of Kevin pushing me down comes back to me and I could vomit from it. I shove against Dean's chest. My body reacts reflexively, trying to protect me.

"It's me," he says as I wrap my arms around my shoulders and try to get away.

I'm numb and shaking.

"It's me. It's okay. It's okay." Dean keeps speaking lies.

It's not okay.

It's never been worse.

Kevin's body is at an odd angle on the floor and as I try to back away, Dean's boot hits Kevin's leg. And it moves easily, lifeless.

I didn't mean for him to die.

It's all I can think. I swear. I wanted the world to know who he was and what he was capable of.

I wanted him to pay for what he did to Sam.

But I never intended this.

"I'm sorry," I say, the words whispered from my lips and Dean stiffens beside me. It's the first time I really look up at him.

His hair's disheveled and his eyes are narrowed and deadly. I should be scared of him, but all I can do is cling to his side.

"You didn't do anything." His t-shirt seems to tighten around his broad shoulders, the cotton stretching as he takes a heavy breath.

But didn't I? The pain and regret all mix with everything else. It's a whirlwind of chaos.

Right there beside us is the undeniable and crushing truth that I've brought Dean into this. I led him here. The one person who made me question it.

My heart stutters in my chest, refusing to believe this is real and not wanting to admit any of this. I just want to go back to that night in the hotel room and tell him everything. I want to beg for his forgiveness. To let him walk away and save him.

It's too late.

The whisper hangs between us as I say, "What have I done?"

"You were fighting him," Dean says and struggles to control his breathing. I can feel his eyes piercing into me but I can't look him in the eyes. "You were fighting him and screaming," he repeats.

I nod my head.

"He was hurting you." His voice cracks on the last word.

I finally look up at him with tears welling in my eyes. The pain has apparently won. Of all things, pain is the most damaging. "He was trying to..." The words are slow, achingly slow and the worst word of all stays trapped in the back of my throat.

I'm going to be sick.

My stomach churns and I try to stand but my head's foggy and I slip backward, almost touching the dead body.

With the image of him pushing me down, I try to get away and Dean's there, holding me, pulling me away from the nonexistent threat. *This wasn't supposed to happen.*

"I'm here," he whispers and holds me as the faint sound of a siren in the distance sneaks in through the broken front door. "It's okay."

"Dean, it's not okay." I look into his eyes as I speak and I'm so wounded. None of this is okay. It hasn't been. But it wasn't supposed to become this. This isn't right.

What have I done? Please, I just want to take it back.

My heart pounds in my chest. The fear is crippling.

"No." The word bubbles from my lips repeatedly as the reality hits me. There's no way I could have known this is what would happen. I didn't know. I swear I didn't know and I didn't want this.

"It's okay. You're okay," Dean keeps saying even over the sound of the sirens growing louder by the minute. As if anything could be okay.

"You don't understand," I plead with him to listen but my

throat is scratchy, and I hiccup over my words. "I'm so sorry," I whimper, covering my face as the tears pour from me.

"Stop saying you're sorry!" Dean yells as he grips my shoulders, forcing me to face him. His strong hands pin me where he wants me with a force that almost makes me collapse. If I did, I'd collapse into his arms. "You didn't do anything wrong," he says and his voice is full of sympathy, but so much more than that too. He keeps saying that but he doesn't know the truth.

"You don't understand," I say, the words full of agony as I remember Samantha's broad smile. She was so beautiful. So full of life and happiness. It's a smile that will only live in my memory. I've let everyone down. Everyone I ever loved. Sam. *Dean.*

"Did you want him to do that?" Dean questions with hate, with denial, with jealousy in his eyes and I shake my head furiously.

"Never," I tell him quickly. "I didn't. I swear."

"Then stop it!" he commands me. He doesn't understand.

"I knew he would," I say, the words coming out strained. "When I let him in—" It's only a part of a confession and it's cut off by Dean's fingers digging into my arms as he shakes me slightly.

My cheeks feel hot as the tears stain them.

"He's responsible for what he did, Allie," Dean tells me, his eyes piercing into my own. "I won't have you say any differently." The sirens are louder now, almost deafening.

"I asked for this," I say weakly, full of shame.

"What did you ask for?" He barely gets out the words as his voice shakes with pain. He shakes his head as he adds, "You didn't ask for this." He's full of denial as the police park in front of the house. I can hear them. There's more than one cop car and the sound of multiple doors slamming shut is mixed with him whispering that this isn't my fault and that I'm okay and that he's the one who's sorry.

But it is my fault.

I asked for this. For vengeance. For justice.

I didn't just ask for it. I prayed for it every day for years. When they taunted her in the hallways. When the other girls declined to sit with her. Every meeting I had with lawyers who refused to take the case, saying it was impossible. Every time I thought of her, I knew I would never be able to stop until someone did something. I prayed for him to pay.

Dean didn't, though. Knowing that, I hate myself even more.

DEAN

My stomach feels hollow.

My body is freezing.

The fucking jail cell is cold, so at least that part makes sense.

The doctor who came in to examine me said I was in shock. Maybe that's what happens when you kill a man. Or when you see someone you love screaming in pain. Maybe the two are the same.

A cell opens and closes, and I barely lift my eyes at the eerie sound of finality.

I killed him.

In cold blood.

This isn't a bar fight I can get out of.

Charges have been pressed and they booked me within hours.

Third-degree murder.

I told them everything. Every bit of what I remembered. There's no way to get out of this and I still don't know how I could do it. I can say I'm sorry and I didn't intend to kill him, and I mean it. I do. I didn't mean to kill the prick. It doesn't change it, though. I can't take it back.

I'm fucked.

I run my hand down my face and try to stop seeing him. Any time the image flashes in my head of him dead on the floor, it's followed by one of him on top of Allie. It's like a sick joke my mind's playing on me. Twisting and coiling the darkness inside my head until it strikes me down over and over again.

"Allie," I whisper under my breath and let my head fall. The door opens at the end of the row of cells and I repeat to myself, "It was to protect her." Wasn't it?

I'm already starting to question it. Just like the cops did. Asking me what I thought of him. If we'd had physical encounters before. How my anger management sessions were going. Whether I tried to pull him away or if I just went in to kill him.

They questioned if he was even hurting her.

I didn't have to keep going, but I swear I couldn't stop myself.

There were so many questions, I couldn't even keep my own answers straight.

"Just let me know when you're ready to leave." I lift my eyes at the sound of the guard's voice and see Uncle Rob standing outside of the bars.

They slide open and he walks through, looking like a ghost of the man I once knew. His hair's silver and the heavy bags under his eyes are either from years of booze or weeks of no sleep.

"Dean," he says my name and my eyes drop from his jeans to his boots, then lower to the cement floor of the cell. I can't look him in the eyes.

The cell door shuts with a loud clink and I hear him walk over to the cold bench to sit beside me.

He doesn't speak as he leans forward with his elbows on his knees.

"Your lawyer's coming," he tells me with a tone of comfort and safety as though a lawyer can get me out of this. I guess I should have asked for one before saying a word. But what's the point?

"I did it," I tell him in a tight voice and tilt my head to reach his eyes. "I killed him." The last sentence comes out strong. I can at least own it. "He was trying to—"

Uncle Rob cuts me off, placing a hand on my shoulder and leaning in closer. "I know what happened. They gave me the report. But that doesn't mean you don't need a lawyer."

His eyes are bloodshot and rimmed in red as he stares at me, begging me to hear him out.

"I don't see the point. I told them what happened. They know he tried to rape her." My voice goes tight. "I only did it to save her."

"It's Jack's nephew. He's friends with the judge. You need a lawyer." His voice is hard but also panicked.

I huff out a breath of disbelief at my uncle's words. "I already know that."

"Listen to me for once in your fucking life, Dean," my uncle shouts at me with exasperation. "He doesn't want his name smeared."

"Smeared?" I can't believe what I'm hearing.

"You don't know how they'll spin it," my uncle says sharply and that gets my attention.

"Spin it?"

"Jack said she set his nephew up."

"She what?" My vision spins.

"That she liked it that way and wanted to make you jealous."

"You believe him?" I stand up abruptly, moving away from my uncle and looking at him with disgust.

"No!" he says and taps his foot nervously on the cement floor. "They're going to try to spin it. They're saying she wanted him and that you caught them in the act."

"But she's a witness, she can testify. Shit, a neighbor heard her screaming!" My voice bellows in the cell, my anger bouncing off the hard, unforgiving walls.

"Well, there's some damning evidence, Dean. You need to hear it. You need to be prepared for it."

"Hear what?"

"Your anger, your arrests. Pictures of the two of you and testimonies of her being *more than friendly* with some of your friends." My heart slows with each word.

"None of that has anything to do with this."

"Maybe not to you, but your opinion doesn't matter. If they think she's lying, her testimony doesn't matter."

"It's the truth!"

"It doesn't matter," he says in a flat voice.

"She didn't want him to rape her."

"You have to prove it was rape."

"Her word isn't enough?" I spit back at him with even more contempt.

"Not when she's made her intentions questionable. The DA has to decide—"

"Get out!" I say and seethe. "I don't need you or your lawyer." My voice comes out even and confident, and I have no fucking clue how. I'm trembling with anger and sickness.

"I'm not leaving you," he tells me with a shaky voice. "You needed me back then, and I failed you. I won't fail you now. If you don't want me here, that's fine. I'll respect that, but I'm getting you a lawyer for the arraignment."

ALLISON

$\mathcal{I}$'ve been waiting for one phone call.

The one where a stranger on the end of the line will tell me I can go see him. They told me I needed to leave. That I needed to wait and stop calling. So, I'm trying to be patient.

I have to tell Dean first. He has to know.

And then I can tell everyone else. They'll let Dean go after I do. They'll have to.

It's my fault. I'm still in disbelief. I can't believe it happened.

My tired eyes lift from the dead violets on the windowsill to the front door. The window's open and I should have heard someone pull up to the house, but I didn't.

"Allison?" a soft voice says hesitantly and I press my palms into my sore eyes.

"Mom?" Through my tears, I think I see her. She's hazy and the white blinds swirl in front of her before she can walk in and shut the door behind her, but I hear her voice.

"You didn't answer your phone." She talks quickly as she walks toward me with uncertain steps. "I had to come see you," she whispers as I get up from the floor with shaky legs.

"Mom?" I can't stop repeating myself.

My feet move on their own, guiding me to her and when I finally get close enough, I cling to her. Burying my face in the crook of her neck, I hold on to her with a tight grip.

"Mom," I say between the sobs.

"I'm here," she says and holds me back just as tightly, the keys in her hand dropping to the floor and clattering together. The noise makes my shoulders shake, but everything makes me jumpy now. I don't care.

I've broken down so many times in the last week. I thought I was done with crying. I thought I had nothing left, but as she cries into my hair and rocks me, they come again. They're merciless.

I deserve it.

"Are you okay?" my mother asks me although her grip doesn't loosen. I can't nod and I can't speak, so I don't say anything until she holds me at arm's length.

"Talk to me please," she begs me and I shake my head. Her eyes are red and puffy with dark shadows beneath them.

"I'm not okay. I'm not okay," I tell her as my shoulders shake.

"It's okay, I'm here," she says, just like Dean did. As if mere words can make it all right but they can't. "I heard what happened," my mother says and my body tenses, but all she says is that it will be okay.

"It's all my fault." The words pour from me even though I'm not sure they make sense. I'm not sure she can even comprehend them.

"Shhh." Hushed words won't keep me quiet. Not anymore.

"You don't understand," I say and the words come out quickly, the rest begging to follow. To confess.

"I do understand. I know that boy's name. I know who he is," she says and her gaze turns hard and full of worry. "You can't tell them you knew. They won't look into it. Don't tell them you knew." Her throat's tight as she swallows and it takes a moment for the realization to hit me with full force. She knows. Maybe not all of it, but she knows.

"I have to—"

"It's not your fault," she says, cutting me off. "What happened to Sam wasn't your fault either and—"

"Yes, it was!" I scream at the audacity of my mother saying such a lie. Especially now. How dare she! I shove against her, knocking myself backward and scramble to leave her comfort. "When will you admit it?" I shout at her, letting the pain and anger twist in my gut. "I knew the truth and I didn't fight for her! I didn't help her!" I practically hiss, the shame and regret all-consuming as I say, "I walked away because you told me to."

My mother shakes her head, denying it as she always has. Her hands are up in defense as if she's approaching a wounded animal ready to run. Her blonde hair brushes back and forth around her shoulders. "It wasn't your fault," she tries to say again but her words are lost as she cries into her hand. "None of this is your fault and I'll protect you, baby. They won't find out."

"If I hadn't texted her," I say then gulp in air and my body shudders. "If I hadn't told her you didn't want me to see her anymore …" I close my eyes, remembering how I sent the text in anger. I was so upset that my mother would treat Sam the same way everyone else did. Like it was her fault that Kevin had hurt her. Like she was lying about what he'd done to her.

My mother blamed Sam. And I spread that blame to my friend. My friend who was struggling. Who just needed someone to love her. I broke Sam by telling her that. I know I did. I didn't agree with my mother. I wasn't going to leave her. But I wasn't given the chance to show her. I sent that message without thinking what it would do.

My mother was just like them. She said Sam was trouble, and I should never have turned my back on Sam. I should never have acted so rashly.

That was the last text I sent to Sam. And the last one she read before she killed herself.

"Admit it," I demand with a note of finality in my voice. "Admit it, Mother!"

"It's not—" she starts to say but I cut her off, refusing to listen to her denial after all this time. Her shoulders shake with a sob she tries to silence.

"Why avoid me then? Why walk around like you're guilty? So quiet and afraid to say anything to me like your words will break me? Why!" I scream at her. I was quiet for too long. All of this waiting to come out and instead it only festered inside.

Both of us were so aware of how our words had killed, that neither of us spoke. I hate her for it. So quiet, I became dead inside. She's the one I blame because I'd rather blame her than myself.

"For years, you hardly spoke to me. You let me get away with anything and everything. You avoided me. You know how much you meant to her. You knew how it would hurt her. And you didn't care! You didn't care about her and now she's dead!"

My voice is hoarse and the words echo in my head. I didn't care about Sam when I sent that to her. I was just angry at my mom for not believing me. I didn't think about how it would destroy Sam. It was my fault for telling her. It's always been my fault.

"I'm sorry!" my mother wails. "I wish I could take it back, Allison, but I can't and I'm sorry." Her face is bright red, and she struggles to swallow as she waits for my response. "I'm so sorry. I didn't want to hurt her. I never wanted to hurt her. I just wanted to save you."

It's the first time she's ever told me she regrets it. It's so late. Too late for what really matters but still, it's something I desperately want to cling to.

How could I ever be saved in a world that allowed this to happen? In a world that makes a victim feel like they could have stopped it when there wasn't a damn thing they could have done to prevent the inevitable. There's nothing that can save me.

"Please stop hating me," she begs, her bottom lip wobbling and her frail shoulders shaking. I always thought she was so strong. I thought I was the weak one. Maybe we're both weak.

"I never hated you," I tell her but I can't be sure that it's honest. Pain turns to hate so easily. "I wasn't okay, though. It's not okay. It never will be."

"Please forgive me."

I nod my head although I flinch when she tries to hug me, and it breaks her. I can't help it. There's so much more. And the truth begs me to speak it.

My voice is eerily calm and my mother just nods her head once, staring at the pot of withered violets and avoiding my gaze. Or maybe my judgment.

"Mom, I have to tell you something."

My mother's eyes whip to mine. Maybe because the tone of my voice has changed. From pained to haunted.

"When Grandmom died, that very week, there was an article."

My mom wipes her face with the sleeve of her shirt, but I know she's listening.

"There was a name I recognized." My hands clench at my side as I remember seeing it. "The name of the boy who hurt Sam." The words hurt as they leave me and the article flashes in my memory.

"You don't need to tell me this." There's hesitation in her voice like she's scared to know.

I hear her and I know she already assumes, but she should know. I want the world to know what I did. "Just about alumni, about tradition. It wasn't anything that should have made me angry, but it did. I was the angriest I've ever been." I admit to her something I've never said out loud. Jack and Kevin Henderson, the proud alumni nephew. Smiling in an article.

The boy whose uncle was friends with a judge.

The boy who said she'd made him think it was what she wanted.

The boy who went back home and kissed other girls and smiled, knowing he'd get what he wanted. *No matter what.*

That boy never paid for what he did. He smiled at me. "Sam could never smile again, but there he was, smiling."

"Allison?" she says, and my mother's tone holds a warning. Like she knows what's coming. Like she's followed my train of thought.

"I'm not done," I tell her and her expression changes. I force my clammy hands to unclench.

"I came here because of that article. I came here because I wanted him to do to me, what he did to Sam."

"No," she says and shakes her head, denying it, the puzzle pieces firmly falling into place for her. *I asked for it.* Her head shakes as I continue my story. She can say those words now like she did back then. It'll be true this time.

"I wanted the world to see him for the person he was. I wanted them to know she wasn't lying." My words get louder as I speak. More frantic, more saddened. "She deserved some kind of justice. I came here and I sought him out on purpose."

Her cries are all that stop me from telling her more. She covers her mouth with both hands and shakes her head.

I won't deny it. I won't pretend things aren't as they seem.

"I knew what I was doing, Mom. I wanted him to hurt me. Because if he did it to me, he'd be punished. Sam would finally have some sort of justice. It wouldn't make it right, but she'd have something." I croak out the last word, the tears slipping down my face to my chin and falling hard on the floor beneath me. Each one feeling heavier than the last.

I walked away six years ago, perfectly fine on the outside. Nothing happened to me. I was saved by circumstance. But what happened to Sam, not only that night but the weeks after, forever changed whatever it is that makes a person a person.

Death changes people.

So does hate.

That's all I've been since Sam died. Hateful.

I know my hate came from fear, it came from regret. It was bred from sadness.

In six years, all I've been doing is suffering. *Until I met Dean.* It hurts. Whatever heaviness was lifted from my shoulders by my confession comes crashing back down tenfold.

"You can't tell anyone, Allison," my mother speaks with tears brimming in her eyes. She cups her hands around the sides of my face like a mother does and pleads with me. "They can't know. Don't tell them. Don't give them a reason to blame you."

"But Dean," I start, and my voice is tight. The second I say his name, my phone rings.

DEAN

*E*xhausted isn't even close to the right word. Terrified doesn't do it justice either. Both are nothing compared to the concoction that flows through my veins as I sit here. Still, I don't feel either. All I feel is the pain for my Allie Cat, sitting on the other side of the plexiglass wall.

"You only have ten minutes," the guard reminds me before stalking off. I don't turn to look at him. Instead I take in Allison, the darkness under her eyes and the dress that hangs delicately on her slender frame. Her hair's brushed back and falls around her shoulders. She tried to look good for me. Although her mascara doesn't stay in place when she wipes under her eyes before desperately reaching for the phone. One on her side, one on mine. There are eight other stations like this. Only two others are being used, though.

I don't make her wait long before picking up the phone and breathing her name.

"Are you okay?" she asks but her voice is strained, and then she lowers her gaze, closing her eyes tight. *Don't look away. Please.*

My hand against the glass brings her attention back to me and she's quick to put her hand on the other side. As if magically the barrier between us would vanish at her touch.

She swallows thickly and tells me, "I know you're not. I'm so sorry, Dean. I—"

"I'm all right," I say, cutting her off and remind her, "I've done this before, you know."

"It isn't the same."

"I know."

"I'm so sorry," she cries even though I shush her. She keeps saying it as she unravels in front of me.

Even on the phone, the sound of her swallowing thickly is audible. "Dean, I have to tell you something," she says and her voice begs for mercy she doesn't think she deserves.

"Is it about the case?"

"Yes and—"

"Don't say a word."

"I have to—"

"No." My voice is sharp and her eyes strike me with both surprise and pain. As if the single word was venomous too.

"You won't say anything here. Where there are other people who can hear you. record you."

"Dean, you don't understand," she says then pulls her hand away from mine as she shakes her head, but I keep mine in place.

"I do. I understand more than you realize, Allie Cat." My expression softens and when it does, hers mirrors mine, softening with a sadness. Her bottom lip trembles when I say her nickname and my throat goes tight as I swallow down the pain of it all.

"Give me something I can dream about in here and I'll make whatever it is come true when I'm out," I tell her and even though it's spoken like a command, I'm desperate for it.

The tips of my fingers slip on the glass and they get her attention. She's quick to put her hand back and her head drops down, her eyes never leaving mine, though.

"Don't let me see you sad, Allie," I say, consoling her in a whisper over the phone. "I need something to dream about."

Removing her hand for only a moment to wipe under her eyes, she sniffles and then tells me, "I miss you in bed at night."

"Oh yeah?" I comment with an asymmetric smile and she heaves in air, attempting to keep herself from crying although it doesn't work.

My heart breaks a million times for her and it'll break a million more with every tear she sheds.

"I miss you too. At night and always. I miss your sassy mouth and stupid jokes."

She huffs a laugh and wipes her tears again. "Mine aren't stupid, yours are stupid." Her rebuttal makes both of us smile.

"You should get a big pillow. Like one of those long ones while I'm gone."

"Dean." She says my name like it pains her, closing her eyes tight.

"Look at me, Allie Cat." She responds to my command without hesitation, waiting with her lips parted and her body at the ready.

"Get a long pillow, and hold it at night." I force a grin when I tell her, "It's the only thing allowed in your bed until I get out of here. You hear me?"

She barely laughs and the sound is saddened, but she does and presses her hand against the glass again, its warmth coming through to me.

"It's only you, Dean," she confesses, her voice lowered and full of sincerity on the line. "You're the only man I want and love."

The itch at the back of my throat and the prick at the back of my eyes is hard to hide, but I do it for her. "About time you told me," I respond and a genuine smile paired with a huff of a laugh from my Allie Cat is my reward. "I love you too, Allison."

She's got to know I love her. And that makes this worth it. I would do anything for her.

ALLISON

"We just have a few more questions." There are two detectives in the room and I can tell the men apart from their voices and picture exactly how their lips move with each word without looking up from the pile of chipped nail polish I picked off in the last hour I've been sitting here.

"Explain the altercation again," the other cop, Detective Massing asks and then the other, Detective Ballinger, adds, "At what point, exactly, did your ex decide to pick up the lamp?"

My mother begged me not to come in at all. She said I legally could decline. She's afraid I'm going to say something I shouldn't. Truth be told, right now I'm afraid too. I made a promise to her though, that I wouldn't tell them. That's because I'm going to tell them all the truth when I'm on the stand. I have to. My eyes prick with tears. It's the only way to save Dean. I have to save him. That's the only reason I've been sitting in this chair.

"I told you, he didn't decide." My voice cracks and my eyes gloss over remembering the haunted look on his face. "I was screaming before the door burst open and when I looked up, he saw what was happening. He ripped him off of me without thinking at all." I watch it all unfold again, barely breathing. I see it every night, a memory that will stay with me forever.

"And then?"

"And then he picked up the lamp and I yelled for him to stop from where I was, but he was so fast and ..." I trail off and my eyes lift to meet theirs as I continue, "it was over before I could even breathe."

"And then what did he do? Did he attempt to conceal the weapon?"

"He didn't even seem to know what he'd done. Dean approached me and tried to reach out for me and there was so much blood on his arms."

"From bludgeoning his friend to death," the asshole one says. Ballinger. I ignore him and my response is only a whisper when I say, "It was like he didn't realize."

"How is it Dean entered your place of residence?"

I blink at him. "He opened the door.

"So you didn't have it locked?"

"I ..." I have to think back to whether I did or not and Kevin's eyes stare back at me.

Do you want to come in? Was that what I asked him? My bottom lip quivers with the visions playing in front of me.

"I asked if you had it locked," Ballinger repeats with a hardened tone. As if reliving the moment just before trauma and tragedy doesn't take more than a second to get through.

Swallowing thickly, I answer him, I didn't even close the door. The vision of Kevin kicking it shut as I tried to sway, deliberately appearing drunk takes over.

"So he didn't need a key to get in."

"No, anyone could have opened that door to help me."

They don't like it when I say *help me*. They quiet down and share a glance each time I say it. But that's what Dean was doing. He came in to rescue me because I was screaming and in return, I made him a murderer. I don't know how he'll ever forgive me.

But so long as he doesn't pay for my sins, I'll be able to sleep at night. At least I pray I will.

"You said you were screaming," Massing starts then takes a long inhale. The air conditioner kicks on in the quiet room with a click. It's empty except for us, another uncomfortable as fuck chair next to me, and a folder containing Dean's rap sheet sitting in the middle of the table. "And that's because Kevin was on top of you?"

"Yes, he was forcing my clothes off."

"And did you at any time, help him?" Ballinger asks and I peer up at both of them, unflinchingly looking back at me.

"Help him?"

"To remove your clothes," he clarifies. I've never felt so disgusted and the emotions that swell up inside of me are a mix of raw pain and fear and anger. It's all of it, all at once.

"I want a lawyer." My statement is simple and I damn well mean it. My throat is sore and the words raspy, but clear.

"You don't need one; you haven't been charged with anything."

"So I'm free to go then?" My voice is flat, my lips pressed in a thin line.

"We have more questions."

"I won't be answering any without a lawyer." For the first time since I walked in here, I speak with authority.

"Why is that?" Massing asks.

"Do you have something to hide?" Ballinger says with a sneer.

My entire body is tight with a pain neither of these two pricks will ever know.

"You aren't just questioning me. You're questioning what I already told you ... maybe that's your job, but mine is to get a lawyer."

DEAN

*S*o many eyes are on me as I sit here in the hard wooden chair. There's only one gaze that calls to me, though. One that begs me to look back.

Allison.

She's so close, yet unreachable. All I can hear as my lawyer and the district attorney go back and forth in front of the judge is my heart racing, begging me to turn to her and ease the worry and pain I know she's feeling.

She's staring at me like that day in class when I first got the balls to talk to her. That day she gave into me. I can feel her staring at me like I did her, but I can't resist her the way she did with me. I never could.

When I turn to face her, I can't stand the look in her eyes. It's clear she blames herself. I would give anything to go to her, but I have to rip my gaze away.

I don't know where we stand. If she hates me. Condemns me. Loves me. *Please God, let her love me still.* I'd do anything for her.

My throat's tight, as is the pain in my chest when my lawyer argues in my defense. It's only an arraignment and my lawyer said the case they have is weak.

A plea of not guilty by reason of temporary insanity is my best bet for surviving this and I don't object to it.

Judge Hubert is an old man. The years are shown through the wrinkles around his pale blue eyes and the white beard around his scowl.

His gaze lingers on me while the prosecutor reads the statement from the psychologist who examined my initial confession.

It's more evidence but at least the shrink supports my case. Not that the prosecutor sees it that way. He's doing his damnedest to make sure this goes to trial. A plea of temporary insanity isn't applicable, according to him. Every time his hard voice booms in the courtroom, my hands clench into fists. If he were in my position, I can't imagine he'd do any different.

I just want to get out of here. In my head, I imagine them letting me walk out right now so I can go straight to Allie. So I can finally talk to her.

I don't know if she's all right. I know she refused medical help. I know he didn't get a chance to ... I have to clear the lump in my throat at the thought, a chill rolling down my spine and making me that much more tense. I overheard some cops talking about it. For that reason alone, all of this is worth it. Even if it weakens my case.

At least I saved her from that.

Still, I need to hear her say she's okay. I need to hear it from her.

I'm only able to take a quick glance, just one. As soon as our eyes lock, hers well up with a sadness I hate. With a pain I wish I could take from her. And she apologizes. *Again.*

"Your honor, our case is strong. There was nothing my client could have done given his mental state when he arrived on the scene." My lawyer, Nina Abbot, speaks clearly and confidently. As if there's no greater truth than the words she's made echo throughout the courtroom. "He was unaware of reality. In that moment, he was not aware of what he was doing. Only his motions, not what they would result in."

I force my gaze back to the wooden table in front of me. It's smooth and smells like lemon as if it was just polished before we came out here.

It's difficult to breathe as she places her hand on my shoulder. "It's obvious given my client's testimony and the report just read from Dr. Agostino that given the situation, Mr. Warren was not in his right mind to control his actions."

"That only holds true if in fact the testimony from both Mr. Warren and Allison Parker are reliable, and there are questions surrounding the validity of Miss Parker's statement." The prosecutor's voice rings out and my fists turn white knuckled. I keep my gaze down, refusing to look at him and his tailored suit. The image of his face is clear in my mind as I keep my shoulders and neck stiff. His jaw is hard and cleanly shaven. His eyes cold and unforgiving. He's a man who will fight to put me behind bars at all cost. The very thought should be terrifying as I sit here, because I did it. I murdered him. But I did it for her. *And I'd do it again.*

"With all due respect, Miss Parker's statement is irrelevant. Mr. Warren's mental state was determined by his perception when he arrived on the property. The same perception that the third witness, Mrs. Clemons, the adjacent neighbor who witnessed the end of the act, gave. As far as my client and Mrs. Clemons could both tell, Miss Parker was in imminent danger. Whether or not she's even capable or willing to testify is irrelevant."

The sound of the courtroom doors opening beg me to look behind me, but I resist. My body's tight and my muscles coiled. I hardly trust myself to breathe. I can still feel Allie looking at me. I refuse to move unless it's to go to her.

It's only when my lawyer turns away from me and the soft whispers of furious voices make the rest of the room turn silent, that I force myself to look in my periphery.

The sound of two people walking down the aisle draws my attention more. A skinny young woman, dressed in black slacks and a loose, cream blouse, is hidden by the silhouette of the man beside her but as they walk, her face comes into view.

I think her name is Angie. She has the same chem lecture as Allison and me and I've seen her around a few times. She stands just past Mr. Beck, the prosecutor, and next to another man in a suit. I turn my head to make sure it's her. Her blonde curls dangle in front of her face and I'm sure she's doing it on purpose.

She's ashamed. Even as she stands there, clasping her hands in front of her, she starts to cry. Silent tears that she quickly wipes away.

"Your honor, new evidence has just come to our attention and we'd like a recess." Mr. Beck finally addresses the court, although his voice is laced with something that gives me hope.

Defeat.

"What is this new evidence?" the judge asks, his pale blue eyes moving between Angie and the man who brought her in.

"The prosecution's defense rests heavily on the questionability of Miss Parker's statement that Mr. Henderson was forcing himself on her. A witness has come forward stating the action of Mr. Henderson is a repeated offense."

"As in, he attempted to rape her?" the judge clarifies and Angie lowers her head, tears falling freely, and this time she doesn't brush them away.

"Charges were pressed in early August, but the case was never brought to court. The charges were dismissed." The quiet air of the room changes, turning to whispers and murmurs. Back in early August I hadn't been accepted into the program yet. But Kevin was here then at his parents' place.

"Your honor," Mr. Beck says, "the case was never—"

"They settled out of court?" the judge asks, cutting off Mr. Beck and the district attorney shakes his head no.

"The witness refused to testify and dropped the charges."

215

The judge taps his pointer finger on the gavel in front of him, considering her and the new information.

"I'm sorry," I hear Angie say in a tight voice. She's trying to whisper but it's useless in a room where everyone's watching her. Her shoulders are hunched and trembling as she pleads with Allie to understand, "I should have told you sooner. I was so ashamed. I didn't want anyone to know."

ALLISON

$\mathscr{T}$he air is cold for only being October. It doesn't help that it's late, dark, and I'm standing in the shadow outside of the jail.

Even with the chill in my bones and the wind whipping around my face, I'm hot. It's from the anxiety.

I don't even think I can feel anything really. At least, I wasn't until the double glass doors open and Dean walks out of them.

My eyes don't stray from the entrance as he strides forward, looking to his left and right. I don't recognize the clothes he's in; they must be new or maybe the lawyer brought them to him so he had clothes to leave in. Dark jeans and a crisp white polo look odd on him as he passes under the streetlight just outside of the doors, but he's never looked better to me. I've never wanted him more.

He's free. Free to go with no charges pressed. There isn't enough evidence to support a trial for what they charged him with.

I want to take him away before anyone can say anything differently.

All I have in me is a shaky half step forward, but I can't move any farther. He may be free from all of this but I'm not, and I don't deserve to be. The sheer terror of what this confession will do to me is enough to keep me cemented in place.

It's enough that he sees me. The small motion makes him look at me and when he does, everything changes.

"Allie." The way he says my name frees me from the spot I've been chained to. I run to him as quickly as my body will allow. Crashing my chest against his and holding him with a fierceness I've never felt before. As if letting go of him would mean losing him. I can't lose him. *Please God, let him love me still.*

"Are you okay?" we both say at nearly the same time. His hands travel from my cheeks to my arms, then lower. As if checking every part of me and making sure I'm all right. Apart from a few bruises, there's nothing on the outside that's hurt.

I can barely nod as I look him over. He spent days in jail and was charged with murder. All because of me.

"Everything's okay. It's over. It's okay." He repeats himself as he kisses my hair. As if it really is but I know all too well that it's not. With a heavy inhale I get a whiff of his scent and I hold onto him tighter, refusing to let go. I have to tell him. He deserves to know it's my fault. He wanted the truth and I owe him that much.

"Dean." When I say his name, my voice cracks and his eyes spark with slight fear. The same fear that runs through my own blood.

"Let's get out of here," is his only response as his dark eyes pierce into mine. "Let's just go."

"Where are you going?" I ask him as my heart pounds and I barely get out the words. The dreaded sickness stirs in my belly. I have to tell him. That's why I refuse to let his hand go. It may be the last time I ever hold him.

The sound of a passing car in the street behind us catches my attention, but I feel Dean's gaze and it never leaves me.

"I don't care. Anywhere," he says while still staring deep into my eyes.

"It sounds a lot like running away to me," I tell him honestly with a shaky breath. The bitter wind of the cold night whips by us and it only makes each of us move closer to the other. I'm on the edge of falling again but this time, I don't want to stop myself. I almost don't want to tell him. I want to run away with him. So long as I'm with him.

"Maybe sometimes," he says then pauses and takes my hand in his, taking a step closer to me. I have to lift my head to look him in the eyes. "Maybe sometimes it's okay to run away."

"I thought we were only supposed to run toward something?" I remind him.

"I don't give a fuck what you call it, Allie. As long as I'm running with you, that's all that matters to me."

My eyes close and I lean into Dean's hard chest. His strong arms wrap around me and I cling to him. "Can we forget the past?" I ask him softly, my question lingering in the heat between us. "I don't want to remember any of it anymore."

I can feel the urge to lie. To keep it all a secret. My heart begs me not to speak the truth. It wants Dean too much.

"Whatever you want to forget, I'll help you," he whispers and his voice sounds pained. He still loves me. The pitter-patter in my chest hurts.

My fingers skim along his shirt and my conscience begs me to confess to him, at war with everything else. The moment my lips part, his finger slips down against my lips.

I shake my head away from his fingers, refusing his protest to not say it. It's now or never, and I can't let it be never.

"Dean, I have something I have to tell you," I say and swallow thickly, hating myself in this moment. I hate what I've become. How revenge and justice consumed me. My obsession changed who I was. For years.

I'm only vaguely aware of where we are and how someone could overhear, but I'm so afraid that if I don't tell him right now, I never will.

"Is it about what happened?" Dean asks me, his voice hard and I can only nod. The words pile up in the back of my throat, suffocating me. "Then you don't have to say it."

"You have to listen," I plead with him. "It's about me," I start to say, and my words come out scratchy as my throat closes. "It's my fault."

"You didn't make him hurt you." Dean's shoulders tense as he looks at me without holding back any emotion. The air turns bitter cold between us. "I don't care if you feel like you should have known. Fuck, I don't care if you were drunk and passed out naked with the door wide open." Dean's words are harsh as he lets the anger slip out. "I don't care if you blame yourself. I don't care if the world thinks you should have known. I don't give a fuck."

I worry my bottom lip between my teeth as tears prick my eyes.

"He didn't do it just once," Dean says and I can't hold back anything anymore.

I let out a hard, ugly sob, the images of Sam going up the stairs flashing through my mind. Shouldn't we have known back then? I wish we had. God, I swear I wish we had. "I want to take it back," I sob, barely getting out the words.

"Allie Cat, don't cry." Dean's words come out softly and he pulls me into his arms again.

"Please," I beg him as if he alone has the power to go back. I need him to listen. To hear me, and to understand.

He kisses my temple, my hair, rocking me as my tears slowly subside. I sniffle and try not to get his shirt wet and smeared with mascara, but he doesn't let me pull away.

"I'm not innocent," I tell Dean, looking him in the eyes and feeling the confession right there. "I'm telling you when I opened that door—"

"You let him in," Dean says and cuts me off. "That's all opening that door did. You let him in."

"I knew who he was." I let out the first part of the confession, the dark dirty secret spilling out in small pieces.

"All you did was let him in." He responds as if he didn't hear me.

I gave him the chance he needed. There's an evil in the eyes of those who cause pain. It won't be influenced. I should know. I knew when I opened that door that I was staring into the eyes of a man who would hurt me. And I welcomed him.

"I wanted him to come in. I wanted him to hurt me." My words are strangled, but Dean hears them.

His grip on me loosens as he looks down at me with an expression of disbelief, but it's quick to harden and he shakes his head.

"My friend Sam. He raped her," I say but have to stop and cover my mouth with my hand as I gasp for air. My eyes close as I try to calm myself down and Dean holds me, begging me to just come with him, but I need to get it out.

"Dean." I barely manage to look him in the eyes as I cling to his forearms and confess. "I came here knowing who he was. I wanted him to hurt me, so I could get justice for what he did to Sam." It's her name on my lips that makes my voice tremble and the tears fall. "I knew what I was doing, but I didn't want this."

Dean doesn't speak as the night gets colder and darker and a gust of wind pulls my hair behind my shoulder, baring my neck and letting the chill travel down my spine.

"So, if you want to run, I don't know that you'd really want me to be the one beside you. I'm not a good person, and I haven't been in so long. I hated him, Dean. I wanted him to pay ..."

Dean takes a step backward and the chill instantly replaces what's left of his warmth, but I can't stop myself from telling him everything.

"I came here," I say then pause as my vision clouds with tears and my shoulders shake. "I came here to set him up. I knew he would do it again ... not like that. I didn't know that would happen but I just had to give him the chance. It's my fault."

"He already had," Dean says although his gaze is vacant, and his words fall flat. "That girl in our class ... he already had."

"I didn't know," I say and then wipe under my eyes with the sleeves of my sweater. I can barely look Dean in the eyes.

"There's so much I didn't know. I didn't know I would meet you, let alone ..." I hesitate to admit what's between us. Or what was between us. It's odd, sensing the sickness of the truth being quickly replaced by emptiness. It's all that's left as I wait for Dean's judgment. But he doesn't say anything.

"Please talk to me." I have no right to speak to him, but I still beg him. If he hates me, I'll deserve it.

"Say it," Dean commands me. "Tell me."

"Tell you what?" I grasp at anything I can to give Dean what he wants. "I didn't know I'd fall for you. I didn't think this would happen."

"You didn't think I'd kill him?" he asks as if he really thinks I'd set him up for that. I shake my head violently, praying that he'll believe me.

"Never. I never thought for one moment that you would get hurt."

"You thought you could let him hurt you like that and that I'd be okay?" he asks me, his eyes narrowed and his hands clench and unclench. He's on edge and for the first time, I'm scared.

"I thought you were done with me," I whisper and hearing the words and feeling the reality of them in this moment, makes a sharp pain tear through me, regret seeping into my veins.

"How could you ever think that?" Dean asks me in a single breath.

I can't answer. I don't have the words or the logic. "I just wanted him to pay for what he did to her." That's the truth. The need for him to get what he deserved outweighed everything else.

"I already knew, Allie," Dean says and swallows harshly as if he's the one confessing. "I had a lot of time in my cell to think. About what I knew about Kevin. About what I knew about you. Samantha Jenkins. She's the girl who claimed someone raped her at a party I was supposed to go to years ago. They never told us who the charges were against and I didn't know it was Kevin."

Disbelief grips me. He knows?

"I heard about it on the news when she killed herself but the details were missing and I was already so far gone … but sitting in jail with nothing to do but think will help put the pieces together. The way you were with him that day outside the locker room … I figured it out myself, Allie."

My eyes widen and I struggle to breathe. To say anything. He knew and he wants me? How could he?

"You will never do that again," Dean commands. "And you'll never talk about this again," he says and my breath halts. "Never tell anyone else. No one."

I nod my head, clasping my hands in front of me and with my posture as still as can be. My heart races and a flicker of hope lights inside of me. Dean looks at me for a long time, as if judging what he believes and what he finds lacking. *Please believe me.* My body trembles as I try not to grip on to him. As I wait for whatever it is he needs. Whatever it is, I'll give it to him.

"Is that everything?" he asks me. "Tell me now."

My bottom lip drops but I don't know what he's asking, or what he wants.

"What else are you hiding?" he asks in a raised voice and I cower as I shake my head and insist, "Nothing, nothing."

"You won't lie to me again." His voice is hard.

I almost tell him that I never lied, but that wouldn't be true. I kept the truth from him, and that action in and of itself was a lie.

"Is there anyone else that you *want* to hurt you?" he asks me, and I can't stand the anger that's there. "Because I swear to God I don't know what I'll do if anyone tries to hurt you."

"No. No. I'm sorry," I tell him in a croak, shame washing over me.

"Do you realize what could have happened? What he would have done to you?" Dean asks and his own voice cracks.

"Not until he was," I start to say and remember how heavy his body was, how much it hurt.

My eyes squeeze shut tight, but not tight enough. I just want it all to go away. "I wish I could take it back. I'm so sorry."

"I would do it again, Allie. I'd kill anyone who tried to hurt you."

"I didn't mean for that to happen."

"Don't keep anything from me, do you hear me?" he asks me, and his voice is consoling this time.

"I promise," I tell him with all sincerity. "I have no more secrets."

"Good, because I still love you. I love you, Allison."

I finally breathe, a large gulp of air that's nearly too much as I fall into him. His arms wrap around me tightly, holding me just as fiercely as I hold him.

"And I want you to come with me." His words are whispered into my hair.

I can only nod, I can't speak anymore. I have nothing left to give, but if I ever I do, it's all for Dean.

Before I'm ready, Dean pulls me away from him, letting the cold air come between us and for a moment, I think he's changing his mind. But then he speaks.

"Just don't stop loving me," he says as he stares deeply into my eyes.

"Never," I breathe out the word quickly, desperate for him to know how true it is. I love him. I love him more than he'll ever know.

DEAN

"How many boxes?" I ask Allie as I pull the clear packaging tape down the center of the box.

"Fourteen," she tells me, appearing from the kitchen doorway with a cup of tea in her hands. "It all fit in fourteen boxes," she says, leaning her hip against the wall and then blowing over the cup.

She kept the empty cardboard boxes, breaking them down and stacking them neatly in the pantry. Like she knew she was going to need them before long.

Every time I'm reminded of why she came here, the very thing that brought her to me, my chest aches with a pain that runs deep. A pain I don't think will ever leave me.

"You sure you don't want a cup?" Her small voice carries into the room and snaps me out of the dark thought.

When I glance up at her, ready to say no again, the hint of happiness is on her face. Or maybe it's hope. With her hair draped over her shoulders and wearing nothing but a pair of panties and one of my old rugby shirts, she looks perfect. The shirt clings to the middle of her waist when she stands like that. Everything about her makes me want to take her into my arms and never let go.

Partly because she needs it, but mostly because I need her.

"Maybe I will," I tell her and drop the roll of tape on the floor, turning the box upright. We have two boxes packed and within just a few hours, Allie's place will be cleared out. I want to pretend we were never here and rewrite our story, but that's life. You don't get to rewrite it.

As I stand, my back cracks and my stiff neck and shoulders ache. I haven't slept for shit, not since I got out of jail and I don't think I will again until we leave this place, this city … all of it. A fresh start is what we want and need. Wherever that might take us.

Her bare feet pad against the floor as she heads back into the kitchen.

I follow the sound of her running the faucet and then opening and closing the microwave. She's in front of it, gripping the counter and staring absently ahead when I walk in.

"Allie Cat." I barely speak her name. Her green eyes search for mine instantly. Every time I move or speak, she's there waiting for me, on edge and waiting for something. That's the way it's been since I've been back here. It's like she's afraid I'm going to run or that one day I'll wake up and think she isn't worth it. That loving her costs too much. It fucking kills me. I'll hold her and love her every day until she knows I'm here for good and staying.

She doesn't know what lies ahead, and neither do I.

But I know it'll be all right, so long as she's with me.

In three strides I'm beside her, silencing the microwave with the mug of water in it for tea and pulling her into my arms instead.

"I want to hear you tell me you're all right," I whisper, cupping her chin in my hand and forcing her eyes to mine. She doesn't have a trace of makeup on and under her eyes are dark circles, although she's been sleeping all right; better than she was before.

"I couldn't be with you because I didn't want to be okay and you made me so much more than just okay."

"You know I love you," I tell her. It's not the first or second or third time I've told her since I've come home to her. And I'll keep telling her until the look in her green eyes reflects that she knows they're true.

"I love you," she says back in barely a whisper, her expression changing to one of complete sincerity but also laced with pain. Her eyes close as she lets out a breath and presses her cheek into my hand.

I knew she was hiding something and that's what drew me to her. From the very beginning, she was a mystery.

The dark secrets I didn't expect. Who could've ever expected this?

Allie peeks up at me, the hurt and worry still in her eyes.

She's walking on eggshells. She's been this way for days and I hate myself for even feeling slightly angry toward her.

Even though she should have told me.

I love her.

I'd kill again for her. And she knows I would.

Sitting in that cell with nothing to do but think on how it came down to this, the pieces slowly fell into place.

The reason why she kept pushing me away even though we both knew we fit together just right.

The reason she seemed off to me when I first met her, the reason I was drawn to her.

It was meant to be this way. As tragic and horrific as it is. I should have been at that party to stop it, but fate found another way, the two of us too broken to prevent the pain. I'll take her however I can have her.

"Come sit with me?" I ask her and she's quick to give me the trace of a smile when I take her small hand in mine. She's eager to make things right and to make me happy, I can feel it in everything she does. Every small look and move is cautious and eager to please.

I sit cross-legged on the floor of the dining room. The sofa's already in the truck, so the barren floor will have to do.

"When did you become so shy, Allie Cat?" I ask her as she settles in my lap.

"Shy?"

"I feel like you're hiding from me," I tell her honestly.

"I'm just ..."

"Ashamed?" I say the word I hate to think is the truth.

"And afraid," she tells me softly in a single breath.

"Of what?"

"I don't want to lose you, but I know I don't deserve you." Thank God she's at least confessed what I already knew.

"You're wrong." My heart beats quicker, my blood runs warmer. All from fear of losing her. I swear I'll never let her run again.

"I never meant for you to get hurt," she tells me again. I don't know why she feels the need. I believe her. Every word.

"I think it was supposed to happen this way," I say and pull her soft body closer to mine. "I'm not mad at what you did." I'm careful with my words as I add, "I'm upset you didn't tell me but I'm not mad, and I don't hold any of this against you."

She only nods her head, casting her gaze down and picking at the hem of the shirt she's wearing. My shirt. "What I did wasn't okay," she whispers.

I force her chin up with my hand on her jaw. "You only did it because something had to be done."

"I did it out of anger," she's quick to admit. As if acting out of anger made her intentions worse.

"You did it out of pain," I say.

Her eyes water and she closes them, not wanting to cry in front of me. Or maybe not wanting to cry at all anymore.

"I'm sorry about Sam, and I'm not sorry that Kevin's dead."

"I'm not sorry he's dead either," she says, closing her eyes and letting the tears seep into her thick lashes.

"I love you, Allison. I love you so fucking much. And it kills me that you never told me."

"I didn't know if you'd believe me," she says, and it cuts through my heart. "But I also didn't want you to stop me." That's the real truth. And I get it. I understand it. I still hate it, though. "She needed this. Sam needed this," she says and then breaks down in my arms.

"Where do we go from here?" I ask her. We want each other. But there's no roadmap for what the future holds and that's terrifying for her.

"Forgive me, and I'll go wherever you want. I'll run away forever. I'll do whatever you want," she says, brushing the tears away and leaving her cheeks reddened.

A heavy breath leaves me in a huff. "I've already forgiven you, Allie."

"I love you. I'm so sorry," she says hurriedly.

"Stop saying you're sorry." I plant a small kiss on her lips, tasting the hint of salt from her tears. "And I love you too," I whisper against her lips.

A moment passes before she questions me.

"You really love me? Even still?" she asks me, and I hate that she questions it.

"Of course I do." I brush my knuckles across her cheek and gently push the hair out of her face. "That's not something I can stop," I say before lowering my lips to hers.

She softens, eagerly accepting my kiss and parting her mouth for more.

"Please don't stop," she tells me when I pull away and at first, I think she means the kiss, but then she adds, "I can't lose you ..." Her voice skips and she takes in a quick breath. "I don't know what I would do if you stopped loving me."

"I never will," I tell her with a small smile playing on my lips. My voice is upbeat, but it doesn't echo what I feel. That first day I saw her in class, a piece of me recognized something inside of her and now that I have it, I can't lose it. I can't lose her.

"You love me and I love you. That's all we need," I say, and she doesn't know how raw my promise is.

She rises from her seated position, crashing her lips against mine with a desperate need.

For forgiveness. For love. For a life without pain and regret.

Her grip is tight as her nails scratch through my hair as she intensifies the kiss. For the first time in days, I want more. I want to feel every bit of her. I want to give her everything and make her mine again.

She parts the seam of her lips, granting me entry and I'm instantly hard for her. Desperate for more of her to be bared to me.

She only pulls back from our kiss to breathe.

"Please," she says and nuzzles against me. "I need you." Her voice is laced with anguish.

Her small hands slip under my shirt. They're warm and her fingers are gentle as she moves them to my back, eager to touch every inch of me.

"I need you," she says again, her eyes wide and pleading. "I need to feel you," she adds. She kisses the little dip at the bottom of my throat and then my neck.

It's been tense between us but more than that, I haven't touched her since everything's changed.

"Please," she whispers with need and I'm quick move her out of my lap and lay her on the floor, my hands moving under her shirt to her hips, looping around the thin panties and pulling them slowly down her thighs.

Her eyes are closed, her lips parted as she pants.

It doesn't take me long to strip down and settle myself between her thighs, all the while leaving kisses along her jaw, her neck, that little dip beneath her collarbone. Every inch of her skin that I can kiss, I do.

"I love you," she murmurs over and over, and when her eyes finally open and reach mine, she says it with a strength that can't be denied.

I slam into her, filling her completely in one swift stroke. Her bare back rubs along the hardwood floor as I thrust into her, again and again. It's an unrelenting pace. Her head thrashes and her eyes close tight as I grip her hips and pin her down.

I have to brace her to take the force of my thrusts.

She's so tight, so wet.

Her gasp is coarse; her nails dig into my wrists. With her eyes shut tight, her body tenses. She shakes her head and I know this is wrong.

She's thinking about it.

About what happened.

"Allie," I murmur and brace my arm behind her back, pulling her up to sit on top of me. I kiss her ravenously with her on top of me. "Look at me," I command her and instantly her eyes open. She holds on to me with a fierceness, wrapping her arms around my shoulders and burying her head in the crook of my neck. Emotions or her memories getting the best of her.

I wasn't sure how she would react after what transpired, but holding her now, I hate it. I hate that she's not lost in pleasure and that the thoughts of what one man did to her have dared to come between us.

I stay as still as I can, still buried inside of her, but not wanting to move yet.

"Look at me," I tell her again more firmly and she does slowly.

"I'm sorry, I thought I could ..." her voice trails off and her shame comes back, but it's gone the moment my words hit her.

"You're mine." I say the words reverently, our shared gaze heating with raw vulnerability. "No one else will ever touch you." My heart beats hard and heavy, but slowly. "I'll take it all away."

"And you're mine," she says and runs her fingers through my hair. Her touch gentle but possessive. I love it.

With her on top of me, I move my hands to her hips and rock her. Our eyes still locked. Her clit pressing against me with every motion.

"Slow at first," I tell her and pump my hips once, burying myself inside her, but still letting her lead. She gasps a moan as her hands fall on my chest. Her small fingers dig into my shoulders.

She nips my bottom lip, letting the tip of her nose brush against mine as she pulls away slightly, but rocks her hips again, making her body shudder with pleasure.

My hand moves to the back of her head, and only then does she look at me. "We'll get through this," I tell her, searching her eyes to make damn sure she believes me. "I've got you."

Whatever she asks for and however she needs it, that's how it will always be with us.

Always and forever.

EPILOGUE

Allison

"How are things going now that you're settled in?" Dr. Robinson asks me. I like his office; it's cozy with the dark furniture and a thick rug under my feet. I like it more when Dean's with me.

"Well, really well," I answer, letting out an easy breath as I pick my feet up and slip them under me to get comfortable.

"Moving was a good change, a new environment for both of us."

"So everything went smoothly?"

"Better than I thought. Daniel took over the lease at the place I'd been renting."

"And Daniel is Dean's friend?" he asks me.

"Yeah, he's a good guy," I say and my heart races as I talk. Because I'm hiding the truth. I'm keeping what I overheard just yesterday to myself. Daniel has his own demons, but that's not my story to tell. It's his and he'll get through it. I know he will.

He nods in approval although he doesn't write anything. The book stays on his lap, the pen sitting on top. My eyes keep flickering to it; I always wonder which parts of our session Dr. Robinson deems worthy of recording.

"We got a golden retriever," I tell him. "He's just a fluffy puppy, but he's sweet."

"You got him together?" he asks me.

"My mother got him for us."

"And how does that make you feel?"

"You sound like a shrink when you ask me that," I tell him.

"And you sound like you're deflecting." He's quick to call me on my shit.

My eyes fall on the coffee table and I feel a tug at my heart-strings. "I feel like he's too good for me." I speak without looking up at Dr. Robinson, but the telltale sign of his leather notebook opening makes me huff a small laugh. I guess anything that hurts my heart is worthy.

"My grandmother used to say, find someone who loves you just a little more than you love them." My eyes water, remembering how she said it. And how she meant it.

"And is that how you view your relationship with Dean?" he asks me.

I shake my head, nearly violently, as I wipe the tears away from the corners of my eyes. "No," I say quickly, the word coming out scratchy. "But I'm afraid that's how he'll feel because I'm not good at loving anymore. That's what really matters. It's not about the truth. It's all about what people think."

"Why do you say that?" he asks me.

"Because it's so obvious he'd do anything for me. And I'm scared he doesn't think I'd do the same for him." I would. *I'd kill for him, die for him. Dean is my everything.*

"No, why do you say you aren't good at loving anymore?" Dr.

Robinson says. He adds before I can answer, "Dean knows you love him. It's something that's clear to him. And to me,."

It soothes me like a balm on my aching chest, calming the anxiety and nerves that keep me up at night. "Why do you think you're not good at loving?"

"I haven't done it before. Not like this. And I'm scared," I say, the confession coming out in a single breath.

"Scared of what?" he asks me.

"That one day he'll leave me, and I won't survive it." I sniff, reaching for the tissues on the coffee table and keep talking without looking him in the eyes.

"I don't know how he can forgive me so easily. He says it's love, but I still don't quite feel like I deserve it."

"Because you were protecting yourself."

"If I had trusted him sooner," I start to say the same thing I've been saying for weeks. I stop myself and pick under my nails, staring blindly ahead. "I can't change the past."

"And your past is where it belongs, behind you. What you have now is someone who loves you and who you love in return. Someone who wants to grow with you. Someone who knows the shadow side of yourself and you know his. There isn't much that could be more ideal than that. To love and be loved for every part of you."

"I feel like I can never show Dean how much I love him."

"Maybe that's a good thing. I want that to be your homework."

"What?"

"I want you to write down ways you show Dean how you love him and how he loves you."

I nod my head easily, feeling relieved slightly. Even if I could write it all down, Dean will never know exactly what he means to me. He knows everything, my darkest secrets, and he still loves me, without judgment. He gave me a new life and it's complete with him in it.

I don't think it's possible to feel more love for that man than I do.

"Do you believe in fate, Dr. Robinson?" I speak without thinking.

"Why do you ask?" he answers my question with a question of his own and a small laugh bubbles up as I trace the edge of the coffee table with my fingers. It's hard and unforgiving as I let my thoughts surface without fear of his judgment.

"Dean was supposed to be at that party." It takes a moment for the good doctor to realize what I'm saying and when he does, his brow raises with surprise.

"If he hadn't gotten suspended and in that fight with his step-dad, he would have been there."

"And what do you think about that?" Dr. Robinson asks me.

"I think he would have hit it off with Sam." My answer comes out choked.

"Do you think he would have ended up with her and not you?"

"I think none of it would have happened." The words pour from me. "I don't think any of that night would have happened." The thought of that night being erased eases a pain inside of me, but then it comes back full force knowing that wish will never come true.

"Maybe we were supposed to be together, like fate."

"Or soulmates," he says.

"Whatever you want to call it." I shrug and then add, "Maybe that's why we felt the way we did toward each other when I first came here. Like somewhere deep down inside we knew, and Dean knew it long before me because he wasn't as broken."

"Do you still feel broken?" Dr. Robinson asks me and it's such a ridiculous question.

"Of course I am." Once you're shattered, you can be mended but the cracks are still there. "Both of us were flawed, but together we make sense, don't we?" I ask Dr. Robinson, and never in my life has someone's judgment meant more to me. He simply nods as his timer goes off.

It's time to go.

Time for a fresh start.

The End.

AFTERWORD

A note from the author

I hope that you enjoyed this book, that it spoke to you and that you felt what I felt as I wrote it.

We give so much power to four small words. *She asked for it.*

I hate the power they have. I hate what those words have done to so many women.

I hate that the saying even exists.

But if it must, it will have a different meaning for me.

I hope after reading this book, those four words mean something different to you than they did before. And if you ever feel the need to reach out to someone because those words, or thoughts are too much, don't hesitate to seek out help. There's too much love in the world to ever feel anything but.

As always, best wishes and happy reading,
Willow xx

POSSESSIVE

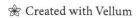 Created with Vellum

DEDICATION

Dedicated to Jerry.
I miss you already.

PREFACE

Addison

It's easy to smile around Tyler.

It's how he got me. We were in calculus, and he made some stupid joke about angles. I don't even remember what it was. Something about never discussing infinity with a mathematician because you'll never hear the end of it. He's a cute dork with his jokes. He knows some dirty ones too.

A year later and he still makes me laugh. Even when we're fighting. He says he just wants to see me smile. How can I leave when he says things like that? I believe him with everything in me.

My friend's grandmother told me once to fall in love with someone who loves you back just a little more.

Even as my shoulders shake with a small laugh and he leans forward to nip my neck, I know that I'll never really love Tyler the way he loves me.

And it makes me ashamed. Truly.

I'm still laughing when his bedroom door creaks open. Tyler plants a small kiss on my shoulder. It's not an open-mouth kiss, but still it leaves a trace on my skin and sends a warmth through my body. It's fleeting though.

The cool air passes between the two of us as Tyler leans back and smiles broadly at his brother.

I may be seated on my boyfriend's lap, but the way Daniel looks at me makes me feel like I'm alone. His eyes pierce through me with a sharpness that makes me afraid to move. Afraid to even breathe.

I don't know why he does this to me.

He makes me hot and cold at the same time. It's like I've disappointed him simply by being here. As if he doesn't like me. Yet there's something else.

Something that's forbidden.

It creeps up on me whenever I hear Daniel's rough voice; whenever I catch him watching Tyler and me. It's like I've been caught cheating, which makes no sense at all. I don't belong to Daniel, no matter how much that idea haunts my dreams.

He's twenty-one now and I'm only seventeen. But more importantly, he's Tyler's brother.

It's all in my head. I tell myself over and over again that the electricity between us is something I've made up. That my body doesn't burn for Daniel. That my soul doesn't ache for him to rip me away and punish me for daring to let his brother touch me.

It's only when Tyler speaks to him that Daniel looks away from me, tossing something down beside us.

Tyler's oblivious to everything happening. And suddenly I can breathe again.

My eyelids flutter open, my body hot under the stifling blankets. I don't react to the memory in my dreams anymore. Not at first, anyway. It sinks in slowly. The recognition of what that day would lead to growing heavier in my heart with each second that passes. Like a wave crashing on the shore, but taking its time. Threatening to engulf me as it approaches.

It was years ago, but the memory remains.

The feeling of betrayal, for fantasizing about Tyler's older brother.

The heartache from knowing what happened only three weeks after that night.

The desire and desperation to go back to that point and beg Tyler to never come looking for me.

All of those emotions swirl into a deadly concoction in the pit of my stomach. It's been years since I've been tormented by the remembrance of Tyler and what we had. And by the memories of Daniel and what never was.

Years have passed.

But it all comes back to me after seeing Daniel last night.

CHAPTER 1

Addison
The night before

I love this bar. Iron Heart Brewery. It's nestled in the center of the city and located at the corner of this street. The town itself has history. Hints of the old cobblestone streets peek through the torn asphalt and all the signs here are worn and faded, decorated with weathered paint. I can't help but to be drawn here.

And with the varied memorabilia lining the walls, from signed knickknacks to old glass bottles of liquor, this place is flooded with a welcoming warmth. It's a quiet bar with all local and draft beers a few blocks away from the chaos of campus. So it's just right for me.

"Make up your mind?"

My body jolts at the sudden question. It only gets me a rough laugh from the tall man on my left, the bartender who spooked me.

A grey shirt with the brewery logo on it fits the man well, forming to his muscular shoulders. With a bit of stubble and a charming smirk, he's not bad looking. And at that thought, my cheeks heat with a blush.

I could see us making out behind the bar; I can even hear the bottles clinking as we crash against the wall in a moment of passion. But that's where it would end for me. No hot and dirty sex on the hard floor. No taking him back to my barely furnished apartment.

I roll my eyes at the thought and blow a strand of hair away from my face as I meet his gaze.

I'm sure he flirts with everyone. But it doesn't make it any less fun for the moment.

"Whatever your favorite is," I tell him sheepishly. "I'm not picky." I have to press my lips together and hold back my smile when he widens his and nods.

"You new to town?" he asks me.

I shrug and have to slide the strap to my tank top back up onto my shoulder. Before I can answer, the door to the brewery and bar swings open, bringing in the sounds of the nightlife with it. It closes after two more customers leave. Looking over my shoulder through the large glass door at the front, I can see them heading out. The woman is leaning heavily against a strong man who's obviously her significant other.

Giving the bartender my attention again, I'm very much aware that there are only six of us here now. Two older men at the high top bar, talking in hushed voices and occasionally laughing so loud that I have to take a peek at them.

And one other couple who are seated at a table in the corner of the bar. The couple who just left had been sitting with them. All four are older than I am. I'd guess married with children and having a night out on the town.

And then there's the bartender and me.

"I'm not really from here, no."

"Just passing through?" he asks me as he walks toward the bar. I'm a table away, but he keeps his eyes on me as he reaches for a glass and hits the tap to fill it with something dark and decadent.

"I'm thinking about going to the university actually. To study business. I came to check it out." I don't tell him that I'm putting down some temporary roots regardless of whether or not I like the school here. Every year or so I move somewhere new ... searching for what could feel like home.

His eyebrow raises and he looks me up and down, making me feel naked. "Your ID isn't fake, right?" he asks and then tilts the tall glass in his hand to let the foam slide down the side.

"It isn't fake, I swear," I say with a smile and hold up my hands in defense. "I chose to travel instead of going to college. I've got a little business, but I thought finally learning more about the technicalities of it all would be a step in the right direction." I pause, thinking about how a degree feels more like a distraction than anything else. It's a reason to settle down and stop moving from place to place. It could be the change I need. Something needs to change.

His expression turns curious and I can practically hear all the questions on his lips. *Where did you go? What did you do? Why did you leave your home so young and naïve?* I've heard them all before and I have a prepared list of answers in my head for such questions.

But they're all lies. Pretty little lies.

He cleans off the glass before walking back over and pulling out the seat across from me.

Just as the legs of the chair scrape across the floor, the door behind me opens again, interrupting our conversation and the soft strums of the acoustic guitar playing in the background.

The motion brings a cold breeze with it that sends goosebumps down my shoulder and spine. A chill I can't ignore.

The bartender's ass doesn't even touch the chair. Whoever it is has his full attention.

As I lean down to reach for the cardigan laying on top of my purse, he puts up a finger and mouths, "One second."

The smile on my face is for him, but it falters when I hear the voice behind me.

Everything goes quiet as the door shuts and I listen to them talking. My body tenses and my breath leaves me. Frozen in place, I can't even slip on the cardigan as my blood runs cold.

My heart skips one beat and then another as a rough laugh rises above the background noise of the small bar.

"Yeah, I'll take an ale, something local," I hear Daniel say before he slips into view. I know it's him. That voice haunted me for years. His strides are confident and strong, just like I remember them. And as he passes me to take a seat by the bar, I can't take my eyes off of him.

He's taller and he looks older, but the slight resemblance to Tyler is still there. As my heart learns its rhythm again, I notice his sharp cheekbones and my gaze drifts to his hard jaw, covered with a five o'clock shadow. I'd always thought of him as tall and handsome, albeit in a dark and brooding way. And that's still true.

He could fool you with his charm, but there's a darkness that never leaves his eyes.

His fingers spear through his hair as he checks out the beer options written in chalk on the board behind the bar. His hair's longer on top than it is on the sides, and I can't help but to imagine what it would feel like to grab on to it. It's a fantasy I've always had.

The timbre in his voice makes my body shudder.

And then heat.

I watch his throat as he talks, I notice the little movements as he pulls out a chair in the corner of the bar across from me. If only he would look my way, he'd see me.

Breathe. Just breathe.

My tongue darts out to lick my lips and I try to avert my eyes, but I can't.

I can't do a damn thing but wait for him to notice me.

I almost whisper the command, *look at me*. I think it so loud I'm sure it can be heard by every soul in this bar.

And finally, as if hearing the silent plea, he looks my way. His knuckles rap the table as he waits for his beer, but they stop mid-motion when his gaze reaches mine.

There's a heat, a spark of recognition. So intense and so raw that my body lights, every nerve ending alive with awareness.

And then it vanishes. Replaced with a bitter chill as he turns away. Casually. As if there was nothing there. As if he doesn't even recognize me.

I used to think it was all in my mind back then. Five years ago when we'd share a glance and that same feeling would ignite within me.

But this just happened. I know it did.

And I know he knows who I am.

With anger beginning to rise, my lips part to say his name, but it's caught in my throat. It smothers the sadness that's rising just as quickly. Slowly my fingers curl, forming a fist until my nails dig into my skin.

I don't stop staring at him, willing him to look at me and at least give me the courtesy of acknowledging me.

I know he can feel my eyes on him. He's stopped rapping his knuckles on the table and the smile on his face has faded.

Maybe the crushing feeling in my chest is shared by both of us.

Maybe I'm only a reminder to him. A reminder he ran away from too.

I don't know what I expected. I've dreamed of running into Daniel so many nights. Brushing shoulders on the way into a coffee shop. Meeting each other again through new friends. Every time I wound up back home, if you can even call it that, I always checked out every person passing me by, secretly wishing one would be him. Just so I'd have a reason to say his name.

Winding up at the same bar on a lonely Tuesday night hours

away from the town we grew up in … that was one of those daydreams too. But it didn't go like this in my head.

"Daniel." I say his name before I can stop myself. It comes out like a croak and he reluctantly turns his head as the bartender sets down the beer on the wooden table.

I swear it's so quiet, I can hear the foam fizzing as it settles in the glass.

His lips part just slightly, as if he's about to speak. And then he visibly inhales. It's a sharp breath and matches the gaze he gives me. First it's one of confusion, then anger … and then nothing.

I have to remind my lungs to do their job as I clear my throat to correct myself, but both efforts are in vain.

He looks past me as if it wasn't me who was trying to get his attention.

"Jake," he speaks up, licking his lips and stretching his back. "I actually can't stay," he bellows from his spot to where the bartender, apparently named Jake, is chucking ice into a large glass. The music seems to get louder as the crushing weight of being so obviously dismissed and rejected settles in me.

I'm struck by how cold he is as he gets up. I can't stand to look at him as he readies to leave, but his name leaves me again. This time with bite.

His back stiffens as he shrugs his thin jacket around his shoulders and slowly turns to look at me.

I can feel his eyes on me, commanding me to look back at him and I do. I dare to look him in the eyes and say, "It's good to see you." It's surprising how even the words come out. How I can appear to be so calm when inside I'm burning with both anger and … something else I don't care to admit. What a lie those words are.

I hate how he gets to me. How I never had a choice.

With a hint of a nod, Daniel barely acknowledges me. His smile is tight, practically nonexistent, and then he's gone.

CHAPTER 2

Daniel

$\mathcal{M}$y father taught me an important lesson I'll never forget.

Never let a soul know what you really feel.

Never express it.

Only show them what you want them to see.

I hear his voice as I slip my hands in my jacket pockets and keep walking down Lincoln Street with my heart pounding in my chest and anxiety coursing in my blood. Two more blocks and I'll wait there. The alley is the perfect place to wait and collect myself.

Until then, my blood will pound in my ears, my veins will turn cold and my muscles will stay coiled. But I won't let anyone see that. Never.

I remember how my father gripped my shoulder when he looked me in the eyes and gave me that advice.

His dark stare was something no one ever forgot. It was impassive and cold. I lived many days wondering if my father loved me. I know my mother did. We were family and his blood, but he would never show any emotion and after that night, neither would I.

I was fourteen years old. And standing only a few feet away from the body of someone I once knew. I don't even remember his name. A friend of my father's. He worked in the business and gave the wrong person the wrong impression.

When you reveal that fear, that anger, that emotion, you give someone a hint of how to get to you. And that's what my father's friend had done. When someone gets to you, you end up dead.

My shoes slap on the concrete sidewalk as I slow down at the intersection, as if I'm merely waiting for the cars to stop at the red light so I can cross. It's not a busy night, so only a few people are walking down the street. A man to my right lights up a cigarette and leans against the brick wall to a liquor store.

I make my way around the block, replaying what happened in my head. It was supposed to be a simple, easy night. Another night of waiting for Marcus to show for the drop-off or waiting to hear word about what's going on with the deal between my brother and the cartel.

She caught me off guard.

Addison Fawn.

She's always been able to do that. She gets to me in a way I despise.

She makes me remember.

She makes me weak.

Another step and I see her face. Her high cheekbones and piercing green eyes. I love the way her hair falls in front of her face. There's always something effortless about it, like she doesn't put an ounce of work into looking as fuckable as she does.

The cool night air whips past me as I round the corner. The next alley will take me where I want to go. Directly across from the lot where her car must be. It's the only parking lot on this street for three blocks.

I swallow thickly, checking my phone again. It's been three minutes since I've left.

Three minutes is more than enough time for her to pay the tab and walk off.

I don't know if she will though.

It's been years since I've felt like I've known who she is.

Years since I've heard her say my name.

The corners of my lips turn up in a smirk as I hear the hesitancy in her voice replay in my memory and I let it. Like she was scared to say my name out loud.

It echoes in my head as I lean against the wall of the dark alley and gives me a thrill I haven't felt in a long time. *Too long.*

The alley is narrow, the type of passageway built decades and decades ago before the world knew better. Before humanity realized they were inviting sins in the night with small spaces like these.

My phone vibrates in my pocket, and I take a quick look around me before pulling it out.

There are four cars parked in the dirt lot. The streetlight on the right side illuminates the area easily, as do the headlights of a passing car.

My eyes flicker to the text on my phone and the amusement from only moments ago leaves me instantly.

Who's the girl? Jake texted and I'm reminded that I upped and left as if she mattered. As if her existence would cause an issue.

And of course it does. More than anyone could know.

My shoulders rise as I draw in a deep breath and let it out slowly, releasing the anger from letting her get to me and I focus on regaining control. Control is everything.

No one, I write him back but think better of it. It's obvious she's someone to me and Jake needs to be reassured. *My brother's ex,* I add.

My body tenses as I wait for him to respond. I keep my posture relaxed, although I'm anything but.

Off limits? Jake must have a fucking death wish.

I can't help the way my teeth grind as I text a response and then delete it before finally firing off a quick message.

For now. If Marcus comes tonight, tell him I'll be back late. I'm smoldering with rage as I realize how stupid it was to risk missing the meet with Marcus all over a quick emotion I couldn't suppress. Shock, anger ... fear even. She's only a girl. Inwardly, I can hear myself seething.

Alright, Jake messages me, making the phone vibrate in my hand. I almost ask him if Addison is still there. My fingertips itch to push for information.

But it's not needed.

Even as Jake continues to text me about the drop-off, I watch the skirt sway around Addison's hips. It's the color of cream and loose on her, not giving me any hints of how her ass looks right now. But her legs are on full display.

I've always thought of Addison the same way, even after everything that went down. From the first day I met her until this very second. She's a sad, but beautiful girl. You can see her pain in every bit of her features when she doesn't know someone's looking. Like I often did. From the way her full lips pout delicately, to the way her eyes seem to stare off in the distance, even when she's looking right at you it's as if she can see through you.

Those eyes have haunted me. The beautiful shades of green and brown are like the sunset over a forest. Like flecks of light peeking through and enhancing the darkness that's soon to come.

She runs her hand over her soft porcelain skin and through the modest waves in her thick dark hair. Even those slight movements and the swing of her hips as she walks carry a sadness with them. It never leaves her. It defines her. But it suits her well.

More than sad, and more than beautiful, Addison is memorable. *Unforgettable.*

Her car beeps as she unlocks it, a shiny new black Honda from the looks of it, and the sound echoes in the alley. She's parked in the third spot in the row of cars lined up under the streetlight. She looks to the left and right, cursing as she drops her keys in the gravel.

My dick stirs in my pants, straining against the fabric and I let out a low groan at the sight of her bent over. Her hair is swept to one side and the strap of her top is falling off her shoulder, giving me a view of that soft spot in the crook of her neck.

I adjust my dick and memorize the curves of her hips and waist until she opens up her car door and slips inside.

Every second my breaths come in heavier. The air around me feels as if it wants to suffocate me. Her tires kick up the gravel in the lot and I have to take a step back into the alley to avoid her headlights as she turns out onto the street.

I tell myself it's only out of instinct that I take a picture of her license plate as she drives off.

Well I try to, but I'm a poor liar.

When she's gone from view, I step back out onto the concrete sidewalk, staring down the desolate street and letting the brisk night air cool my hot skin.

Addison is back.

The only question on my mind is what I'm going to do with her.

CHAPTER 3

Addison

I've hated Daniel for a lot of things. I've never really tallied them up before.

The silent drive back to this tiny apartment provided plenty of time to recount each and every moment that bastard has made me feel inadequate, embarrassed ... undeserving.

I take in a deep, calming breath then toss the keys onto the small kitchenette table and head right for the wine.

This day was going so well.

The thought settles me as I open the fridge and quickly grab a half-full bottle of red blend. I use my teeth to pull out the cork and pour the wine into a bright yellow coffee mug with sunflowers engraved on it. It's the closest thing to me and all my glasses are still packed in boxes.

It'll do fine to hold the wine, I think as I take a small sip. And then a large one.

I don't have a buzz yet, but in fifteen minutes I'm sure I will.

As I lick the sweet wine off my lips, I stare aimlessly at the glass bottle. I have to be careful not to fall into old patterns. It's been a long time since I've needed wine to sleep. But I can see myself relying on that bad habit tonight. *That's what some memories will do to you.*

I take a good, hard look at the bottle. It's more than halfway empty as it is. I'll be fine.

Leaning against the counter, I let the past flicker in front of me and trace the outline of the flowers on the mug.

Each memory is accompanied by another gulp of wine, each one tasting more and more bitter.

So many times Daniel's left me feeling less than. And it's my fault.

Even the first time was my fault.

The sudden memory of Tyler both warms my heart and makes my vision blur as my eyes gloss over with tears. I can't think of him for long without feeling a deep pain in my chest.

He was my first. My first everything.

Just like his brother Daniel and just like the rest of the men in their family, Tyler Cross was stubborn. And he didn't let up until I finally caved and said yes to being his girlfriend.

I told myself he was nice and that it felt good to be wanted. And my God, it did. When you're an orphan, you learn rather quickly people don't want you.

It's a hard thing to unlearn.

And at sixteen years old and in my fourth foster home, I didn't believe Tyler wanted anything more than a kiss, or to cop a feel. To get into my pants. Just like the previous foster dad wanted from me. He was a rotten bastard.

I run the tip of my finger along the edge of the mug, remembering how Tyler didn't give up on making me feel wanted. I only stayed with the Brauns, my fourth foster home in three years, because of how Tyler made me feel.

I didn't want to move to another school district.

I finally wanted to stay somewhere.

The Brauns would get their check and I would be a good kid, I'd be quiet. I'd put up with whatever it was I had to do in order for them not to send me back.

All because Tyler genuinely made me feel wanted. Even if it was obvious the Brauns, like the other foster parents, only wanted to get paid. Having to watch over a teenager with hormones and homework wasn't on their wish list.

Looking back on it now though, I don't much mind Jenny and Mitch Braun. They were okay people. Maybe if I hadn't run away when everything happened, I'd have a relationship with them. Or a semblance of one.

They didn't like Tyler though. They were probably the only people on the face of the earth who didn't like that boy. I can't blame them, since he did in fact want to get into my pants when they eventually met him.

I cover my mouth with my hand as I let out a small laugh at the memory.

He had to meet my guardians before I'd go anywhere near his house.

I have to give Tyler credit, he put up a good showing.

And then I had to face his family.

There was one big difference though. One massive separation between what he had to do and what I had to do in our little agreement.

Tyler had a real family.

That was so obvious to me. Actual relatives. Like I had once. It's an odd feeling standing in a room with people who belong together. Especially when you don't, but you want to. You desperately want to.

It was wrong of me. Every reason I had for staying with Tyler was selfish.

I was young back then. Young and stupid and incredibly selfish.

I know that now and it only makes the shame that much worse.

I remember how I could hardly look at anyone as Tyler wrapped his arm around my shoulders. Like he was proud of me and I belonged to him.

His mother had died years before, something Tyler and I had in common. His father was in the leather recliner in the living room, seated in front of the television although I'm certain he was sleeping.

Tyler told me his father worked late nights, but I could read between the lines. I knew the type of family the Crosses were. I knew by the way people spoke in hushed voices around them with traces of both fear and intrigue. And I heard the whispers.

There were little clues too. Tyler and his brother Jase were always being handed money under the cafeteria table and making quick exchanges. Certain people avoided them, certain red-eyed and scrawny potheads, to be exact.

It didn't matter to me.

In fact, I liked that their family was doing some type of business that meant his father would be asleep when I was forced to meet them all. Five boys in the family and Tyler was the youngest.

One less male to have to endure was fine by me. Declan, the middle boy, gave the impression of being disinterested in life in general. Let alone his brother's girlfriend. He was the first of Tyler's brothers I met, and even he seemed to be kind, if nothing else.

And that continued as I met his other brothers. They all welcomed me. There was no hidden agenda, no sneers or snide comments about where I was from or what the Brauns did at the local tavern two weeks ago.

That's one thing people liked to gossip about at school when I first got there. Foster parents aren't supposed to be drunks. Funny how that type of talk died when Tyler staked his claim on me.

Yet another reason I stayed and gave more and more of myself to a boy who could never have all of me.

It was so obvious that he never would. Especially that first day he brought me home.

The moment I thought I could relax, I met the last brother.

Daniel.

Tyler knocked on the door to his room, tapping out song lyrics and telling him to open up.

I remember exactly the way my polish had chipped on my thumbnail. I'm a nervous picker and I was busy chipping away at it when the door opened.

"What?" The word came out hard and my body stilled. I could feel the anger coming off of him from being interrupted.

He gripped the doorframe, which made his shoulders and height seem that much more intimidating. It was his toned muscles and the dark stubble lining his upper throat and jaw that let me know he was older.

And the heat in his stare as he let his gaze wander to where I stood that let me know I wasn't welcome.

That was the first time Daniel made me feel the same way I do now.

And the first time I knew I'd never love Tyler the way he deserved.

But I stayed with him. Deep inside I know it's because a very large part of me wanted Daniel to want me back. I wanted Daniel to want me the way that I instantly wanted him.

CHAPTER 4

Daniel

The back door to Iron Heart Brewery is propped open a couple inches with a brick. There's a small stack of them next to the dumpster and I've seen a few of them used for a number of things.

The door creaks open slowly as I take a look to my left and right. It's pitch black out now and deserted. It's been four hours since I left. Enough time to pass for me to get my shit together and figure out what it is that I want and how I'm going to handle this.

The entire town is quiet now that everything on Lincoln Street is closed.

I sneak in the back, hearing the clinking of glass around the corner and past the stockroom. The fresh scent of hoppy beer in this place never gets old.

I've only been here a couple months and I thought I'd get bored fast. So far there's not much action or competition. For a college town, it's surprising. But feeling out this area and waiting on information about future deals for my brother hasn't been the pain in the ass it usually is.

Other than Jake. He's not good for a damn thing other than asking for a beer or who comes around here when I'm away. He knows this place is used for drops, but that's as far as our relationship goes.

Jake's got his earbuds in, he's not paying attention in the least. My shoulder leans against the wall closest to the far end of the bar, and just enough so I can see the table where Addison sat earlier today.

I let the memory linger for a moment before speaking loud enough for Jake to hear over the music blaring in his ears.

"Marcus show up?" I call out and Jake startles, hitting his lower back against the counter and dropping a glass to the ground.

It breaks, cracking into a few large pieces rather than shattering.

Pushing off the wall, I take a few steps closer to him.

"Shit, dude," he tells me as he slowly lowers himself to the floor, catching his breath, and starts picking up the shards. "You scared the shit out of me." He starts to ask, "How did you get—" before stopping and looking past me to answer the question himself.

"Sorry," I offer him and crouch down to pick up the single piece of broken glass that's left. It's a solid piece a couple inches long with a sharp tip. I slide my finger along the blunt, slick side of it, toying with it as I talk to him. "Didn't mean to startle you." It's hard to keep the grin off my face, but it's easier if Jake is somewhat relaxed. He needs to know to fear me, but only so much that he doesn't do anything stupid. So long as he's easygoing, so is everything else that goes down here. He can keep looking the other way and I can keep everything moving as it should.

"No worries, man," he says as he stands up and deposits the chunks in his hand into a bin under the counter. He's still shaking and instead of reaching out for the piece I'm holding, he takes out the rectangular basin and offers it to me.

I hold his gaze as I toss it in to join the rest of them.

"What's going on?" he asks as he sets it back into place and pretends that he's not scared. That he doesn't look like he's going to piss himself.

"How long was the girl here?" I ask him and take a look around the counter. This section of the bar is small and narrow. There's a lone window on the other side and it's cracked open, letting in a small breeze.

"Addison?" he asks, saying her name out loud and I don't trust myself to speak as the anger swells inside of me, so I wait for him to look at me and give a short nod.

"Not long," he answers and gets back to wiping down a few of the glasses still lined up on the far side of the sink. "She left right after you."

"What was she here for?" I ask him and pray it wasn't for a meet. They're all done here. It's the perfect place, in the perfect town. Any necessary conversations can happen right here. And any arguments can be settled in the back ... with those bricks. But this city may be more useful and profitable. Time will tell.

"Just coming in for a drink."

I nod my head and remember how I've found a few guys I know sitting at the bar, completely oblivious to what was going on around them. Like Dean. He had no idea; he was too wrapped up in his own story to realize what was happening here.

"Who is she?" Jake asks, interrupting my recollection.

"A girl," I answer and then go back to being the one asking the questions. "She come in with anyone?"

"Nope, she's single. She didn't say she knew anyone or that she was looking for anyone." He replies with the information I was hoping for. It was just a coincidence that she was here. But the way he answers it doesn't quite sit right with me.

He's a funny kid and a good guy in some ways, but he's the type who looks the other way and likes to pretend everything's friendly and fine and nothing fucked up is going on.

I don't have any problems with him. *Yet.*

"Is that so?"

"Yeah, she's looking at going to the university. New to town. You know, that kind of thing."

"Hey Jake," I start and wait for him to look up at me. "How do you know her name?" My body's tense and tight, even though I don't think he has a clue how badly I'll fuck him up if he hit on her. He's a flirt, young and carefree. He gets plenty of action from girls coming in here to get a drink and drown out their problems with alcohol.

The fucker looks up at me like it's a given and says, "From her credit card."

I don't like his tone, or the ease with which he talks about her. But my body's relaxed, and the smile on my face grows as I tell him, "Of course. Sorry, she's got me a little wound up."

"I could tell." My back stiffens at his confession. "I mean I get it, she's hot," he says, completely oblivious to how my hand reflexively forms a fist. He shrugs and dries off the last glass. "You want me to keep tabs on her?"

The correct answer is no. But it's not the word that slips from my tongue. "Yes," I reply and it comes out harder than it should, with a desperate need clinging to the single syllable.

Jake pauses and takes in my appearance.

"I have a soft spot for her," I tell him and inwardly I hate myself. Both for the lie and for the hint at the truth. He nods his head and hangs up the dish towel in his hands.

"So she's going to the university?" I ask him and he returns to his normal easy self.

"I didn't get much information from her. She'd just gotten here and Mickey was at the bar."

"Well, don't worry about it. But if she comes in here again, text me."

"No problem. You need anything else?" he asks and I remind him of my earlier question.

"Did Marcus come?" I already know the answer. He hasn't shown up yet. Carter, my brother, messaged me to let me know not to waste my time in the bar tonight. But I know Marcus is a lot like me. He likes to know people's habits and if I tell him I'll meet him, I want him to know I'll be there.

This isn't my first run-in with him. Last time it took weeks before he finally showed.

There aren't a lot of men I'd wait on, but Carter says this is important and Marcus and I have history.

"He didn't. I don't know why he- "

"Looks like you're almost done," I cut him off with a trace of a smile on my lips. "Sorry to keep you."

"Not a problem," he says to my back as I turn and leave the bar.

The bright light of the Iron Heart sign casts a shadow beneath my feet as I walk toward the barren parking lot with only one thing on my mind—how to find little miss Addison Fawn.

CHAPTER 5

Addison

*D*aniel's a prick.

Why is it that the assholes stay in your head, rankling and festering their way into your thoughts while the nice guys are passed over?

I went shopping on the strip downtown to distract myself. I spent a pretty penny on décor for this apartment and on the softest comforter I've felt in my life.

One tweed rug, two woven baskets and a dozen rustic wood picture frames later and my living room is acceptable. Snapshot after snapshot I post the different angles on Instagram, where I have my largest following and where I sell most of my photos.

But it's all done absentmindedly. And it's not like these are for sale, just pictures that serve as an update to let my followers know I've found a new place.

I don't have an ounce of interest flowing through me.

I came here to settle down. To finally give myself a reason to stay and possibly take formal classes to breathe new life into my business.

And instead I've been pushed back to when I was only seventeen.

No home.

No life.

No reason to do anything at all.

My throat tightens and my eyes prick, but I refuse to let a single tear fall.

It's all because I'm still not worthy enough for Daniel fucking Cross.

My phone pings and I go into the messenger app on Facebook to see who it is.

Another person wanting me to photograph their wedding.

I don't do functions.

I politely message back that I don't do shoots. I only photograph the things around me and tell my own story. Not other people's. In other words, I'm not for hire. Photography is my business, but also my therapy. I photograph what I want and nothing else. It's the only way I've survived and I won't compromise that.

That's how I've made a living for the past few years. Little sales here and there. Enough to keep my head above water and to keep moving from place to place.

Searching for Something is what I eventually called my business.

Not that it started as a business. I was just taking pictures of every little thing that reminded me of Tyler.

All I had was my camera, the only present my last foster mother had ever given me. Tyler told her she should get it for me for Christmas. He said if she wouldn't, he would. He would've given me anything.

And so it started with me wanting to take a photograph of the snow around his old Chevy truck that couldn't run anymore. The rusted-out hood. The flat back left tire.

I started taking pictures of everything, obsessively. It was something Tyler and I had done together and it made sense to do at the time.

I needed something and although I didn't know what that something would be, I took photos of everything on my way to find what I was looking for.

Something to take the guilt away. Something to make me smile the way a boy who loved me in a way I didn't deserve had.

Searching for Something.

What it turned out to be was profitable.

A myriad of photos all priced ridiculously high. In my opinion, at least. But that's what everyone else was doing. The competition's pictures sold for hundreds. And mine looked like a steal simply because of the price tag.

I adopted the "fake it till you make it" strategy. And it's been working. But I don't know shit about running a business.

The random person on Facebook shoots back an apology and I don't bother to respond. My customer service isn't the best either.

Some days are better than others.

Some days are filled with reminders of the past. And those days are the worst for me personally, but the best for the things I see and can capture with a lens. And they sell well. Not just well, like serious money.

The shots I've taken today don't tell my story. It should be a part of my journey, but the pretty images of wooden frames and white tweed with pale blue accents are what I wanted before last night. Before I went to Iron Heart and ran into that asshole.

This is a décor shoot for a new life with new roots. It'll look pretty on Instagram with a soft filter, but that's about all it is. Just a series of pretty pictures.

My phone pings and pings with updates and I put it on vibrate before heading to the kitchen, where I place it on the table.

Next week is the kitchen makeover.

For now, it's all black and white with pops of cherry. A red teapot sits untouched on the stove as I shove my sunflower mug into the microwave to heat up water for tea.

I doubt I'll ever use that teapot.

My phone vibrates yet again, rattling the table just as the microwave beeps. A heavy sigh of irritation leaves me, but I know it's not the messages, nor the headache from stress and exhaustion.

It's because of Daniel. Just like years ago, I'm losing sleep over the asshole. Back then I never said a word. I let him treat me how he wanted, and I cowered away.

I'm older now and last night I should have said something. I should have gotten up and slapped him for being such a dismissive prick. Well, maybe that's taking things a little too far. But he deserves to know how much it hurt me. How I still struggle with what happened and how him treating me like that only makes the pain that much worse.

As the tea bag sinks into the steaming water, an idea hits me to search for Daniel on Instagram.

If not Instagram, then Facebook. Everyone is somewhere online now.

With my feet up on the chic glass table and the mug in my right hand, I search both on my cell phone.

And when both of those prove useless I try Twitter.

The steady, rhythmic ticking of the simple clock across from me and above the little kitchenette gets my attention when my search proves to be futile. I stare at the second hand that's marching along, willing it to give me an answer.

But time's a fickle bitch and she's never helped me with anything.

I take another sip of the now lukewarm tea before getting up for another cup.

As I wait for it to heat, I decide to search Iron Heart Brewery on Church and Lincoln Street.

Slowly a grin forms on my lips. Jake Holsteder stares back at me from a black and white photo where he's holding up a beer in cheers. The bartender from last night is apparently the owner. Jake has links to his social media accounts.

And more importantly, Daniel knows Jake.

It's a stretch, but I send a message to Jake on Facebook and then prepare my second cup of tea.

Nice to meet you last night. Sorry I left early.

It's a simple message and if he doesn't respond, I can always go back to the bar. I'm vaguely aware that I'm chasing after Daniel. After the man whose very existence brings back the ghosts of my past. But I don't care. I live off instinct and everything is telling me that I need to find Daniel. If for no other reason than to tell him he knows damn well who I am.

I add more sugar to the cup this time than last and the spoon clinks against the ceramic edge of the mug as my phone vibrates.

No worries. You leave for any reason in particular?

I chew on the inside of my cheek at his message.

Just had to go. But I wanted to come back and try that beer. I don't even remember what the hell the beer was called, but then I add, *I'd love to take pictures of the place too if that's okay?*

I purse my lips and tap my thumb against my phone before finally sending the message.

Pictures? That's all he answers.

I send him a link to my Instagram and then text, *Your place gives me so much inspiration.*

NICE!

Even if he's only being polite, I appreciate it. *Thanks!*

He writes, *Seriously, these are beautiful. You should try selling them.*

I do. It's what I do for a living and I'd love to take some pics in your bar. The whole place gives me a ton of inspiration. Maybe we can chat too?

He takes a moment and then another to respond. Each second makes my heart beat a little faster and I find myself picking at my nails. *You come by looking for him?*

Him? I play coy.

I thought maybe you knew Daniel? he asks me although it's a statement.

I did, but I haven't seen him in years. I send the message without checking it. Maybe I gave away too much.

You should stay away, Jake warns me and although I know he's right, it pisses me off. All the kids at school told me that about Tyler too—well, more about his family than him specifically, and he was the only good thing I've ever had in my life. And I really don't like people telling me what to do.

I didn't go to your bar looking for an old friend. I pause before adding, *I'm here to make new ones.*

It feels like a hand's squeezing my heart in my chest as an anxious feeling comes over me. The only sense I can gather from it all is that I know I'm only doing this to piss Daniel off. And that's something I shouldn't do; I've done it once before and the memory makes me feel weak.

You can come by anytime. What's your number? he asks me and although it's forward, I send it over. Jake knows Daniel. So maybe I can get some intel at the very least.

Daniel was always the possessive type. Even if he hated me, he hated anyone who showed me any attention more. So maybe finding out Jake has my number will piss him off. I can only hope.

I feel petty as I walk away from the phone, listening to it vibrate in time with the ticking of the clock.

As I peek out of the sheer white curtains and down onto the street below me, an eerie feeling washes through me. It slowly pricks along my skin until the hairs on the back of my neck stand up.

It's a feeling like someone's watching me. I'm slow as I turn so I'm facing my living room. There's no one else here in my studio apartment. Not a soul.

My hand wraps around the hot mug and I pull the curtains shut. It's only the memory of Tyler that's brought this back.

I couldn't go anywhere without feeling him there. Watching

me. A shudder runs down my spine as I remember each day. Each photo I took as I whipped around, expecting to find someone lurking in the shadows. There was never anyone there. It was only my shame that followed me.

I hate Daniel even more in this moment.

It took me years to get to where I was days ago. And with one look, I've gone back to being the girl I was trying to leave behind.

CHAPTER 6

Daniel

"It's been long enough, hasn't it?" my brother's voice asks on the other end of the phone.

My eyes close as I try to push down the irritation. Madison Street is busy today in the quiet town. Cars pass and I can hear the hums and rumbles with the windows opened in the diner as I lean back in the booth. The vinyl coverings protest as I lean forward and wave the waitress away before she can offer me another cup of coffee.

"We go through this every few months, Carter." I close my eyes again as I continue, "Do you really want to have the same conversation again?"

Across the street is a coffee shop. And inside it, Addison. She's hunched over in the corner with her laptop on a small circular table as she sits cross-legged in a chair. Some things never change.

I watch her from a distance in the safety of the diner. I'm

within view; she could see me if she wanted to. But that's the thing about Addison. She never wanted to see me.

"How long are you going to keep this up?" Carter asks me. He's older than me by a year, almost on the dot. Irish twins, so to speak. I don't bother answering him and instead I remember the details of her address that Marcus gave me.

Funny how he can't show up to deliver the package from the Romanos. But one encrypted message from me to him with Addison's license plate number sparks enough interest for him to respond.

I suppose he hasn't forgotten. Marcus has a good memory.

"Whatever, I just need the package." Carter sighs on the other end of the phone. "I need to know what we're getting into before we decide…"

He doesn't continue, but I know what he's getting at. It's best not to speak those things where others can hear.

"He'll show. You know how he is."

"He's a pain in my ass."

The corner of my lip kicks up at his comment. "So many things are a pain in your ass, Carter. It's hard to believe you can sit down without wincing," I joke as I watch Addison take a large drink from her coffee cup. It's the tallest size the shop has and it looks like she's almost done.

"You're fucking hilarious, you know that?" I laugh at Carter's comment even though he says it with disdain. He runs the family business now. What started as a way for my father to make extra cash became an empire formed from ruthless and cutthroat tactics. Carter's the head, but I do his bidding more from a vague obligation that we're blood than anything else.

"Are you coming home after this? As soon as this package arrives? There's no reason for you to stay away and we need you here."

Her name is on the tip of my tongue. *Addison.* I may deal in addiction, but she's the only addiction I've ever had and the only one I desire.

"Well?" he presses.

"I'm curious about something," I answer my brother.

"What's that?"

"Something of personal interest," I mutter and the words come out lower than I intend them to. He's quiet for a long moment. And my focus is momentarily distracted. A man in a thin leather jacket walks past the coffee shop slowly, but his gaze is on Addison.

My eyes narrow as he stops in his tracks and glances inside the place. I shake off the possessive feelings. I'm only projecting.

Carter's voice brings my attention back to him. "With that shit your friend Dean pulled, there's too much heat around you." He ignores my earlier comment and I decide it's for the best. There's no need for anyone to know what I'm doing.

I'm quick to answer him. "Which is exactly why I need to stay. Leaving would raise suspicion."

A line of cars pass on the street in front of me, temporarily blocking Addison from my view. At their movement, she peeks up through the large glass windows of the shop.

Her hair brushes her shoulder and falls down her back as she takes a break to look out onto the street. Her pouty lips are turned down. They always are. There's a sadness that's always followed Addison. It's only a matter of whether or not she's trying to hide it, but it's always there.

Her green eyes are deep and even from this distance they seem to darken. Her hand moves to the back of her neck, massaging away a dull ache from sitting there for hours now. With each breath, her chest rises and falls and I'm mesmerized by her. By all of her.

More so by what she does to me.

The hate and anger I felt toward her years ago has numbed into something else each minute I sit here.

Curiosity maybe.

"Just get the package from Marcus. You've been gone long enough and we could use you here."

"I don't know if I want to come back," I tell him honestly and flatly.

"It's not a matter of want," he replies but his words come out hollow and with no authority although he wishes he had it. "We're your blood." He plays the only card he has that can get me to do his bidding.

"You never fail to remind me."

My phone vibrates with a message and I'm more than happy to end this call.

"I've got to go." My phone vibrates again. "I'll update you when I can." I don't wait for him to acknowledge what I've said, let alone tell me goodbye. I've never been close to my brothers. Not like they are toward each other. I'm the black sheep, I suppose.

I crack my neck as my phone vibrates for a third time. Before checking it I glance back at Addison only to see she's gone, although her laptop is still there. My heart stills and my body tenses until I see her by the counter, ordering something else.

Annoyance rises in me as I realize how much pull she has over me in this moment. I've turned back into what I hate. My teeth grit as I pull up my texts and that annoyance grows to an agitation that makes me grip the edge of the table to keep me from doing something stupid.

Three messages, each from Jake.

Marcus isn't coming tonight. He said there are complications.

I have your girl's number though if you want it.

And I think she's coming here tonight.

Jake wants to die. That's the only explanation. He literally wants me to kill his ass.

My glare moves from the cell phone in my hand back to the coffee shop across the street. Addison's cardigan dangles loosely around her as she moves back to her spot. Her jeans are tight and I can just imagine how they'd feel against my hands as I ripped them off of her. It'd be difficult, but I would fucking love it.

"Do you …" I hear a small, hesitant voice next to me and I have to school my expression before I can look back at the waitress.

She's an older woman, with soft lines around her eyes. A stray lock of dark hair with a line of silver running through it falls from her bun and into her face as she offers me a smile and holds up a pot of coffee. "You're all out this time," she says, like it's a reason to have another.

"Sure," I say and smile politely as she fills the cup.

The hot coffee steams and I stare at it as she leaves me be.

So Addison is giving her number out.

I wonder if she would have given it to me. I replay that scene in my head and instead of leaving, I slip in beside her.

I don't deserve Addison. That's a given.

But I'll be damned if I let some asshole like Jake get his hands on her.

CHAPTER 7

Addison

$\mathcal{I}$t took three days to actually go through with it and go back to Iron Heart Brewery.

Three days and this feeling in my gut that won't leave.

Three days of fiddling with images in Photoshop and hating each and every one because I can't focus.

And worst of all, three nights of not sleeping.

Every night I keep dreaming of the bar and every time the scene ends differently. It starts out how I'd have liked for it to have gone. With him giving me the time of day. With him offering to get me a drink. But then it turns dark and wicked. Daniel grabs me. Or worse. I hear Tyler tell me to stay away.

And I wake up shaken.

I feel just like I did that winter I ran away.

And I hate it. I hate Daniel even more for making it all come back. And if I can find that asshole I'm going to tell him exactly how he makes me feel. Not just the way he made me feel the other night, but also the way I felt all those years ago.

Part of me wants to run. But I already did that. I can't keep running forever.

I open the heavy glass door to the bar with the buzz of the late traffic behind me. This is an old town, but on weekends everyone is out and about.

I'm immediately hit with the aroma of pale ale lingering in the air and the chatter of everyone in here. The air outside was crisp, but only two steps in and the warmth lets me slip off my cardigan.

"Addison," Jake says my name from his place behind the bar. It carries over the hubbub and a man seated on a stool by him turns to look back at me.

Jake's smile is broad and welcoming as he gestures to an open seat at the bar.

For a small moment I forget the churning in my gut. I think that's what really happened these past couple of years. I slowly forgot. And if that isn't a tragedy, I don't know what is.

"You alright?" Jake asks with his forehead creased and a frown on his lips

"Sorry," I tell him and shake my head as I fold the cardigan over the barstool and then slip on top of it, resting my elbows on the bar. "Been a long few days."

"What's bothering you?" he asks while passing a beer down the bar to an old man with salt and pepper hair and bushy eyebrows that are colored just the same.

The man waves him a thanks without breaking his conversation. Something about a football game coming up.

Letting out an easy sigh, I pull the hair away from my face and into a small ponytail although I don't have a band, so it falls down my back as I talk. "Oh, you know. Just moving and getting settled." I smile easily as I lie to him. "So, how's it been going for you?"

Even as I ask him I'm almost painfully aware of how I couldn't care less. I'm eager for information and that's all I want. I rest my chin in my hand and lean forward, pretending to give him my full attention even though my mind's on all the questions on the tip of my tongue.

How often does Daniel come here?

Do you think he'll be here tonight?

Do you know where I can find him if he doesn't come?

Instead I smile and laugh politely when I'm supposed to; all the while Jake chitchats about the bar and points to the pictures on the wall. Occasionally he answers his phone and texts or gets someone a beer.

Although it's crowded and I'm having a real conversation for the first time since three nights ago, I've never felt more alone.

"So we go around from place to place, collecting all of them we can find," Jake wraps up something he said that I was only half listening to and then takes a seat on his side of the bar.

"What's really bothering you?" he asks and it catches me off guard. My simper slips, and my heart skips a beat.

"What do you mean?" I ask him as if I haven't got a clue and then quickly follow up with, "I'm just tired." It sounds phony to my own ears, so I'm sure I sound like a bad liar to him too.

"You seemed a little shaken the other night," Jake says softly, leaning forward. Someone calls out his name and he barely acknowledges them, holding up his hand to tell them to wait. "Maybe you came in looking for something?" he asks me with his eyes narrowed.

The playfulness is gone, as is the sound of all conversation in the busy bar. In its place is the rapid thumping of my heart.

"Or someone?" he says as somebody else calls out his name again, breaking me from the moment. I turn to the man with the bushy eyebrows as Jake tells him, "One minute!" in not the most patient of tones.

"So what is it?" he says and waits for me.

"I didn't come in here looking for anything or anyone." I tell him the truth. My voice is small, pleading even.

"But you found something," he prompts.

I only nod my head and he pushes off of the bar, standing up and making his way back to the draft beers to satisfy the old man's order.

"If you don't want to see him again, you should leave now," Jake speaks without looking at me and then smiles and jokes with the man at the end of the bar.

"Why's that?" I call after him, my voice raised so he can hear me and the bar top digging into my stomach as I lean over it to get a good view of him.

Just as Jake opens his mouth to answer me, the door to the bar opens and I can feel the atmosphere change.

No one else stops talking. No one else turns to look over their shoulder.

But I do. I'm drawn to him and always have been. It's like my body knows his. Like my soul was waiting for his.

Daniel's always had an intensity about him. There's a dominance that lingers in the way he carries himself. A threat just barely contained. The rough stubble over his hard jaw begs me to run my hand against it. The black leather of his jacket is stretched over his shoulders.

Thump ... thump ... my heart ticks along and then stops.

Daniel's dark eyes meet mine instantly. They swirl with an emotion I can't place as they narrow, and I can't breathe until he takes a step. We both hang there for what feels like forever. He must know I've come here for him.

I watch as he moves, or rather stalks toward me. Each movement is careful, barely contained. Like it's taking everything in him just to be near me. I know he wants to appear relaxed, but he's faking it.

And with another step toward me, I can finally tear my gaze away.

I look forward, my back straight and my eyes on the beer in front of me as he walks behind me. I can hear each step and the scratch of the barstool on the floor directly to my left as he pulls it out.

I remind myself I came here for him. No, not *for* him. To see him. To clear the air.

I came here to this small town for me because I finally had my life together.

And he ruined it. The memory of his cold reception and dismissal hurts more and more with each passing second. I'm not a little girl for him to shove aside anymore and treat like I'm some annoyance.

The thought strengthens my resolve and I turn sharply to the left just as he takes his seat. He's so close my breasts nearly brush his bicep and it forces the words to a grinding halt as I pull back.

I'd forgotten what he smells like, a woody scent with a fresh-ness to it. Like trees on the far edge of a forest by the water. I'd forgotten what it feels like to be this close to him.

To be too close to what can ruin you is a disconcerting feeling.

"Addison," he says and although his voice is deep and mascu-line, in that smooth cadence my name sounds positively sinful. The irritation in his tone that was constant in my memory is absent.

"Daniel." I barely manage to get his name out and I clear my throat, slowly sitting back in my seat to grab the beer in front of me. "I was wondering if I'd find you here," I admit and then peek up at him.

A genuine grin grows slowly on his handsome face. I swear his teeth are perfectly white. It's a crime for a man to look this good.

"You came here looking for me?" he asks me with a cockiness that reminds me of a boy I once knew and again, for the second time, my confidence is shaken. As I lick my lower lip to respond, I fail to find the words.

"Do I intimidate you, Addison?" he asks in a teasing voice and I roll my eyes and then lift the beer to my lips. I assume he'll say something else as I drink, but he doesn't.

As I set the glass down, I look him in the eyes. "You know you do and I hate it." There's a heat between us that ignites in an instant. As if a drop of truth could set fire to us both. I can barely breathe looking into his dark eyes.

"Do you now?" he asks again in that same playful tone. "So you came here looking for me because you hate me?"

"Yes," I answer him without hesitation, although it's not quite truthful. That's not why, but I'm fine with him thinking that.

His brow raises slightly and he tilts his head as if he wasn't expecting that answer. Slowly he corrects it, and I can feel his guard slowly climb up. It's this thing he always did. It's odd how I remember it so well. For only moments, only glimpses, I swear he let me in. But just like that it was gone, and a distance grew between us, even if we hadn't moved an inch.

"Don't do that," I tell him as soon as I sense it and his eyes narrow at me. "I don't hate you. I hate that you were rude to me."

"I wasn't rude."

"You were a dick." My words come out with an edge that can't be denied and I wish I could swallow them back down.

"I'm sorry," he tells me and he looks apprehensive. It's weird hearing him say those words. I can't think of him ever speaking them to anyone before. "You came looking for an apology?"

"No, not really," I tell him and shrug, wanting to take a step back from the tense air, but my ass is firmly planted on this stool. He turns to his left and I look back at the glass while I continue, just wanting to get it out of me before he's gone again.

"I just wanted to talk." The words finally come out, although they're not quite right. I want to spill every word that's inside of me. From the last night I saw him all those years ago, to everything that's happened up until this moment. There aren't a lot of people who can relate to what we've gone through.

He still hasn't said a word. His gaze is focused on me as if he's trying to read me, but can't make out what's written. If only he'd ask, I'd tell him. I don't have time for games or secrets, and our history makes up too much of who I am to disrespect it with falsehoods.

"Are you going to run off again?" I ask as he only stares back at me.

"Do you want me to?" he asks me in return.

"No," I answer instantly and a little too loud. As if what he'd said was a threat. I'm quieter as I add, "I don't want you to go." The desperation in my voice is markedly apparent.

"Well what do you want then?" he asks me and I know the answer. *I want him.* I take in a breath slowly, knowing the truth but also knowing I'd never confess it.

"I haven't been able to sleep since the other night," I confess and my gaze flickers from the glass to his eyes. My nail taps on the glass again and again and the small tinkling persuades me to continue. "I had a rough time for a while, but I was doing really well until I saw you." I don't glance up to see how he reacts; I'm merely grateful the words are finally coming to me. "When you didn't even bother to look at me, much less talk to me ..." I swallow thickly and then throw back more of the beer.

"It was a shock to see you." Daniel says the words as if he's testing them on his tongue. Like they aren't the truth, although I'm sure they are. I look into his eyes as he says, "I didn't mean to upset you."

"What did you mean then?" I ask him without wasting a second.

He hesitates again, careful to say just what he wants. "I didn't know what to say, so I left."

"That seems reasonable." Or at least that seems like the version of Daniel I remember. I take another sip of beer before I say, "It hurt though."

"I already said I was sorry." His words are short, harsh even, but they don't faze me.

"I wasn't looking for an apology. I only wanted you to know how you make me feel."

He responds quickly this time, still looking over my expression as if he's not sure what to make of it. "And how do I make you feel now?"

I swear his breathing comes in heavier, and it makes mine do the same. "Like I have someone to talk to."

That gets a huff of a laugh from him. A disbelieving one. "I'm sure you have better options for that."

I shake my head and answer before taking another sip, "You'd be wrong then."

It's never felt pathetic before. The fact is I don't talk to many people and the one friend I have is thousands of miles away. But admitting that to him and seeing the trace of the grin fall on his lips makes it feel slightly pitiful.

I muster a small smile although it's weak, and time grows between us. The seconds tick by and I know I'm losing him, but I can't voice any of the things I'm feeling.

"It's been a while," he says and I nod my head as I answer, "Since the funeral."

I don't think I've ever said it out loud and it's the first mention of Tyler between us. The air turns tense but not in a way that's uncomfortable. At least not for me. I even have the courage to look back at him. I can see hints of Tyler in Daniel. But Tyler was so young and he looked it. Still, there are small things.

"You remind me of him, you know?" All while I speak, Daniel stares at my lips. He doesn't hide the fact in the least. I think he wants me to know. I swallow and his gaze moves to my throat, then he leans in just slightly before correcting himself. The hot air is tense and as he finally looks me in the eyes again, the noise of the bar disappears from the pure intensity of his stare.

"You do the same for me, I think."

"You think?" I ask him to clarify.

"You bring back certain things," he says icily, so cold it sends a chill down my spine.

My shoulders are tight as I straighten myself in the seat, again looking into the glass of beer that's nearly gone as if it can save me. Or as if I can drown in it.

It's only the sound of him standing up that makes me look back toward him. "Are you leaving?" I ask him like an idiot and then feel like it.

He only nods and I'm sure he's going to walk off, but instead he steps closer to me. He shoves a piece of paper in front of me onto the bar and then grips the barstool I'm sitting on with both of his hands.

He's so close I can feel his heat as he whispers to me, "I'll see you soon, Addison."

CHAPTER 8

Daniel

Five years ago

The wind howls as it whips past us. We're all dressed in black suits, but the shoes we spent all last night shining are buried beneath the pure white snow. The ice melts and seeps between the seams, letting the freezing cold sink into what was once warm. It's fitting as we stare at the upturned dirt in front of us.

We're the last ones here. We stopped on our way back from the dinner since the sun has yet to set, and there's still a bit of light left.

The sky beyond us is blurred and the air brutally cold, the kind that makes my lungs hurt each time I try to breathe.

One of my brothers cries. It's a whimper at first but I don't move to see who's the weakest of us. My muscles coil at the thought, hating how I've judged. Hating how I view strength. I'm pathetic. I'm the weak one.

Jase, the farthest from me, sniffles as his shoulders crumple and then he covers his face.

He was the closest to Tyler but now he's the baby, taking Tyler's place. The air turns cruel, biting at the back of my neck with a harsh chill as his cries come to a halt. My throat's tight as I try to swallow. It makes me bitter to be standing here, knowing I need to leave and can't stay here. That I'm the one who gets to continue breathing. That fate chose to take one of the good ones, and leave the ruthless and depraved behind.

Five brothers are now only four.

Four of us stand over Tyler's body. Six feet in the ground.

All of us will mourn him. The world is at a loss for not knowing him. I finally get the expression about how it's better to have loved and lost than never to have loved at all.

Tyler was good through and through. He would have lived his days making the world a better place. He'd try to start a conversation with anyone; just to get to know them, just to make them laugh if he could.

All four of us lined up and saying our final goodbyes will never be the same after losing our youngest brother.

But only one of us knows the truth.

Only one of us is guilty.

THE WORST PART is when I leave. I'm the last of us to finally part from Tyler's grave, but when I leave, my gaze stays rooted to where her car was. Where Addison had parked. My memories aren't of my father crying helplessly against the brick wall of the church, refusing to go in when he couldn't hide his pain. The images that flash before my eyes as my shoes crunch against the icy snow aren't of all his friends and teachers and family who have come from states away to tell us how sorry they are and how much Tyler will be missed.

All I can think about is Addison. How she stood so quietly on the fringes of the crowd, her fingers intertwined, her eyes glossy. How even as the wind ripped her scarf from her shoulders, carrying it into the distance

292

and leaving her shoulders bare, she didn't move. She didn't even shudder. She was already numb.

The picture of her standing there motionless, staring at the casket is what I think about as I leave my brother.

I DIDN'T KNOW THEN how dangerous that was. Or maybe I did and I didn't want to believe it. But Addison would haunt me long after that night, as do so many other things.

She's only a girl. One small, weak girl.

Her red cheeks and nose and windblown hair made her look that much more tempting. Everything about her is ruined. At least she appeared to be that night. But I knew she had more left in her. More life and spirit. More emotion to give.

I may be cruel and unforgiving, but I'm right. I'm always right.

CHAPTER 9

Addison

The night Tyler died, I saw it all happen.

I was there and I heard the tires squeal.

At the memory, I can practically feel the cold raindrops from that night pelting my skin. I turn on the faucet to the hottest it can go and wait until steam fills the room. I step into the shower, ignoring how the sounds of water falling are so similar to the rain that night as I stood outside the corner store. He called my name. My eyes close and my throat feels tight as I hear Tyler's voice.

The last thing he said was my name as he stepped into the street.

It takes a lot to leave someone because you fell in love with somebody else. Somebody who would never love you back.

It takes even more of your heart to witness the death of someone who truly deserved to live. More than I'll ever deserve it.

And to know that they died because they were looking for you …

God and fate are not kind or just. They take without reason. And the world is at a loss for Tyler being taken from us.

I thought I was doing the right thing by leaving Tyler. I didn't know he'd come looking for me. If I could take it back, I would.

The water hits my face and I pretend like the tears aren't there. It's easier to cry in the shower.

I was fine until I saw Daniel again. It took me years to feel just okay. That's the part I can't get over. Maybe this is what a relapse is? One moment and I've lost all the strength I've gained over the years. All of the acceptance that I can't change what happened and that it'll be okay. It's all gone in an instant.

I lean my back against the cold tile wall and sink to the floor. The smooth granite feels hard against my back as I sit there, letting the water crash down on me as I remember that night over and over. Just a few moments in particular. The moment Tyler saw me, then the moment he spoke my name and moved toward me.

The moment I screamed at the sight of him stepping into the road.

The car was right there. There was no time.

It didn't matter how I threw myself forward, racing toward him even as the car struck him.

I swear I acted as fast as I could. But it wasn't good enough.

My head rests on my knees as my shoulders shake.

Life wasn't supposed to be so cruel. Not to him.

"Deep breaths," I tell myself. "One at a time," I say, brushing at my eyes even though the water is still splashing down.

Standing up makes me feel weak. The water's colder, but the air is still hot.

Just breathe.

As I open up the shower door to inhale some cool air, I hear something. My heart stops and my body freezes. The water's still on but my eyes stare at the bathroom door.

The mirrors are fogged even though I left the door open slightly. A second passes and then another.

My body refuses to move even after I will myself to reach for the towel. My knuckles turn white and keep me where I am. I know I heard something. Something fell. Or something was pushed. Something beyond the door. *Something.* I don't know what, but I heard something.

I force myself to take one step onto the bath mat, and then another onto the tile floor.

I keep moving. I take the towel in both hands and then wrap it around myself although I can't take my eyes off the door.

Water drips down my back, but I don't bother with drying my hair. I make myself open the door and it groans in protest as I do.

The second it's open wide, I feel foolish.

It's only a picture I'd put up with hanging tape strips. It's fallen and the paint on the wall where it was hung, a Tiffany blue, is marred.

I should have used nails or screws to hang it.

Even as I pick up the picture and roll my eyes, my body is still tense; my heart still races. The frame is cracked and broken. When I place it onto the dresser, I catch a glimpse of the piece of paper Daniel gave me. It's a ripped portion of something—maybe a bill, I'm not sure. But on it is his number. The number I texted so he would have mine and to ask when we could meet. The number that didn't answer, even though the message was marked as read.

I leave the paper there with the broken frame and head back to the bathroom to finally turn off the water. But I stop just shy of entering.

Peeking at the door to my bedroom, a chill travels down my spine.

I don't remember leaving it open.

CHAPTER 10

Daniel

I would say I don't have time for this shit, but I do. I really do.

I would make time for it if I didn't already have it in spades.

I'm cradling my chin while I drum the fingers of my other hand in a rhythmic pattern on the sleek mahogany tabletop. The soft sound doesn't even reach my ears, mixing with the chatter and hum of small talk and the clinking of silverware in the restaurant.

The Madison Grille has gotten a facelift recently. It's obvious. From the new wood beams that make the place smell like cedar, to the industrial lighting with exposed bulbs. I deliberately chose a place that wasn't too expensive or elegant so this wouldn't seem like a date. But it's better than a bar. There's privacy here that I'm eager to take advantage of. I waited to message her until only hours ago. Last night took a lot out of me, but once I decided, there was no turning back.

"Would you like anything while you wait?" The waiter already has his pad out and pen ready to go. There are a lot of things I'd like right now. Addison bent over the table, for one. Simply for inviting me back into her life. She may not know how much she taunted me, but she's smart enough to know the attraction was there and still she teased me.

"A whiskey sour and two waters," I tell him and he waits for more, but a tight smile sends him away.

Again my fingers drum as I think about each and every curve of the woman I'm waiting for.

Addison is all grown up.

And that look in her eyes is one I recognize. Desire. My blood feels hotter with every second I sit here thinking about what I wanted to do last night. And what I plan to do tonight.

I can imagine those pouty lips of hers wrapping around my cock and the sounds she'd make as I shoved my dick down her throat.

If nothing else, I can finally get a piece of what I wanted when I first laid eyes on her. Just the thought makes my dick harden and I stifle back a groan as the zipper of my jeans digs into me.

It took everything in me not to take her last night.

When she looked at me like she could see right through me.

When she told me to stop, as if she could command me.

When she spilled her little heart out as if I was the one meant for those words.

I'll be damn sure to make the time for Addison. Finally having her is worth all the fucking time in the world.

Sheets of rain batter against the large front window of this place and crash noisily on the tin roof.

I hate the rain. I hate what it does to me. The memories it brings back.

Addison is out there in the rain right now. Feeling it beat against her skin. Listening to the familiar sound.

And the unwanted memories that come with it.

I should feel a good number of things with the memory of Tyler besetting me right now as I wait for Addison. Shame, maybe even disgust. Swallowing thickly, I replay the memories, but this time focus on *her*. How she looked at me and shied away. How she couldn't talk to me while looking me in the eyes. How she blushed every time she caught me staring. Her reaction to me and only me was everything.

It was never about Tyler and I stayed away back then for him. It was always about Addison.

My thoughts are interrupted by the drinks I ordered being set on the table in front of me.

"Will you be dining tonight?" the waiter asks and I shake my head no and reply, "Just drinks."

"Let me know if I can get you anything else." With that he's gone and I'm left sitting alone at the table in the back. Staring at the entrance and waiting.

The soft lighting is reflected in my watch face as I turn my wrist over, showing the time is nearly ten minutes past the hour. She's late.

My eyes narrow as I look back toward the entrance, willing her to walk through the doors. There's a mix of worry and fear that I'm vaguely aware of. Fate's been a cruel bitch to me and I wouldn't put it past her to take the one thing I've always wanted. The one person I'm so close to getting.

Before I can let the unwanted emotions get the best of me, the door opens and Addison steps inside, huddled under an umbrella that she's quick to shake out over the mat and close. The hostess greets her as I sit paralyzed, watching Addison.

It's still surreal to see her here. I don't know how to react to her.

My fingers long to help her slip out of her jacket, but instead they grip onto the table.

I frown at the sweet smile she gives the hostess for helping her with her things. Addison hasn't given me one. In fact, it falls as she's directed toward me.

The happiness so evident only a second ago is gone as she walks over.

It makes my blood heat to a simmer but I stand anyway, pulling out the chair across from me for her to sit.

"Hi," she offers politely and the scent of her shampoo wafts toward me.

I don't trust myself to say anything, so I only offer her an inkling of a smile. I'm better than this. I know better too. "Thank you," she says softly as I retake my seat.

"I didn't know what you'd like to drink," I tell her even though I know she'll order a red wine. On the sweeter side.

"Oh, I'm fine with anything," she says agreeably and just like that, the bits of irritation slowly ebb and start to fade. She offers me a hesitant smile as she adds, "I'm glad you texted me."

Her smile broadens and she takes a sip of water before the waiter comes by again. And she orders cabernet. She's a creature of habit, little Addison.

"You wanted to talk?" I sit back easier in my seat now that she's here.

"I do, but I don't know how."

A genuine smile creeps onto my face. Little things like her innocent nature have always intrigued me. "Just say whatever you want, Addison."

"Do you hate me?" she asks me quietly. The seriousness is unexpected and catches me off guard.

"No, I don't hate you." I hated that I couldn't have her. But that was then.

"I feel like you should," she tells me although she's staring at her glass. She does that a lot. She looks down when she talks to me. I don't like it. My chest feels tighter and the easiness of tonight and what I want from it tangle into a knot in my stomach. I reach for my drink, letting it burn on the way down.

The words to ease her are somewhere. I know they exist, but they fail me now because the truth that begs to come out is all I can focus on.

I'm saved by her glass of cabernet that she accepts from the waiter graciously.

"Tyler did mean a lot to me, you know?" she asks me as if my acceptance means everything. As if I couldn't see it in her eyes back then. Every fucking time I saw them together it was obvious. He was all she had and I think she hated that fact, but loved him for simply being there for her.

"That was never a question," I tell her with a chill in my voice. One that I can't control.

"I just feel like," she pauses and swallows, then takes a sip of wine. With her nervous fidgeting, she's clearly uncomfortable and it's pissing me off. "I'm just afraid of what you and your brothers think. Your dad, too."

"My father died two years ago," I tell her and ignore the twinge of guilt running through me plus the pain of the memory. The knot seems to tie tighter.

I went home for the first time in years only to watch him being put in the ground next to my mother, just twenty plots down from Tyler's grave. And I haven't been back since. It's funny how guilt spreads like that. How it only gets worse, not better.

"Oh my God," Addison gasps and reaches her small hand out on the table for mine. "I'm so sorry." One thing I've always admired about Addison is how easy it is to read her. How genuine she is. How honest. Even if the things she was thinking were less than appealing.

"My father liked you, so he told Tyler that you would come back." I don't know why I tell her that. The memory doesn't sit well with me and the conversation isn't going where I'd like it to. Uncomfortable is an emotion I don't often experience. I suppose it makes sense that I am now though. Yet again ... that's Addison's doing. But I allow it. It would be easy to get up and leave, to not have to deal with this conversation. But having Addison tonight is worth it.

Barely catching a glimpse of the starched white shirt of the waiter, I hold up my hand just in time to stop him.

"Yes?" he asks and I order two rounds of black rose shots, which are a mix of vodka and tequila and the restaurant's drink of choice. Plus another whiskey sour. I greatly underestimated this conversation and the need for alcohol to go along with it.

"Anything else?" the waiter asks and Addison pipes up. With her hands folded in her lap, she orders the bruschetta.

It's only once the waiter's left that she leans forward, tucking her hair behind her ear and says, "I didn't eat much today."

"Get whatever you'd like," I tell her easily and keep my gaze from wandering straight down her blouse. It's only a peek. Only a hint at what's under the thin cotton, but I can see the lace of her bra and it begs me to look.

"I have to get this off my chest." Her words distract me and looking at the serious expression in her eyes I'm irritated again, but I keep my lips shut tight. It will be worth it when it's over with. It better be.

"I just ... even that day when I left, I didn't want you to think that I didn't appreciate everything."

She has no fucking idea. How is it even possible that she could be so blind?

She lived under our roof. It was off and on for nearly a year while the two of them dated. Tyler insisted. And the nights she didn't stay felt off toward the end. Each and every time she left I thought it was my doing.

But she always came back.

Tyler wasn't one to make demands, but he wanted her there with him. He wanted her protected and cared for. And when he told us why, when he told us what she'd been through, my father agreed.

It wasn't just that she had a tragic backstory. That she'd lost her parents and had no one.

It was the story of her previous foster father that changed my father's mind.

You could see it in the way Addison shied away from everything and everyone. And how she didn't want to go back to a stranger's house and hope nothing like that ever happened again.

She was safe with us. Even if she felt like she was intruding, every one of us wanted her there.

Even more so after we paid that sick fuck a visit.

It wasn't in Tyler's nature to want to hurt someone. Addison had a good way of bringing out a different part of him. She's good at that, at bringing out facets of your personality that were dormant before.

Carter was the one who decided when and how we'd take care of the asshole who'd touched her the year before. He was forty years old with a fifteen-year-old girl under his care.

Carter decided all five of us would go together while Addison was at class. The drive was only three hours away. Too long to do it at night, because she'd have noticed. But we had plenty of time during the day.

Carter always has a plan, and I was supposed to go around the back. Which is right where the asshole was raking up leaves.

I'd never killed anyone with gardening equipment before. I still wonder what it would have been like had I used the sharp tines of the metal but the damn thing broke in half. The spike of the splintered wooden handle worked well enough.

He got out one scream, if you can even call it that. More of a pathetic cry.

My family may have sheltered her.

I killed for her.

Tyler should have told her back then, and I have a mind to tell her now. But I don't break promises, not even to the dead.

So I keep that little bit of our history to myself.

The memory gives me the strength to look her in the eyes as I tell her, "You care a lot about what other people think. You'd be happier if you didn't."

"I'm not sure I would be," she answers softly with the corners of her lips turned down.

Again, the alcohol saves the conversation. The shots hit the table one by one.

"I think you need a drink."

I sure as fuck do. I didn't have her come here for a heart to heart. This isn't going how I'd planned. Wine and dine and fuck her is what I wanted. The first two I could take or leave, but the last I've needed for so long.

"I could use one ... or six," she jokes and pulls her hair over her shoulder, twirling the dark locks around her finger.

Addison's entire demeanor changes as she watches the dark purple shot swirl in the glass.

"Thank you," she says as she smiles up at the waiter.

"Cheers." I tilt my shot toward her in jest and down it before she can say otherwise. No salutes to the dead, or to anything else for that matter.

When my glass hits the table, Addison's is just reaching her lips.

Everything about the way she drinks it turns me on. From the way her slender fingers hold the glass, to the way her throat moves as she swallows.

A million images of how she'd look as she sucks my cock are going through my head until she speaks again.

"You make me feel ..." she trails off and hesitates to continue.

"Scared?" I offer her. I'm used to making certain people feel that way. Only when I need them to remember what I'm capable of.

"No ... unworthy." I'm struck by her candor.

"If you think that, it's because you've come to that conclusion on your own."

"You've always made me think that. Even back when I was with

Tyler." My spine stiffens hearing her bring him up so casually this time. Like it's easy to use his name in conversation.

"Your bruschetta," the waiter says, setting the plate down in the center of the table. I've never wanted to kill a waiter for delivering an appetizer before. Not until this moment.

He starts to speak again and I cut him off. "We're good here, thank you." My words are rushed and hard and I pray for his sake he takes the fucking hint.

My gaze moves from him to Addison, and her expression makes me regret it.

"You made me think that when I got here." Addison looks as if she's debating on eating. I guess the topic has ruined her appetite. It takes me a second to remember what she even said ... *unworthy*.

"You were late."

"I got here as soon as I could," she protests weakly. As if she's truly apologetic and the part that pisses me off the most is that I know she is.

"If you don't want me to be angry, then don't make me wait." I'm wound tighter and tighter by the second. It's amazing how a girl like Addison can tempt my self-control.

"You didn't have to wait. You can go," she retorts, saying each word while staring straight into my eyes. Daring me.

I smile. "I don't want to leave."

The anger in her features softens at my response. "I just hit traffic."

A heavy breath comes and goes as I settle back in my seat, watching for her reaction. This tit for tat is different for me. "It's fine," I tell her, hoping to end it. And move back to the plan.

"Why do you look at me like that?" she asks me and I still.

"How is it that I look at you?" I ask her to clarify. It's usually so easy to manipulate others into seeing me how I need them to. But Addison is observant beyond measure. She always has been. And she's always been different.

"Like you don't trust me. Or maybe you don't know what to expect from me."

I shrug. "I don't trust anyone. Don't take it personal."

She laughs and her shoulders shake slightly. "Maybe that's because of the people you hang out with?" she suggests and quirks a brow at me.

"I don't hang out with anyone." I answer her simply, with no emotion. Merely stating a truth.

She hums a response and reaches out for a piece of the toasted bread. As she bites into it, the bread crunches loudly and diced tomatoes fall into her hand. She actually blushes, and after she swallows she says defensively, "You should eat some, it's weird with you just watching me."

I let a rough chuckle vibrate up my chest. "I'm not hungry."

"I hate being rude and eating it all myself, but the alcohol is already hitting me."

Good. I don't say the thought out loud.

As she wipes her hands on her napkin, I ask her, "What is it that you want from me, Addison?" My hands clench under the table as I wait. I know exactly what I want from her. To fuck her out of my system. To be done with an obsession from long ago.

She shoots me a sweet, genuine smile and the blush grows hotter on her face. "I think it's the alcohol talking."

Her smile is addictive and I feel my own lips twitch up into a lopsided grin. "Why's that?"

"Because I want to tell you I've always wondered what it would be like to kiss you."

I feel myself swallow. I feel everything in this moment. Watching her blush and smile at me like that, I want more of it. I don't know if it's the vodka, the tequila or the wine. Maybe a combination of the three. But whatever's making her blush, she needs more of it.

My heart beats rapidly and my cock hardens to the point where it's nearly unbearable.

As she covers her face with her hands, the waiter walks by casually and I reach out, fisting his shirt and stopping him in his tracks.

The look on his face is a mix of shock and fear. But I'm quick to loosen my grip and tell him, "More shots."

CHAPTER 11

Addison

*W*hen I'm drunk, I have some odd thoughts. Some do make sense. For instance, how many shots did we have? That one seems like a logical thought, and I'm not sure of the exact answer, but at least three. Which is probably three too many but with how tense and awkward I was at the start of dinner, maybe three was just the right number.

Also, what happened to my car? I should be concerned about that. But I'm drunk, so walking seems smart. I keep my feet moving, one after the other even though I sway slightly. Only slightly though.

The thought that matters the most and the one I keep coming back to is whether or not Daniel can see how my hands keep trembling.

I'm sure the heat in my cheeks is obvious. And the butterflies in my stomach aren't staying where they ought to. They fly up and mess with my heart. Fluttering wildly and with an anxiousness that makes it feel like they're caged and trying to escape.

Maybe it's normal for what I'm doing.

When you want to kiss someone who's obviously a dick, it makes sense that your body would feel anxious and like you should run, right? Not to mention I'm sure he's still dealing. When your family's business is crime, you don't exactly walk away from that life. This heated nervousness won't leave me. I can't stop fidgeting with my hands and I'm sure it's ridiculous, but what else could be expected of me?

And then there's the fact that he's my ex's brother. An ex who's gone. And in many ways, it's because of me. It should make me feel worse than I do. But in a lot of ways, it feels the same way as running has. Only this time, I'm running to Daniel. A man I've dreamed for so long would comfort me and tell me these feelings were alright.

Obviously, that never happened. And I'm not sure it ever will.

There's a part of my mind that won't stop picking at that fact. A part that wonders how Daniel can even stand to be around me. A part that wonders if he's only toying with me. Like he's waiting to get his revenge and tell me how he truly feels.

And that's the part that scares me when I look up at him. I don't care how many times he'll tell me that no one blames me. How could they not?

I don't know what's happening, but I'm too afraid to stop, because I really want to find out. I'm too eager to finally know what it feels like to be wanted by him.

"You're so nervous," he says as if he's amused.

"Aren't you?"

His smile dims and he runs his hand through his hair, looking to his left at the stop sign. "Let's go to my place."

We're standing on the corner of Church and Fifth and I know I just need to go six blocks and I'll be two streets over from my apartment building ... I think. There are bus stops everywhere in this college town. So even if I get lost, I could find my way back home by just hopping on a bus.

"Your place?" I question him while squinting at the signs. I'm more than a little tipsy. But everything feels so good.

"Let's go," he answers and then takes my hand in his, pulling me across the street even though the sign at the crosswalk is still red.

"Still a rule breaker," I tease and I think that one is from the alcohol. I must find it funnier than he does though, because once we're on the other side, I'm the one smiling at my little joke while he stands there. Staring at me like he's not sure what to do with me.

"So you aren't nervous?" I ask him, daring to broach the subject again. I don't mind what he does to me. I crave it. And I'll be damned if he tells me he doesn't want me. I can see it in his eyes.

But what exactly he wants me for? That I have yet to know for sure.

A good fuck seems to be first on the list though. And I can't argue with that.

"I don't get nervous."

"Everyone gets nervous." The words slip out of my mouth and I tell him about a study my friend Rae told me about. She's a psychology major and she told me about public speakers and how even professional public speakers' adrenaline levels spike when they get on the stage. Everyone gets nervous. "There's no denying it."

"If you say so, Addison." That's all I get from him as the night air seems to get colder and I shiver. That's when I notice he's still holding my hand.

"This doesn't make you nervous? It doesn't make you question if ... if we should be doing this?" I lift up our clasped hands and he lets me, but he doesn't stop walking.

"Why shouldn't we?" he responds, but I hear the hard edge in his voice. *He knows.*

"There are so many reasons," I tell him and look straight ahead.

"Can I tell you a secret?" he whispers and the way he does it makes me giggle. A silly little girl giggle that would embarrass me if I wasn't on the left side of tipsy.

"Anything," I breathe.

"I was jealous that Tyler got to have you."

I nearly stumble and my smile slips. That erratic beating in my chest makes me want to reach up and pound on my heart to knock it off.

He continues once I get my footing back. "You were too young and Tyler got to you first."

I walk with my lips parted, but not knowing what to say or do.

Daniel's arm moves to my waist as his steps slow and I look up to see a row of houses. Cute little houses a few blocks from the university campus. They're the type of houses that come equipped with white picket fences and for the second time in fifteen minutes, I nearly trip.

"How drunk are you?" Daniel questions with a serious tone.

"Sorry, not that drunk," I answer him as we walk up the paved drive to the front door of a cute house with blue shutters. My heart won't knock it off, but I ignore it and change the subject. "This is your place?"

"Just renting."

I nod my head and as much as that makes sense, it's also one less thing to question. And now I find myself on the front steps of Daniel's place, with his hand on mine. Drunk after I've confessed to him how I feel.

Not the smartest thing I've ever done, and not the best decision I've made in my life.

But maybe I'll wake up in five minutes, and this will just be another one of my dreams.

My breathing comes in pants as Daniel lets his hand travel lower down my back and I instantly heat everywhere for him. My heart pounds and my blood pressure rises. I'm almost afraid of how my body is reacting so intensely. He has to see it, but if he does, he doesn't let on.

I don't need Rae or a shrink or anyone to tell me I'm going to regret this. I know that already.

Maybe I can blame it on the alcohol.

Or the sudden flood of memories.

Sleep deprivation, that's a good excuse too.

I don't care what I blame it on. So long as it happens. I wanted him for so long, even if it was from a distance. An unrequited and forbidden lust, not love. I refuse to believe it was love.

I lost the chance long ago to have what I always wanted. There's no way I won't push for it now.

I watch as Daniel reaches for the doorknob but stops, dropping his hand and directing his gaze to me.

"What are you thinking?" Daniel asks me and instinctively I look up at him, swallowing hard and licking my lips. I love how his eyes flicker to them and I hesitantly reach up, spearing my fingers through his hair.

And he lets me.

He lowers his lips and gently brushes them against mine although he doesn't kiss me yet. The lingering scents of whiskey and vodka mingle with my lust and love of bad decisions, giving me a heady feeling.

"I ALWAYS KNEW you were bad for me," I whisper against his lips as he bends down to kiss me. To actually press his hot lips against mine this time. His tongue demands entrance, licking against the seam of my lips and I grant him his wish. The heated kiss is short-lived and I'm left breathless.

I can feel his smile as he pulls away, taking the key from his pocket and licking his lower lip. I love how he does it like that. Slow and sensual and like he's hiding a secret that thrills him to no end.

"Bad for you doesn't even begin to cover it, Addison."

CHAPTER 12

Daniel

*B*arely contained.

Everything about me is barely contained. All I can think about is ripping off Addison's clothes and finally getting inside her tight cunt. I know she wants me. She's sighing softly every time I let my skin touch hers, filling the night air with her little pants of need.

Tiny touches. It started out as a way to tease her as we walked back to the house I'm renting. Little caresses that made me smile at her desperation.

She's so responsive. So needy.

I can't fucking stand it.

I've always known I was selfish. It's something my father said I inherited from him. He looked at me with pride when he said it too.

Tonight I'm going to take advantage of that particular trait of mine.

The front door swings open and it's pitch black inside. I don't waste my time stumbling for a light in the foyer.

I'm fucking her in my bed. I've already decided that.

"Daniel--" Addison gasps my name as I pick her up with one arm, forcing her legs to wrap around my hips. The door slams shut and I lock it as I crush my lips against hers.

My name. She's gasping my name. She'll scream it too. Hearing that hauntingly sweet voice say my name as if it's the only word meant to fall from her lips is everything I've ever wanted. Fucking music to my ears.

She moans into my mouth and then pulls away to breathe, her neck arching as I press my stiff erection against her heat, pushing her into the door and nipping at her neck.

"Upstairs," I groan against her hot skin although she doesn't have a choice in the matter. I've only said it to remind myself that I'm not fucking her here.

Not just yet. Only seconds away. Only seconds.

I take the stairs two at a time, making her cling to me. My heart feels as though it's losing control, beating chaotically. All the blood in my body must be in my dick. Her lips crash against my neck over and over and her nails dig into my shoulders through my shirt.

"Daniel," she moans and my name on her lips is a sin. I kick the bedroom door open and moonlight is shining through the blinds, giving me everything I need to see all of this.

I want to remember every detail. I can barely breathe and the alcohol is coursing through my blood, but I will remember every fucking detail of this night.

The bed groans with her surprised gasp as I toss her onto it and pull my shirt over my shoulders. She's still trying to get her balance as I kick off my pants and crawl on the bed to get to her. My breaths are coming in short and frantic. I'd be embarrassed, but Addison is just the same. She's just as eager and there isn't a thing in this world that could make me feel more desire than the way she stares back at me with nothing but lust.

Something tears as I pull at her dress, ripping it off her shoulders and down her body. Before I take her panties off her to join the puddle of clothes by the bed, I cup her hot pussy as I kiss her again. And this time it's me that moans into her mouth.

My dick is already impossibly hard, and precum is leaking from me at the feel of the silken fabric beneath my fingers, hot and damp with her arousal.

I don't bother to take them off gently. But I never thought I would either. Shredding them with my hands, I ignore her gasp of surprise and quickly lower my mouth to her cunt.

She falls back onto the mattress, spearing her fingers through my hair as I lick her from her entrance to her clit.

So fucking sweet. Sweeter than the shots. Sweeter than the trace of wine on her lips as she kissed me.

There's not enough time in a single night for everything I want to do to her. I barely pull myself off her clit to shove two fingers inside of her. I'm not gentle as I finger fuck her, thrusting as deep as I can go.

Her back arches, threatening to pull her pussy away from me, but I pin her hip down and curl my fingers up to stroke against her front wall. The sweet, strangled moans are everything I need and everything I've ever wanted.

I pause for only a second to watch her reaction. How her eyes are half-lidded but she's staring at me. Her dark green eyes meet mine and I press my thumb to her swollen nub to see her throw her head back in pleasure. Her pussy clenches around my fingers with need.

"So tight," I say with reverence.

"It's been a while," she breathes out while writhing.

· · ·

I almost ask how long. *Almost.*

There's a small voice in the back of my head that keeps hissing that she doesn't belong to me and when she utters those words, I'm acutely aware of how my brother had her first.

He might have been her first, but I'll ruin her.

I'll make her mine and make her forget about any other man who's touched her.

My dick throbs with a nearly unbearable pain from the desire to be inside her. To thrust into her and take her exactly how I've been picturing since I saw her four nights ago.

My fingers wrap around her throat, and at the same time I palm my dick.

"I want you to look at me," I tell her although I'm breathing heavily. I feel her swallow against my grip and then she nods. Lining up my dick, I press the head between her folds and she shudders beneath me.

Her soft moan vibrates against my hand and then I slam all of me inside of her. Every bit of me, and I watch her eyes widen and her mouth drop open with a sharp gasp.

Fuck! She feels too good and she immediately spasms around my dick. I can't move or breathe. If I do, I'll cum with her without a second thought.

It takes every ounce of control I have to keep my eyes on hers. To watch her so I can remember this forever.

Her body trembles as she tries to bow her back, but I'm holding her down, making her take it all. Her hands reach up to her neck. Her nails are digging into my fingers as I thrust again and again, tightening my grip but still letting her breathe. *Yes!* I love how she lets me own her body. *Mine. All mine.*

Her cunt tightens around my cock to the point where it's fucking strangling me the way I am her. The room is filled with the noises of me fucking her relentlessly.

I loosen my grip as I pound into her and she sucks in a deep breath. Feeling her pant and struggle against me, my lips slam against hers. With her chest pressed against me, I can feel her heart beating just as hard against mine.

Her nails rake down my arms and I can tell she isn't sure if she wants to cling to me for dear life or shove me away. I lift my lips from hers to breathe and she screams out my name with reverence. Her reaction only makes me fuck her harder, with every ounce of energy in me. *Mine.*

My fingers dig into her hips as I keep up my ruthless pace, each stroke taking me higher and higher to a pleasure that nearly makes me cum. My toes curl and I struggle to breathe, but I put every bit of energy into looking into her eyes.

As she screams out my name, her teeth clench and her heels dig into my ass. Her nails break the skin at my lower back as she cums violently on my dick.

My body begs me to give in and bury my head in the crook of her neck as I cum inside of her, but I can't. Not yet.

Mine. The word slips from my lips as she screams out my name again. Her back arches while she struggles beneath me, shoving against my chest.

"Look at me," I command her as I shove myself deep within her, all the way to the hilt, pausing for the first time since I've entered her. My dick slams against the back of her warmth, stretching her and forcing her lips to make a perfect "O."

Her eyes meet mine, dilated with a wildness to them I've never seen. I brush my pubic hair against her clit, angling just slightly and rocking. Just to see how much she can take.

"Daniel," she whimpers my name as she thrashes her head from side to side, cumming again even though I've stilled inside of her. Her pussy clenches and tries to milk my cock. And I groan from deep in my chest at the sensation. "Fuck," I mutter then hold my breath and tense my body.

Not yet. I can't cum yet.

It's only once her release has passed and her body is still that I move again.

One more. One more is all I can take.

My forehead rests on the mattress above her shoulder and I gently kiss her soft skin although she flinches from the sensation. Even that's too much for her. She's already cumming again.

I ride through her orgasm, pounding into her heat and with each thrust the word mine escapes between my clenched teeth.

Even as I cum deep inside of her, not breathing, not moving with the only exception being the pulsing of my dick. Even in that moment I whisper the word against the shell of her ear. *Mine.*

* * *

I'VE NEVER BEEN able to sleep well.

Some people aren't meant to be heavy sleepers.

So instead of trying to sleep, I watch Addison in the dark. My eyes adjust easily and with the moonlight shining through the slats of the blinds, I can see every feature of hers clearly. I can see the gentle rise and fall of her chest with her steady breathing and the little dip in her collar that begs me to kiss it.

I'd forgotten how badly I wanted her all those years ago. The thrill of having her near and the desire to hold on to her outweighed the memories. But seeing her beauty so close and the beast inside me sated, there's no denying the attraction.

No one has ever held my attention like Addison. No one makes me forget like she does. Nothing else matters when she's near me. Only the need to make sure she knows that I see her, that I feel her, that I want her.

And now I have her.

A deep rumble of satisfaction leaves my chest. Addison mirrors me in her sleep, a sweet moan slipping through her lips as she nuzzles closer to me. But then she stiffens.

My body tenses at her reaction.

I watch her lashes flutter and the realization show in her expression. Shock is evident on her face as she slowly lifts up her body, bracing herself on one palm. Covering her chest with the sheet, her lips part and her forehead pinches. She clenches her thighs and I've never been so proud in my fucking life.

There's a warmth in my body, knowing how I took her as if her body was mine alone to ruin.

It's been hours, hours of me simply watching her so close to me and memorizing the curves of her body. And she can still feel me inside of her.

With the ghost of a whimper on her lips, she slowly slips off the mattress, ignoring how it dips and could wake me. As if she wouldn't mind me waking.

My heart stutters and the hint of happiness in my expression falls. She's leaving? The fuck she is.

"What are you doing?" My voice is sharp in the still night air and it startles her. But only enough that she turns to face me. With one hand splayed across her chest and the other covering her bare pussy, she looks from me to the pile of her clothes on the floor.

Seeing her naked, and even better, trying to hide that nakedness from me makes my spent dick hard in an instant. I'm already eager for more of her. The slit of my cock is wet with precum and my thick shaft twitches at the thought of taking her again. I can keep her here. She'll stay. I fucking know she will.

"I have to go," she speaks softly, her words a murmur.

"You don't have to do anything but get back in my bed," I command her and then let my eyes roam down her body, making sure she knows exactly what I want. "Lie down."

She hesitates, but only for a moment. And then she lowers herself slowly, first leaning on her elbow and then nestling into the covers. That warmth comes back as soon as she's back where she belongs. The trace of the fear of losing her and the sickening feeling that she's leaving are both still present, but muted.

As soon as she's settled, staring up at me in the darkness with the moonlight highlighting her face, I lean down and kiss her on the lips. Not a gentle kiss, and not a goodnight kiss either.

She's breathless when I pull back and my own chest heaves for air, but I speak calmly, with the control I've come to expect.

"Spread your legs for me," I tell her and before her back is even settled, she does as she's told. Her thighs part so easily as a blush covers her skin and her eyes shine with the same hunger I remember from so long ago.

I take her by surprise, shoving my hand between her thighs and thrusting my fingers into her cunt. Slamming my lips down on hers, I silence her screams. Her back bows and she squirms under me, trying to get away from the intensity.

Pinning her hip down, I keep her where I want her and finger fuck her until she's screaming into my mouth. My teeth sink into her lip and then nip along her jaw, all while I'm enjoying her cries of pleasure and how tight her pussy gets when it spasms around my thick fingers. With my thumb on her clit, I don't stop until she's breathless and can no longer make a sound as she cums on my hand. Her body's still trembling when I finally thrust myself deep inside of her.

And it's my name on her lips.

My dick wrapped in her warmth.

My bed she sleeps in.

All mine.

CHAPTER 13

Addison

Five years ago

I know I should stop this. My belly aches with this disgust. I
hate myself for it.

For using Tyler as a distraction.

*We go out every day, taking pictures of all sorts of things. The project
is over, but he keeps asking if I want to go. And I never tell him no.*

It's better than going back to the Brauns' place.

*"Let's go over there," Tyler says and points toward a run-down path in
the woods behind the park. We're at the far end of the park and I know
this area. In front of us is the creek and if we go left and walk half a mile
or so, we'll end up at the highway line and can follow that back to the
parking lot. There are running trails along the way too. Although I don't
like to run. I just walk and take pictures. I like doing that with Tyler.*

One step to follow him. Two steps and he reaches for my hand.

I slip mine inside of his and he squeezes tight when he holds it. It's a little thing, but he really holds my hand like he means it. And that sick feeling in my stomach feels like nothing compared to the bitter-sweet sensation in my heart. I'm not sure if it's really pain or what it is.

I want more of it though.

A part of me knows it's selfish. That part's quiet as fallen branches crack beneath our weight and we stop at a clearing on the edge of the creek.

"It's beautiful," I whisper, staring out at the bubbling brook. It's the softest shade of blue although it gets darker where it's deeper.

"Like you," he says and gives me a charming smile. When he lets go of my hand to take his jacket off and lays it on the ground, those feelings mix, and the resulting brew is something I don't know how to handle.

But Tyler knows my secrets, and he's seen me in those moments I wish I didn't have. The ones where I cry and sometimes it's hard to know what's caused the outburst.

I swear I used to be happy. I used to be normal. But I'll never be normal again.

Although Tyler's jacket is laid flat, he sits next to it in the dirt and beckons me, patting the fabric and looking up at me with big puppy dog eyes. He doesn't ask much of me, but I can't help feeling like today may be different.

My shoulders hunch in a little as I sit down and tuck my hair behind my ear.

It takes everything in me to look at him. To look at Tyler and try to gauge his intention.

"Do you want to sleep with me?" I ask him bluntly.

He lets out a bark of a laugh and rests his forearms on his knees as he looks out onto the creek. Looking back at me he answers, "I read once, I think in a biology book, that teenage guys are horny as fuck."

I can't help the smile that cracks on my face at his joke. That's the way Tyler handled anything serious. He'd just make a joke and deflect.

"Seriously though," I say then wipe the palms of my hands on my

knees instead of looking at him as I continue, "I don't get why you keep coming out with me."

He shrugs. "I like spending time with you," he tells me.

"So you don't want to get into my pants."

"I definitely want to fuck you."

I'm shocked by his candor. Tyler's ... careful around me. I feel like he considers each word carefully before speaking to me. Like if he says the wrong thing, I'd run. And that's not too far from the truth.

"You haven't tried anything ... though."

"Don't confuse my patience for a lack of interest." The second the words slip from him, Tyler lets out a genuine laugh. "Of all the dirty things I could say, that's what gets you to blush?"

It's only then that I feel the heat in my cheeks. It matches other places too.

Minutes pass with both of us taking small glances at each other, watching the sunset descend behind the forest with shades of orange and red in the clear blue sky. He even tosses a few twigs and rocks into the creek. He tries to skip them, but he's not very good at it.

"I think you'd like it if I kissed you here." He almost mumbles his words when he catches me staring at him. They're spoken so low and nearly absently.

His lips brush along my neck and desire sweeps through my body unexpectedly. Both of my hands move up to his chest and I push away from his overwhelming touch with my lips parted, my breath stolen.

He blinks away the lust in his gaze and slowly a smile forms on his face. "I knew you'd like it."

As I bite my lip, he leans forward cautiously, judging my reaction and then he does it again. His lips kiss over every part of my neck and up to the soft spot behind my ear.

...

AND THAT'S why I slept with Tyler. He said and did everything that made sleeping with him feel like it was right and meant to be.

As soon as we started walking back to his truck, that sick feeling returned. And I began to think that tomorrow he'd be different. That he'd gotten what he wanted, so he wouldn't want to be with me anymore.

But I was wrong again. He held me tighter. Talked to me sweeter. And loved me harder than before.

Tyler was patient. He didn't look at me as if I was broken, but he treated me like breaking me would be the worst sin in the world.

I could never tell him no.

Even if I still thought of his brother in ways I shouldn't have.

* * *

YOU SHOULDN'T COMPARE LOVERS.

Certainly not brothers.

It was a fantasy come alive to feel Daniel's skin against mine. To finally know what it's like to writhe under him.

But that's all he can ever be. A fantasy.

One that I'm prolonging by letting the days blend together in a whirlwind of alcohol and sex. He messages me where to meet and I go. We drink. We fuck. There are no more awkward conversations of our past, but the reminder stays deep in the pit of my stomach.

I'm not stupid. Daniel's no good. And this thing between us is merely two people giving in to a pipe dream we had long ago.

It's all-consuming and I wouldn't have it any other way.

But the moment this cloud of lust and bliss dissipates, I'll be left with the sobering truth.

I've given myself to a man who's only ever seen me as a plaything.

I've slept with someone who should truly hate me for being the reason his brother is dead.

And the events I've allowed to occur are something that should shame me for a lifetime.

There's no getting around those hard facts. But it's nice to ignore them for a while and in the moments when Daniel's with me, it feels different. It feels like nothing else exists.

And when your world is made of nothing but painful memories you're constantly trying to outrun, it's a relief for nothing else to exist.

Well, nothing but this flutter in my chest and this ache between my thighs. I love it. I love feeling this way even if nervousness and tiny bits of fear creep in.

It was better than I ever could have imagined. Even when I woke up alone in the morning. Even as I took the bus home with my hair a mess and still in the clothes from the night before.

A walk of shame had never felt so fucking good.

I bite down on my lip to keep the smile on my face from being too smug.

It was something I know I'll regret, but right now all I'm going to do is love this horrible mistake.

Over and over again.

The spoon clangs against the ceramic mug as I stir in the sugar for my tea. I need caffeine badly. I've slept soundly for the past three days, two of them in Daniel's bed, only to be woken up on occasion and fucked into the mattress. It feels good to be back at my apartment though, where I can rest undisturbed. He had a meet last night so I slept alone, which is a good thing. I'm too sore for any more of Daniel right now.

A smile graces my face as I lift the mug to my lips.

I blow across the top of the mug, breathing in the calming smell of the black tea and avoiding the hot steam. With my eyes closed I feel like I could go back to bed right now.

My little moment is interrupted by the sound of my phone going off. It's a distinct noise and I know exactly who it is by the tone. It's from an app that allows you to text people overseas for cheap. Which means it's Rae.

The mug hits the counter a little more aggressively than I'd like, sloshing a touch of tea on the counter as I reach for my phone.

"Shit," I mumble under my breath, but I don't bother with it. I need to talk to Rae.

How are you love? Miss you.

She always calls me *love*. She says things like *cheeky* and *cow* too. I love the diction of the United Kingdom and their accents. A very big part of me misses her and the small farm town she lives in. But it will never be home for me.

I message her back, *Miss you to pieces. How's your mom?*

I wait with my eyes on the screen and my lips pursed. She doesn't write back quickly so I busy myself with cleaning up the spill and having another sip of tea. Rae's mom is going through some health issues. I know it's been a pain in the ass for both of them. Or *arse* if it's Rae talking about it.

Mum's fine. Happy for now and enjoying the time off work. How have you been?

I start to text her everything from the very beginning, but then delete it. And then I try once more, but the words don't come out quite right. Before I can even message her anything, she texts again.

I'm thinking of going back to that bar in Leeds and having another go at the boy bands there. Made me think of you.

The reminder makes me smile and spreads a sense of warmth and ease through me. Enough that I reply simply, *I think I'm seeing someone. But I'm not sure if it's good or bad.*

"Seeing someone" might be a stretch. It's just fucking. I'm smart enough to know that.

She writes back quickly this time. *Spill it.*

You already know him. Well, of him. It's Daniel.

I feel a momentary pang of guilt, like I've betrayed him. As if saying what's between us out loud will ruin it. Because no one else will understand.

. . .

327

TYLER'S BROTHER?

I stare at her response and feel that spike of chagrin and shame I should have known was coming.

Yes.

It's all I can write back. The mug trembles slightly in my hands, but I ignore it, taking a drink although now the heat feels different on my lips. Less soothing and less comforting. Even if it isn't luke-warm yet.

Seeing him? she questions.

I put the mug back down and gather up the courage to try to make her understand. She knows everything. Including how I left Tyler because of what I felt for Daniel. What I thought was one-sided and an indication of how awful a person I was. All I had to do was love Tyler back. Instead I ruined what we were over dirty thoughts I couldn't stop.

We ran into each other. And I told him how I felt about him.

A moment passes, and then another. And that feeling in my gut and heart keeps at it. Twisting and squeezing until I feel wrung out. I wish I could say I don't care what she thinks about this. But she's the only person I have left. I'm careful not to get too close to anyone. Everyone I love dies. So it's best I don't let people in. Rae is the only exception.

How do you feel about it?

I let out a single chuckle, like a breath of a laugh at her response. I text back, *You sound like a shrink.*

You sound like you might need one.

Her response makes the small bit of relief wash away. *Maybe I do.*

I just worry about you, she texts me and then adds, *I know it has to bring back memories and other unpleasant things.*

It does. But it also feels like a relief in a way. And so much more than that.

Are you dating? she asks.

I roll my eyes at that question. She knows better. *I don't date.*

She sends back an emoji rolling its eyes and a genuine snicker leaves me.

Just take care of yourself, will you?

She's a good friend and I know better than to think she'd be anything other than concerned.

You burst my bubble, I tell her and I really mean it.

* * *

Five years ago

TYLER'S LIPS *slip down to the crook of my neck. He knows just the spot that makes me wet for him.*

My palms push against his chest and the motion makes my body sink deeper into the mattress beneath him.

"Spread your legs." He gives the command against my skin, making me hotter ... needier. But my eyes dart to the door and then back to him.

"But your brothers," I whisper as if my words are a secret.

Tyler pulls away, breathless and panting with need. He always makes love to me wildly. Like it's all he needs. Each time is quick, but he takes care of me first. I bite down on my bottom lip as he hovers over me and then looks over his shoulder at the door.

"They don't care," he tells me and I can only swallow the lump in my throat.

One brother cares. I know he does. He looks at me like I'm a whore whenever I stay over here. And I haven't even slept with Tyler under the Cross roof yet.

"I don't want them to think I'm staying over just so we can have sex."

"They don't think that." Tyler smiles and brushes the hair from my face as I pull the covers up closer around me. I still have my nightgown on; Tyler's just pulled the fabric up around my waist.

"What if they think I'm using you so I don't have to go back home?

Like I'm spreading my legs just so I can have a place to stay." I heard a girl say that at school a week ago and the thought hasn't left me. It's true I don't want to go back. But I'm not a whore either.

"I have to fucking beg you to stay here, Addie. They can hear that. They know that. And we've been dating for how long now?"

Almost six months to the day he first tapped on my shoulder in science class.

The uneasiness still doesn't leave me and I stare at the door until Tyler's hand cups my chin.

"We can be quiet," he whispers and lowers his lips to mine.

My eyes close and I let myself feel his warmth and comfort.

"Just kiss me," he tells me as he slips his hand between my legs, parting my thighs for him.

I keep my eyes shut and try to be quiet. My muffled moans carried through the walls though and so did the unmistakable sounds and steady rhythm of Tyler fucking me.

I know because of the way Daniel looked at me late that night when I snuck into the hall to use the bathroom.

My hand was on the doorknob when he opened his bedroom door. Caught in his heated gaze, I couldn't move; I couldn't breathe. He let his stare trail down my nightgown before looking back into my eyes.

I'll never forget the way my body heated for him and how my heart pounded. I thought he was going to punish me, to pin me against the wall and make me scream. That's the way he would have fucked me. The kind of sex where you can't keep quiet.

Instead of doing or saying anything, Daniel turned around, going straight back into his room.

I sat in the bathroom for the longest time, feeling like the worst thing in the world. Like a whore and a fraud and an ungrateful bitch.

I snuck out in my nightgown, with my clothes clenched into a ball in my hand and drove home as quickly as I could.

I didn't go back to the Cross house for weeks. And the next time I let Tyler fuck me in his bed, I wasn't quiet about anything.

CHAPTER 14

Daniel

* * *

It's cute how she keeps looking at me like she's waiting for me to walk away. Like how yesterday she was surprised that I told her to come over. I'll never forget the shy look on her face. How her eyes scanned mine and she was hesitant to come back in.

So long as I'm in this small town, she needs to be in my bed. Every second I can have her. Our one-night stand turned into one week ... turned into two.

I've waited for so long to have her. Did she think I'd have my fill of her so quickly?

As she stretches on my bed, the sheet slips and reveals more of her back, along with the curve of her waist.

I could get used to this. Waking up with her in my bed, going to sleep alongside her.

If I could keep her here forever, I would.

"That was nice," she whispers as she rolls back over and lays her hand on my bare chest. Her finger traces up to the dip below my throat then moves lower, and lower still. Stirring my already spent dick back to life.

"Be careful what you ask for," I warn her in a rough timbre as I hold back a groan.

I can feel her smile against my shoulder and then she laughs sweetly.

"I think I need a shower first," she says.

"You'll need another when I'm done with you." I don't miss the way her legs scissor under the sheets at my comment.

"Shower first," she says as if she's decided. Had I slept well at all last night, I'd slip my tongue between her thighs and convince her otherwise. But the meeting location changed yesterday and then again. It seems the message I've been waiting on Marcus to deliver has changed as well and Carter's on edge with what's coming our way.

The unwanted thought is what motivates me to get up. I've been in a daze with Addison. She's a distraction.

I crack my neck and stretch my arms before getting out of bed with a twisted feeling in my gut.

With my back to Addison, she traces the small scar on the bottom of my shoulder. A scar I've long since forgotten. There are a few really, but they're faint. Only one is easily seen.

"How'd you get that?" she asks me and I clench my jaw as I stand up.

She always liked my father. He was a good man ... to her at least. And maybe the family business wouldn't have survived if he hadn't been so hard on Carter and me.

"I popped off to my father," I explain, keeping it short and simple as I get off the bed and grab a pair of boxer briefs from the dresser. My voice sounds strained even to my own ears.

My dick's already hard and wanting more of her, but the unpleasant reminder of my childhood makes me want to bury

POSSESSIVE

myself in work. I have an encrypted file I should look over with details for a big shipment coming in next week. It includes a list of new hires and Carter always gets wary when it comes to new people unloading stock.

"You popped off?" she asks and I turn around to the sound of her saddened voice. My stomach twists when I see her expression. Like she can't believe my father would have ever struck me.

She has no idea.

"I should have known better." My words don't do a thing to change the look in her eyes and when they move from the thin scattering of silver scars on my back to my own gaze, all I see is sympathy. And I don't fucking want it. Not from anyone, and sure as fuck not from her.

"Leave it alone, Addison." I move back to the dresser for pants and a shirt, opening one drawer and slamming it shut before moving to the next.

"What did you say?" I hear her ask softly as I shut a third drawer, still not finding what I'm looking for. The fourth drawer slams shut harder than I intended.

"It doesn't matter." My response doesn't faze her.

"I wouldn't have thought he'd ever-"

"He saved that side of himself for Carter and me," I say, cutting her off sharply before I can stop myself. Apparently the anger is stronger than I thought. Up until now I assumed the animosity was buried with him when he died.

"I'm sorry," she says softly and it only amplifies my agitation.

The air is tense in the bedroom as I slip on a t-shirt and pajama pants, an old plaid flannel pair.

"Pass me one?" Addison asks, apparently ready to move on from the revelation that my father wasn't the saint Tyler made him out to be.

I almost toss the black cotton Henley toward the bed, but instead I walk it to her. Letting her take it from me and when she does, her slender fingers brush against mine.

333

There's nothing sexier than watching her pad around this place in nothing but my t-shirt. Her occupation means she can work anywhere, which means her ass is staying right here with me. *For now.*

Gripping her hand as she takes the shirt, I pull her closer to me and steal a quick kiss. And then another as I release her.

She props herself up on the bed, getting onto her knees and deepening the small kiss. As she bites gently on my bottom lip, she tangles both of her hands in my hair. I let myself fall forward, bracing my impact with one arm on either side of her.

She doesn't open her eyes until she gives me a sweet peck right where she bit me. Her green eyes stare back at me for only a moment before she closes them again and brushes the tip of her nose against mine.

My fucking heart is a bastard for wanting to believe the kiss has anything to do with the conversation we just had. But it flips in my chest as if that little nudge and the fact that her eyes were closed meant everything in the world.

I've always had a bastard heart when it comes to her.

"I have to work," I tell her and quickly bend down to plant a quick kiss on her temple. I'd better leave before I wind up doing nothing but staying in bed.

"So you don't want to come with me to check out the campus?"

"I'm not sure there's a polite way to say this, but fuck no." It amazes me how easy it is to be candid with Addison. Maybe it's because just like now, she isn't offended or taken aback. She simply takes what I have to give and smiles.

"So you think I shouldn't go here?" she asks and from her tone I know it's a loaded question.

"Why would you?" I offer in rebuttal.

She breaks eye contact and shrugs, picking at a thread on the comforter. "It seems like a business degree would make sense."

"You already have your business set up and it's successful, isn't it?"

"I'm doing well. How'd you know? You look me up?" she asks playfully, but I ignore her and the twinge in my chest.

"Then why bother?"

She peeks up at me over her shoulder with a defensive look on her face. "Well, why do you bother?"

Leaning forward, I lower my voice to answer her. "I don't. I'm not staying."

"You're going home?" she asks and the very idea of home doesn't quite sit right with me, but neither does the expression on her face. The hurt one that she can't hide although I'm not sure she would bother even if she was aware of how transparent her emotions are.

"I'm working and that might lead me back to where we grew up."

As I lower myself back onto the bed slowly, I question being so honest with her. The coy and curious nature I've come to enjoy from her turns timid. Like she's walking into dangerous territory.

"Should I ask?" Her voice is quiet and she doesn't look me in the eye.

"That depends on what you want to know." She hasn't asked a single question since we've started hooking up. She's smart enough to know. Maybe smart enough to know not to ask too.

Finally, her gorgeous green eyes look back at me and she presses, "Would you tell me the truth if I did? Tyler never did."

"Tyler wasn't ever involved in anything serious." I ignore how everything in me turns cold at the mention of his name. Being with Addison ... knowing he was her first. It hurts to swallow as she keeps talking. Especially after the memory of my father. *I don't like to remember.*

She answers me, "Your version of serious and mine are different, I think."

The time passes as I fail to come up with a response. She doesn't need to know about any of this shit. It would be better if she didn't.

335

Another second. Another thought.

"Is that why you left him?" I ask her and although it hurts deep down in my core, I need to know if her idea of what he did for work is what made her leave him. I don't say his name though.

"I don't want to talk about that night." Her answer comes out sharper than I expect. With a bite and a threat not to question her. It only makes me that much more curious.

"The night you broke things off?" I ask her to clarify. That night isn't the one that haunts me. That's not the night that's unspeakable to me.

Addison stands on shaky legs with her back to me. Finding her packed bag and unzipping it as she speaks.

"I just don't like thinking about how the last couple of times I saw him I was turning him away," she says with a tinge of emotion I don't like to hear. The kind of emotion that's indicative of love.

A love I know for certain he had for her.

"You weren't the first seventeen-year-old girl to end a high school relationship," I remind her and also me. It was puppy love. That's all it ever was.

"Yeah well, I didn't know what it would lead to," she says and her voice trembles as she slips on a pair of underwear and sweatpants.

I'm not sure I want to know the answer, but I have to ask. "So if you could go back?"

Addison's quiet at my question and I walk toward her although her back is still to me. "If you could go back, you'd still be with him?" Her hesitation makes my muscles tighten. My fist clenches as a tic in my jaw spasms.

I've been kidding myself to think otherwise. Of course she'd be with him and not me. My breathing comes in ragged as she answers.

"If he were here now--" she starts to say, but I cut her off.

"He's not, and he never will be." The anger simmers. Everything that's been pushed down for so long rises up quickly. All the years of control and denial.

The hate that my brother was taken from me. And the pain of knowing it was my fault and that I've never told a soul. I could tell her now. But I never would. It's too late to confess.

Addison turns to face me with wide eyes. "Don't say that."

Maybe it's the denial, the guilt that plagues me. But I sneer at her, "You think it's easy for me? You got over his death far easier than I did."

I don't see the slap coming until the sting greets my cheek. My hand instinctively moves to where she's struck me. I flex my jaw and feel the burn radiate down the side of my face.

Her beautiful countenance is bright red with anger and her eyes are narrowed. I've never seen her this full of rage. Never.

Her hands tremble as she yells at me.

"You don't know how many nights his death haunted me!"

I do.

Her voice wavers and I know she's on the verge of tears. The kind that paralyze you because they're so overwhelming. But instead of giving in to grief, she screams at me

"You don't know how I blamed myself to the point where I begged God to just kill me and let me take his place." She takes each breath in heavily.

I do.

Adrenaline rushes through my blood. The hate, the shame, and the unrelenting guilt surge within me. And I can't say anything back. I can't have this conversation with her.

When I don't say anything, when I feel myself shutting down, she snaps. "Fuck you," she tries to yell at me but her voice cracks as she grabs her bag and storms out of the room.

She doesn't have her shoes on and she's not wearing a bra under my shirt.

"You're not leaving?" It's meant to be a statement but the question is there in the undertone. All because I said she got over his death easier than I did? It's a fact. I fucking know it is.

"Yes, I am," she snaps as she turns around just as I walk up behind her. I have to halt my pace and take half a step back as she cranes her neck to bite out, "How dare you tell me that it was easy for me."

"You don't know-" I try to tell her that she has no idea how well I relate to her pain, but she doesn't let me finish.

"Leave me alone."

She angrily brushes under her eyes as she quickly descends the stairs with me right behind her. The front door is right there and she makes a beeline for it.

She's out of her fucking mind if she thinks I'm letting her leave here like this. "Addison. Wait a fucking minute."

"Don't tell me what to do," she yells back and tries to whip open the door. My palm hits it first, slamming it back shut.

"You're not leaving like this," I warn her. My muscles are coiled, but it's the fear making me wound so tight. She's leaving. And she's not coming back.

I can feel it in every inch of me.

"Yes, I am," she replies, though with shaken confidence.

"The fuck you are." My words are pushed through clenched teeth.

"If you respect me in any sense of the word, you will let me leave. Right now."

"Addison, don't do that."

"I mean it, Daniel. I need to be alone right now."

"I want to be there for you." I don't know how true the words are until I've said them. And oh, how fucking ironic they are.

"Well, you can't." She shuts me down.

Her green eyes stare up at me and all I can see is the same look she'd give Tyler when he was being clingy. The look that so obviously said she needed time and that she was overwhelmed. I get it now why he always hovered.

I'm afraid if I let her go now, she's never coming back. I can't lose her. Not again.

"I'm coming by tonight." I give her the only compromise I'm capable of.

I lower my arm but she doesn't respond. With a swift tug she pulls the door open and walks out, bare feet and all.

I stand in the doorway and watch her reach in her bag for flip-flops then put them on at the corner of the street.

She keeps looking over her shoulder, maybe to see if I'm coming for her.

And I am. She knows better than to think otherwise.

But I'll let her get a head start.

* * *

Five years ago

HE HOVERS. Constantly hovering.

We all know why. It's so fucking obvious every time he brings her around.

She's waiting to run.

She's cute and sweet, but there's something about her that makes it almost painfully apparent that a kid like Tyler could never hold on to her. It would take a man to keep that cute little ass.

Just thinking that as I stand in the kitchen, watching the two of them in the dining room makes me feel like a pervert. She's only sixteen, although her curves make her look like more of a woman and less of a girl.

He gives her little touches as they sit next to each other watching something on his laptop. Her laugh makes him smile.

He's foolish to think she'll stay with him. Girls like that don't stay with men like us. He can keep pretending if he wants to. He can keep bringing her home and cuddling up with her because he doesn't know how easy it is for people to shove you away.

She'll shove, she'll push, she'll leave. And I can't blame her.

Her shoulders shake as she laughs and leans into him. His broad smile grows and like the kid he is, he wraps his arm around her shoulders.

The smile dies when Addison leans forward and away.

He doesn't know she needs space.

It's not his fault though. Tyler has a lot to learn. Hard life lessons.

Like the ones I've had to endure.

Cancer took our mother and left us a bitter father who likes the belt a little too much. Not to mention a pile of bills that a single person couldn't possibly afford. It's taken years to turn my father's small-time dealing into a thriving business. Years of destroying what little life I had left.

"Let's not," I hear Addison say and when I look up her eyes are on me. Caught in her gaze, I hold her there, but it doesn't last long. Tyler's always there to reclaim her attention.

A sense of loss runs through me, followed by disgust.

I haven't been a good person in so long, maybe I've forgotten how. Or maybe I never was a good person to begin with.

"You and Carter going out tonight?" my father asks as he interrupts the view I have of Tyler and **his** girlfriend.

It's only ever Carter and me. Never my other brothers. We're the oldest, after all. The ones who need to pick up my father's slack. The ones who pay these bills and make the business what it is.

We're the ones who have to shoulder the burden. And really it's Carter's hard work and brutal business tactics that make any of this possible. It sure as fuck isn't my father. He's good at hiding his pain. But every time he remembers my mother, I know he copes with a different addiction. One that makes using that belt easier.

Only ever for Carter and me though.

"Yeah," I tell him and wait for him to hint that he wants us to bring some of the supply back for his personal use. Friday marks four years since our mother's been gone and I know a relapse is coming. He'll disap-

pear for days, maybe even weeks. It was worse when she first passed. I guess I should be grateful that he's better now than he was then.

"Be careful coming home. I heard there's a patrol on the east side so maybe come up the back way after you get the shipment."

A second passes and then another before I nod.

Some days I wonder if he cares for me anymore. He was always a hard man. But when Mom passed, he was nothing but angry. The years have maybe changed him to be less full of hate. But it doesn't mean he has anything in him to take its place.

I give him another nod and look past him as the sound of Tyler and Addison getting up from the table catches my attention.

My father glances over his shoulder in the direction I'm staring and then turns back to me. He only shakes his head and makes to leave, but I hear him mutter, "She isn't yours."

I hate him even more in this moment. Because he's right.

The sad, pretty girl doesn't belong to me.

No matter how much I think she'd take my pain away.

CHAPTER 15

Addison

I wonder what the girl I used to be would think of me.

The girl who still had both her parents and a life worth living for.

I think she'd make up excuses for my poor behavior. She'd say I was sad, but she has no idea how pathetic I am.

Grief isn't static. It's not a point on a chart where you can say, "Here, at this time, I grieved." Because grief doesn't know time. It comes and goes as it pleases, then small things taunt it back into your life. The memories haunt you forever and carry the grief with them. Yes, grief is carried. That's a good way to put it.

I pull a pillow on the sofa into my lap and stare at the television screen although my eyes are puffy and sore and I don't even know what's on.

Playing with the small zipper on the side of the pillow absently, I think about what happened. How it all unraveled.

I think it started with his scar, the past being brought up. But just like scars, some of our past will never leave us. The old wounds were showing. That's what it was really about.

I always knew Daniel was broken in ways Tyler wasn't. But I didn't know about his father. I didn't know any of that. I don't even know if Tyler knew.

But what happened between Daniel and me, that … I don't even have a word for it. It was like a light switch being turned off. Everything was fine, better than fine. Then darkness was abrupt and sudden, with no way to escape.

MY EYES DART to the screen as a commercial appears and its volume is louder than whatever show or movie was playing. I sniffle as I flick the TV off and look at my phone again.

I'm sorry. Daniel messaged me earlier and I do believe he is, but I don't know if that will be enough. My happy little bubble of lust has been popped and the self-awareness isn't pretty.

I'm sorry too. It's all I can say back to him and he reads it. But there's nothing left for either of us to say now. I wonder if this will be the end of us.

We can't have a conversation about the bad things that have happened. That's the simple truth. It's awkward, tense. And we can't escape the moments coming up in conversation. There's no way getting around that.

It's easy to blame it on my past. On things I had no control over and things I can't change.

It's a lot like what I did when I left Dixon Falls. But really I was running, just like I had been since the day my parents died. Tyler was a distraction, a pleasant one that made me feel something other than the agonizing loneliness that had turned me bitter.

And then there was Daniel. He left me breathless and wanting, and that's a hard temptation to run away from.

I'm woman enough to admit that.

So sure, I can blame it on our past.

It's easy to blame it on grief, but it's still a lie. It's because neither of us can talk about what happened.

I startle at the vibration of the phone on the coffee table.

My heart beats hard with each passing second; all the while a long-lost voice in the back of my head begs me to answer a simple question. *What am I doing?*

Or maybe the right question is, *What did I expect?*

My gaze drifts across each photo on the far wall of the living room and it stops on three. Each of the photos meant something more when I took them. There are a little more than a dozen in total. Each photographed in a moment of time when I knew I was changing.

I keep them hung up because they look pretty from a distance; the pictures themselves are pleasant and invoke warm feelings.

More than that, the photos are a timeline of moments I never want to forget. I refuse to let myself forget.

But the three I keep staring at are so relevant to how I feel in this moment.

The first photo was taken at my parents' grave. Just a simple picture really, small forget-me-nots that had sprouted in the early spring. There was a thin layer of snow on the ground, but they'd already pushed through the hard dirt and bloomed. Maybe they knew I was coming and wanted to make sure I saw them.

In the photo you can't even tell they've bloomed on graves. The photo is cropped short and close. But I'll always remember that the flowers were on my parents' grave.

Tyler was with me when I took it. It wasn't the first, second or even the third time we'd gone out. But it was the first time I'd cried in such a long time and the one friend I'd met and trusted was there to witness it. I thought I was being sly asking him to drive to a cemetery hours away. Back to where I'd grown up. I hadn't been there in so long, but on that day when Tyler said we could go anywhere, I told him about the angel statue at the front of a cemetery I'd once seen that would be perfect for the photography project.

I didn't tell him that my parents were buried there, but he found out shortly after we arrived.

Part of me will forever be his for how he handled that day. For letting me cry and holding me. For not forcing me to talk, but being there when I was ready to.

Like I said, I never deserved him.

The second is a picture of the first place I'd rented after I ran away from Dixon Falls. I went from place to place, spending every cent I'd gathered over the years and not staying anywhere any longer than I had to. Until I found this farm cottage in the UK and met Rae.

She's such the opposite of me in every way. And she reminded me of Tyler. The happiness and kindness, the fact that she never stopped smiling and joking. Some people just do that to you ... and because of it, I stayed. For a long time.

She's the one who took me to the bar in Leeds where I kissed another boy for the first time after Tyler's death.

She's the one who showed me how to really market my photography and introduced me to a gallery owner. She made me want to stay in that little cottage I'd rented for much longer than I'd planned. But feeling so happy and having everything be too easy felt wrong. It was wrong that I could move on and it made me feel like what had happened in the past was right, when I knew without a doubt that it wasn't.

It would never be right and that realization made me see Tyler everywhere all over again. I needed to leave. It was okay to remember, but it wasn't okay to forget. And I did leave. Each place I stopped at was closer and closer to Dixon Falls. At first I didn't realize it. But when I picked this university, I was keenly aware that I'd only be hours away.

The third picture is only a silhouette I took in Paris.

I don't know the people.

It's the shadows of four men standing outside of a church with a deep sunset behind them.

From a distance, all I could see were the Cross boys. And I took picture after picture, snapping away as quickly as I could. As if they'd vanish if I stopped. I wanted them back badly. I wanted them to forgive me and tell me it was alright. After all, they were the only family I had for a long time and just like my parents, I lost them.

That picture hurts the most. Because there should be five people in the shot. And because when the men did leave the hilltop behind the church and come closer, they weren't the Cross boys and I knew in that moment I'd never see them again. Daniel was never going to show up for me to stare at from a distance. It would never be them, no matter how much I prayed for it to happen.

Three pretty pictures, mixed in with the others. All hues of indigo, my favorite color, and all seemingly serene and beautiful. But each a memory of something that's made me the person I am.

My phone vibrates with the reminder of the most recent message. It's Daniel, of course. *Come over.*

I need to work, I text him and snort at his immediate response. *No you don't.*

I do, in fact, need to work. I could easily work at his place. That's what I've been doing and I actually enjoy it. I love it when he kisses my shoulder and tells me what he thinks of the photo I'm working on. He makes me feel less alone and he understands how I see the pictures and why they mean so much to me.

I want to apologize.

You did and I get it, I tell him even though it makes the ache in my chest that much deeper.

Please, just give me another chance.

Please is another word I'm not used to hearing from Daniel and as much as I want to give in, I need a little time.

I really do have to work. We can meet up next week. As I press send, I realize I'm caving in. Simply prolonging what is sure to end. But then I remember the men by the church. If I could go back in time and make them stand there forever so I'd never have to face the fact that they weren't the Crosses, I would.

It hurts deep in my chest. Denial is a damning thing.

And that's what this is, isn't it? Just a futile attempt to deny that we could ever exist without our past tearing us apart.

The phone sits there silent, indicating no new message from him although I know he sees my response. Picking up a tissue from the coffee table, I dry my nose and pick myself up off the sofa.

Life doesn't wait for you. That's something I've learned well.

Before I can take a step toward the kitchen to toss the tissue, a message from Daniel comes in. *I promise I will make it up to you.*

I don't know what to write back. There's no way to make this right.

So instead I focus on the work that's waiting for me and choose not to respond.

I've barely been active online for a week now. Instead I've been taking pictures. Lots of them. Some of Daniel in abstract ways. Others of little things that remind me of him from when we were younger. I haven't posted those yet though. I'm not sure I will either. No matter how beautiful I think they are.

I haven't answered messages or sent out any packages. I don't even know how my sales are going. When you run a business all by yourself, you can't afford to take time off. For years I've buried myself in my passion and work, although really I'd just been running from reality. From my past.

Staring at the message from Daniel, the black and white text that's so easy to read, I can't answer the one question that matters.

What am I doing?

* * *

Six years ago

347

"HEY ... HEY ..."

I hear a persistent voice but I ignore it. No one in this school has said a word to me. At least not to my face.

With a tug on my shirt, I'm forced to turn around and face a boy. A boy who's nearly a man. He doesn't have a baby face, and I can tell he shaves, but there's a kindness about him that makes him appear young. And likable. Which is something I haven't felt in the last two years.

"What are you doing?" he asks me and my forehead pinches.

I lift the pencil in the air and point to the chalkboard in science class as I say, "It's called taking notes."

The handsome guy laughs, a rough chuckle that forces me to smile. Some people's happiness is simply contagious.

"No, I mean tonight."

I don't bother to respond other than to shrug. I do the same thing every night. Nothing. My life is nothing.

"My brothers and I are having a little party."

"I don't really do parties," I answer him and nearly turn back around in my seat, but his smile doesn't falter and that in itself keeps my attention.

Shrugging, he says, "We can do something else."

"I don't really do much," I tell him honestly. I don't really feel like doing anything. Each day is only a date on a calendar. That's all they've been for a long time now.

"What about the assignment for art class? We could take some pictures for the photography project?" It takes me a moment to place him, but now that he's mentioned it, I think I did see him in the back row yesterday in art class.

"It's not my day for the camera." The budget for the art department is small, so we have to take turns checking out the equipment.

"I've got one we can use—well, it's my brother's."

"Your brother?"

"Yeah, his name's Daniel." It all clicks when he says his brother's

name. I've seen him. It must be him. I've watched as this boy I'm talking to waits outside at the entrance to the school and another boy picks him up. Except he's not a boy. There's no question about that. Daniel is a man and it only took one glimpse of him to cause me to search him out each and every time the bell rings and I'm waiting in line for the bus.

"Now I know your brother's name, but I don't know yours."

"It's Tyler." I repeat his name softly and when I look at him, I see traces of his older brother. But where Daniel has an edge to him, Tyler is warm and inviting.

"I'm Addison."

"So what do you think, Addison?"

"I think that sounds like fun. I wasn't doing anything anyway."

MAYBE FATE KNEW I wasn't going to be able to keep Tyler. It was going to take him from me. So it gave me Daniel to keep me from loving Tyler too much.

I don't know for sure and there's no point in speculating.

All I know for certain is that Daniel will consume me, chew me up and spit me back out.

I need to end this before I get hurt … well, before it gets worse than it already is.

CHAPTER 16

Daniel

I'm losing it.

I can feel myself slipping backward into a dark abyss.

Addison and I are alike in more ways than she knows. In ways I'd never dare to whisper out loud. She's lying to herself when she says she needs space.

She doesn't.

She needs me, just like I need her. She's the only thing that takes the pain away and I do that for her too. I know I do. I can feel it. I can see it in her.

The light from the computer screen is the only thing that saves the living room from being in complete darkness. I've been staring at it, waiting for him to see I've been logged in for hours.

I'm trying to stay away from Addison. I'm trying to do what's best.

It's been a long time, Marcus finally responds. It's not his name or his alias in this chat. But I know it's him.

Three years now, I answer, leaning back into my seat with my laptop on my thighs and trying to ignore the shame that rings in my blood. It's been three years since I've logged into this black market chat and sought him out. Three years since I've felt the urge to watch over Addison every second of every day. Three years since I've had a hit of my sweet addiction.

What brings you back? he asks me and I swallow thickly.

She came back into my life. But you already know that.

She, as in Addison? he asks me to keep up this charade.

The keys beneath my fingertips click faintly as I type. It's odd how I find it comforting, the soft sounds tempting me to confess my sins.

I wasn't stalking her or trying to find her. The first time was a coincidence.

How many times have there been? he asks me.

A lot, I admit but then add, *but she's been with me this time. It's not me hiding in the shadows. She sought me out.*

Do you think that makes it healthier? The text stares back at me on the brightly lit screen and I want to answer yes. Of course it is. This time isn't anything like what happened years ago. He doesn't wait for me to answer before he poses another question.

If she knows, does that make it okay to allow your interest to grow to obsession?

Obsession may be the wrong word. I think possessive is better. She's mine. My reason to move on from what happened before. My desire for more. My only way to cope.

It's different this time. This time she wanted me there.

Wanted? he presses, and the shame of why I'm even here in this anonymous chat makes my chest feel tight. *As in past tense?*

She asked me for time apart and I'm having difficulties. I'm slipping back into old habits.

It's called stalking, Daniel.

I'm aware of that, Marcus.

I use his name, just like he uses mine. No one else knows it's him, but I do. Because years ago, when I watched Addison finally sleep without crying, when she could say Tyler's name with a sad smile instead of barely restrained agony, he was there for me. All those years ago when she moved on and I was still struggling to cope with the guilt of Tyler's death, Marcus is the one who stopped me from pulling the trigger with a gun pressed to my head.

It took nearly two years before it came to that point. A year and a half of following her, of watching her and living out my pain vicariously through hers. And months of slowly losing myself and any reason not to end it.

She kept me sane in a way she'll never know as I watched her grieve with the same pain I had.

But as the months went by, she started to smile again.

It made me feel worse than the day Tyler took his last breath.

She got better, when I didn't. Every laugh, every bit of happiness made zero sense to me.

I could only cope through her sadness. I understood it; I needed it.

Does she know about the past? he asks me.

She'll never understand, I type into the chat box, but I don't send it.

I shake my head, remembering how I followed her everywhere after Tyler's death. How I watched her run and that alone was enough to take my pain away. She loved him after all and felt responsible like I did. And if she could move on, so could I. But I could never move on from Addison.

* * *

Five years ago

I TELL myself the only reason I'm on this train is to speak to her.

To tell her it's not her fault and I'm the one to blame.

That's the reason I've followed her, stalking her in the shadows and silently watching her as she struggles with what to do.

I tell myself that, but I don't move. I'm struggling too.

The train comes to another stop and my grip tightens on the rail as I wait to see what she does. Where she goes, I'll go.

I need to make sure she's okay, that she doesn't have the same thoughts I do. I'll protect her.

Her hoodie is up, hiding her face as she leans against the wall of the train. Unmoving.

My body tightens, wanting to go to her. To hold her, to check on her and make sure she's still breathing. She saw him die like I did. That changes you. There's no way to deny it or to recover.

It will forever be with us.

CHAPTER 17

Addison

*I*t's funny how time moves.

It crawled along for years before and after Tyler came into my life. Each day's only purpose was to be a box on a calendar I could cross off with a deep red marker. If I bothered to even count.

But the days with Tyler, when I was really with him? They flew by. Because time is quite like fate, it's a bitch.

And the same thing happened with Daniel. The days were whirlwinds of moments that made me feel like everything was alright. Like it was okay to simply live in his bed and sleep in his arms. Like the selfishness of ignoring everything else was how life is supposed to go.

But the past few days without him … it's been worse than the slowest pain. There's a coldness that feels like it's just below the surface of my skin. As if my blood refuses to heat. And the nights are filled with memories designed to play on my weakest moments.

Knock. Knock. Knock.

My focus is shifted to the front door of my apartment as I sit cross-legged on my sofa with my laptop cradled on me. The screen's gone black and I don't know how long it's been like that.

He knocks again. There's only one person it could be. *Daniel.*

Every day and night since we last talked I've thought about him. And about what I need to do. Each text he sends is met with a short response that makes the pain in my chest grow.

I'm no longer in denial. It's time to move on. That means moving on from everything, including Daniel. And that hurts. But it's supposed to.

My neck is killing me from bending over the computer for hours. I have a standing desk; I should really use it, but I don't. I spend hours a day sitting on the sofa with my computer in my lap while I Photoshop my pictures. There are at least three dozen more I want to edit and post before going out and searching for my next muse. Although I don't know if I'll find it here. Maybe it's time to move on already.

My sore body aches all over when I stand, but that pain is temporary, so I don't mind it.

Each step to the front door makes me feel like I'm running in the opposite direction from where I was going days ago. I've come to the only logical decision there is and I've never liked breaking up with anyone. The way Daniel made me feel is unlike anything I've ever felt. Wild and crazy, I suppose. Thanks to the late night sex and not caring about anything, not even our next breath so long as our skin was touching and our desires seeking out refuge in each other.

Pausing with my hand on the doorknob, I let out a deep breath. He'll understand. He's probably here to do the same. This thing between us could never last.

I feel like I'm being stabbed in the heart, but the moment the

355

door is opened, the pain dims and that other feeling, that fluttering sickness I have trouble describing takes its place. The kind of pain that I want more of, but it scares me.

"Daniel." I whisper his name as his dark eyes meet mine and then soften. His leather jacket creases as he puts his hand on the doorframe and leans in slightly.

"You still mad at me?" he asks with a deep timbre to his voice that speaks to vulnerability and I answer him honestly, shaking my head.

"I'm not mad at you." Forgiving others is easy. It's forgiving myself that's hard.

Daniel lets out a breath and starts to come in, but I can't do this. It's better to stop it now and not do the easier thing. Which would be to fall back into bed with him and numb the pain with his touch.

It's not healthy.

My palm hits his chest and his expression turns to confusion, but he stops just outside the threshold.

"I've been thinking," I start to tell Daniel and he tilts his head, his eyes narrowing.

"This sounds like the *we have to talk* conversation." There's a trace of a threat in his voice.

"It kind of is," I say softly and the pain in my heart grows. "I've just been thinking about every way this is going to end."

"End?" he asks incredulously, moving forward and closing the distance between us. He's standing on the threshold now.

It's hard to speak, but I have to be honest with myself and him. I have to protect myself.

"I'm not sure we should do this at all."

Stunned is how I'd describe the look on Daniel's face, and it surprises me. "It doesn't make sense for us to continue this-"

"You don't want me?" Daniel asks, cutting me off in a voice devoid of anything but sadness. I've never heard the sound from his lips before. The tone pains my heart in a way nothing else ever will. I know it for a fact. Some things simply break a piece of you that can never be mended.

"That's not what I meant. Not at all. I didn't anticipate this happening," I try to explain. What I thought would be a simple conversation ending with Daniel leaving me behind escalates to something I hadn't anticipated. "I didn't think you would care." My words come out rushed.

"You thought I wouldn't care that you're done with me?"

"I'm not done ... I could never be done with you. But this," I gesture between us, "this is something I know is going to hurt me. And both of us know will never last."

"I'm not Tyler. That's why?" Daniel's words should be cutting. They should hurt me. But I only hurt for him. How could he think that?

I have to swallow hard before I can tell him, "I want you." I almost say Tyler's name. I almost tell him how I wanted the love Tyler gave me and how I wanted to love Tyler back but never did. But I can't. I can't bring him into this. "It's not that at all, Daniel. I've wanted you for the longest time and I hated myself for it. We can't even have a simple conversation about anything before..." I swallow hard, the lump in my throat refusing to let any more words pass.

"You hate yourself for wanting me?" The sadness is gone and anger quickly takes its place. Suddenly I'm suffocating, finding myself taking a step back and then another although he stays in the doorway, radiating a dominance barely self-contained.

"You're scaring me," I whisper and Daniel flinches. The emotions cycle through him one by one. The anger, the shock, the frustration from not knowing what to do.

And I've felt them all, I've also suffered the torture of not knowing what to do for so long. Every day that I felt loved by Tyler but knew I loved Daniel more. I know his pain as if it was my own. But there's no way to make this right. And the sooner this is over, the better.

"I want you Daniel, but it's wrong."

"It's not wrong," he says and his words come out strangled, his breathing heavier. He almost takes a step forward and then stops himself, gripping the edge of the doorframe and lowering his head, hanging it in shame. I'm reminded of the day I first met him and that makes the agony that much worse. "I don't know how to ..." he trails off and swallows thickly.

"There's no way this is going to be more than ... than what we were doing."

His head whips up and his dark eyes pin me in place. Daniel's always been intense, always been dangerous. For others, I'm sure it's similar. But they'll never feel *this*. Not the way I feel for Daniel.

"Why does it need to be *more* right now? Why can't we hold on to what we have?"

"It's not good for either of us, Daniel," I whisper and wrap my arms around my chest. I don't know how else to explain it and how he could fail to understand that.

The silence grows. All I can hear is my own breath as Daniel stands there stiffly, staring at the faded carpet beneath his feet. Finally, he looks me in the eye again and the intensity and pain there shatter me to the very center of my soul.

"I know that you belonged to Tyler first, as much as I hate to admit that. I hate to say his name. I don't want to imagine what used to ..."

"Daniel, please don't," I say and reach for him, my heart hurting for his and I hate myself in this moment. Why did I have to do this?

"We can't change the past, Addison. I wish I could. But it's over now. And right now I want you."

There was never a point in my life where I thought I'd hear those words from Daniel. And the shock, the sadness, and the conflict of not knowing how to protect myself and what I should do keep the words I'm desperate to say trapped in my throat.

I want to believe what he's saying. But he's already said the words I need to hold on to the conviction of leaving him. *There will never be more.*

"You know where to find me if you want to see me." Daniel's last words are flat, with a defeated tone.

I can't form a coherent thought as he turns his back to me and walks off. This isn't what I wanted or how I'd planned for it to go. "I didn't mean for this to happen," I say, but my choked words are barely audible to me, let alone Daniel as he disappears in the distance.

I worry my bottom lip and a storm brews inside of me. A storm that feels as though it's never left, like it was only waiting in the darkness. Preparing for when it could come out and destroy the little piece of me that remains.

It's not until Daniel's gone that I close the door, lean my back against it and fall to the floor on my ass.

I've made a mistake. More than one. But I can't keep going on like this, making mistake after mistake and running from them.

Helplessness overwhelms me and I've never felt weaker. Why is it all so complicated? Why can't love and lust be one, and right and wrong easier to decipher?

CHAPTER 18

Daniel

Five years ago

*E*very small movement makes the pain spread deeper. I shouldn't
have called him a drunk. I shouldn't have yelled back when my
father yelled at me. I know better. I brought this on myself.

I let out a deep breath, but even breathing hurts. Carter will cover for
me. He always does. I swallow thickly as I hear heavy footsteps coming to
my door and my heart pounds for a moment, thinking it's him. Thinking
I fucked something up.

Like I did last night, losing thousands of dollars. Thousands and
thousands of money and merchandise are gone. Stolen off the truck. And
it's my fault. I'm the one who opened it, getting the fucking CD Addison
left in there and not remembering to lock it back up.

This is all because of her.

There's only a slight bit of relief when I hear Tyler yell out my name as he bangs on the door.

I struggle to put my shirt back on, but do it through clenched teeth while wincing. It was only a belt, I grit out with the part of me that thinks I'm pathetic. That I deserve all of this and more.

I open the door without thinking of the cuts on my back and the pain sears through me.

"Why do you have to be such an asshole all the time?"

Tyler's question is met with nothing from me. Not a single emotion that I can give him.

"You don't have to make her feel like she's not welcome."

Anger makes me swallow hard. I still don't respond.

I'll never tell him how I feel about her, but at least now I know how she feels about me.

"Are you going to say anything?"

My lips part and I want to give him something, anything. But the fact that I went out of my way for her last night ... maybe that's why. Maybe she knows I want her. The idea hits and steals my words from me.

"She's a good person," Tyler tells me as if that's why I stay away from her.

"I love you, Tyler. God knows it. But you're a fucking idiot."

I should have kept my mouth shut, but everyone has their limits.

"She loves me and she's not going anywhere," he tells me with a confidence I've never seen in my baby brother.

My baby brother who's oblivious to what we really are and what goes on here.

My baby brother who's never been struck once by my father.

My perfect baby brother who wants to make everyone around him smile because he's never known pain like I have.

"She only loves you because she has no one else who loves her." My gaze pins him where he is as I say the words. "Remember that."

* * *

LONELINESS IS a bitter pill to swallow. I know I've brought it on myself, but still. A sarcastic, humorless huff leaves me as I grab the bottle of whiskey and take a swig.

It must be karma.

I left Addison to her loneliness so I could survive.

Now she's leaving me to mine to ruin me.

Touché, little love.

The whiskey burns as I take another heavy drink. And with it every possibility of where I lost her flashes in my mind. The times from back when we were younger and I held back so much, to only moments ago when I didn't hold back a damn thing.

I lick my lower lip and then pick the bottle back up, but a timid knock stops me from chugging back more of the amber liquid.

"Daniel," I hear Addison's voice from beyond the door. Hope flickers deep inside of me, flirting with a darkness that's nearly consumed me.

My heart pauses. So do my lungs. It's only when I hear her again that they both decide to function again. She's here. *She came to me.*

My blood buzzes as I stand up and make my way to the front door. All while I stride to the door the alcohol sets in, and I hear her call out again. "Please open the door, Daniel."

She's mid-motion of knocking again with her mouth parted and more to say when I pull the door open. She looks shocked and even flinches slightly.

"Daniel," she says my name with a hint of surprise, but quickly her expression and tone change. "I wanted to explain."

And that right there is why I didn't let that hope grow. The coldness in my chest puts out the small flame. It's hard to school my expression. It's hard to hide it from her. But a part of me is screaming not to. To let her see what she's doing to me. To make sure she knows she's destroying me bit by bit.

"Explain?" The question comes out with a bit of anger and I

have to readjust my grip on the door and look away from her for a moment.

"You don't owe me anything, Addison," I tell her and turn to walk down the hall, but I leave the door open. I let her come to me willingly.

When I hear the door shut and her following me inside, a smile slowly forms on my face. It's only a trace of genuine happiness. But at least I know she can't let me go as easily as she thinks she can.

"Daniel, please," she says as she catches up to me in the living room, gripping my shirt and making me turn to face her.

"What is it you want to explain?" I ask her and almost call her little love. Almost.

"I didn't think that you wanted anything but a good fuck." God, she does something to me when she talks like that. When foul and dirty words come out of that pretty little mouth of hers.

My own indecent thoughts keep me from responding quickly enough. So she storms over to the leather chair in the corner of the room and sits down angrily, crossing her legs and then her arms.

Of course that's what she thought. It's what this started out as. But she's fooling herself if she thinks what we have could ever be anything so shallow. Even I can admit it. "I'm not leaving until you talk to me," she demands and it's cute. She's so fucking adorable thinking she can make demands like that. My bare feet sink into the rug as I make my way to the chair opposite hers.

With the blinds closed, the only light in the room is that of the tall lamp in the corner.

"Say something, please. I feel awful. I didn't expect you to react the way you did." She leans forward and grips the armrests of the chair. "The last thing I wanted to do was hurt you," she confesses and I know she's telling the truth. Addison isn't a liar.

And that gives me hope.

"I don't know what I want, other than you." My voice comes out rough as I lean forward and put my elbows on my knees so I can sink down to her eye level.

"What does that mean?" she asks breathlessly. Her chest rises and falls as if my answer is everything she's ever needed. The only thing she's ever desired.

Licking my lower lip, I stare into her eyes but the words don't come. I don't know how else to say it. I want her.

I want her to be mine. It's all I've ever wanted.

Not just in my bed. I want her touches, her kisses, her intentions. Moving forward, I want each piece of her. Every little piece. I want them all.

More than that, I want her to give them to me.

Her words spin chaotically, as do her emotions. "I need something to hold on to, Daniel, and this, this is intense and overwhelming and emotional-"

"But do you want it?" I cut her off, asking the simple question.

"Why did you come get me in that bar? Don't lie to me. You knew I'd be there, didn't you?" she asks me and I don't know if she knows more than she should, or if she's just that damn good at knowing who I am.

I lean back in my seat and decide to be careful with my words as I slowly say, "I wanted you for so long."

"So that's all this is? You wanted to fuck me, so you finally did?"

"You already know that's a lie." My words come out like a vicious sting and she drops the act. "I know you feel this too." I finally speak the words that feel as if they'll break me. But they're true. "There's always been something between us."

Addison's expression is pained.

"I know you feel guilty admitting it, Addison. I do too. I'm just as much to blame." She doesn't know how true those words are.

Time wears on and more than a moment passes. Addison pulls her knees into her chest and all I want to do is grab her ass and pull her into my lap. But my fingers dig into the leather, pinning me where I am until I have the only answer I need from her.

"Do you want me?" I ask her.

"It's not that easy," she whimpers. Torn between the desire she feels and the guilt she won't let go of.

My body tenses and the rage from knowing the past may forever darken my future takes over as I lean forward. "The fuck it isn't."

I have to close my eyes and focus on what I want, what she needs to hear. I speak so low I'm not sure she can hear me, but I pray she can. "I can't tell you what will happen a week from now, but I know I'll still want you." I open my eyes to find her watching me intently as I continue, "I've always wanted you. It's not going to stop, and I don't care about anything that happened yesterday as long as I get you tomorrow."

"When did you turn into this man?" Addison's question is quiet, but full of sincerity. "I don't remember any of this from you."

The answer is right there. So obvious to me.

Because she wasn't mine and couldn't be.

"You were young, and belonged to someone else." I can't bring myself to speak Tyler's name. The alcohol and thought of losing her if he comes up again is too much.

Before she can respond to the omission I ask her the only thing that matters, "Do you want me?"

Her green eyes shine with sincerity as she barely whispers the word, "Yes." She bites down on her lip as I rise from my seat and make my way to her. Slowly and carefully, with each step knowing I'm so close to keeping her.

"If you stay here Addison, I swear I won't let you leave." I swallow thickly and clear my throat when she searches my eyes and knows I'm speaking the truth. "This is your last chance to run from me." I owe her that at least. One last chance to run.

"I've never wanted to run from you." Her words are laced with raw emotion and she reaches up to cup my face. "We're doing this?"

"You can't leave me, Addison. You have to promise me, no matter what happens," I say and hope she can't hear the desperation in my voice. "No matter if we fight." I start to say more, but I choke on the obvious. *No matter if Tyler comes up again.*

I can barely breathe as she strokes the stubble of my jaw with her thumb and whispers, "I promise."

She falls into my lap so easily. Her warmth and soft touches light every nerve ending in me on fire. But so much more than that too. The pounding in my chest. The need to be close to her. To be skin to skin and show her she's mine again.

I'm dying inside, needing to take her, but I move so achingly slowly. Cherishing every second of something I almost lost. Every second of *her*.

"DANIEL?" Her voice is hesitant, but raw. As if the question itself will break her as I kiss the crook of her neck and let my fingers barely graze her skin, just a whisper of a touch.

"Addison?" I answer her with a playful air and smile against her skin when she breathes easily.

"I'm scared," she whispers into the air and when I pull away from her, her face is toward the ceiling with her eyes closed tight. Her fingers dig into my shoulders as I nudge her chin with my nose to get her attention.

"I won't hurt you," I whisper when she doesn't respond. My heart races, though not in a steady rhythm. But when she lowers her gaze, her green eyes finding mine, it steadies and slows. It's lost without her.

Addison nods, a small nod of recognition, but the hesitancy is still there. Her slender fingers pull at my shirt and I help her, leaning back and pulling it off. Then I remove hers, and move lower. We strip each other slowly, each movement met with the sound of our breathing. Kisses in between each garment being tossed to the floor, each turning more desperate, more breathy. *More.*

And when I finally slip my fingers between her folds, she's

soaking wet with need and rocks her hot pussy into my hand. Her eyes are still closed as she rides my palm and my thumb presses against her clit. Groaning against her throat, I grab my dick and push myself inside of her until I can let go and grab her hips as I fill her tight cunt.

Sucking in a breath, her fingers move to my shoulders, her blunt nails digging into my flesh.

Her wide eyes meet mine and I'm entranced.

Every thrust up, I dig my fingers deeper into her shoulder. My abs burn as I fuck her like this over and over, as deep as I can while I stare into her eyes.

The need to kiss her is all-consuming. But I can't break her gaze either.

Her lips part just slightly as her pussy flutters and then spasms on my dick. My name slips from her lips as a strangled moan. And it's only when she shudders and an orgasm rips through her that she breaks my gaze. She falls forward in my arms as I keep up my pace, riding through her climax.

I kiss her shoulder, her neck, her hair, every bit of her ravenously, worshipping her as she grips on to me for dear life.

My release comes in a wave so strong, I'm not ready. I'm not at all ready for this to end. But I swear I hear her whisper against my skin, her hot breath sending a chill down my spine as the intense pleasure rocks through me. I swear I hear her whisper as her lips graze my neck.

I love you.

My arms wrap around her and I don't move; I don't let her move either. I can't say the words back. And I don't know if she'll say them again. But I swear I heard them.

I swear I heard her say those words to me.

To me.

CHAPTER 19

Addison

*D*aniel Cross is my boyfriend.
How high school. But still ...
That's all I sent to Rae this week. I'm used to giving her long descriptions of where I'm going next. It's all I've ever considered and she loves to hear stories of what new places are like. But this town brought me Daniel and I don't want to share a ton of details. He's mine.

A snicker makes me lean back from the laptop as I read Rae's response to my email.

How big is his dick? is her opening line. Leave it to Rae to relieve the tension.

I've been worried about what she's going to say. And knowing that she isn't judging me makes everything so much easier to accept. She even said, *As long as you're happy, I'm happy.*

That's all I wanted. As I click out of the email, ready to close the laptop, I see my subject line again. *Daniel Cross is my boyfriend.*

I cover my smile with my hand as I pull my heels up onto the sofa. With my pillow snuggled up close to me, I'm in for a night of binge-watching housewives and reality television.

But I couldn't really care less about any of that. I can't get into a show to save my life— or work, for that matter. All I keep thinking is that Daniel wants to be … *mine.*

It's been over a week and that's still the case. Nights of hanging out, watching TV or looking over photographs I've taken. It's almost normal.

Those stupid butterflies in my stomach won't quit and it makes me feel childish and giddy. But even in the eye of the storm that surrounds us, I want him and he wants me.

That should be all that matters, right?

As I reach for my glass of wine sitting on the coffee table, I can't help but feel like the bottom is going to fall out from under us. Like there's something waiting on the edge of all this. I can feel it with everything in me.

Life doesn't work like this. You don't get what you want simply by asking for it.

I swallow a sip of the wine and the sweetness I was feeling only a moment ago tastes bitter with the last thought.

Daniel feels like everything. Like there was nothing before him even though I'm fully aware there was. There's no way with our history that there will be more between us, no matter what he says and how well we play house together. There won't be any family dinners with his brothers or any sense of normalcy in that respect.

No matter how much I wish that were the case.

Every day I'm waiting for Daniel to tell me he was wrong and it's over. Or that he's ready to go home and that I'm not welcome there. I like to think that my guard is up and that it won't hurt when he does it. But each day that passes is another crack in that armor.

He fucks me like he owns me. He holds me at night so tight; like if he lets go, he'll lose me forever.

And he kisses me like he's dying for the air I breathe.

We don't talk about the one thing that plagues me. About how we're supposed to just ignore our past. He thinks we've said enough, but if that were the case, I would be able to sleep without the memories haunting me.

It's hard to explain how I feel. I want to be happy and grateful. But it's obvious I'm being naïve. This is too good and I know good things always come to an end.

"You want anything while I'm out?" Daniel asks, interrupting my thoughts as he steps out of the hall to the bedroom and strides toward me. It's odd seeing him in my apartment still. I'm more used to his place, but tonight he'll be gone for a while and I need the space.

The fresh smell of his body wash follows him into the room and I find myself humming in agreement although I didn't quite hear him. He's too distracting when he's dressed like this. Black jeans and a crisp white button-up with one sleeve already rolled up while he works on rolling the other. Freshly shaven with his high cheekbones and strong jaw on display, it almost makes me wish he was always cleanly shaven. But that stubble ...

Either way, he looks like a fucking sex god. He fucks like one too. *My* sex god.

"I might be out for a while, but I can bring back something for breakfast if it's too late."

I watch the muscles in his forearm as he rolls up his sleeve and as I do, the desire is slightly muted by his comment.

That's another thing we don't talk about. We don't talk about what he does late at night. I was quiet whenever Tyler would leave to go do something early in the mornings or skip school because he had to do something for "work."

But we aren't children anymore, and what Daniel's involved with isn't a high school game.

"Is this stuff for ... back home?" I'm careful with my words as he grabs his keys off the kitchen counter. The jangling is the only sound in the room.

Well, and the ever-present clicking of the clock.

"Back home? As in, the family business?"

My gaze is on the tile in the kitchen. Soft gray with dark gray grout. It's nothing special, but I can't bring myself to look at Daniel and meet his gaze that's obviously on me, so I keep my eyes right where they are.

He works for his brother Carter. Dealing drugs and God knows what else.

He'll leave one day. Soon. He keeps mentioning it. The one question I ask myself every time he leaves is simple. Do I stay? Or do I go with him?

"Yeah, that's what I was asking."

"You know better than that, Addison," Daniel reprimands me and that's what gets me to look at him.

"Better than to be careful about who and what I involve myself with?" My tone dares him to question that logic.

"You already made your choice, didn't you?" The way he speaks to me simultaneously strikes a bit of fear in my heart and heats my blood with lust.

"There are lots of choices, Daniel." I know in my mind he's right. I've already decided I'd go with him. I don't want to be alone again and I crave the feeling of family and acceptance I once had with the Cross brothers. But that was then, and this is now. I don't know what it would be like to face them knowing I'm now with Daniel. It feels like a betrayal of the worst kind.

"Only one when it comes to me. Don't forget that you're the one who started this. You're the one who came back to the bar. You're the one who came to my house after you ended it. I don't like being played with."

"Funny, because you sure do like being the one doing the playing."

My comment rewards me with a charming smirk on his lips.

"With you?" he questions as he stalks toward me and grips my chin between his fingers. "Always."

My eyes close as he plants a kiss on my lips. Mine mold to his and my body melts. It's over too soon and I find myself sitting up a little taller to prolong it just slightly.

Daniel keeps his grip on me and a crease forms on his forehead as he looks down at me with a question in his eyes.

"Are you thinking of leaving me?" he finally asks and I reach up to take his hand in mine.

"No," I tell him, practically rolling my eyes and getting more comfortable in the corner of my sofa.

"Good," he says although he still eyes me curiously.

"If I hadn't come to your place, would you have let me leave you?" I don't know why I feel so compelled to ask in this moment. Maybe I already know the truth and I just want to see if he'll tell me or not.

His dark eyes seem to get darker, although his voice stays even as he answers me, "I would have tried."

I chew the inside of my cheek and look away at his response.

"Why does that disappoint you?"

"Can't you feel it?" I barely whisper the words. He makes me feel weak and foolish. But admitting there's something undeniable that pulls you to someone like it does no one else isn't weak at all. It takes every bit of strength in me.

Daniel's eyes leave mine for a moment and I begin to doubt myself. I can barely swallow until he says, "I said I would try. I didn't say I was capable."

My eyes close and I wish I could will all of this overwhelming emotion away. But that's what Daniel's always done to me. Overwhelmed me.

"I'll keep you safe. Always."

My heart soars and plummets with his words. That's how it feels and the relief on my lips falls with it.

"I just know … your job … is dangerous." I hate how my throat feels tight as I speak. "I knew what I was getting into. It's different when you wait at home alone wondering …"

"But I'm a dangerous man, Addison. I know what I'm doing."

I search his dark eyes for reassurance and it's there, but still I can't help adding, "Don't die. Everyone I love dies."

"What if it's more like anyone who loves you dies?" he questions and it doesn't help me feel any better at all. He shrugs and points out, "Then I'm dying anyway, so you might as well love me back."

Although I realize the words were spoken in a lighthearted way, the acknowledgement is there. That there's something more between us and we both feel it. We both recognize it for what it is. I don't dare to speak it again. I'm too caught up in those flutters in my chest. The ones that hurt in the best of ways. My eyes start to gloss over and I shove all the emotion away.

"Just be safe, my dangerous sex god." My voice is playful and nonchalant as I reach for the remote, ending the conversation. It's too much, too soon. But it feels like everything that's always been missing. It feels right. It feels like home. And I'm so afraid to lose it.

Daniel chuckles and leans down to cup my cheek and plant a soft kiss in my hair. "I'll be back as soon as I can," he whispers and it tickles me enough to make me pull away and snatch a kiss from his lips myself.

It's only been weeks, but this is everything I've ever wished for.

As the door clicks shut, leaving me alone in my apartment, I remember a certain saying.

Be careful what you wish for.

CHAPTER 20

Daniel

Five years ago

I knew something was off when I walked in at 4 a.m. and the dining room light was on. The yellow glow carries into the kitchen and I follow it to see Tyler at the end of the large table, head in his hand staring at the screen to his laptop.

I expect to hear something, maybe see him watching a video. But the screen has gone black and that's when I see his expression. Defeated and exhausted.

"You still up?" I ask him, which is a stupid question. It gets his attention though, although his exhaustion makes him blink several times before he can answer me. It's then that I see his eyes are puffy, not with sleep, but with something else.

"Yeah, couldn't sleep," he answers and then visibly swallows as he closes the laptop.

My jacket rustles as I slip it off and hang it over the chair in front of me. I still feel like an asshole for snapping at him the other day. Of everyone living under this roof, Tyler's the last person who needs my shit. "Everything alright?"

He sits back and lets out a heavy breath, but instead of answering verbally, he only shakes his head no.

"You want to talk about it?" I ask as I grip the back of the chair and prepare myself for the answer I know is coming. Addison isn't here and Tyler can't sleep. She left him.

"You were right," Tyler says and then turns away from me.

"I was an asshole who was trying to be an asshole. I'm never right. You know that?"

He lets out a huff of a laugh and wipes under his eyes.

"What happened?" I ask him.

"She said it's too much for her. That she needs space."

I nod my head in understanding. "Nothing wrong with a little space," I say and try to make it sound like it's not a big deal.

"I know her, Daniel. I know it's her way of putting distance between us so I'll be the one to leave."

The legs of the chair scratch along the floor as I pull it out and take a seat. A heavy breath leaves me as I put my elbows on the table and lean closer to him. "Girls are hormonal," I say to try to make him crack a smile. He's the one who's good at this, not me.

"I think she's done with me, but I don't know why."

"She loves you," I tell Tyler although it makes a spike of pain go through my heart. She does love him. I know it by the way she kisses him. It's obvious she does.

"I don't know," he says in a whisper, shaking his head.

"Just give her a day or two, cut class if you have to. Give her time to miss you." I hate that I'm giving him this advice. But I hate to see him like this more.

"What did Mom used to say, huh? If you give someone love, they'll love you back. Right?"

He nods his head, although he still doesn't speak. It's been a while since I brought up Mom. And it still doesn't feel right, but Tyler was her baby boy. He may have been younger when she got sick, but it hit him hard. He didn't understand.

"I promise you," I tell him as I pat his back. "Come with me for the next two days. I have to make a trip to Philly for a shipment. Come up with me and let her miss you."

He's reluctant for a moment but then he nods. "I could use the distraction, I guess."

"Perfect." I stand up quickly and leave him be as fast as I can. "Get some sleep," I say over my shoulder and I don't stop walking or respond when he tells me thanks.

As I climb the stairs to go pass out, loneliness settles in my chest.

The idea of Addison never coming back hits me hard. The possibility of never seeing her again.

It's very obvious to me in this moment that I don't like it.

More than I don't like how she's younger than me.

More than I don't like how she looks at me the way I look at her when I know she's not looking.

More than I don't like that she's Tyler's.

* * *

EVERY DAY there's a memory I've forgotten. Haunting me. Showing me how I could have stopped the inevitable. Or at least changed our fates.

Late at night, holding Addison as she sleeps, I wonder if Tyler would still be alive if I had done something different. Or if I'd be the one buried in the ground now.

Fall has arrived and each step I take down Rodney Street is accompanied with the crunch of dead and withered leaves. My steps are heavy tonight because I know Marcus is going to be here.

He's finally come with whatever it is Carter's been waiting for. I know Marcus' patterns. He spends weeks scouting out a place and making sure you go to one location he has constant eyes on. And when he's found where he's comfortable, he delivers.

He's found that place at the park on the corner of Rodney and Seventh.

After tonight I have no reason to stay here. Addison will either come with me, or leave me. It's too good right now to think she'll refuse me, but she's run before and it's entirely possible she'll do it again.

I glance down the side street to see what block I'm on and my heart freezes.

The man in the black leather jacket, the one who stopped to look at Addison. That first day I watched her in the coffee shop and saw him staring at her. It's him. I swear I saw him melt into the shadows down the street.

"Hey!" I call out, more to see if he'll move than to actually get a reaction. But there's only silence. I barely glance to my right to check for cars as I run across the street. The cool air does nothing to calm my heated skin or the anxiety rushing through my blood.

I'm ready for a fight when I get there, but the shadowy corner is only a dead end. And no one's there.

A chill flows over my skin and I look all around me. It's no one. There's no one here.

It's hard to swallow as I walk back across the street. *It's just paranoia*, I tell myself. It's nothing. But still, all of my thoughts lead back to Addison. To her being alone.

She's messing with my head.

I think about every way she's consumed me with each step I take.

I can't see anything other than her when she's around me.

Every breath she takes depletes the air from my lungs.

I hated her for it back then, back when she was with Tyler. When she smiled at him instead of me. She tempted me, and I couldn't do a damn thing about it.

But time changes everything.

Every step she takes closer to me makes my fingers itch to grab on to her and never let go.

Fate simply waits for men like me. So it can fuck us over until we fall to our knees and admit there isn't a damn good thing about us.

Addison has no idea what she does to me.

She'll be the death of all that's good in me. I would lose focus of everything just to have a miniscule piece of her attention. I'd steal for her. I'd kill for her. I already have.

Goosebumps still cover my body as I get to the empty park. It's in the back of a small church that's surrounded by woods. I guess for Sunday school.

My gaze scans the perimeter of the park, but there's no one there. It's empty.

Marcus is never late. I check my watch and make sure I'm on time.

A minute passes as I walk toward the church and then back. It's not a good look to loiter and I don't need anyone getting suspicious.

Another minute and my anger and anxiety start to get the best of me.

A flash of white catches my eye as the breeze goes by; the squeaks of the swing's rusty chains make me turn toward them.

A note. I walk toward it without hesitation. Marcus and his fucking games.

There's a message on the swing.

Another address.

Tomorrow night. Check the mailbox. That's all you'll need.

Gritting my teeth, I hold back the urge to scream out toward the forest in anger. I know that fucker's in there watching. Making sure I got the memo.

The paper crumples in my hand as I stare out into the forest and wonder why he didn't meet in person.

Marcus always meets me in person. I've heard tales of him not showing and only leaving notes. Everything is fucked after. Marcus doesn't like to meet with you if he knows you're about to be fucked over.

A chill runs down my spine.

The only guess I have is that it has something to do with Addison. She's the only thing that's changed.

He knows everything. He knows about what happened the night Tyler died. He knows about my obsession. And he knows she's back.

My eyes flicker to the woods, searching him out but coming up with nothing. Every small sound of a branch breaking or the wind rustling the leaves reminds me of that night, the images flashing in front of me.

The night that Tyler died.

I'd just finished a meet with Marcus. It was an easy transaction for a hit we needed. He seems to like those better than being a messenger. He responds faster.

He knows that on my way home, I saw Addison in the diner.

I saw him across the street watching me after I'd sent the message to Tyler. She was in pain and I knew Tyler could take it away.

Marcus followed me as I followed Addison. I couldn't leave her, knowing Marcus saw me watching her. I didn't trust him. So I followed her from place to place. The diner, the bookstore and finally the corner store. And Marcus was there, every step of the way. I told myself it was only to satisfy his sick curiosity.

And worse than anything, Marcus was there; he was the closest when Tyler died right in front of us.

Marcus knows everything and he's not coming to see me in person. That leaves a bad taste in my mouth.

Deep breaths come and go.

This doesn't have anything to do with her. It's about Carter. It has to be about Carter and not about the shit Marcus knows about Addison.

Part of me questions if I should confess to her and tell her the truth before someone else does. She blamed herself for so long and I know she did. But I'm the one who sent Tyler after her.

He knew where she was because of me.

He went to see her because I told him he should.

It's all my fault. It was never hers.

CHAPTER 21

Addison

It's been strange.

My fingers hover over the keys and I delete my last words. I don't know how to tell Rae what's going on. I shift on my sofa, feeling uneasy. This whole day has felt different. Daniel hasn't touched me since yesterday morning. And things have been off since he got back from his meeting. It's also when the word "love" was said. Maybe he didn't realize he'd said it until after he left.

I've gotten short kisses, but nothing else. It feels different.

It's a way that makes me feel uneasy.

It's a way that makes me feel like the end is here and I was right all along.

All the flutters stop and the butterflies fall into a deep pit in my stomach.

That's the way he's making me feel.

The hall light flicks on and Daniel's large frame takes up the opening of the narrow passage. He doesn't look at me as he strides to the kitchen, walking right behind the sofa. He's not talking to me, but he doesn't want to leave either.

I can't take this. I prepare myself to type up the email telling Rae what I'd like to say to Daniel. Before I can even type a word I get fed up and slam it shut, turning sideways to face him. All of my frustration and nervous feelings snowball together into nothing but anger.

This time he's looking right at me.

"Something's wrong." That's all I can say and instead of answering me, Daniel reaches for a mug from the cabinet.

"Could you give me something?" I ask him with all this pent-up frustration and shove the laptop onto the coffee table. "You've barely looked at me, spoken to me, or touched me. Something happened or something's wrong, and if it's us I need to know."

Silence. I get silence in return. "If it's just work, you can tell me." My voice cracks and I hate that I'm so emotional while he gives me nothing.

It would be easy for him to simply say it has nothing to do with us. I can accept that. But he doesn't and that's when the sick feeling that's been twisting my gut all day travels to my heart.

I'm already halfway to him, determined to get some answers when he finally says something.

"I have to leave tomorrow night."

My bare feet stop on the cold tile floor in front of him. "That quick?"

"Either then or the next morning at the latest."

I swallow down my heart and breathe out somewhat in relief, but it's short-lived as I cross my arms over my chest. "You have to leave?" I ask him that question because the other one is too scared to leave me.

What happens to us?

He answers the unspoken question. "I want you to come home with me."

"Home?" I say the word with a humorless huff and pull out one of the chairs at the kitchen island. I don't know where home is. Taking a seat, I tell him, "Are you sure they'll even want me there?"

It's hard to swallow when I look at him. I can say goodbye to the idea of college, or at least this college, easily. But facing his brothers? That's something else entirely.

"They'll be happy to see you again." He says the words with compassion, but there's something there, something else that he's holding back.

"When did you find out you need to leave?" I ask, prying for more answers.

"Last night." He clears his throat and adds, "It's not my brothers that I'm worried about. It's you … deciding to leave me again."

"Stop it," I snap at him and then correct myself. "Why would you even say something like that?"

"I've done some things," he says and then leaves the empty mug on the counter. It's quiet and all I can hear is the sound of my heart beating as he takes a seat on the sofa in the living room. Although I know something bad is coming, I follow him, taking the cue to sit next to him.

"You're scaring me again," I whisper to him with a pleading voice and wait for him to look at me.

With his elbows on his knees, his head is just a smidge lower than mine as he turns to look at me and says, "It's because I'm a bad man. That's what bad men do. They scare people."

"I told you to stop it," I tell him as I reach up to put a hand on his broad shoulders. His shirt is stretched tight, making him seem caged beneath it. "You're a good person inside. I know you are."

"You think I'm good?" he says with an air of disbelief and then he turns to look straight ahead. When he speaks again, it's as if the words aren't directed at me. "I'm sure you think you can see the good in everyone."

"I don't like you talking like this. Seriously. You need to stop." I find myself struggling to speak. "I don't know what's making you say these things, but you have to stop."

"I think I should tell you something." Daniel speaks as he runs his finger around the lip of the coffee table in front of him. He focuses on it as the silence stretches out and I wait.

"Whatever it is, you can tell me." My heart flickers, the light going out for a moment. Maybe from fear, or maybe from knowing it's a lie I've spoken. There are so many things Daniel could say that would destroy me. But he knows that already.

"You're so breakable, Addison."

I huff a laugh, although it's drowned out by relief. "Is that the big news? Because I knew that already."

His dark eyes lift to meet mine and the intensity swirling within is something I haven't felt for a long time.

"No, that's not the news, but it's why I don't want to tell you."

My shoulders rise with a heavy breath. "If you have something to tell me, then I want to hear it."

Daniel relaxes his posture, sitting back and sinking into the cushion of the sofa as he stares at me. His hands are folded in his lap and I can tell he's deciding. Judging. And I allow it.

Because he's right. I am breakable. And the last person I want to break me is him.

He clears his throat, bringing his fist to his mouth and then looks at the decorative pillow that's next to him. I suppose it's just so he doesn't have to look at me. He runs his thumbnail over the fabric of the sofa as he talks, busying his hands. "When Tyler died, you left and didn't say goodbye."

I nod my head and ready myself to answer, leaning forward and even scooting slightly closer. He has to know how ashamed and riddled with guilt I was. I could barely speak to anyone.

I wanted to tell them all goodbye, but I couldn't even look them in the eye.

POSSESSIVE

My words are halted when Daniel continues, not waiting for a response from me at all.

"And when I went to your house," he pauses and licks his lips before moving his gaze to mine. "I could lie to you here, and say you were already gone."

My heart beats hard and my breathing halts from the danger that flashes in his stare.

"But you hadn't left yet and so I watched you pack. I wanted to pack too. I didn't want to stay where Tyler had just walked, just sat. Where I'd just listened to him tell me about that beat-up truck he wanted to fix but never would." Daniel runs his thumb along his lower lip as his eyes gloss over. "I wanted to run like you wanted to, but I didn't think I would be capable until I saw you do it."

"You watched me leave?" I ask him, not knowing where this is going, but fearing what he has to say because of his tone and bearing. Because of how the air thickens and threatens to strangle me. As if even it would rather I be dead than for Daniel to destroy me with the history between us.

"I wish it were as easy as that," he says with a smile that doesn't reach his eyes. "I watched you board the train with that heavy suitcase, and I got on too. I watched you check in to a motel four cities over. And I requested a room next to yours."

Every word he says makes my heart feel tighter.

"I watched you for days before finally breaking myself away from you to call Carter and tell him I wasn't coming back. I'd decided to spend my time doing one thing." The heat in his eyes intensifies at the memory and his gaze feels like fire against my skin. "Watching you."

"You stalked me?" I ask him although the words stumble over each other and barely come out as a croak. I can't deny the fear that begs my body to run, but I'm frozen where I am, waiting for his confession to release me.

"I watched you because I needed to. You blamed yourself and your pain was so raw and genuine. So full of everything that I

385

didn't have. Of course I hated every bit of who I was because Tyler had to die, while God chose to let me live. I wanted to cry and mourn like you did. A very large part of me wanted you to cry harder as you hugged your pillow to your chest in the dark. Some nights you couldn't even stand long enough to make it to the bed."

He cocks his head as he looks me in the eye and asks, "Do you remember how you'd sleep on the floor even when the bed was so close?" His last words come out as a whisper and I can't answer. I can hardly breathe as tears leak from my eyes.

"I thought about picking you up and putting you in the comfort of your sheets-"

"You came in?" I cut him off and suck in a deep breath. "You broke in to my room?"

"Addison, I couldn't be away from you." His admission elicits a very real fear that makes my body tremble as I shy away from him. Scooting farther away on the sofa, but not quite able to run.

"Not until you started getting better," he adds and then stands up. I cling to the cushion, cowering under him and backing away when he tries to touch me.

The tears fall freely as the extent of my fears from so long ago is realized. I swear I heard things. I heard someone walking in my room in the darkness. I swear I felt eyes on me. "I thought it was him," I cry out and cover my burning face. I thought Tyler was with me for so long. And it took me years to think that it wasn't because he wished me harm. I thought he hated me and wanted me to be scared. And then I loathed myself that much more for thinking so poorly of such a good soul.

"I needed to watch you, Addison. I'm sorry."

I stand up quickly, and I'm close to him. So close I nearly smack the top of my head against his chin as I stand. "I need to get away from you," I sputter, crossing my arms over my chest and walking around the sofa although I have no idea how I can even breathe, let alone speak and move.

I can barely see where I'm going, but I know where the door is.

Gripping the handle, I swing it open and face him. My legs are weak and I feel like I'm going to throw up. He made me crazy. It was him all along.

"I never did anything to hurt you, Addison, and I didn't want to." Daniel speaks calmly, the other side of him starting to emerge. The side that's okay with Daniel dropping his defenses. The vulnerable side that wants me to understand and isn't pushing me away. But that's exactly what I need to do right now. I need to shove him far away.

"I want you to leave," I tell him and sniffle, swiping under my eyes aggressively, willing the tears to stop. I'm shaking. Physically shaking.

"You need to go," I tell him because it's the only truth I know. My mind is a chaotic storm and everything I'd been keeping at bay, all the fear and sorrow are screaming at me until I can't hear anything. I can't make out anything. The exception being the man standing right in front of me who's the cause of my pain.

"Who did you think I was, Addison?" he asks me as if this is my fault.

And maybe part of it is.

"You knew I wasn't a good man back then, and you know that now."

"Get out." They're the only words I can say.

"It was years ago."

"I said get out!" I scream at him, but he only gets closer to me until I shove him away. He can't hold me and make this right.

"You stalked me." I can barely get the words out. I'm in disbelief and terrified, although I'm not sure which reaction is winning.

"You had hope," he says back hard as if it justifies everything. "You had happiness. You had everything I wanted. You were everything I wanted. You can hate me for it, but you can't deny that. It's the truth."

"I want you to leave."

"Please don't make me leave," he tells me as if it's only just now getting through to him. He looks at the open doorway and then back at me. The hall is empty and cold and a draft comes in, making me shudder.

"Get. Out." I can't look at him as he stares at me, waiting for me to say something else.

"Addison-"

"Out!" I yell as loud as I can. So hard my throat screams with pain and my heart hurts.

Even over my rushing blood I hear each of his footsteps as he walks away from me.

"You said you wouldn't leave me," Daniel grits between his teeth as he stands on the threshold of my door.

The words leave me as I slam the door shut in his face. "I lied."

CHAPTER 22

Daniel

The heavy pit in my stomach is why I don't give people a damn piece of myself. That sick feeling that I swear is never going to go away is why I play it close to the vest.

I thought she was different.

I close my eyes, swallowing although my throat is tight and listening to the busy traffic on Lincoln Street. I'm close to the address Marcus gave me. Close to being done with this town and having no reason to stay.

It's only when the street quiets that I open my eyes and force myself to move forward. Going through with the motions.

She *is* different. She does know better. She knows who and what I am.

She just doesn't want to accept it.

And how can I really blame her? I don't want to accept it either.

I didn't even get to tell her all of the truth. I didn't get to take her pain away from thinking she's to blame.

And that makes everything that much harder to swallow.

Passing a corner liquor store, I make sure I track the movements of the few people scattered around me. I keep to myself, heading south down the street. It's late and only the moon and streetlights illuminate the road ahead of me. But dark is good when you don't want to be seen.

I try to focus, but with the quiet of the night, I can't help but to think of Addison. She's always comforted me in the darkness.

I finally had her. Really had her. I felt what I always knew there could be between us. And I let her get away. I lost her by confessing.

Maybe that's why it hurts this fucking bad. She loved who I am, but hates what I've done. And there's no way I can take it back.

She saw the truth of what I was, but I could have sworn she knew it all along.

Maybe I should have just hinted at it. And let her ask if she wanted to know more.

You can't change the past. If anyone knows that fact all too well, it's me.

Give her time. I close my eyes, remembering the advice I gave Tyler once. If only it was that easy.

The chill in the autumn air is just what I need as I steady my pace with my hands in my jacket pockets. The metal of the gun feels cold against my hand as I glance from house number to house number.

55 West Planes. In the mailbox.

That's what Marcus said. Simple instructions. But an easy setup if he's planning one.

They say he's a man with no trace, no past, and nothing to use against him. A ghost. A man who doesn't exist.

He knows everything and only tells you what he wants when he wants to deliver it. But he's a safe in-between for people like us to use. Because if Marcus tells you something, it's because he wants you to know it.

And that's a good thing, unless he wants you dead.

I brush my hair back as I glance from right to left. There's a group of guys on the steps of an old brick house across the street and on its mailbox is 147.

I cross the street after passing them, so I'm on the odd-numbered side. The block before this was numbered in the two hundreds. So one more block.

The adrenaline pumps in my blood and I finger the gun inside my jacket pocket.

I have to will away the thoughts of Addison, no matter how much they cling to me and plague me every waking second.

My father taught us all to pay attention. Distractions are what get you killed.

A huff of a laugh leaves me at the memory of his lesson.

I guess when you don't care if you live or die, the severity of his words don't send pricks down your skin like they did when you were a child.

Tyler wasn't with me that day. I wonder if my father ever bothered to give Tyler that advice. Addison was as big of a distraction to him as she was to me.

With the tragic memories threatening to destroy me, I halt in my tracks, realizing I wasn't even looking at the numbers.

And I happened to stop right at 55. The mailbox is only two steps away.

The cold metal door of the mailbox opens with a creak. The sound travels in the tense air and the inside appears dark and empty. I dare to reach inside and pull out only an unmarked envelope. Nothing else.

My forehead pinches as I consider it. It's thin and looks as if it's not even carrying anything. But it's sealed and this is the right address.

All of this for one little envelope.

Slamming the door to the mailbox shut, I walk a few blocks, gripping the envelope in my hand and looking for a bus stop.

I text my brother even though I don't want to. I don't want him to know it's done. That I have what he's been waiting for. *It's just an envelope.*

It's marked as read almost immediately and he responds just as quickly.

Good. Come back home.

Staring at his text, that pit in my stomach grows. I'm frozen to the cement sidewalk, knowing I have to leave and hating that fact.

I know I need to move and not stay here, lingering when Marcus will be watching. But with the phone staring back at me with no new messages or missed calls, the compulsive habit of calling Addison takes over.

The phone rings and rings and goes to her voicemail.

I haven't stopped trying and I don't intend to.

I stayed as long as I could outside her door. I listened to her cry until she had nothing left. I don't know if I should have tried to talk to her and made her aware that I was still there wanting to comfort her, or if it would have only made her angrier.

A heavy burden weighs on my chest as I slip the envelope into my jacket, careful to fold it down the center and keep moving in the night.

I have no choice but to take this back to Carter. There's no way I can stay.

For the first time in a long time, I feel trapped. Suffocated by what's coming.

I can't leave her again.

I can't watch her walk away, and I can't leave her either.

But it was never my choice.

It's always been hers.

CHAPTER 23

Addison

J can't count the number of times I swore I was haunted. Not the hotels I stayed in or the places I moved. But me. A Romani woman in New Orleans once told me that it's not places, it's people who are haunted.

And since the day Tyler died, I swore up and down that he decided he would haunt me as I ran from place to place, never finding sanctuary.

From the creaks in the floorboards, to small things being misplaced. Every time I tried to find meaning in those moments. Each time I thought it was something Tyler wanted me to know and see.

There were so many nights when I cried out loud, begging him to forgive me. Even when I couldn't forgive myself.

I wonder if Daniel heard my pleas.

My phone pings on the coffee table and out of a need to know what he has to say this time, I reach for it. I haven't answered a single call or message from him. I don't know what to tell him.

It's fucked up. He's fucked up.

He hurt me beyond recognition.

I should tell him how I couldn't move for days on end. But the bastard knows that already.

I truly loved him, but a lie from years ago makes me question everything. He could have helped me heal. He could have shouldered the burden of my pain and I would have done the same for him. But just like when Tyler was alive, he was silent. He gave me nothing.

I'm surprised by the hurt that ripples through me when I see it's Rae and not Daniel.

It's a shocking feeling. And it takes me a moment to realize what I really want. I want him to beg me to forgive him. I want him to know my pain.

I let the idea resonate with me as I ignore Rae and click over to Daniel's texts. Six of them in a row.

I'm sorry.

I was wrong.

I couldn't help myself.

If I wasn't with you and watching you it was too much for me to take.

I wish you would understand.

I would never hurt you. I never will.

I read his texts and the anger boils as I text back. *You'll never know how much it hurt to go through that alone. And you made it worse for me. You sat in silence while I was in pain. How could you ever think I'd forgive you?*

I realize I'm more disturbed that he didn't try to help me than the fact that he stalked me. I guess that's not so different from what he did when I was with Tyler.

I press send without thinking twice. And then I click over to Rae, who wants to know how it's going. *Fucking priceless*, I think bitterly.

I roll my eyes, letting a shudder run through my body and tears roll down my cheeks. Instead of answering her, I move to the kitchen for a bottle of wine.

I still haven't unpacked my wine glasses and I know it's because part of me was already envisioning leaving with Daniel. I knew he wasn't staying long and I'd go anywhere with him. I would have done anything he wanted to be by his side.

My phone pings again as I bend down and grab a bottle of merlot by the neck from the bottom shelf of my wine rack. I pretend I'm going to let the phone sit there, but I'm too eager to see what he has to say. I'm a slave to his response.

He writes back, *Because I was in pain too. And I'm sorry. It wasn't to hurt you. It was only to distract me from the guilt I felt.*

Pain and guilt and agony and death make people do awful things. But it's no excuse.

I write back instantly, *You used me.*

I did.

I hate you for it. I stare at the text message and with the pain in my heart, I already know it's not hate. It just hurts so much that he watched and did nothing.

Can you love me and hate me at the same time?

I'll never forgive you.

He types some and then the bubbles that indicate he's writing stop. And then they continue, but suddenly stop again. All the while I grip my phone tightly.

Instead of waiting, I write more. My hands shake and the anger in me confuses itself for sorrow.

I needed someone and I had no one. I wanted you, you had to know. I blamed myself for everything when there was no reason to think otherwise. You could have helped me, but you only watched. You made my pain so much worse than it needed to be.

I send it to him and although it's marked as read, nothing comes. Minutes pass and the ticking of the clock serves as a constant reminder of every second going by with nothing to fill the gaping hole in my heart.

The moment I set the phone down on the counter and reach for the corkscrew, the phone beeps. I have to read it twice and then reread the message I'd sent him before the sob escapes me.

That's the way I felt every time you kissed him.

My shoulders shake so hard that I fall to the ground, my phone falling as well, although the screen doesn't shatter. I cover my face as I cry, hating myself even more and not knowing how to make anything better.

My phone pings again, but I can't answer it for the longest time. Even though it feels pathetic, I cry so hard it hurts every piece of my heart. The piece I gave Tyler when I gave myself to him. The piece I thought I'd left behind when I walked away from him. The piece that left me when he was laid to rest, and the piece I gave Daniel. There are many pieces. Pieces from years ago, from only days ago and the very big piece he just took.

I want him back instantly. I want him to hold me. There's a part of me that knows it's weak and pathetic to feel this desperate need for someone else. But deep inside I know I'd live my life happily being weak and pathetic for him. Isn't he weak for me just the same?

Sniffling and wiping at my face, I somehow get up, bracing myself against the counter and reaching for the faucet. My face is hot and I can still hardly breathe.

I don't think you ever get over the death of someone who's taken up space in your soul. It isn't possible. There are only moments when you remember that you're a pale imitation of what you could be if they were still with you. And those moments hurt more than anything else in this world.

As I turn off the faucet, I swear I hear something behind me and I whip around, a chill flowing over my skin and leaving goosebumps in its wake.

It takes every ounce of strength in me to lower myself to the ground, although my eyes stay on the skinny hallway where the noise came from.

It's silent as I pick up the phone, barely breathing, and quickly message Daniel. *Are you here now?*

It was a long time ago. I promise you. I wasn't well. I'm sorry.

I stare at his answer, feeling a chill flow over my skin and the hairs on the back of my neck raise.

So it's not you? I will myself to keep my eyes on the hallway, my back to the counter as I type. I can barely breathe.

Someone there?

I don't answer him and a series of texts come through. Ping. Ping. Ping. Each another sound that echoes down the hall.

Without looking at the messages I text, *I'm fine.*

His answer comes through before I look back to the hall. *I'm coming over.*

At his response I push forward, forcing myself to walk down the hall and to the loft bedroom. There's only one door and I push it open, telling myself it's nothing as the phone pings in my hand again.

It pings again as I take in the bedroom, cautiously stepping forward until I see a picture has fallen from the collage on the far side of the room.

My phone pings a third time and I can finally breathe. It's only a photo that's fallen.

I read his latest text and roll my eyes. *Answer me.*

My heart nearly jumps out of my chest as the phone rings and I drop it on the floor. It takes the entire time it's ringing for me to catch my breath and when I do I pick up the phone to text him. *It was only a picture falling.*

I'm on my way.

Don't come here, I text back while I'm still on the floor and I hope he can feel the anger that's still there. I add, *I don't want you here.*

It hurts me to tell him that. Partly because it's a lie. It hasn't even been twenty-four hours and I can already see myself forgiving him.

Addison please. Don't shut me out.

It took us long enough to admit what we needed.

I miss you. I need you.

If you're scared I need to be there.

With the fear and regret and everything else that's tortured me today, I just want to give in to him after reading his rapid-fire texts. But I won't.

I just need sleep, I reply and then add, *Don't come.*

Please forgive me, he finally texts and I can't respond right now, so I shut the phone off and fall onto the bed. I don't know how long I stare at the wall or at what point I decide I have enough energy to clean up the fallen picture, but I know it's longer than I'd like.

The command tape is stuck to the wall this time. I swear I'll never use it again.

Just like I'll never let myself give in to Daniel again.

Some people you're meant to miss.

They're just no good for you.

I think the words, but I don't know if I really feel them.

With that thought in mind I move to where the picture frame lays facedown on the ground and lift it carefully. Luckily there's no broken glass.

I almost feel okay as I turn it over to inspect the frame.

But then I see the picture that fell. One I took myself, five years ago.

A still life of Tyler's rusty old truck.

And that's when I lose it all over again. I'm forced to come to terms with the fact that some wounds never heal. And they aren't meant to be forgotten.

CHAPTER 24

Daniel

The phone rings and rings as I throw a zipped up bag into the corner with the rest of the luggage. I've packed light for years, but it's never bothered me before.

Looking at the small pile that comprises everything I own, I've never felt so worthless. Or so tired. I didn't sleep at all.

The phone goes silent and instead of calling Addison again, I scroll to Carter's number and call him. I could easily text him to let him know I'm on my way, but I don't want to. I want him to hear the defeat in my voice. And I need to talk to someone. Someone real. I'm losing everything, slowly feeling it drain from me.

I need someone. Desperately. I stayed awake outside Addison's apartment all night. I had to make sure she was okay. But time doesn't wait, and I had to pack ... and now I have to leave.

It only rings twice before he picks up, greeting me with my

name although it comes out as a question. And I know why he'd be confused to see I'm calling him.

I don't call anyone ever. I don't care to talk to him or any of my brothers, and they're the only ones alive I love. *My brothers and Addison.*

"Do you miss him?" I ask Carter without prefacing my question. "Not like Mom and Dad, where we knew it was coming and it made sense." Carter tries to talk on the other end of the line, but I keep going, pinching the bridge of my nose and sitting on the end of the bed. It protests with my weight. "The kind of missing someone where it feels better to pretend they're coming back? The kind of missing where you talk to them like they can hear you and it makes you feel better?" I know why I don't go home. It's because he's there in my head. I know what home is, and he's there. I refuse to accept otherwise. I can't.

I tell him I'm sorry every time I'm reminded of him. I hate going south, too many old trucks. I could never tell the difference, but they were Tyler's thing. He was an old soul like that.

"Every day," Carter says as I sit there quietly.

"I did something," I start to confess to Carter but stop myself. I'm too ashamed, so I settle on something else. "I ran into Addison." Her name leaves me in a rush, taking all the air in my lungs with it.

"Tyler's Addison? That's what brought this up?" he questions me and I nod my head like an ass, as if he can see.

"Yeah," I almost repeat, *Tyler's Addison.* But she never belonged to him. As much as I love him, she was always mine. Maybe he was meant to be her first, but I'll be her last. My throat tightens and my heart hammers in my chest. She's not his anymore. She's mine. And telling Carter feels like a betrayal of the worst kind. It feels like I'm telling Tyler. And as much as I thought it would be easy to admit it, I don't want them to hate me. They have to understand.

"And?" Carter presses and I'm not sure where to begin.

"When I left ... after Tyler died five years ago ... when I left you and the family, I followed her." The words spill from me. "Watching her cry made me feel normal. She gave me hope that I wasn't broken, because she felt the same way. But she stopped crying, Carter. She moved on without me."

"Daniel," Carter warns and I hate him for it.

"You'll listen to me," I seethe with barely concealed anger. He will listen and accept it. There are no other options. I can't have it end any other way. "I have no one."

"You chose no one. You left us."

"You know why." They gave Tyler's phone to Carter after the dust settled. Carter saw. He never spoke it out loud. But I was there and I know he saw that I was the one texting him.

I'm the one who led Tyler to his death.

"You didn't have to go." His voice is sincere, but soft and full of sympathy.

"Well I'm coming back now," I tell him.

"Does she know?" he asks me and I answer him with, "I shouldn't have told her."

"She knows you followed her? Is she going to press charges?" he asks and I huff a humorless laugh and then stare at the ceiling fan that's perfectly still.

"I don't think so," I say and it's only then that question becomes a possibility. I've only been thinking about what I can do to make her forgive me.

"She has to forgive me," I tell him with words stronger than I feel.

"She doesn't have to do anything," Carter answers me and the silence stretches as my disdain for him grows.

"What did she say?" he asks me just as I'm ready to hang up.

"That she hates me." It doesn't hurt me to say the words today like they hurt me yesterday. There's hope, only a small piece, but it's there. "She didn't mean it," I tell him.

"Did you do anything else?" Carter asks me with a tone that's cautious, like he already knows.

"I've done lots of things, brother."

"With her. With Addison." My gaze wanders to my shoes by the bed and I bend down to put them on and lace them while I tell him, "I tried to stay away from her, but she sought me out ... before she knew."

"Did she fuck you?" he asks me and it strikes me as if he's said it backward.

"I fucked her, yes." The irritation gives me strength and I stare at the pile of shit next to the door that I'll take with me back home and nearly leave it behind. It's all meaningless.

"Is she ..." Carter hesitates to ask.

"She's mine." The words leave me quickly, whipping out as if they're meant to lash him, hating how he questions it. *She's always been mine.*

I almost tell him that she'll forgive me, but the doubt in me stops the words on the tip of my tongue.

"I'm coming home. I've been running away for a long time."

"If you bring her, tell me so I can tell the others."

"Why tell them?" Although I don't give a shit what they think, I know Addison will.

"She was like a sister to us, Daniel. She didn't just leave Tyler, she left all of us."

She didn't just leave us once. She left us twice.

When I heard her break up with Tyler in the kitchen, I could hear every word. I stood by the window, watching her leave.

I can't let her leave a third time. I can't let her go.

Before I can stop myself, I speak into the phone, "I'll let you know."

Staring at the closed door to this rented house, I can see Addison so clearly all those years ago. Driving away and I never bothered to stop her or tell her how she wasn't allowed to leave.

She could never leave.

She was meant to be there.

Not with Tyler, but with me.

Maybe if I had bothered to tell either of them that, Tyler would still be here and none of this would have happened.

CHAPTER 25

Addison

*T*his coldness won't go away.

It follows me everywhere. Even burying myself under the blankets doesn't take the chill away.

I can't sleep. I can only wait for updates from Daniel. He texted me all night. He's really leaving.

It all feels so final and I have no time to process anything. There's a heaviness in my chest and a soreness in my lungs that I'm so painfully aware of. They won't leave me alone.

Another message, another plea from him.

Please meet me, he begs. *I can't lose you again.*

Looking at his message stirs up so much emotion. I don't want to lose him. That's the worst part of all of this. It's the fact that I don't want to be alone and without him again.

But how can you forgive someone for watching you suffer when they knew they could save you?

I'll wait outside. I'm on my way and I'll wait for you, but I can't wait long. Please Addison.

The seconds tick by as I stare at his message.

Tick-tock. Tick-tock.

It's early in the morning; the sun is still rising. A new day.

I can tell him goodbye. Just one last kiss. A kiss for the love we had. The love we shared for another too. A final goodbye that I should have had years ago.

I can pretend that's what this will be, but I already feel myself clinging to him.

Some people you're meant to say goodbye to, and others you aren't.

I don't text him back. Instead I head to the bathroom. I look exactly how I feel, which is fucking awful. I half question getting myself somewhat put together to see him.

But I don't want him to remember me like this if it really is the last time I'll see him.

I take a few minutes, each one seeming longer and longer even though hardly any time has passed. And when I look up, I see a pretty version of me, with mascara and concealer to hide the exhaustion. I can't hide the pain though.

I'll try to let him go and move on.

Because that's what I'm supposed to do. Isn't it? It's what a sane, strong woman would do.

The zipper seems so loud as I close the makeup bag, as does the click of the light switch. There's hardly any light from the early morning sunrise as I make my way out and down the stairs to the side entrance of the apartment.

Each step feels heavier than the last and my heart won't stop breaking.

It's a slow break, straight down the center. My heart hates me, but yet again, it's something that seems so fitting.

There's a large window on the side entrance door and I'm staring out of it, looking for Daniel's car when I push it open. He isn't here yet. Not that I can see.

I want more time before I have to say goodbye and it makes it painfully obvious that I don't want to speak the words. But I can't be weak and I don't know that I can forgive him.

The cool air hits my face as the wind whips by and I walk slowly down the stairs. I take my time, not wanting this to end but knowing it's so close and there's nothing I can do to stop it.

The second I hit the bottom step and see Daniel's car pull up to the curb, a large hand covers my face at the same time that I'm pulled back into a heavy wall—no, a man's chest.

A man. Someone's grabbed me. The realization hits me in a wave. I didn't see him coming. I still can't see him.

A scream rips up my throat as I try to swing back and hit him. Daniel! I try to scream, but I can't. The man whirls around and my vision is blurred as I hit a brick wall, my arm scraping against it.

I don't stop screaming; I don't stop fighting with everything I have. My knee thumps against the brick wall as the man sneers at me to be quiet, the black leather glove on his hand making my face feel hot. I kick off the wall with the fear, the anger, and the knowledge that if I don't scream for Daniel, he won't know. He won't be able to save me.

My knee burns with pain as I shove my weight into the man and push at the same time, falling to the asphalt and breaking free for only a split second.

I scream out for Daniel, although I don't know if he heard me. I can't breathe as a man in a black hoodie with bloodshot eyes shoves his hand down on my face so hard that I think he broke my nose for a moment. The pain radiates and tears stream from my eyes.

I always thought the worst thing you could see when you die was the face of someone who loved you, but couldn't help you.

Staring into the black eyes of this man, I question that.

But relief comes quickly.

Through my blurred vision, I see a boot slam into his head, knocking him off of me although I struggle to get myself free and scramble away.

Bang! Bang!

I hear gunshots and I scream out again out of instinct, falling onto my side and huddling into a ball. *Bang!*

One last shot.

One heartbeat.

Another.

Silence.

And then I look up to see the man lying still, but Daniel clutching at his chest. He breathes heavily and then stumbles.

"No!" I cry out as blood soaks through his white cotton t-shirt and into the open button-up layered over it.

"Daniel," I cry out with fear gripping my heart.

He screams at me, even though the strength is gone. "Get inside!"

My body refuses to obey as he pulls his hand away from his chest. There's blood. So much blood.

Daniel's expression only changes from worried for me to angered as he stares at his hand. His focus moves to the man lying motionless on the asphalt and he points the gun at his head, firing.

Bang! Bang! Bang! Each shot makes my body tremble. The man's body doesn't react. His face is one I don't recognize as he stares lifelessly at nothing.

My gaze shifts from his dead eyes back to Daniel as he hunches over and grips his chest, falling to his knees on the ground.

That's the moment I can finally move again. And I run to him as fast as I can with one thought running through my mind.

Everyone I love dies.

Every.

Single.

One.

CHAPTER 26

Daniel

Fuck.

Hot blood pours from my wound and soaks into my shirt as I lean against the brick wall, feeling sharp, shooting pains run up and down my spine. I apply pressure to the gunshot to try to stop the flow.

I can barely breathe through my clenched teeth at the pain.

"Go inside," I try to yell at Addison as she hovers over me. "Now," I grit out and my words come out weak.

"Daniel, get up. Get up!" she yells at me. And it actually makes me smile.

As I try to stand, with her pulling on me and attempting to aid me, I look back down at my hand. It's bright red, not black. That's the first good sign. But when I look down to my chest and see how much it's still bleeding, the lightheadedness nearly makes me collapse.

"Come with me," she begs. "We have to go to the hospital."

"No, no hospital. No cops." I'm still okay enough to know better than that. "You can't stay here; the cops will be coming. You have to go."

"I'm not leaving you," she yells at me with disbelief. "Just stay with me. Hide in my apartment. Let me help you, please," she begs me and that's the only reason I let her wrap an arm around me and guide me back to her apartment.

Thank fuck it's so early in the morning and everything went down in the back alley.

Dark alley.

A man who knew where to be and when.

Someone with information.

Not Marcus ... but it's someone who must know Marcus. My gaze moves to Addison's pale face as she opens the door to her apartment. Someone who wanted her. Someone who wanted to hurt me. And Marcus had to have told them. He's the only one who knew I was with her and what she meant to me.

"Come on." She tries to push me into her apartment and for a moment I hesitate, but if Marcus or someone else is after Addison, I have to be beside her.

It's too late for me to say goodbye.

I feel breathless as my gaze darts from the door behind us to the counter, then to the window. I have to tell Carter. At the thought a pain shoots up my back and down my shoulder, making me grit my teeth.

Fuck! Holding my breath, I put more pressure on the wound.

My steps are wide as I walk in and head for the kitchen. To the tile floor where it will be easy to clean up.

"Was there blood in the alley?" I ask Addison in a pained voice that I can't control and look behind me as I walk. Nothing's spilling onto the floor. Not a drop. My shirt is soaked with blood, but hopefully there's nothing that will lead the cops up to Addison.

"A lot of it," she answers me as she rips open the cabinet door and pulls out a roll of paper towels.

"Did it lead up the stairs?" I ask her breathlessly and then wince from the pain. *Fuck! Make it stop. Please.*

She looks at me wide-eyed before realizing I was talking about my blood. Not the asshole who dared to put his hands on her. She visibly swallows while shaking her head frantically. "No, nothing." She winds the paper towels around her hand before giving me the bundle of them. Her hands are still trembling. My poor Addison.

I take a quick look, as quickly as I can. Looks like the bullet exited cleanly. The wound isn't the problem. It'll bleed, but it'll heal. It's the infection that'll kill me if I don't have one of the guys take a look at it.

"Come sit," she tells me while also reaching for my shirt. "Sit down," she commands again. Her hands are shaking and her voice trembles, but she's trying to be strong.

I reach out and grab her hand to stop her. My blood smears on her soft skin. "I'm fine," I say to try to comfort her.

Addison shakes her head with tears in her eyes. "Sit down and let me take care of you." She swallows her tears back and adds, "If you won't go to the hospital, it's the least you can do."

A breath leaves me and makes me feel weak.

Another and my hand releases hers, but she doesn't look at it. She doesn't even wipe the blood away; she's still searching my eyes for approval.

Nodding, I take a step back and push the chair at the kitchen island far back enough to sit.

I watch her face the entire time she helps me pull my shirt off. She cares about me still. I know she does. *She'll forgive me.*

"Didn't you say you'd hate me forever?" I ask her. Maybe I'm delirious. I don't know why I push her.

"I said I'd never forgive you," she tells me flatly and doesn't look me in the eyes. Instead she pulls the wad of paper towels away, which are mostly soaked with blood and she quickly balls up more and presses against the wound.

"But you came down to see me," I say without thinking. "It had to mean something." The hope in my chest falters with her silence.

And when she does speak, its light dims.

"It means I was ready to say goodbye."

"I don't believe you," I tell her without hesitation and she looks up at me teary eyed.

"Don't cry," I command weakly. "I didn't want to upset you."

She sucks in a breath and blinks the tears away, but pain is clearly written on her face.

"I'm sorry," I whisper as she wipes the tears from her eyes. "I didn't mean for this-"

"Oh, shut up. You couldn't have known that this ..." her voice breaks before she can finish and she closes her eyes and struggles to calm her breathing.

"It's fine, Addison," I try to reassure her, reaching out even though it sends a lance of pain through my chest. I run my hand down her arm and then pull her in closer, positioning her between my legs.

"It's okay," I whisper into her hair and then plant a small kiss on her temple as I hear sirens outside. She opens her eyes and looks to the far side of her living room, where the alley is just below.

"They may knock, but you don't have to answer," I tell her softly, and she only nods once, her eyes never moving.

"I'm sorry. I can't say goodbye to you," I tell her as I wish I hadn't ever come back to the bar. I wish I hadn't brought this on her. She doesn't know. I'm sure she thinks it was a random mugging or attempted rape. She has no idea. But I know there's no way it's a coincidence.

"I wish I could say goodbye to you again. I wish I could tell you I'll let you go, because it really is what a good man would do."

"Here you go with words about good and bad men when you

don't even know the difference." Addison's tone is flat but there's the hint of a smile waiting for me. I can feel it.

"Thank you for taking care of me," I speak as she pulls the wad of paper towels away and there's less blood. I try to take a deep breath, but it hurts and I wince.

"Let me clean and bandage you," she says although I'm not sure she really wants a response. I swallow thickly and let her work. She can do whatever she wants to me, since I'm just grateful that she's here for me.

I don't deserve her. I know I don't. And that's all I can think about as she tapes the sterile gauze in place. Even as she poured rubbing alcohol over my wound I barely felt a thing.

"I need you to go lie down." Addison speaks with authority although she looks like a beautiful mess herself.

The desperate need for sleep begs me to listen to her, although Carter is expecting me. He knows I'm coming.

As if reading my mind Addison says, "It can wait. You can't drive right now anyway."

"Will you lie down with me?" I would give anything to feel her soft body next to mine and hold her right now. The thought sends a warmth through me, but it vanishes when I look up.

Her sad eyes meet mine with something they haven't before. Regret, maybe? Or denial? I'm not sure, but I'm certain she's going to tell me no.

"Please," I add and my voice trembles. "Even if it's only a little while?"

She's reluctant to nod, but she does and my throat closes with a pain that's sure to haunt me forever.

At least I have one more night. But I know in my heart, it's only one more night.

CHAPTER 27

Addison

I don't want to wake up. I don't want to move.

Because right now I have a man I desperately want, and it doesn't make me weak to be with him. But when this moment is over, that's what I'll be. It's not about forgiving him anymore; it's accepting who I am if I'm with him.

I'm not sure how long we've been in bed, but the knocks at the door from the cops came and went. And at least hours have passed, because my eyes don't feel so heavy, only sore.

"You're awake." Daniel's deep rumble makes his chest vibrate. And it's only then that I realize how close to him I am, how I'm curled around him and his arm is behind my back, holding me to him.

I roll over slightly, only enough so my head is on the pillow and not his chest. There are so many things to say. And so little time.

You can want a person but know they're bad for you. That's the person Daniel's been for me since I've met him. And it's not going to change.

Daniel lifts the sheet and checks his gunshot wound. I can only see a faint circle of blood and I try to gauge his reaction, but he doesn't say anything.

"Are you going to be okay?" I ask him and try to swallow down my worry.

"Are you going to leave me if I say I'll be fine?" he asks, turning his face toward me and his lips are only inches from mine.

I huff a small laugh and a trace of a smile is there for a moment, but the pain of the unknown is quick to take it away. The smile on my lips quivers and I have to take in a deep breath.

"I don't know where we go from here." It's hard to tell him the truth.

I hear him swallow and then he looks up at the ceiling, rather than at me.

"I still want you," he says in a whisper although I'm not sure he meant for it to come out that way. "I can't let go of you," he says and puts his gaze back on me, assessing my reaction.

I can't explain how it feels to hear him say the only words I want to hear. I want to beg him not to let go of me because I'm so afraid to lose myself with him, but I don't ever want to be apart.

A second passes, and then another. And I don't know what to do or think or say. I only know time is running out.

"I'll never stop watching you, Addison. My heart thinks you belong to me and it always has. Whether I want it, whether you want it. It doesn't matter–I'll always feel this need to watch over you."

"It's not the watching part," I try to tell him and then shake my head. My hair slides against the pillow and I struggle to speak, but somehow I do. "It just hurts."

"I'm sorry." He says the same words as before, but the pain is so much more real now as he turns over slightly and puts his hand on mine.

"Do you want me?" he asks me and then adds, "Do you want to come home with me? I'll make it better. I swear I will."

He squeezes my hand and I don't know what to say. I just want everything to feel better and to not hate myself for running back to him.

"I don't want you to come with me because you're lost or lonely or scared. If you want me, I want you. I can't help it and I can't stop it. I tried and when I finally let go of you, there was nothing left of me."

My heart aches for him and for me. I know exactly how he feels. Tears prick my eyes and I can hardly breathe.

I can't answer him, so instead I tell him what I'd planned on saying when I was ready to say goodbye.

My words come out in shuddered breaths. "If you'd come to me back then, I would have let you in. Instead of watching me in pain, I would have loved you for being there for me and I would have been there for you too."

"You're blind to how you were back then. You may have had feelings for me. But you loved him."

"I loved you too though." My voice cracks as I protest and I heave in a breath.

"You wouldn't if you knew the truth. It was my fault-"

I cut him off, pressing my finger to his lips to silence him. "I'm done with the past, Daniel. I don't need to know every horrible thing you once did. I only wanted you to know that I would have let you in." I almost add, *just like I am now*. I can feel myself falling back to him after nearly losing him. After almost seeing him die. There's no way I can let him go again.

Something lifts in my chest. A lightness that gives me more room to breathe. It's the truth, and knowing that makes me feel anything but weak.

He pauses, considering what I've said and looks past me at the window to the bedroom before speaking again. "You think you would have, but I couldn't take the chance that you'd turn me away. I never had a chance, Addison. Even after he was gone you still loved him, and I hated myself for even thinking about taking his place in your heart. I don't care anymore. I already hate myself, but at least I can have you. I can love you better than anyone else."

He swallows thickly and adds, "I can promise you that."

"Love is a strong word." I'm still afraid to tell him I love him. I don't want him to die. More than anything else, I can't lose him. I know deep down inside, I love Daniel Cross and always have.

"It's the right word for what we have, but we can pretend to go slow?" he questions as if I've already forgiven him. As if I've agreed to go back home with him.

"So you think I'm yours again?" I ask him as I wipe under my eyes and sniffle. "Just like that?"

He holds my gaze as he tells me, "You've always been mine."

And I don't have any words for him in return.

It's true.

Daniel says that he's the one who never had a chance back then. But the truth is Tyler never did.

I was always Daniel's and I don't think I had it in me to say that out loud. Because I don't know if Tyler could have ever forgiven me if he knew.

Daniel leans closer to me with the intent to kiss me. But just before he can cup the back of my head, he winces in pain.

"Shit," the word leaves my lips quickly and I hover over him. "For the love of God, lie down and rest." I pull up the sheets to check on the wound, but it looks the same.

"No, I need to kiss you," he says softly and when my eyes meet his, he smiles weakly and pleadingly.

"I need to kiss you too," I whisper and tears prick my eyes.

I lean down to press my lips to his. I mean it to be soft and sweet, but it deepens instantly and naturally. One of his hands cradles the back of my head, his fingers spearing through my hair. The other grips onto my hip, holding me there as his tongue sweeps over mine and his hot breath mingles with mine.

My body heats, feeling completely at home in his embrace.

"I need you," he whispers against my lips with his eyes closed. My pussy clenches at his words and it's then that I feel his erection against my thigh. The agony breaks and I wipe under my eyes.

"You're hurt," I tell him as I weakly shake my head and cup his strong jaw in my hand.

"Doesn't matter, I'll always need you. Always want you."

My heart pounds and pounds again. Recognizing how true it is, because it's the same for me.

"I love you," I say the words in a whisper even though they frighten me. "I can't lose you."

"I love you more," he tells me and I lean down to kiss him again and shut him up before he makes that pain in my heart grow even more.

CHAPTER 28

Tyler

Five years ago

I feel so fucking stupid.

I don't know how I didn't see it before.

It took him texting me where she is for me to realize it.

Daniel's in love with Addison.

And she's in love with him.

It all makes sense now.

I check the map on my phone to make sure I'm going the right way, although every step makes my heart hurt more.

He doesn't know that I know. Neither does she, but I can do them both a favor and tell them.

I want to kiss her one last time though.

I know it's wrong. But it's just a goodbye kiss. Something to remember her by. Something to let her know that it's okay. That I'm okay with her loving him. I just want her to be happy. She needs it more than anyone. I can see it in her eyes.

My throat feels tight as I walk past Fourth Street. The rain starts coming down harder and it feels fitting.

I pull up my hoodie around my head and listen to my sneakers squeak on the sidewalk as I make my way closer to heartbreak.

I thought her telling me that she couldn't be with me anymore was the worst thing I'd ever feel.

But knowing she loves my brother and wants him more than she wants me? Fuck, it hurts. It hurts so fucking much.

My phone vibrates and I look down to see a text from Daniel. She's gone into the corner store now and Daniel said it looks like she's been crying. She's been doing it at school too. But she won't let me near her this time. She won't let me comfort her when she needs it so badly.

This isn't the first time she's dumped me. My brothers don't know because I'm too ashamed to tell them.

But each time she did, I'd find her crying somewhere and she'd let me hold her to make it feel better.

I just loved her, hoping she loved me back. And I know some part of her does. But I never thought she didn't love me fully because there was someone else.

I thought it was just the way she is. That she just pushes people away and that I would have to handle her more gently. I should have known by the way she avoided Daniel and the way he asked about her.

How was I so fucking stupid?

Do you want me to go to her? *Daniel texts me and I stop one block over from where she is. Where both of them are. So close, I can see the window of the store. The light is dim in the sheets of rain. So close, but so far away.*

I should tell him yes. I should let him go to her. I bet she'd let him comfort her.

But I just want one last kiss. Just one more time before I let her go.

It's all I want. Just one last kiss before I let her go.

CHAPTER 29

Addison

"*I* don't think I can breathe."

"I'm not inside you right now, so you should be fine," Daniel quips as the car door shuts behind us. He leaves his black Mercedes in the paved horseshoe driveway as we step up to the Cross estate. The stubborn asshole wouldn't let me drive. The painkillers definitely helped him. But I'm looking forward to someone taking a look at him. Someone who knows what they're doing.

"It's different from the other house," I state, ignoring Daniel's joke and how easy this is for him. It's not just different. It's massive. They used to live in a small house off the backroads. This is ... something else.

"Home looks different when you're different," he tells me and walks forward, leaving me standing in the shadow of the large white stone house. Is it even a house? It looks like a mansion.

"Who lives here?" I ask Daniel and he wraps his arm around my waist. "It's for all of us."

I haven't seen any of his brother's since the funeral and on that day, I couldn't look any of them in the eye. I could barely speak to them. I could barely do anything because the guilt was so strong. My pulse quickens as he pushes me forward.

"I don't know ..."

"I know you can. And you'll feel better when you do. Both of us will feel better when we go in there." His eyes plead with me—not just to go in for him, but to be *with* him.

He holds out his hand for me, leaving it in the air until I finally grip on to him.

"Don't leave me," I whisper and stare into his eyes.

A tight smile is the response I get, followed by him leaning down to kiss me once on the lips.

His hot breath tickles my skin in the crisp fall air as he lowers his mouth to the shell of my ear. "I know this isn't ..." He trails off and I can hear him lick his lips. "This isn't a fairytale. But there's nothing for me in there if it isn't also for you," he finally says and then pulls back.

My heart clenches with a pain that I think I love. A pain of a shared past, but of knowing we can have a future together.

Standing in front of the estate, with his thin black cotton shirt stretched tight across his shoulders, a shade of black that almost matches the darkness in his eyes, how could I deny him?

"They know you're coming. They know you're mine." He speaks with a conviction I feel in my soul.

It's not the first part of what he said that comforts me. It's everything in the second part.

I want to be his, and they know that I am.

I swallow thickly and ignore the churning in the pit of my stomach as we walk up the stairs to the entryway.

It's safe. Everything is alright. I'm with Daniel.

The thoughts are comforting enough to give me the strength to breathe as he opens the large front door and leads me inside.

Each step is harder to take and I feel myself pulling away from him. I don't want to face his brothers. I'm too afraid of what they'll think. I'm afraid of their judgment and hate. Because I've only ever had love for them. Not the kind of love I had for Tyler, and not what I have for Daniel. But love nonetheless. They gave me a home when I had none. They were my family.

And right now … I can't bear for them to send me away.

"It's okay," Daniel says and holds me in the quiet foyer. "It's going to be hard at first. The memories are the hardest part, I think, and there are a lot between us all."

"I don't know if I can do this," I admit to him, wiping under my eyes to see a blurry vision of mascara smeared on my fingertips. I sniffle and then wish I hadn't come.

"We'll have good days and bad days, like everything else. And if it gets to be too much, we'll leave for a while, however long we need. We can go wherever you want to go. We don't have to stay here. I'm fine as long as we stay together. All that matters is that you stay with me." His eyes search mine as we hold each other.

I'll stay with him. Daniel is where my home is. "I'm not going anywhere."

"I've wanted you for far too long to not have you forever now."

"I'm yours," I promise him.

"You've always been mine."

The sound of footsteps is drowned out by a voice that echoes down into the open space. It's grand to say the least, but I can't take it in. I can only watch two men walk into the foyer.

"Addison," one of them says, catching me by surprise. It takes me a long time to realize it's Jase. I almost cry when I do. He looks so much more like Tyler than Daniel does. They always looked alike. Daniel tightens his grip on me as my voice cracks. "Jase."

I clear my throat as Jase stands tall in front of me.

"You look so different," Jase tells me.

"You don't," I say quickly but then take it back. "I mean you do, but you don't."

He smirks down at me and runs his forefinger and thumb over his chin. "Funny, I don't remember you being this shy."

I can only shrug; I don't trust myself to speak and I can hardly keep eye contact as I remember all the memories together. Jase and Tyler were close. The closest. And unless Tyler wanted privacy, Jase was there. Like an annoying brother.

Part of me is still aware that I'm holding on to Daniel with a white-knuckled grip. And that part of me wants to let go, so I can hug Jase.

"It's good to have you home. Everyone else thinks so too, trust me."

"Do you-" I falter and pick worriedly at the pocket of my jeans with the hand not being held firmly by Daniel. The questions I have are all begging to come out at once.

Do you hate me for leaving him?

Do you blame me for what happened?

Do you forgive me? That's the one that lingers. That's the only one that matters. "I'm sorry-" I start to say, but the words are tainted with a small cry.

"Addison." A voice to my right startles me before I can gather the strength to chance the apology. "So how'd you get him back here?" a deep voice asks me and I know immediately it's Declan.

Daniel pulls me in closer, planting a small kiss on my temple in front of both of them as we stand in the foyer. It's all too much, but none of them seem taken aback. Neither of the brothers is looking at me as if anything is off.

As if I'm not a reminder of what they've lost. Not an outsider. Not an enemy.

My lips part and I'm not sure what to say, but I'm grateful. I'm so grateful that I'm welcome. And that I get to see them again.

I never thought I would.

"Where's Carter?" Daniel asks Declan, wrapping his arm

around my waist and pulling me in more just slightly, but still easy and casually. His thumb hooks into my jeans and gently caresses my hip as he talks to both brothers.

I try not to make it awkward.

It takes everything in me not to cry upon seeing both of them.

I'm surprised when Daniel loosens his grip on me and whatever they were talking about comes to a halt.

I'm even more surprised when Jase leans in close.

"It's good to see you, Addie," Jase says and hugs me hard, so hard that Daniel has to take a step back. Finally letting my hand go as Jase pulls me to him. It's been a long time since someone's called me Addie. They all did back then. All of them but Daniel. I was always Addison to him.

The hug is short-lived and I'm still numb from it along with the shock of everything when Daniel asks for a minute. As soon as his brothers turn away, I press my palms to my eyes and try to calm myself down. It's emotionally taxing to see those you've mourned because you thought you'd lost them forever.

"I'm okay," I tell Daniel weakly as he rubs my back.

"I promise I'll love you forever." Daniel whispers words that frighten me. Words that threaten to take him from me one day. I hesitate to say it back and he adds, "Just stay with me."

It's a plea from the lips of a man who could destroy me.

Sometimes when you walk into a darkness, a place filled with both what terrifies you from the past and what will forever haunt you in the future, you get a sick feeling that washes over you.

Like you know bad things are coming.

"I love you too," I whisper to Daniel and let him take my hand.

He squeezes lightly as I step further into the Cross estate.

It's brightly lit, but it doesn't fool me. The darkness is here.

There's a certain feeling in the pit of your stomach. I felt it when Tyler brought me to his home all those years ago.

It's a feeling that tells you you're doing something wrong. Something you know you shouldn't, but it tempts you and whispers all the right things; it promises you that you're meant to be here.

Not unlike what I've felt since the moment I met Daniel. This force of needing to be with him. Of knowing I was supposed to be his all along.

Even if the very thought of being his was enough to send a chill over me each time he dared to breathe near me.

That feeling is supposed to warn you, to keep you safe.

Daniel kisses the underside of my wrist as I let the feeling settle through me.

Sometimes that feeling is terrifying.

Sometimes that feeling is home.

MERCILESS

Carter

$\mathcal{I}$'m not used to the anxiousness ringing in my blood.

But times have changed and until this shit is settled, I'm going to be on edge.

I need all the help I can get.

And judging by the way Daniel can't take his eyes off of Addison, he's not in the right mindset.

But the important thing is that he's back.

Daniel cranes his neck to look up at me from where he's seated with her in the den.

Addison Fawn. I never thought I'd see her again. I thought I'd lost her when I lost my brother.

"Do you have a minute?" I ask him, getting their attention. Addison glances between Daniel and me, and I give her an easy smile. I've barely spoken to her, but it's only because of everything else. The war that's starting. That's what has my attention. That, and whoever decided to fuck with us.

Whoever decided to touch Addison and fuck with Daniel.

It's only a matter of time before we know who. Although the thought of Marcus being involved sends a chill through my blood.

Daniel winces as he stands, reminding me of the gunshot and rekindling that anger inside of me. He bends at the waist to kiss Addison. My eyes stay on her, noting how she pulls back slightly, but his hand on the back of her neck keeps her there. Her doe eyes look back into his and he brushes the tip of his nose against hers. And then she reaches up to kiss him this time.

I don't know what she did to my brother, but it's been a long damn time since I've seen him care about anything other than himself.

It's a good look for him.

"I was wondering when you were going to come for me," Daniel says as we walk back to the office. I keep him in sight even as he looks over his shoulder to check on her.

"You think she's going to run off?" I ask him jokingly, but it only makes his expression harden. Maybe he's still blind to it. But it's obvious she loves him. It was obvious five years ago too.

Silence escorts us until I close the door to the office with a loud click.

Daniel takes a seat in front of the large desk and rather than sitting at the head of it, I take the seat across from him, feeling the worn brown leather beneath my hands.

"I need that package," I tell him and wait for whatever the hell it is. He's already been here for hours, but Addison needed him for a little while. I could afford them that.

With a nod, Daniel slips the envelope from his back pocket. My teeth grind against one another. Hundreds of thousands of dollars in trades and a war between drug lords are on the line over whatever the fuck the Romanos are offering us.

And it's only a thin envelope, folded and creased down the center.

Our fingers brush as he hands it to me, but he doesn't let it go.

With my arm outstretched I look back at my brother, waiting for what he has to say, but nothing comes. A second ticks by and he releases it, sitting back in his chair but still not saying a word.

"What's gotten into you?" I ask him. Ever since Tyler died, Daniel's been a shell of who he once was. Until recently. Until she came back and brought him with her. I have too for reasons no one knows, but I'm damn good at hiding it.

"She reminds you of Tyler?" he asks me.

"She reminds me of what you were like when he died," I answer him without thinking. And it's true. "You were on the edge of going one way or the other back then, but it looks like you've come back around."

"What do you mean?"

"I thought you were going to take care of her back then." I bite my tongue, wondering if I should tell him what Jase told me when Addison broke up with Tyler. When she said her goodbyes, she could hardly even look at Tyler. Instead she kept looking upstairs toward Daniel's room.

Everyone knew how Daniel felt about her. She was only seventeen and we had bigger and better shit to concern ourselves with. But that day it was more than obvious why she was leaving.

It was only the three of them who were blind to it.

Daniel shakes his head as if what I'm saying is ridiculous. Even after all these years he can't admit it.

"It doesn't matter. You're back, and she's with you. I don't care about anything else and neither does anyone else."

It's quiet for a long moment and Daniel runs his hand down his face, letting his head fall back and looking at the ceiling before he breathes in deep. The memory of Tyler and the pathetic look on Daniel's face forces a vice to tighten around my heart. I fucking hate it. I hate the pain of our past more than anything else.

"Do you think he'd ever forgive me?" he asks me.

"Tyler forgave everyone," I answer him quickly, ready to rid this anxious feeling coursing in my blood. He was the only good one of us. Of course he's the one who died young. "And Tyler wanted her to have a home. To have a family."

He nods his head, although it takes him a long moment before he looks back at me.

"It feels too good to be true," he says softly and I know why.

"Did you tell her the truth?"

"The truth?" he asks as if I don't know.

It only takes me glancing at his side where he was shot for him to understand my question.

"She has no idea. She thinks it was random. A coincidence."

"Is it Marcus?" I have a bad feeling in my gut, but he's the only person that this leads to.

"Yeah." His answer is quick and met with a simmering anger that I recognize from him. There's the brother I know and love. "I told him about her. I needed his help."

"You told Marcus. Who else?"

"He's the only one I told. It had to be him or someone he told."

"Why did you tell him anything?" I keep the accusations out of my tone. Daniel's been reckless for Addison. He always was but this ...

"I had her license plate and nothing else."

My thumb rubs in circular motions over my pointer finger as I take it all in.

He adds, "I couldn't lose her again." I know he could have told Jase. Jase could have looked up her information. But I don't remind him of that. He holds on to guilt too much and I've only just gotten him back. I need him here... especially knowing what's coming.

I have nothing but silence as I think of any reason that Marcus would come for us. He's not a man I want as an enemy, but I'm also not certain it's him.

"It wasn't supposed to happen like that. It will never happen again." He strengthens his resolve and leans forward, daring me to object. But I do.

"And what if she leaves you again?" I ask him and he stares back at me, his chest rising and falling with determination. "What if she finds out something she shouldn't?"

He doesn't say what I expect him to, that she won't. Instead he merely answers, "Then I'll follow her."

My breath leaves me slowly, words failing me.

"She's mine," he says as if nothing else matters. And maybe it doesn't.

I nod my head once, ending the conversation.

The hands of the clock in the office are all I can hear as I run my thumbnail under the flap of the envelope and stare back at my brother. "She's changed you."

"How's that?" he asks me. Again he's on the defensive, and it makes me smile. I like to see him showing something that's real.

"It's hard to pretend when you'd do anything for someone you love."

His gaze flickers to the envelope in my hand and he stares at it as he says, "I didn't come here for a heart to heart, Carter."

"You didn't open it?" Although the words come out with disbelief, the corners of my lips kick up with amusement. He's so consumed with Addison he didn't give a fuck about the one thing I've been losing sleep over for weeks.

"Marcus said it was a message of what's to come," he tells me as I finally open it. The paper tears easily and inside I'm surprised to find only a one-by-one-inch square photo. It falls into my palm facedown and I toss the crumpled envelope onto the desk, then flip the small piece of photo paper over.

"I went through all that shit for that?" Daniel asks, but I ignore him, too drawn to the picture.

I trace the curve of her porcelain face. I let the rough pad of my thumb run along the edge of the photo as I note her beautiful smile and the way her dark hair is lit with the sunshine in the image.

My heart pounds hard and I can't hear what Daniel's saying. I can't hear anything but the conversation I had with Tony Romano in the basement cellar months ago. The man who I've been avoiding, and the man who reached out to Marcus to deliver the message rather than tell me himself.

The dimly lit, cold and dark room was as unforgiving and unmoving as I was when he made his case and I turned him down.

Then he started bartering with things that didn't belong to him.

With women the Talverys were shipping off. His enemies. He wanted me to help him in a war against the Talverys and he was offering their property as payment. There was no way I'd ever accept.

"What is it?" Daniel presses, barely interrupting my memory.

"The gift from the Romanos." I don't know how the words come out strong as I gently place the photo onto the desk. "They want us on their side of this war they're starting."

I remember the way the heavy knife felt in my hand as I picked it up from his desk and stabbed it down onto the splintered wood in front of him. The sharp tip struck the paper in front of him.

The photo of the enemy family.

"If you give me any woman to start a war, it better be this one," I sneered in his face. I remember the stale stench of whiskey and cigars as I turned my back on him, leaving the knife where it was. With the tip of it stabbing the shoulder of the enemy's daughter. The shoulder her father's large hand was clenched around tightly.

His pride and joy, and one and only heir.

I didn't think Tony would ever have the balls to take her and offer her to me.

"A gift?" Daniel questions with his brows raised and then picks up the photo.

"Yes," I answer him impatiently, quick to hide my depravity.

The photo of the one thing I asked for—Aria Talvery.

"In exchange for a war … she's mine."

The End.

A KISS TO TELL

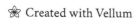 Created with Vellum

PROLOGUE

Chloe

*T*he kiss was bruising, just like his presence always was.

On the last Tuesday before school let out for the summer, and my ninth-grade year was over forever, Sebastian Black kissed me. No. He devoured me.

He destroyed everything I had in that moment. He took every bit and he made it his. *I* was his for that all-consuming kiss. My first kiss.

I still remember it so well. I couldn't breathe. I couldn't do anything but let the heat and electricity rip through my body as Sebastian pinned me against the wall. The rough brick scraped harshly against the small of my back, but I hadn't even noticed. I wouldn't notice until hours later, standing under the stream of water in a scalding shower. The sting I felt proved his kiss had left more than one mark on me.

His tongue was hot, his grip intense and his presence dominating as ever. When he followed me outside as I tried to hide around the corner behind the school, I didn't even see him coming. The chill in the air struck against my heated face as soon as the door swung open, and I could barely manage to feel anything but the cold sensation that flowed over my skin. I needed to hide. From the other kids, from the teachers who didn't care... from reality. I was always good at that.

I didn't expect anyone to follow me. No one had for the past few days. Each day proved harder than the last, although the nights were the worst.

I was still carelessly wiping away my tears—they were an unwanted nuisance just like how everyone else saw me—when I heard his hard steps behind me.

The sudden spike of fear I felt, paled in comparison to the effect Sebastian had on me. The sound of my startled gasp was dwarfed by the feel of my heart racing rapidly against his as he pinned me where he wanted me.

He always took what he wanted.

But I'd never once thought he wanted me.

His warm breath flowed over my face, and suddenly the iciness in the air was nonexistent. Nothing existed but him. Not even the air that separated us.

If I hadn't been stunned, the confusion would have shown on my face. I'd always wondered what it would be like to be kissed by a boy like Sebastian. I'd assumed it would always be nothing more than a passing thought. But every time he walked by me, every time I caught him staring at me, I knew there was something between us. His piercing gaze seemed to capture me in place while also looking right through me.

I was no one, but I wanted it that way. Not being noticed was the best thing that could happen when you lived where I did. Unless you were Sebastian, and then everyone noticed you and everyone feared you just the same.

He pulled away from me before I could react to his lips on mine, both of us gasping for air.

I'll never forget that his eyes were closed, or how slowly he opened them to paralyze me with those steely blues of his. A mask of indifference slipped over his face, but I know my expression showed my awe, my shock... my lust that I had so painfully hidden since the first day I'd laid eyes on him.

"Stop crying," he said, and his command was harsh as if my tears were an insult to him. As if my pain had anything at all to do with him. His nostrils flared and the rage he was so well known for was evident on his handsome features.

But just as it had never affected me before, it didn't affect me then either. I knew he was forbidden. I knew I was supposed to be afraid of him. Maybe I was just stupid because I never felt anything but desire for him.

"Stop fucking crying," he gritted out between his clenched teeth, "and don't tell anyone I did this. Not a single fucking person," he threatened. He brought his lips even closer to mine in a gesture that should have been menacing, but I'd be damned if it didn't make me hot for him where I'd never felt heat before. His eyes searched mine.

"Or else I'll make you cry those tears harder than you can imagine." His words caused my gaze to move from his lips to his cold stare. He would never know how hard I had cried in the middle of the night. He didn't know what had really happened and how guilty I was.

I shook my head gently and replied, "You can't."

His grin was accompanied by a huff of masculine laughter like he thought it was a challenge, but before he could say whatever was on the tip of his tongue, I cut him off.

"You won't make me cry. I know you won't," I said and shook my head, meeting his gaze with every ounce of sincerity I could muster. "And I won't tell anyone." The last bit broke my heart in two, but I don't know why when there wasn't a single soul to tell anyway. There was no one I wanted to run to. No one but the boy who had lost control, kissed me, and obviously regretted it.

I watched as he swallowed, his throat tightening. The bit of stubble that ran up his neck tempted me to touch it. Whatever it was that had caused him to kiss me, whether it was only to silence my crying or something else, was gone. And I knew he'd never kiss me again.

Letting out a long breath, my lips still parted, I said nothing and let him walk away.

The masculine scent of a boy I should have feared and a boy I should have never wanted, was all that filled my lungs as I tried to steady myself. I sagged against the brick building and tried to make sense of what had just happened.

I stopped crying that day and didn't shed another tear. Not that week, and not at the funeral. Not when my uncle let me move in with him, so I would have a place to stay.

I never spoke of what happened and I started to question my sanity when he never spoke of it either.

Nothing changed in the way he acted, or in the way he looked through me.

But I remember the way I touched my lips as he stalked away.

I remember how it felt and how it was everything I needed in that moment.

HE COULD NEVER HAVE KNOWN what he'd done to me that day.

But neither of us would ever forget.

CHLOE

Five years after the kiss

andom streetlights going out is something that used to terrify me.

I hate the feeling that comes with the sudden flicker signifying what's about to happen. Then the light burns out, and all you're left with is darkness. Even just remembering how it's happened before makes me shudder.

One night two years ago, it took place in quick succession, the bright lights flickering briefly and then suddenly there was no light at all. It happened on my way home from old man Bailey's hardware store. I'd gone only an hour before sunset and spent longer than I thought I would. Some asshole had kicked in my front door the night before and there was no way I was going to leave the store without a new lock. I bought two just to be on the safe side.

And so, I was walking home alone in the dark when the lights went out, one after the other. I couldn't walk fast enough to get to the next light that hadn't burned out; I nearly ran to it.

I don't like to be outside at night, not unless I'm on my porch. But even then, I'd rather stay inside, where the idea of safety used to mean something.

Either way, I'd spent too long at the store and with the plastic bag dangling from my wrist, I quickened my pace when the first bulb died. I remember how I stared straight ahead at the next one, praying it would give me light long enough to get home. As if it was listening to my fears and wanted to mock me, the light vanished before my eyes.

Fear of darkness is reasonable. But the kind of inevitable dread that lingers when a light goes out while you're watching it used to follow me everywhere.

It haunted me during the day and never hesitated to steal my sleep at night.

I don't know when things changed, but as I make my way down Peck Avenue, the light flickers on my right and I don't miss a step, I don't even dare to look at it. In my periphery, I see shadow consume everything behind me. My fingers wrap a little tighter around the strap of my purse, but it's more instinctive than a conscious response.

My heart races and then steadies to the sound of my heels clicking rhythmically on the pavement.

One more block and I'll be home. In darkness or in light, it doesn't matter anymore. I've been through both.

I keep my eyes fixed straight ahead and think about the mundane task awaiting me at work tomorrow. I spent all day organizing Mr. Brown's new clients, and my back is killing me from leaning down to the filing cabinet and then looking at the computer, time and time again. A few more days and the new system will be in place. At least until he decides to change it again.

I used to think Marc Brown changed the system so frequently

out of boredom, but after looking at his client list, I think the lawyer is a crook. Everyone in this city is, so it shouldn't have surprised me. I'd work for anyone else, doing anything else, but my options aren't exactly overflowing.

I have my high school diploma, but after trying for the last two years since graduation to get into any college at all and being rejected, a diploma is all I have and all I'll ever have. And that piece of paper is useless here.

My phone pings in my purse and I'm more than eager to pull it out.

I could use something to keep my mind from wandering back to the shit job I have. As I pull out my phone I see the old book I'd stowed in my purse earlier this week, ready to read the novel again. For the dozenth time.

A court-mandated shrink gave it to me five years ago. She loved to draw, although I remember thinking she wasn't really good at it. I used to have a picture from her of a duck she drew with a pencil. I don't know where it's gone, not that it matters much. I still have the books she gave me and, more importantly, a love of books. I wasn't so much into the drawing, but that shrink—I think her name was Rebecca—gave me a handful of fiction. She gave me a way to get lost in someone else's world. It wasn't long before I started writing as well, trying to create an escape from this life. I couldn't give two shits about her artwork, but I'll always be grateful to her for giving me a love of reading and writing.

Forgetting about the book and everything that happened back then, I focus on the text message.

You'll never guess what happened last night.

It's Angie, a friend from work. Well, I think she's my friend. She's new and doesn't do much but read magazines and chew gum while she tells off clients who want their paperwork faster than she can print it out, but she tells me all the details of her Tinder dates. I'm the only one she talks to at the office.

Mr. Brown exclusively hires girls in their twenties—and

younger. Of the five of us, Angie likes to only talk to me. I get it, sort of. I don't care for the other women either. For the most part, they ignore me, which I'm used to, but they also stop their hushed whispers the moment I walk into the room. At first, I thought it was all in my head, but no, they like to talk about me. About the rumors of what happened years ago. *How sad it is.* They can go fuck themselves.

My family has history here, but it's no secret. Every person in this damn city comes from circumstances of shame. Luckily, I don't work with them much; it's usually Angie who I get paired with, and I should really be grateful to Marc for that.

What? I text her back, curious about the escapade of last night.

After dinner, I took him home and he was fucking amazing in bed. I think I'd use the word... enthusiastic.

My brow raises at the last word.

What does that mean? I ask her.

He did things to me I had no idea I even wanted.

I can feel my blood heat just thinking about what she may have done. I've never done anything with anyone. Having sex simply isn't on my to-do list. I'm not interested, not from anyone in this city. My phone pings again, and I look to see what else she's said.

He choked me.

I stop in my tracks for a moment, staring down at the glowing screen in my hand and rereading what she wrote.

And he told me he was going to take my ass and holy shit Chlo, anal is e v e r y t h i n g.

If anyone could see my face, they'd see the shock. I don't know how she can even surprise me anymore. My fingers reach up to my throat as I swallow, wondering why he'd want to do that to her and how she could enjoy it. The choking part. I watch my fair share of porn, but that's one I don't really understand.

I'll tell you more on Monday, but I had to tell SOMEONE. I read her text as if she'd spoken it to me, sprightly voice, and all.

Can't wait to hear all the deets. My reply can't convey my gratitude at being informed via text about the choking, so I can hide my naivety and shock from her at the realization she's into that.

You almost home? she asks, and a soft smile plays at my lips. A warmth I'm not used to courses through me and slowly I find my pace again.

One block to go, I answer her and wait for her to respond with the same thing she wrote a few nights ago. For me to tell her when I get in.

Last week I told her I live just outside of Fallbrooke, and she kept pushing to know where exactly. When I told her I'm from Crescent Hills, the same city as Mr. Brown's office, her face paled. She's not from around here, but she knows the reputation of this place and what it's known for. Everyone does. If you want a taste of sin, Crescent Hills is where you'll find more than your fill.

I'm used to the embarrassment, but not from someone who chooses to work in this city. She doesn't have to be here any longer than a nine-to-five, and honestly, I don't know why she even chose to work in this run-down area when she lives in the big city. And that's exactly what I challenged her with when she told me I shouldn't be walking home.

I'm grown. I'm aware. I'm also broke and on my own since my uncle died two years ago, leaving me with bills, a mortgage, and no job to pay for any of it, so I told her she could take her high horse and shove it. But maybe not in those exact words, and maybe with a choked voice of shame.

The silence lasted only a minute or so, but it felt like an hour. She offered to walk me home and when I declined, as politely as I could, she snatched my phone from my desk. Before I could ask her what she was doing, she texted herself before handing it back, so we would have each other's number.

Text me when you're home, she told me, but I didn't answer her. When she texted again, apologizing, and asking if I'd made it home all right, I answered only because I thought she was genuinely worried. And things have been normal again ever since.

It's a small act of kindness, but it means more to me than it should. I'm smart enough to know that I shouldn't let it get to me like this. I can't rely on anyone or trust anyone. Outsiders come and go here. Even Ang said she wasn't planning on staying at the law firm for long. I should know better than to think of her as a friend.

But when she sends texts like the one that just came through, I can't help but feel a little camaraderie. I smile as I reread the text. *See you Monday, prepare to be scandalized!*

My heels click on the asphalt, worn rough from years with no repairs. In the distance, I hear a siren, and farther down the block, a few kids are screaming at one another. It's nearly ten at night, but this is normal.

Just like the streetlights going out.

Back when I would have childish fears about the darkness swallowing me up, I also used to dream. I used to dream of leaving here. Of going anywhere but here and never returning. I wish I could forget those memories. But they cling to me like the filth that clings to the gutters on the side of the road.

I used to dream of running away. Mundane things like bills have a way of robbing you of your fantasies. At least I have my books and my writing. Even if I never escape this place, I can still escape into the worlds I build for myself in my stories.

Years ago, when I was still in school, I told my uncle that I'd leave here one day. I remember the sound of the porch swing as it swayed, how my fingers felt as they traced the rusted chain that held it in place. He told me this city didn't let anyone leave. It kept them rooted to this place.

I didn't know what he meant until he passed and there was no one here to pick up the pieces. No one but me.

My feet stumble and I come to a halt as I try desperately not to fall forward. The combination of rubble on the ground and the sight of someone's shadow laying across the very porch swing I'd just been thinking about are what almost cause me to trip.

My chest aches with a sudden pounding of anxiety. No one comes to visit me. It's one of the blessings I've been afforded by being the sad girl with her sob story. I keep my head down and I mind my own business. No one likes me, no one but Ang, and no one fucks with me either. Why would they? I have nothing.

But someone's there. I can't see their face, but the shadow is there and unmistakable.

The paint on the porch swing is weathered, and no one ever sits on it anymore, but I watch the empty seat move back and forth and then a man steps away from the shadows.

A man I see from time to time, but always in passing. Except for when I think of him late at night. Unfortunately, it happens more than I'll ever admit.

He's a man I used to want because he made me feel something I'd never felt before. A mixture of hope and desire. Like the silly dreams of getting away from this place, I used to want to be his. To be pinned down by his hands while his eyes held me in place.

I used to dream of him pressing his lips to mine and stealing my breath with a demanding kiss. I knew he could do it; I'd felt it once before.

His stubble-lined jaw looks sharper in the night with only the neighbor's porch light and the pale moonlight casting shadows down his face. My heart beats slower, yet faster all at once. Knowing Sebastian is on my porch waiting for me, I can hardly breathe, let alone move.

His steely blue eyes are next to come into view, and they immediately capture me. Staring straight at me, they pierce through me and see more of me than anyone else can. He must. I can feel it deep in the pit of my gut. He's always been able to do it. There was never a moment where Sebastian didn't have that power over me.

With clammy palms, I try to move my hands, but my fingers are as paralyzed as my body. It's not from fear, although I know that's what this man should elicit from me. That's the reaction he has on everyone else.

No, it's not fear. As a gust of wind blows, I sway gently in the breeze and it seems to free me from the spell his sharp blue eyes have placed on me. I refuse to look back into his gaze.

Instead, I stare at the chips in the old cement stairs that lead to my porch and feel my heart squeeze harder and tighter than it has in a very long time.

"What do you want?" I ask Sebastian in a hoarse voice, barely louder than a murmur.

His shadow shifts in my periphery, but I don't look up at him.

He's a man I would let do whatever he wanted to me. I would let him do completely as he pleased. There's no reasonable explanation for it. No justification. I'm fully aware that he'd chew me up and spit me out.

Maybe everyone has a person like that. That one person you know can destroy you, and you pine for it despite yourself. I crave what he's capable of. I want the bad things that come with the promise of being his. That confession alone is enough proof I belong in this shit city.

I can feel the danger, the dominance, the overwhelming presence that never leaves with Sebastian Black. I can even smell his masculine woodsy scent that sometimes filters into my dreams. With my lungs full of it, I close my eyes, letting it intoxicate me, but doing my best not to show it. I won't give him that satisfaction. Not when he chooses to give me nothing. Not when he pretends that I'm nothing to him. Although maybe I am. Why would I ever be more than nothing to a man like him?

"Why are you here?" I ask, hardening my voice, raising it, and daring to finally look at him. His shoulders fill the entrance to my front door. My *open* front door. It creaks and the sound echoes in the chilly night air as Sebastian looks me up and down, the hint of a smirk on his face until his gaze reaches mine again.

"I thought you were smarter than that, Chloe," he says and his deep voice rumbles. It's rough, and the way he says my name sounds dirty, even though he's only said it in the same manner as always. With a wanton heat building in my core and my breathing picking up, I stare into his eyes as he adds, "I'm here for a little chat... with you."

SEBASTIAN

Chloe looks so damn tired. It's obvious that her hair must have been up all day; I can still see the impression of where a band was wrapped around her wavy brunette locks. She swallows thickly, and I swear I can hear the faint sound even from where I am feet away from her. Even with the clamoring from the Higgins kids yelling down the block. With a heavy breath she looks up at me, and I can see she's biting her tongue in reaction to me telling her I came to chat. She's done it for years. The questions shine in her doe eyes though. They stare back at me with the well of emotion that runs deep between us.

The bags under her pale blue eyes only make her look that much more beautiful. I don't know how that's possible.

Every time she comes to mind, I tell myself I'm picturing her differently than she is. That whatever it is that attracts me to her, plays tricks on my memory and makes me think she's more gorgeous than she really is.

And every time I'm proven wrong when I see her.

"You going to let me in?" I ask her with a smirk on my lips. One that makes her eyes narrow.

"Seeing as how my door's already open," she starts off strong but has to take a heavy breath before she finishes, "why don't you be my guest?" She gestures and the purse on her shoulder slips down her arm. Although she struggles to grab on to it, she doesn't take her eyes off mine.

The tension between us is thick, but it's always been that way. From the second I saw her in tenth grade, until this very moment, there's something about her that draws me in like a moth to a flame. I know I get to her too, but only one of us can be the fire.

"After you." I push open her door a little wider and wait for her to pass me. She takes the stairs slowly and then quickly walks by me as if she's trying to get away from me as fast as she can. It's not the first time she's done that and the reaction it sparks in me is the same.

The desire to chase her.

The first time it happened, it didn't come over me until the school year was almost over, and I knew I wouldn't get my weekly dose of fantasizing about Chloe Rose from across the lunchroom anymore.

I gave in and went after her, and it only made the sweet, sad girl who stared back at me that much more desirable.

Kicking her front door shut and locking it, I keep my back to her until the light flicks on. I can hear her drop her purse and then continue walking to the back of the hall. She leaves me at the front door in silence, so I have to turn around and face her.

Her house is just like the rest in this area. All the townhouses here are original and were built by the same company that ran the steel mill. They were made for the workers employed by the mill.

Until it shut down, just like the coal mines did, leaving everyone in houses they couldn't afford, with jobs they didn't have anymore.

The slate floors have gouges in the corner; my guess is something heavy hit them, and then I remember what happened two years before. The tension I'm feeling evaporates and anger comes flooding back at the reminder. I take a quick look over my shoulder toward the door, but even through the somewhat recent coat of paint, I can see where the wood broke when it was kicked in. The main lock's been replaced, and there's an additional one above it.

I wonder if she thinks of that night every time she locks the door. I thought about telling her who did it. Marley was an addict who picked houses at random for items to fence to support his habit. Stealing anything and everything he could was his method. He got his last hit the night he stole from Chloe, leaving fear behind that didn't stray from her eyes for months.

He got his high and then fell to the bottom of the river where I dumped him.

Everyone in this city knows I have my limits. They didn't know Chloe was one of them until that night. I stayed away to keep the target off her back, but people don't forget in this city.

I may be young, and I may work for a man who doesn't venture into this territory, but I run these streets where she lives. No one owns Crescent Hills. If I wanted to take it though, there's not a single prick here who'd stand in my way.

But I don't want this city any more than it wanted me.

I want Chloe Rose. The thought catches me off guard. I've always known it's true, but I don't like to admit it. There's something about her that begs me to be something more for her.

That's the part that kills me though; there's nothing more to me than what she sees, what everyone sees. A ruthless man who's angry at life and makes his living by beating the piss out of pricks.

She's not like me. She's soft and kind and needs a gentler hand than I can give her. She deserves better.

"How'd you get in?" Chloe's voice is soft, although the edge of defiance is still there. Bringing my gaze back to her, I take her in again. From her long legs and skinny waist to those wide hips that beg me to bend her over and give her a punishing fuck, the sight of her makes even the misery of why I'm here vanish for a moment.

She crosses her arms as if she doesn't agree with what I'm thinking, but all that does is put a strain on the blouse she's wearing and push those gorgeous tits of hers together. They may be small, but all I need is a mouthful. My dick stirs, and I have to look away, heading to the living room and glancing around at her place as I go.

"I picked the lock," I tell her, although it's not true. I have a set of keys, got them the day she ordered them from the hardware store. It kept her waiting longer than she should've been there, but I had to do what I had to do. And that meant sneaking in later that night to make sure she was sleeping. Which she never did, but Chloe has a habit of missing sleep.

As do I.

So, she laid there quietly in bed and stiffened at the sound of me moving about, but she never turned around, she never dared to check. She has a habit of that too. Of thinking if she ignores the monsters she conjures in her head, they'll go away. The sad fact is sometimes those monsters in the dark aren't imaginary, but damn does she like to convince herself they are.

She huffs out a laugh that's flat and then brushes her hair back as she leans against the side table in the hall. "You making yourself at home?" she asks, daring me to keep walking and make my way to the living room. I don't answer her, still taking everything in and noting that it's all the same.

She hasn't changed a thing. Not one thing in this place for two years. For some fucked up reason, it sends a ripple of pain through my chest, more than the broken door did. The walls of the hallway still have the same framed photos her uncle had put up after she moved in with him.

Her uncle was more of a parent to her than her own mother was. Him taking her in after her mother's death was the best thing for her, but he was supposed to help her get out of this shit life, not have a heart attack and leave her here all alone.

"Come on over here and have a seat with me," I tell her as I sink into the large sofa that takes up half the room. The edges of the armrest are worn, but it smells like her. Exactly how I remember Chlo. A soft peach scent and some kind of flower. Nothing but sweet.

My fingers dig into the cushion as she stalks slowly to the opposite side of the sofa and seems to consider sitting down as she stands in place. She smooths out the back of her skirt as she stares at the seat and then kicks off her heels, letting the silence pass.

All I can do is stare at her, even as she refuses to look back at me. It makes me think about different possibilities. If we lived in a different city. If our lives were different. If any of that were the case, I never would have let her think she was anything but mine. There's something in my soul that recognizes her as belonging to me. She's mine to protect, to take in my bed, to give the world.

Brushing the rough pad of my thumb along my lip, I have to remind myself that's not the world we live in and she's not mine. Life is better for both of us that way.

I'm a threat to those who have control of the neighboring territories. And that little fact never leaves me. Especially after what happened last week.

I'm no good for Chloe.

She needs someone to take her away from here, and away from me.

Finally, she sinks back into the sofa, sighing and taking a peek at me. "Just tell me what you want, Sebastian."

Those eyes transfix me. It's like she sees through the bullshit, but she always has.

What I *want*. That word sends a wave of warmth and desire through my body. I want her. But that's not what I'm here for and she's something I'll never have.

"Have you been watching the news?" I lean forward as I ask her the question, resting my elbows on my knees. Her small body stiffens as she shakes her head. As if watching the news is a sin.

She's a horrible liar. The worst liar I've ever fucking met.

Maybe that's why I feel so drawn to her. She can't hide from me. But I can't hide from her either. There's something so freeing about that simple fact. Something that makes being in her presence addictive.

Even if it's for a shit reason.

"Barry turned up yesterday, did you hear about that?" I ask her and immediately feel the waves of anxiety rolling off of her. Anything that triggers memories of her past causes her pain which is easily seen by anyone who would bother to look.

"I don't give two shits about Barry." Her voice turns harder as she pulls her knees into her chest. She stares straight ahead, and I follow her gaze to the peeling wallpaper.

"Do you know who did it?" At the question, her head whips in my direction with a bolt of anger flashing in her eyes.

"I don't know shit," she bites out and her defensiveness is exactly what the police will latch on to. "I'm going through a lot right now," she adds, but her voice wavers. Her gaze falls as she visibly swallows and tucks a lock of hair behind her ear before peeking back up to the wallpaper. "I don't want to think about any of it." Her voice lowers to a murmur as she says, "Sure as shit, not Barry."

As time slowly passes, her anger diminishes, and I watch as she returns to her typical quiet state. She's nestled in the sofa with the sad smile she always carries gracing her lips. Picking at the hem of her skirt, she glances at me thoughtfully. "Is that really what you wanted to know?"

"How are the nightmares?" I ask her, feeling my chest get tight as the smile vanishes and her eyes shift to a hollow expression I hate and know all too well. She's good at hiding. Hiding her pain behind a smile. Hiding her reality behind the thought that one day she'll get out of here. Well, she used to, anyway. She used to be good at all of that.

Time changes a lot of things.

She starts to answer me, but she can't hide the emotion in her

453

voice. Before she can lie and tell me she's fine, her voice hitches and she turns her gaze toward the empty hallway.

"Why do you care?" Her words cut deep. Chloe's pain is clear, but does she really think I don't care about her?

She's smarter than this. It's the second time tonight I've had that thought. "You know I care," is all I give her. But for the first time since I stepped foot on her porch, I feel the mask slip from me, letting her see what's inside without putting up a wall for her to break through.

She can see it all anyway. If I stop trying to hide, maybe she will too.

She still hasn't answered my question though.

"So how are you handling them? The nightmares?"

"They're back. I've had them every night since Saturday," she tells me. Saturday. The day they caught her mother's killer. She's back to fidgeting with the hem of her skirt as her gaze flickers between me and the floor.

"How did you know?" she asks, peeking up at me and I almost allow myself to get lost in the pain reflected in her baby blues. I'd rather be lost in hers than mine.

"You look tired," I answer her honestly. She drops her gaze though, sighing deeply and pressing the palms of her hands against her eyes.

"Well if you wanted to know if I knew who killed Barry, I don't. So, you can go now, and I can get some sleep." She stands up and hugs her chest, although her posture is more aggressive than defensive.

For nearly a year, I could feel her watching me whenever I was near her. The pull to be at her side was stronger than anything else. Nothing could compete with her, but I resisted. I couldn't let her get caught up in this shit.

Now she's the one pushing me away. Fair enough, I suppose. It doesn't change the fact that this is a small world, and I know she still feels that draw, just like I do.

"I have something that can help you," I tell her as I stand with no intention of walking out just yet. She can pretend that she has the ability to tell me what to do. We both know that's not the case, but I respect her too much to rub it in her face. Besides, I can't let her push me away when I have something she needs.

"What is it?" She's wary but curious. That's the Chloe I know.

Reaching into my pocket, I pull out the vial I prepared before coming here and roll it between my fingers. "It's something to make you sleep."

"Drugs?" she scoffs and shakes her head at me, letting out a sarcastic laugh like I've gone mad.

"It's something you could get at any pharmacy," I offer her, letting a smile slip onto my lips.

That's not completely true. A friend gave it to me to see if there'd be any interest for it on the streets, but people in this city want harder drugs. Drugs to help them forget, to escape, even if just for a short time. I thought it could help Chloe though.

She's a good girl, but she needs this. The sweets will knock her out and give her the rest she so desperately needs. I would know.

"You're a bad liar," she says, and the irony doesn't escape me.

"I'll put a few drops in your tea," I tell her as I walk past her, brushing my arm against hers and feeling that familiar combination of heat and want seep into my blood. Her quick intake of air is all I need to keep moving forward, walking to her kitchen before I hear her take even a single step.

I go right to where I know she keeps her mugs and tea as I hear her walking toward the kitchen.

"I don't drink tea at night," she tells me, and I know she's lying again. Glancing at the box in my hands, I show her the label then pull out what I know is her favorite mug. She picked it up at a used bookstore last year. If she's not working or home, she's always at that bookstore.

"Decaffeinated tea then?" She only crosses her arms aggressively again and leans against the small table in the kitchen. "I'm getting tired of you lying to me tonight," I add with my back to her as I fill the mug with water and put it into the microwave.

When I turn to her, the hum of the microwave filling the room along with the tension between us, she meets my gaze with a hardened expression.

"How many years will go by this time? You know, before you barge into my life, then pretend I don't exist the next day?" She sounds bitter, but I know it's fake.

I cluck my tongue, keeping my eyes on her face instead of her chest. But with her arms crossed like that, she's not helping me. "Would you really want me to make this a habit?" I ask her, not realizing how much I actually care what her answer is until silence is all I'm given.

I already know the answer; I shouldn't have asked the question.

"What do you want from me, Sebastian? It wasn't to ask if I'd heard about some asshole getting mugged."

"It was." I wouldn't have come to see her if I didn't think I really had to be here. I don't like what she does to me. How she takes over every sense of reason and consumes my thoughts long after we've parted ways.

"The cops are going to question you about his death. I need you to tell them you don't want to talk about it. Because otherwise, you'll look guilty." The microwave goes off and I go back to making her tea when she starts to answer me.

"I didn't do it. I--"

"I know you didn't. But you look like you're lying when anyone brings up anything that has to do with your mother. Which is why it could be pinned on you."

With the bag of tea steeping, I stiffen at my own words. A sick feeling stirs in the pit of my stomach. I know what it's like when someone brings up shit you don't want to hear. How all of a sudden, you feel a coldness and pain all over like it's taken over everything inside of you.

I reach for the sugar on the counter and stir some into her tea.

She doesn't object or ask how I knew she would want it. The spoon clinks gently against the ceramic and Chloe still hasn't responded, but when I turn to her, her eyes are glossy with unshed tears. I feel like a prick.

"This doesn't have anything to do with that," she says, although she barely gets out the words.

"That's not what the police think. Two bodies were found right after they caught the guy who killed your mom. You don't need to watch the news to know what the cops are thinking."

She starts to object, but I stop her and say, "Just tell me you won't talk to them." Grabbing the vial, I put three drops in her tea, making sure she's watching me, then set it next to the sugar.

"What could I possibly tell them?" Her tone is as tired as she looks, and she doesn't hide the pain that lingers beneath her words. "I don't know anything."

"They're looking for someone to blame. I don't want you to give them a reason to think that someone could be you." I know they tossed her name around as a possible suspect. She has motive, and emotions are raw for her. They want the case closed, and she's an easy target.

My throat feels tight although the words come out steady as I tell her, "If they come around, I need you to tell them you don't know anything, and you don't want to talk to them. That's it."

I hand her the mug I've prepared for her, my palm hot as I rotate it so she can grab it by the handle. "It doesn't matter how they'll push you for more or what they say. They want you to talk, and you're not going to. All you're going to tell them is that you don't know anything, and you don't have anything to say, right?" I ask her, and she nods obediently and with an understanding that supplants the sadness. The cops here are crooked and covering for whoever lines their pockets. Anyone can take the fall, and they'd be perfectly all right with that.

She takes the mug with both hands, letting her fingers brush against mine. The small bit of contact sends electric waves up my

457

arms and shoulders, igniting every nerve ending and putting me on edge. So much so, that my body begs me to either step away or grab her wrist. But I do what I've always done. I resist. I let myself feel the discomfort of not having her but being so close that I could easily have her if I just gave in.

She's closer now, taking a half step toward me, her head at my chest and her gaze on the floor as she blows across the top of the hot cup of tea.

"I understand," she tells me, her lips close to the edge of the mug, but she doesn't drink it yet.

I reach over, one hand on either side of her head, and brush back her hair. She stares up at me with a longing I remember so well. A longing I've dreamed of for so many nights. The air is pulled from my lungs as I stare into her eyes. "Drink your tea and go to bed, Chloe." My words are rough, and it's hard to swallow. The moment her baby blues close with her nod, I get the fuck out of there before I do anything stupid. Anything that would put her in even more danger.

CHLOE

I'll never forget her screams.

The second I hear the front door open as Sebastian leaves, it's all I can think about.

As I set down my tea on the kitchen table, not even Sebastian's lingering heat and scent can provide an adequate distraction. No, the moment he brought up my mother, I knew the memories would come back and they wouldn't leave.

Sebastian never stays for long. Never. No matter how much I wish he would.

Closing my eyes and gripping the edge of the chair, I take in a deep breath. I know I need to lock the door, but I'm desperately trying to calm and steady myself.

At war with the memories of that night my mother died are the thoughts of Sebastian having been in my house just now.

He was here for business. But whatever the reason, he doesn't want me to say anything, and so I won't. I don't have anything to say to the cops regardless, but I am emotional, and I could see myself spewing all sorts of hate for the dead man whose murder could easily be pinned on me.

Whatever Sebastian is involved with, and whatever his intention is behind telling me to keep my mouth shut, I'm grateful for it.

This addition to my tea, however, I don't know what to think about that. I don't know what it is, and I don't believe him when he said it's something I could get at the drugstore. I may be attracted to him for some unknown reason, but I'm not fucking stupid. The thought resonates with me as I turn the locks on the front door.

It was the nightmares that led him to me the first time. Or my reaction to the nightmares really. The constant crying.

It was five years ago when I was in ninth grade and he was in tenth. I turn around as a chill flows up my arm, traveling to the back of my neck and causing every hair in its path to stand on end. I'd sag against the hard door if my body wasn't frozen at the memories.

Her scream. *Screams*. The shrill sound still wakes me up at night, tears streaming down my face as I try to keep my heart from leaping out of my chest.

When it happened, I was cross-legged on the floor of our townhouse one block down from where I am now, and my friend Andrea was on the sofa.

Justice Street. Ironic isn't the right word for the name of the street I grew up on. It's pathetic and riddled with agony that the word is allowed to exist in this city. I know now that she was nearly two blocks away, in the alley right across from both the park and the bars she had frequented.

The fact her screams carried that far, is evidence enough of how desperate she was for someone to help her.

The first scream came at 11:14 p.m. I remember how the red lines of the digital display shone brightly on the microwave's clock.

"What the fuck are you doing?" Andrea asked me with wide, disbelieving eyes as she slapped the phone from my hand. It fucking hurt. The memory brings the sting back, making my left hand move on top of my right. Absently I rub soothing circles over it, staring straight ahead although I don't see the hall to my uncle's home. Technically, it's mine now, but I don't want to feel any sense of ownership for a damn thing in this city.

She coughed on the hit she took from her blunt and I remember the sound so clearly.

All I see is Andrea's angry expression, but fear was also evident as she locked her eyes with mine. My heart beat faster back then, knowing I needed to call someone to help whoever it was that was screaming. But now it beats slow at the memory as if my body wishes I could stop time. As if it's doing everything it can to try to make that happen, to go back.

I heard another faint cry for help and Andrea followed my gaze to the open window. The smoke billowed toward it. I sat there numbly as she quickly ran to the window and closed it.

"We have to call--" I tried to plead with her, knowing deep in the marrow of my bones that whoever was screaming was in agonizing pain.

"No, we don't," Andrea pushed back, waving the smoke from her face. "The cops can't come here," she argued with me. "Someone else will call... if whoever that was even needs help," she told me, but both of our eyes strayed back to the window at the muffled sound of another shrill scream.

I didn't move to my phone.

Instead, I took a shower. Of all the things I could have done, I stepped into a stream of hot water, listening to the white noise of the shower, praying for the water to wash the feelings away. The guilt, the disgust, all of it.

But that's not something water can do.

When I stepped out of the shower, I swear I heard it again, but it sounded exactly the same. Andrea said I was crazy and that it was all in my head. That it was only the one time anyone had screamed at all, which she corrected to two when I stared back at her.

The last faint cry I heard was well after midnight. Andrea

convinced me it was just a couple fighting; the Ruhills were good for that on the weekends as they were both angry drunks who spent their paychecks at the bar, but now I know that's not true.

Over an hour had passed. And no one went to help her. Not me, not a single person in this city.

It was nearly 9 a.m. when the police banged on the door and I answered. I thought my mother had lost her keys and locked herself out. It wouldn't have been the first time. When I opened the door, it still hadn't dawned on me that the screams had belonged to her.

She was the one I didn't help save.

No one did.

Not a single person for blocks around helped her.

Andrea wasn't the only one to close the window and tell the cops that's all they'd done. Screams in this place are a constant. Cries for help come often. And everyone assumed someone else would call the cops or offer street justice. But it didn't happen that way.

That fucker, Barry, the one who turned up dead in the news today, I'll never forget how he laughed at the bar as he bragged to anyone who would listen about how he'd turned up his television because she wouldn't stop screaming. He'd shut the window and turned up the volume until he couldn't hear her cries anymore. He'd heard her, he'd known she was begging for help, and yet he did nothing and dared to be arrogant about it.

It was easier to hate him than it was to hate myself for knowing I could have helped her. I could have tried to help her. I could have done something, anything—rather than listen to Andrea.

I never spoke to her again. Not that she cared much. With my mother gone, there'd be no one to fill my medicine cabinet with what Andrea referred to as the good shit.

The terrors that came with my mother's death are justified. I deserve so much worse. I would do anything to go back. *Anything.*

My numb body finally moves to prevent what's coming next.

The memories of who my mother truly was, an abusive alcoholic who never wanted me. They're joined by the fears I had back when I was a kid, that she was coming to punish me. That I deserved so badly to be punished.

"She's long gone," I whisper as two kids yelling up the street remind me that I'm here, in my uncle's house, only a block away from my childhood home. And even farther away from where my mother was raped and murdered. More importantly, it's years later.

As my tired eyes yearn for sleep, I walk slowly down the hall back to the kitchen. The chill of the memories follows me. It took all this time to find her killer, a fifty-year-old man who'd once been a high school teacher. They found him dead in his house three cities over. They only know it was him because he was being prosecuted for the rape of some other young woman and the DNA matched. He killed himself rather than being taken in last Saturday.

That wasn't even a week ago, and then Amber Talbott died a few days later. She saw and heard everything, yet she did nothing but record part of the attack and send it to her friend. It wasn't enough to solve my mother's murder.

Shot from behind, it only captured the back of the man who'd done it as he viciously punched my mother, shoving her deeper into the alley. Amber had claimed she sent it to her friend because she was scared, but the texts between them implied otherwise. I know the video; I can see it clearly now. It's only half a minute long and was taken from Amber's window across the street.

My mother saw her in those final moments, or at the very least she saw the phone. Up until the moment I saw the video, I thought the worst thing you could see before being murdered would have to be your killer's eyes. But that's wrong. It has to be. Because how horrible would it be if the last thing you ever saw was someone hearing your cries, knowing you were in pain, but choosing to do nothing? Or simply walking away, shutting their window, or worse, filming it for their own amusement.

Amber said she thought the guy had just mugged my mother and then moved along. She told me to my face that she was sorry, and she wished she could have done something else. I didn't believe her.

She could have done something if she'd really wanted to. She was older than me. She was closer, too. She could have sent that video to the cops. Five years later, just days ago, someone mugged her and left her for dead in an alley next to the hair salon where she worked.

No one did anything to help her, either.

And now Barry's dead. Two people who I hated so much for so long, both killed within days of each other and after my mother's killer was found dead.

Barry was an old man who couldn't be bothered unless you wanted to talk about the winning lottery numbers or placing bets. Horses and the tracks were his favorite. I used to like him because he'd show me pictures of the races. But when I heard how cavalier he was when it came to my mother's murder, I couldn't stand the sound of his name, let alone the sight of his face.

I'm glad he's dead. And if I'm being honest, I'm glad Amber's dead too, but it doesn't change the root of my pain.

Nothing can change the past. Nothing can take away the guilt.

I feel empty and hollowed out as I walk back to the kitchen table. The chills refuse to leave me.

Just as the nightmares don't. But I had those even before my mother died. They were my constant companion, just like the bruises back then.

The night terrors got worse after she was gone, but the bruises eventually faded.

Staring at the cup of tea, I reflect on Sebastian. I remember how being around him, being *kissed* by him, took so much of the pain away. Even just thinking about him helped.

But I'll never be okay. It's only a pipe dream. Sebastian may pull me away, pull me closer to him and into his world, but it's only temporary. He's proven that too many times for me to put much faith in him at all.

I grab the cup and dump it in the sink, watching as the dark liquid swirls down the drain.

I don't want to sleep. My mother waits for me there.

SEBASTIAN

I can still feel her fingers against mine. Her touch hasn't left me since last night. My mind wanders to what she would have said if I'd told her I wanted to stay.

The rumble from the engine turns to white noise as I think about all the ways I could take the pain away from her. I imagine lying in bed beside her and taking her how I've dreamed of for as long as I can remember. My grip tightens on the steering wheel and the breeze from the rolled-down window pauses as I slow to a stop at a red light.

The radio station being changed to something else grabs my attention and I have to clear my throat and adjust in my seat to play off what was going through my mind. Carter changes the station again, but he's not going to find what he needs by picking a different song. There's nothing in this world that's going to help take his mind off of the pain.

"You staying with me tonight?" I ask him. His dad kicked him out of the house again. Not that the kid did a damn thing wrong. He's sixteen and involved with the wrong crowd, namely me, but he never does anything wrong. Not since his mom got sick last year.

He flicks the radio off, choosing silence over the commercial on the last station.

"I don't know," he tells me solemnly and then falls back against the passenger seat, staring listlessly out the window. Chewing on his thumbnail, he avoids looking back at me.

Which is fine, because the fucker behind us yells at me to get going while honking his horn. The red light's turned green. One look in the rearview, catching the driver's gaze silences him. He sees who I am, and suddenly the pissed off expression on his face vanishes. I wait for a beat, then another as the assholes settles into his seat and averts his eyes, waiting for me to do whatever the fuck I want to do.

I'm careful as I step on the gas, and more careful with what I say next. "How's your mom doing?"

Even that simple question gets him worked up. Carter shakes his head but doesn't say anything. He tries but he's too choked up.

Carter's mom keeps asking for him to help instead of his dad. It ranges from changing her position in bed and helping her go to the bathroom, to just being by her side to talk. His father doesn't like that though. He's a drunk and a deadbeat.

With five boys and her health deteriorating, I can only guess his mother is hoping that Carter will take care of the others when she's gone. He's the oldest. Hell knows his father won't.

"Let's talk about something else," he suggests as I turn down Peck Avenue. "Like where we're going?"

My lips kick up in a half smile at his response. He texted me earlier, asking me to pick him up, but didn't question where I was taking him. He asks so often now, almost every day. I guess he doesn't care where we go so long as he has somewhere to get away. He always goes home though. For his mother. For his brothers too.

"I want to check on someone," I tell him as I round the corner, passing over a speed bump and slowing down at the weathered stop sign that marks that we're close to our destination.

Carter's brow furrows. I don't know if I've ever told him I want to check on someone before, but when I turn down Dixon Street and slow in front of Chloe's house, he gives me a shit-eating grin. As if I just told him his favorite joke.

"Like old times," he says with a rough laugh. Carter's my only friend and that's because I know who he is to his core. He's six years younger than me, but he's like family, the only family I have.

All he has are his brothers; he's told me that so many times. But it's always followed up with a pat on my back as he tells me I'm one of them. I have to admit, it's nice to feel wanted, and even nicer to feel like you're part of a family. Even if you know deep down that's not really true.

I was eighteen and he was twelve when we met. He got caught shoplifting bread of all things. Dumb fuck couldn't even pick something that fit under his jacket.

Grabbing him by his collar, I yanked him away from the clerk hellbent on beating the shit out of him. If you let one person get away with stealing your shit, everyone will come running with duffle bags.

So you have to send a message, loud and clear. I was in charge of keeping that shop out of harm's way; it was one of my first jobs from Romano.

I looked the clerk in the eye and told him the kid was going to pay for what he'd done. I had a reputation and the clerk was happy enough to let me handle it, knowing he could tell his story about how I'd kicked the kid's ass for trying to steal from his store.

Carter was a scrawny thing and still is, although he's starting to fill out. I picked him up like he was nothing and he didn't try to fight it.

The look of fear in his eyes wasn't there, only a look of disappointment, even as I dragged him around back. I remember how I felt something I hadn't in so long. Something like regret, maybe?

He wasn't like the others, the ones looking for a fight.

Carter already had enough to fight for and to fight against, so to him I was just one more thing he had to endure. I could see the weary resignation in his eyes.

I didn't kick his ass. Instead, I told him to go home. I made the decision to let him go because he wasn't like the others. And also, because the idea of beating up on a lanky twelve-year-old made me sick to my stomach.

That was when I saw his anger and his fight. His passion.

"I'm not going home without it," he told me with determination, even though his voice shook. His hands balled into fists, but he didn't raise them.

"Get home, kid," I told him, walking over to where I'd thrown him and towering over him.

He stared me in the eyes as he shook his head. "I'm not leaving without it."

"For a fucking loaf of bread, you're willing to get your ass beat?" The kid was stupid. I still tell him he's stupid and it's true half the time.

"I have to make sandwiches, my mom told me--" He started to say something else, but I cut him off

"Well your mom can make it herself," I spat back at him, with a pent-up rage he didn't deserve. He was only a kid, and some of the kids didn't know. My mother was a whore. A bitch. I don't have a single nice thing to say about her. Even with her dead in the ground after spending the last minutes of her life with her favorite needle, I can't bring myself to say one good thing about her. I never had a family aside from my grandmother, bless her soul. And I never would. It's as simple as that. It was as deeply ingrained in me as whatever possessed Carter that night.

"She can't!" he yelled at me. I took one step closer to him, and he stiffened. My spine was stiff, my shoulders straight and the aggression and threats evident just from my stare at him.

His bottom lip quivered as he took in a quick breath, but he didn't give up. "I have to feed them tonight and we don't have anything... but I can make sandwiches." He gritted out the last words with tears in his eyes. "I just need bread."

"And what are you going to put on the bread? You going to steal something else too?" I berated him, even though I believed him.

"There's peanut butter already."

"You can eat it with a spoon," I said dismissively, turning my back to him and ready to get the hell away from him. Something about the way he looked and acted bothered me to my core. He wasn't frightened, and he wasn't angry. *He was desperate.*

"She said to make sandwiches for my brothers-"

I lost it again with the kid, thinking about my own mother and how she'd forced me to fend for myself. She never told me to make dinner, I just had to. No one else would. "And why didn't she do it then? Huh? She can dish out orders, but-"

"She's in the hospital. She told me on the phone to make sandwiches and I just need bread." He stumbled over his words, but he never took his eyes from me. "I told him, the clerk," he gestured to the shop, "we'd pay him, but I don't have the money right now." He visibly swallowed and continued, "My mom will pay him when she's back. And it's going to be real soon. She'll be okay real soon." He started rambling on and on and I could feel his sob story getting to me. I could feel myself getting played like I'd played everyone else as I grew up on the streets.

"So, you're stealing bread to make sandwiches for your brothers?" I lowered my head to his. "Here's a hint, kid. When you're told to do something, you don't have to follow it to a T." I licked my lower lip, slipping my hands into my pockets and expecting him to give up and go home already. To leave the corner store alone and my reputation intact and go eat the fucking peanut butter out of the jar like a normal asshole would.

But he didn't get what I was saying.

"Are you dumb?" I asked him as he stood up, faced me and held his ground.

"She said to make them sandwiches. I'm not leaving until I get the bread."

I searched his eyes for the longest time before going in and grabbing the bread for him. But I followed him home, telling him I wasn't going to give it to him until I saw that he was telling the truth. I knew he was one of the kids who lived on the edge of the city. I remembered seeing a bunch of them out that way. I make it a habit to know everyone and for them to know me.

If he was lying to me, he'd learn real quick to never do it again.

I didn't know that he had four brothers, or that their place was a mess because they'd just moved in. I heard they were on the run from where they came from, but I didn't know that their mother was in the hospital because of their grandfather. Apparently, he's who they were running from and he'd found out where they ran off to. Which is how his mom wound up in the ER and why their father in jail as a result of it all, paying Carter's grandfather back for what he'd done to his mother. Leaving five kids alone in a new place without a damn thing to eat.

I didn't know, and I didn't care, not until I saw how happy they were just to eat. Even something as simple as peanut butter sandwiches. I asked him how long it'd been since she went to the hospital.

It had been four days. And they were starving, but he'd promised his mom he would feed them, and he did.

Twelve years old, and he was the oldest of five. She stayed in the hospital for another three days before the doctors would let her come home. Now she's back in the hospital, but not with bruises and broken ribs. Two years ago, she was diagnosed with cancer. She's been fighting it all this time, but Carter's still taking care of his brothers, and now her too.

That was the first time I met Carter, four years ago. I took him under my wing at first, but now he's a friend. A friend who's been through some shit and is still in it. He has a family though and a reason to fight. I've only ever fought to stay alive or to rule with fear. That difference is something I'm not sure he'll ever understand.

"Is she home?" he asks me, and it brings me back to the present. To being on the other side of the city, close to my place and in front of Chloe's.

Letting out a sigh and running a hand through my hair, I shrug like I don't know.

"You like her," he tells me like it's a fucking joke. He doesn't know what's going on. Not entirely, but even if he suspects it, he won't ask. He doesn't like to look for the darkness, not when he's surrounded by it already.

"She doesn't need me asking her out," I mutter under my breath and ignore Carter's eyes pinned on me.

It takes a second and then another for him to start putting the puzzle pieces together.

"You going to tell me why we're here?" he asks me with a brow cocked. He's feigning lightheartedness; concern is clearly etched on his face.

I've told him more than once that he doesn't pay attention enough. That life is shit, it always will be, and either you accept it for what it is and protect yourself, or you fall victim to whatever fate chooses to inflict on us. But given the weight of what I'm hiding, I don't tell him. I don't want it to be real.

I lie to him and say, "I just wanted to see if anyone was snooping around here."

"Cops? Or Romano's people?" Carter asks and the gravity of either of the two options sends a chill down my spine. I can handle the cops, Chloe can't. But neither of us could handle Romano if he decided to go after her. He runs the territory up north and I work for him on occasion. I may be his muscle, but I'm not sure even I know the extent of the shit Romano's involved with.

As I'm thinking about the last fucked up thing Romano had me do, Carter asks something I wish he hadn't, because it's too close to being true. "Is this about that thing Marcus gave you?" His voice is even, but his expression's fallen.

Pushing back in my seat and hiding my anxiety, I tell him, "I told you not to mention that."

He only nods and seems to shrug it off, like it doesn't matter if Marcus is the reason we're here. Both of us know that's bullshit though. Even saying his name is something no one likes to do around here. Romano may run the territory up north from us, he may even make an appearance down here on occasion when he needs something, but you always see him coming and he's only dangerous because of the men he controls.

Marcus is a different sort of threat. By the time you see him coming, you're already dead. He doesn't have a territory, he doesn't have men. When he makes demands, they're always about death. They called him the Grim Reaper when I was younger. He doesn't want money, he doesn't bargain. What Marcus decides is final and there's no room to negotiate. He's only one man, but he's killed every man who's crossed him and even more men simply because they were on his list.

A minute passes before Carter reaches for the radio again and lets the music ease the tension.

"It's fine." My words come out casually as I watch Chloe's house. Not a thing looks out of place. It's not fine though. This shit is exactly why I could never be with her. One day you're on top, the next you're in a ditch. That's how this lifestyle is, and I'll never bring anyone into this shit life if I can help it. That especially goes for Chloe Rose.

"When are you going to ask her out?" he asks with a wide smile. He still has happiness in his soul. Enough to bring a bit of light to every dark situation. One day it'll go out. It always does for men like us. But I'll do my damnedest to keep it from happening.

"I know you want her," he chides again.

He doesn't know the half of it. I've known Chloe for a long

473

time. And I made sure she never knew how I watched over her when her mother died. She wasn't okay. Everyone knew it. Just like they knew I wasn't okay when my mother died.

No one gives a shit though. People die, and somehow you keep going.

Then more people die and one day it's you.

One time I walked up to her porch and peeked in her window after she'd moved into her uncle's. The TV was on and I thought maybe she was watching it. That she'd be okay. It had been weeks. Weeks of nothing but her crying, constantly crying and hating herself. And I despised it. I fucking loathed it. The whole street could hear her uncle yelling at her to stop crying. That he'd lost his sister too and that she needed to stop.

When I looked in, she was still crying, but her eyes were wide open, her cheeks tearstained, and she saw me.

I know she did, not that it changed anything. I knew at that moment when she didn't do anything or say anything, that I was just as dead to her as her mother was. It hurt me like nothing else in this world had to know that just then, I meant nothing to her. I couldn't take her pain away. I was nobody special.

I'd never been more sure of anything in my life. I was nothing that night.

But the next day, I proved her wrong. When she kissed me back, I proved her wrong.

CHLOE

*H*e comes by every day. Friday night he stood in my kitchen. Saturday, he drove by with Carter Cross, Sunday he came alone and now it's Monday night and he's outside again.

I act like I don't see him. I've always done that. Everyone leaves you alone if you act like you don't exist.

The thing about Sebastian though, is that he doesn't leave until he knows I know he's watching me. Or maybe that's just what I think because I feel his gaze on me every time and I have no desire not to look back at him.

I pull back my curtain when the car outside idles and idles. A book is open in my hand, its pages unread. I let it shut as I peek outside to see who it is. The large text closes with a dull thud that matches the single pound in my chest when I see him out there.

I try to swallow but my throat's dry.

Angie said it's an intimidation tactic. I shouldn't have told her anything about Sebastian coming by like this. She concocted about a dozen theories of what's going on with the murders and Sebastian and why he's checking on me and instructing me on what to tell the cops. She was animated, to say the least, but I was more interested in hearing about what she did on Sunday with her new boy toy than anything that has to do with this shit city.

My eyes drift down, meeting Sebastian's and instead of glancing away, I hold his gaze for a moment.

I would feel it, wouldn't I? If his intention was to intimidate me, I'd feel fear, or a chill maybe? I'd feel something other than the quiet stillness that settles deep in my bones, the smoldering heat that simmers in my blood. Just looking at him, my body relaxes.

I swear I even see his lips tug into an asymmetric smile when I don't look away.

My heart does that thud again, and I have to loosen my grip on the thin curtain and let my head fall back against the headboard.

He'll only ever be at arm's length, so this power he has over me, this innate emotion he controls inside of me, can't be good.

The idling stops, fading into the sounds of the night and that warmth and soothing feeling disappear with it. It's sickening that something so small could garner so much emotion from me. As I reach for my book, I see my phone out of the corner of my eye.

I don't have a fucking clue where I left off. My fingers run along the edges of the pages as if my memory can lead me to the right page, but all I can focus on is the phone.

Shoving the book off my lap, I reach for it.

The cops didn't come to question me. I text the number I know is Sebastian's. He's never explicitly said it was him and usually he texts me, but I know it's his number. I want to tell him he can resume pretending I don't exist.

When he doesn't reply, I skim through the previous messages.

The first one reads: *You did good today.* He sent it a few nights after the infamous kiss. The night I first slept peacefully in this house after my uncle took me in.

Who is this? I asked, but he never answered.

When I first moved in, my uncle didn't have a spare room ready for me. We'd had to clear out the cluttered room he sometimes used as an office. Almost all of my mother's things had to be thrown away in the move. Same thing with some of my possessions, not that I had much. This townhouse was already full, and I wasn't even sure if I was staying here for long. No one told me anything. No one but Sebastian in a nameless text.

The phone pinging in my hand scares the shit out of me, spiking my adrenaline and forcing my heart to race up my throat. I nearly slam my head back against the headboard, but somehow manage to calm myself down.

The memories of the week my mother died have always haunted me. That week brought awful nightmares, ones that have come back in full force now that the past is being dredged up.

It's only Sebastian, I tell myself and breathe in deeply, calming every bit of me, although the task feels even more impossible than staying awake long enough to see what he's written.

How are you sleeping?

It's fitting he would ask that just as I rub my eyes with the palm of my hand and feel the sting of the burning need to sleep.

I chew on my lip, my fingers hovering over the screen. I don't want to lie to him here, not on the phone; I don't want to taint these messages that mean so much. After a moment I tell him the truth and see exactly what I expect in return.

Not well.

Have you been drinking your tea?

The vial is on my nightstand, staring at me as if I'm to blame for this shit. I nearly took it last night, but I don't do drugs. Not any sort. I've seen what addiction can do. Although I've also seen what desperation can do. And I'm desperate for one night where I close my eyes and I'm not haunted by memories of the past. I was doing so well for years. Her murderer being found is what set everything off. And the nightmares have come back with a vengeance.

Take it. His message sends a chill down my spine. It's as if he can hear my thoughts.

It takes me longer than I thought it would to write him back. Mostly because I don't know what his answer will be, but I know what I want to read.

If I take it, will you leave me alone? I text him and then grab the vial. I don't have a cup of tea handy, but I have a glass of water. Without even thinking, I put one drop, then another, then the third.

I watch the liquid swirl as I wait for his message. The other night I thought it was clear, since in the tea I couldn't see its color.

But it's pink, a pale, pale pink that quickly disappears in the water.

Before I take a sip, I check my phone only to see he hasn't responded. The lip of the glass feels cold as I bring it up and take the first gulp, wondering what it will taste like.

It tastes like nothing at all. Maybe a tinge of sugar. Just a faint hint.

I'm still considering the taste when the phone goes off on my lap. *You need to sleep.* How typical of Sebastian to respond without answering my question.

He has no fucking idea how badly I need to sleep. I'm delirious.

I chug the rest of the glass and intend on telling him that I drank the stuff he gave me, or maybe telling him something just so he'll stay with me on the phone until I've fallen asleep.

That doesn't happen though. Instead, I stare at the empty glass, feeling lightheaded and drowsy all at once. My sense of time begins to warp, feeling like it passes slowly but quickly just the same.

I barely get the glass on the nightstand before the darkness takes over. I'm able to slip under the covers, feeling the weight of sleep pulling at me. And I give in to it, so easily.

* * *

"YOU'RE LATE." Tamra's voice is clear as can be. She always had a slight rasp in the last word of every sentence and she kept her lips in the shape of that word for what seemed like an odd amount of time.

Where am I? I can feel my brow pinch; this room is familiar, but not so much that I know where I am. The carpet's thin and worn out in front of the television where the car seats are. There are three of them, although they're empty now. No one's here but me, sitting on the sofa that's just as worn as the carpet and Tamra, who's standing in front of the open door.

"He made me stay overtime." My mother's voice drifts in through the tense air. She's agitated and suddenly anxiety runs through me.

"Well, then, this is overtime for me. I can't watch these brats for free."

I'm not a brat. I swear I was good. I was good. I want to tell my mother, but I know to be quiet. With my hands in my lap, I wait stiffly. I'll only move when I'm told, I'll only speak when I'm spoken to. With my throat tight and dry, I wring my fingers around one another and glance at my bookbag at the end of the sofa. It's already packed, and I didn't forget anything. I never forget. If I do, I don't tell my mom and I hope she doesn't find out.

"Of course, you're gonna fucking charge me," my mother spits out her anger at Tamra. Anger which I know will be directed at me on Monday when she watches me again unless she tells my mom she's not going to watch me anymore without being paid early. Which she's done before. In that case, I stay in my room all day and don't answer the door. But Mom got in trouble for doing that once.

"Let's go, Chloe." My mom barges into the living room as Tamra stays where she is, keeping the front door open. It's late and I still have homework to do, but I don't know how to do it. I don't know how to read the words and I need someone to tell me, but Tamra won't and Mom's mad so I know better than to bother her.

I can tell from the way she stomps across the room it would be a mistake for me to do anything or say anything. I get up quickly. But I have to be quicker. If I move fast enough it won't burn when she grabs my arm.

"I'm coming," I tell her as fast as I can, snatching my bookbag and *scurrying to her side even though fear is racing through me and begging me to run.*

I'll be quiet; I'll go to sleep. Miss Parker will help me. It's only second grade, she keeps telling me I have time to do it at school if I get there early, but that I have to learn to read. I'm trying. I promise her I am.

"You see how no one helped me?" I hear a voice from outside this moment, a voice that sounds so close, so real. So full of rage and vengeance. My mother. Fear runs down my skin and up the back of my neck, freezing me where I am as I swear I feel her hot breath at the shell of my ear.

She didn't say that in the memory. She's telling me now.

I look back at Miss Tamra, still trying to keep up with my mother, even though her grip tightens so hard it's going to bruise. My blood runs cold and a scream is caught in my throat at the sight of Tamra leaning against the back wall, her left hand on the sofa. Blood coats her hair where a bullet wound mars her skull and it leaks down to her cheek, dripping onto her collarbone. I blink and suddenly she's standing there, yelling at my mother that she's an ungrateful bitch.

The chill doesn't go away, the sight from just before still stealing my breath and sanity.

The hand around my arm twists, burning my skin where my mother is touching me. It hurts. Mom, it hurts! I scream out, but the words don't come. I'm no longer there. It's dark and the bruising hold changes to something else, feeling like the kiss of a spider climbing up my arm in the darkness. I try to jump back, but I'm trapped, with nowhere to go and I can't see a damn thing.

She's here. My heart races and dread ignites inside of me, but I can't run. I can't see her. I can only hear her so close to me.

"No one ever helped me," she tells me. "They're going to pay for that."

* * *

IT FELT SO real last night, the sensation of my mother being so close to me.

An uncontrollable shudder runs through me as I slowly walk down the stairs. My heart won't stop racing and I can't clear my throat. I feel like I'm suffocating.

It was only a dream.

It's only a dream.

My chest tightens and the fear rips through me anew as I swear I hear something upstairs, something in the bedroom.

"Knock it off," I grit between my teeth.

The floor behind me creaks, loud and heavy. It almost sounds like someone's walking down behind me quickly and not hiding their weight, making me scream and I nearly fall down the last four steps. My back pressed against the wall and my chest frantically rising and falling, I stare behind me. No one's there. No one's here.

"It's only a dream," I remind myself and ignore the flow of ice that rolls over my body and how every hair on my body stands on end as I remember my mother's words. *They're going to pay for that.*

I'm not crazy, but I feel like I am. Crossing my arms over my chest, I feel my blunt nails dig in and remind myself that I'm alive.

The night after my mom died, I had the same type of dreams. The ones where she felt so real, following me even when I woke up.

"Please, go away," I beg her as I fall to the floor, sitting on the steps and wishing the wave of coldness that keeps coming over me would go away. Go away forever.

I told you, I hear my mother's voice, but I know it's just a memory.

She's not real. This isn't real.

The dead don't stay away for long. And they'll pay. Every single one of them will pay.

SEBASTIAN

*I*t's been three years since Romano gave me this job. The knife slams down on the cutting board as the thought hits me. I grab the carved meat and put it in the tub with the rest of the chunks.

I'm the butcher of a shop that rides the line of his territory. When Romano hired me to work here at Paul's Butcher Shop, I thought it meant something different. I thought it meant he was hiring me to be a part of his crew.

Now I know better; he just wanted to watch me. Train me, or maybe mentor me if he ever needed someone like me. The line of customers coming in for their packages distracts me and I glance up for a moment. Eddie, Paul's son, rings them up one by one. I stay in the back with a few other guys, processing all the orders and occasionally we have to stay here later, after closing hours.

Like when Romano has a special order.

Picking up the butcher knife, I slam it down with my teeth gritting together. This isn't his turf, but I'm not ready to start a war or gather an army against him. There's no one here to recruit, just the addicts who camp out behind the line of the highway that separates his area from Crescent Hills.

Most of the meat here is shipped off to God knows where. This place sees plenty of money come in and go out, but the numbers don't actually add up. We're just doing his bidding.

Still, I cut the fucking carcass up like I'm told, and stay on the right side of a would-be enemy while I have to.

I vaguely wonder how long that'll be. And when the time comes, which side I'll be on.

The bells hanging over the front door bells, two cheap bells that ding and then ding again as the door is open and closed quickly.

My gaze rises and goes back down, only to rise again with an unsettled feeling flashing through me, to take another look.

Chloe's not dressed to be out in public. She's in pajama pants and a baggy t-shirt with sneakers that aren't even laced like she couldn't get out of the house fast enough. Her hair's down and windblown.

"What the fuck is she doing here?" I mutter beneath my breath and drop the knife on the cutting board. Before I can even wipe my hands off, she's brushing past Eddie, ignoring him completely. She doesn't hesitate to go around the counter and make her way back here. "Sebastian," she gasps my name with a mix of relief and desperation.

My heart pounds harder as every man and woman in this place watches us. I can feel all their eyes on me as I keep my shoulders straight and head to the sink to wash my hands. I'm trying not to let her or anyone else see what I'm feeling deep down in my gut. This isn't a good look.

"I need you," Chloe speaks before the swinging door that separates the kitchen from the front of this small shop even closes.

The adrenaline pumps harder in my veins.

"Aren't you supposed to be at work?" I ask her although my gaze is focused on Eddie. I try to swallow but can't, so instead, I

483

watch the water run down the drain before turning off the faucet and drying off my hands. She doesn't answer me, but she steps closer to me at the sink.

"What are you doing here?" I ask her in a harsh tone with no room for her to question how I feel about this shit. No one comes here. No one who knows any better. *She* should know better.

Her baby blues flash with something—shock, or anger—I'm not sure which. Her loose t-shirt nearly slips down her shoulder as she takes a step back. The place is silent save the exhaust fans as she takes a moment to look me up and down.

"I need you," she tells me honestly, with a sincerity that everyone could hear, even if only spoken in a whisper. She brushes her wavy hair behind her ear and moves her gaze to the vinyl floor of the kitchen, blinking away the emotions ravaging her. The muscles of her throat tighten as she wraps her arms around herself. "Do you have a minute?" she asks as if she didn't just run back here and disrupt everything while having no consideration for what she's doing. The type of danger she's putting herself into.

With a deep crease in the center of her forehead and a pained expression in her eyes, she tells me again, "I need you." It's the third time she's said it since she got here, but she's never said those words to me until today. Fuck, I can't describe what it does to me. Her left foot kicks the floor as she slowly seems to notice everyone else as if they didn't even exist before.

I watch her gaze as it moves to Eddie, who's looking at me curiously and I give him an icy stare until he looks away.

I know he tells Romano everything that happens and having her come in making a scene like this is something that would get his attention. Talking to me about something as if I can save her... that would get his attention too. Romano needs to know everything, or so he tells us. But I don't plan on telling him shit.

Especially because it's her. And the way she's going about this is going to cause problems.

That anxiety comes rushing back, not just from what everyone else is wondering, but also from what Chloe has to say.

"Aren't you supposed to be at work?" I ask her again and toss the hand towel onto the steel counter.

"Angie keeps asking me that too," she mutters beneath her breath. Swallowing thickly, she looks over her shoulder before gripping my forearm and whispering, "I need to talk to you."

Her pale blue eyes plead with me, sinking deep inside of me like she always does. And for the first time in so long, I wish she wouldn't.

"Did something happen?" I ask her innocently, every hair on the back of my neck standing on end. I can hear people moving again, going back to their business, but they're quiet and slow to move. They're listening to everything.

"Did you see the news?" she asks me, and I stare back at her straight-faced as I shake my head no. I already know what's coming before she keeps going. It's only now that I regret going to see her; I invited her to think she could rely on me. She doesn't know what she's doing though, and all the shit I'm in right now.

"Tamra Stetson is dead," she tells me in the barest of whispers as if she's speaking a sin in the holiest of churches.

She has no idea what she's doing. She doesn't know how everyone is watching her. Watching *us*.

This city will talk, and word spreads like wildfire. That could be dangerous, but I already knew I was fucked. I just can't risk her going down for this.

"Why don't we go out back?" The question is really a demand as I grab her elbow. Her gasp is short-lived as she walks quickly beside me and my grip on her tightens. Using my forearm, I shove open the back door and pull her out back. The heat and the sun are blinding for a split second.

There may be no one out here, but there are plenty of people watching. Listening. It'd be naive of me to think that Eddie is the only person keeping tabs on me for Romano. Waiting to hear something they can use against anyone who has anything they could want.

Like her.

Chloe hisses between her teeth as the door closes with a loud clack. "Did you have to be such a dick?" she asks me with a fierceness I fucking love.

She rips her arm away and the action makes her shirt slip off her shoulder, showing me more of her soft skin and the dip in her collar.

The second she sees me looking there, she pulls it back into place.

"You should know better than to come here," I warn her, keeping my voice low, making sure she hears the threat. She's reckless, beautifully so, but it's dangerous. Right now, I can't have it.

"I need you, and--"

"It can wait," I cut her off, feeling my heart slam harder. Every time she says those words it does something to me. It rips me apart knowing how badly I want those words to be true and how wrong she is.

"But Tamra--"

"No one gives a fuck about Tamra." My answer is brutal, and I bite it out quickly, defensively even. Enough that I notice the change in my tone, but she doesn't.

"You don't understand, I wrote this list." She barely gets the words out before shoving half a sheet of paper against my chest. It's ragged like it was ripped from a spiral notebook and crumpled up before being smoothed out. It looks old as fuck and takes me a moment to recognize what it is.

Seeing the column of names on that piece of paper sends ice through my blood.

"Each in order," she says, and I hear her swallow before she looks back up at me. "It's every name in order."

Amber
Barry
Tamra
Mr. Adler
Dave
Andrea

"I DIDN'T PUT last names, but look at them, look at the list." She doesn't have to explain it for me to know. "It's happening right in order," she continues and struggles to breathe as if every word is suffocating her.

All the recent deaths have taken place according to this list. First Amber, then Barry, and now Tamra. Everyone knows about Jeff Adler. He'd been with Chloe's mother that night in the bar bathroom. He told the cops he'd heard her screaming but didn't feel like dealing with her. He's a piece of shit, always has been.

"Why would you even write this?" I can feel my anger and the tension in my body. The heat that's running in my blood, but the sight of her changes it as her hands wrap around my hand holding the note.

"Tell me it's a coincidence," she begs me with a choked voice. The tears in her eyes linger and she only stares at the paper, rather than returning my gaze that I know she can feel. She struggles to breathe again and then covers her mouth.

When she lifts her eyes to mine, everything in her begs me to answer her with what she wants to hear. "Tell me this is all a coincidence, please. I keep dreaming about them. My mother and..." She trails off, but her regret and remorse are palpable. She shakes her head when I don't answer, as I stand there stunned by the raw emotion and innocence.

"I'm just going crazy, aren't I?" she asks me, and I let the tension between us wane. I give her a moment to calm down as she lets out a hard breath of air. "I'm just having these nightmares and--"

"Was there another name?" I ask her, cutting her off, and rub my thumb against where I can feel the indentations from a pencil. Where it's obvious she put her own name down before erasing it. I know it was there, just beneath Andrea. I know it.

She chooses to go the route she always does with me, she lies, shaking her head and sending her hair swishing around her shoulders.

She grabs the piece of paper, trying to calm herself down and collect her composure.

"I wrote down the names of all the people who I thought deserved to die. I wanted them to die when they said they did nothing to help my mother when they admitted it with no remorse. I wrote it years ago, but just remembered it this morning when I turned on the TV. I was getting breakfast... and.... and suddenly I remembered. And when I saw it..."

The sound of a car backfiring in the distance makes her jump, but then her eyes close as she shakes her head as if admonishing herself. Her eyes open slowly and the pale blues stare at nothing.

"What if someone found this?" she asks although I don't know if she actually wants me to answer.

"It's in your hands," I tell her with strained frustration.

The huff she lets out is short and full of bitterness. Shoving the paper into her purse, she keeps going, keeps letting her emotions get the better of her.

"I've literally gone crazy." She wipes at her eyes although she doesn't dare cry. "I just don't understand. It's three in a row, like a fucking checklist." The anger comes out before she breathes in deep and says softly, "That's not a coincidence."

Spearing her fingers in her hair, she grips onto the roots at her temple. Her shoulders are hunched, and she looks worse now than she did years ago. "It's not a coincidence," she says quietly and her voice is shaky.

It looks bad. It looks really fucking bad. I can see why she'd be freaked out, but this isn't the way she should have handled it.

I can hear her breathe in sharply as I lay a hand on her shoulder, but I make sure to keep my touch gentle, and she slowly melts. Every bit of her is breaking down.

She licks her lower lip and struggles to look me in the eye as she tells me, "Ever since they found him..." She trails off and rolls her eyes although sadness and guilt even, mar her expression.

"Calm down," I tell her as she takes in a breath. "You're all right." I try to pull her in close to me, to be close to her like I was a few nights ago, but she pulls away enough that my hands fall from her.

She looks me in the eyes as she confesses, "Ever since that night, I've had these nightmares... My mom..." She takes in a shaky breath.

"You need to sleep and eat and let it all go, Chloe." I hold her gaze as I take a step closer to her, willing her to let it go. "People die."

"They're being killed," she replies forcefully, although her bottom lip wobbles. Her eyes dart from me to the door as she takes a half step back. "I dreamed of her last night," she whispers darkly. "With Tamra. And the others before."

Letting out a breath, I straighten my back and run a hand through my hair. Behind the butcher's is a mechanic shop and I stare at a patch of rust on an old beat-up hood as a wind gust blows by and the heat lets up for a moment.

"You didn't do this," I tell her without looking at her.

"I feel like I'm going crazy," she says in a sad voice that forces me to look at her. Her doe eyes reach mine. "Truly crazy, Sebastian."

"You're scared and searching for meaning where there is none," I tell her, hoping she'll just drop it already.

"I don't know what to think, but it's not--"

"A coincidence?" I cut her off, staring into her eyes and forcing her to let it go. "It is. That's all this is."

Her head wavers with the smallest of shakes and she looks at me bewildered. "But even you said the cops would think--"

"Jesus," I cut her off again and run a hand down my face. "Is that what got to you?" I ask her, tilting my head and staring at her like she should know better. I can feel my brow furrow as she struggles to come up with an answer.

"Chloe, you can't be doing this. You need to sleep-"

"I did!" she protests.

"More than one night," I add. "And you need to eat. You need to take care of yourself and stop worrying about those assholes."

She lifts her hand up to her shoulder and lets her thumb drag along the collar of her shirt as she looks out onto the mechanic's shop. "It's just a coincidence?" she asks me, although it sounds more like a hopeful statement. I wait until her eyes are on me to tell her, "Yeah, you're just tired, Chlo."

She holds my gaze for a second and I swear if it had been a second longer, I would have had to look away.

"I'm sorry," she says with another shake of her head. Biting down on her bottom lip she looks away from me and says, "I didn't mean to come here and..."

"You definitely shouldn't have come here," I tell her with a seriousness that makes her flinch.

"I..." she starts to respond and then corrects herself, "I said I was sorry." The instant the words slip from her, I can feel her walls start to go up. For a moment I had her, but I'll be damned, I don't want to lose it. Not again.

"Come have lunch with me." I don't offer her an out or a chance to turn me down. Feeling the heat get to me from the direct sun, I wipe my hand down the back of my neck. "You need to eat anyway."

"I don't know that I should," she tells me although her words come out as if she's asking a question.

A huff of disbelief leaves me. "So, you think it's okay to come here and talk to me about people being murdered?" I wait for her eyes to meet mine before I continue. "But going out to lunch is where you draw the line?" I let my expression show a bit of disappointment, even a little sadness. She's always been a sucker for that.

"I'm sorry." Her expression shifts to one of sympathy as she says, "I didn't mean--"

"I know what you meant," I tell her and splay my hand on the small of her back, giving the shop one more look before guiding Chloe around the building to the front parking lot. "You need to eat."

CHLOE

This diner isn't remarkable, but the food is. I think it's all the salt they put on everything. They even put it on the pizza.

Even though it's my favorite place to eat, I'm surprised I was able to eat anything at all.

The fear and paranoia are embarrassing. I'm fucking embarrassed I got so worked up this morning. It's just… finding that list and the nightmares really got to me. I felt like I was drowning in a childish fear that still has its claws rooted deep in my thoughts.

The fear faded to uneasiness when Sebastian talked me down. Just being around him makes me feel safe and protected. If I could be with him always, I would. Because he settles something deep down inside of me. He makes me crave more. More from life, but also more from him.

A different kind of nervousness took over the moment I got into his car. The soft leather was something I didn't expect. The hum of the air conditioner and the occasional clearing of Sebastian's throat were the only noises the entire ride.

This morning, I had to tell someone and he's my only someone, even if that's a pathetic truth. I didn't think twice. He didn't answer his phone, so I went to where I knew he'd be. It made every bit of sense to me at the time.

Until I slipped into his car and was engulfed in his scent. Until I peeked at him as he drove his car with an air of dominance and authority.

In a room with other people, or even in a room I'm used to being in, Sebastian is still the boy who kissed me. But alone, in his car, something changed. And suddenly I lost my voice along with every thought I ever had, except for the dirty ones that crept up late at night about Sebastian doing more than just kissing me.

Today has been nothing but a series of fucked up thoughts running wild in my head.

"What's on your mind, Chloe Rose?" His deep, rough voice breaks into my thoughts and I take my time reaching for another fry, carefully taking a bite before answering him.

"Just wondering about how much can change in a single day."

I can feel the heat rise up my chest and to my cheeks, all the way to my hairline as he leans forward, his broad shoulders stretching out the t-shirt as he tells me, "I would swear you were thinking about something else."

His steely blue eyes seize all my attention and hold me accountable. I can barely breathe, but he doesn't need the confirmation. He's plenty full of himself already, so I simply eat the rest of the fry and shrug. I ignore the butterflies and the desire to push him for more of that teasing side of him. This is the part of his personality I've craved, but I don't want to appear desperate or say something stupid. I don't want to ruin it. I can barely believe I'm here with him. I don't even want to think about it for too long; I'm afraid if I do, it'll all go away.

His cocky half smirk is what makes me look anywhere but at him as I try to remember how I ended up here with him.

Thoughts that I wish I hadn't tried to return to.

Remembering when my mother died, how I felt the same way. Afraid and paranoid. I felt like no one understood why I was so completely distraught. The mix of emotions never felt right, and I never had any control over them. They hit me relentlessly, like the constant blow of boughs as I was forced to run through trees in a forest. Swiping at me, scratching me, taking me by surprise. I was only a girl, but old enough to remember, old enough to know I could have done something.

"I thought I was done with all this," I tell him absently.

"How's that?" Sebastian asks me with his brow furrowed and a look in his eyes that's compassionate and curious. This is how I imagined he'd look when I read those texts all that time ago. It was only an image conjured in my head because I'd never seen anything of him other than the hard, dangerous boy he wanted everyone to see.

"Do you really want to know?" I question him, the uneasiness returning. He nods his head once and I figure, why not? I have no one to talk to and after this, I'm not sure he'll even talk to me again. So why not let it all out?

"I thought I was over feeling like this..." Before I can finish, the air conditioner blows across my skin from above me just then, and a flow of goosebumps trails down my arm and shoulders making me wish I hadn't picked this seat.

"You want to switch spots?" Sebastian asks and again, I'm surprised he would ask me that.

I gently shake my head and try to recall what I was thinking only seconds ago. Before Sebastian destroyed my thoughts again with a mere five words. He's good at that.

Clearing my throat, I stare down at the half-eaten pile of fries and remember the gut-wrenching feeling and sickness of what's to come. The living in fear and agony part. Oh yes, that's what he took my mind from.

"I thought I'd gotten over this feeling of being in constant state of fear and guilt." I don't look at him as I speak this time. If I do, I'm not certain that my mind will stay on course. "Even after you..." I don't mention what he did, and my gaze almost darts up to meet his eyes, but instead, they fall on his lips. "Even after school let out that year," I say, choosing to settle on the time rather than the action we both know I'm referring to. "Even then, at night there was this feeling, but it drifted away. And then when my uncle died, I was just angry." My voice raises at the thought, my breathing coming in faster.

Sitting back into my seat, I look at him and feel as if I should feel ashamed, but I'm not.

"Angry?" he questions.

"Yeah. I was angry. It wasn't fair that I was stuck here." Emotions threaten to come up at my admission. I loved my uncle and he'd passed only two years ago, right before I graduated high school. I was old enough to take the shit debt he left behind. "I know it's not his fault; he wanted better for me..."

I don't finish that line of thinking. "The point is, I thought I was done with all of this. For the first time in so long, I was fine."

"You were relying on yourself. So, of course, you were fine." Sebastian sounds confident in his response, but he doesn't get it. Parts of me are so thoroughly broken that even the idea I have to rely on myself is horrifying. Rebecca used to say it was understandable after the trauma I'd been through. What she called trauma, I just called my childhood. No wonder I turned to books and writing to help me cope. Getting lost in my stories was a lot more enjoyable than facing reality.

"Everyone needs someone," I answer him, holding his gaze and praying he can feel what I mean. That he can know how deeply settled I am in that decision.

"You didn't have a someone, and you were fine."

I almost answer him with, I didn't say everyone *deserves* some-

495

one. Almost. But I decide to swallow it down. I sure as hell don't want his pity.

The ping of my phone distracts me from the conversation. Sebastian's here with me, so it must be Angie. Pulling it out, I see I'm right.

Where the hell are you? Stop being a bitch and answer me!

Angie certainly has a way with words.

I'm not coming in. I send her the response and then think better of it and add, *I'm sorry. I'm just not feeling all that well today.*

Before she can reply, I silence my phone and slip it back into my purse. She wouldn't understand. She'd think I'm crazy. Shit, I think I'm crazy. My heart beats a little faster at remembering the pure fear that ran through me when I saw Tamra died. My name was on the bottom of that list. If someone else made a list like mine, would my name be on theirs too?

The chill from the air conditioner comes back and I let my head fall back with my eyes closed, suppressing the urge to feel anything at all. I'd rather be numb to it all. Goosebumps prick along my skin once again, slowly this time. It's just the chill, I tell myself. It's definitely from the air conditioner.

"Who's that?"

Sebastian's question distracts me from my thoughts and I open my eyes slowly to tell him, "Nobody."

"So, nobody texted you?" Sebastian asks with what feels like a touch of jealousy. I'm ashamed by the way my body reacts. I feel a heat that swells from the pit of my stomach, rising up but also moving lower. Forcing a small smile to my lips, I answer him, "Just a friend."

When his expression doesn't change, I roll my eyes at him and say, "I finally got one of those." My answer is pitiful, but I own it. I don't care that I'm a loner who prefers books and writing and hiding away in my stories. Books are cheap, and the people in them are better than the ones I have left here.

He looks like he's going to say something else, but he doesn't. He finishes his drink and then reaches for his wallet.

"I can buy lunch," I offer. "After all, I kind of ruined your day." He cocks a brow and doesn't answer me. Instead he puts some cash down on the table, more than enough to pay for both of us.

"I said I can get this one," I tell him and reach for the cash to shove it back to him, but he snatches my wrist. Electricity shoots through me, the desire returning with a blazing force.

He releases me slowly and I bring my wrist back to me, staring at it as if it's been singed. I'm reeling in the shivers that flow through my body.

"I pay," is all he says, with a forcefulness that spikes desire through me. I can't break his gaze, I can't speak.

"I want to," he adds in a gentler tone.

"How do you do this to me?" I ask him, but then I think of a different question. "Why are you doing this?"

"Because I want to." He uses the same intensity as before, but somehow his words come out softer, almost comforting. The tension is thick between us and I wonder if he feels the same pull I do. "Why did you come to see me?" he asks me, and the question breaks the spell, my eyes falling to the table and the realization that the lunch is over. That this moment is only temporary, just like Sebastian's presence in my life.

"Because I wanted to," I offer him a similar response, shrugging and then pulling up the baggy sleeves to my t-shirt. How is it that hours have passed, and I've only just now realized I'm in my pajamas? I didn't even bother to put on mascara. I always put on mascara, I look so much younger without it.

"Are you going to tell me why you're doing this?" I ask him again, feeling irritated by everything, especially my reaction to the series of events that happened today.

"I just wanted to have a nice meal with you." Hearing those words from him makes me smile and let out a short laugh. My mirth doesn't wane when he looks at me with confusion, instead, it only makes me grin harder. Maybe I truly am crazy.

"What'd I say?" he asks, and I just shake my head, taking a peek at him while lowering my lips to have a sip of Coke from the straw.

I let the bubbling fizz relax me and then straighten myself to tell him, "Just the thought of you having a nice lunch and then heading off to your nine-to-five job."

The charming grin grows on his face, revealing his perfect white teeth. "Don't you know I'm a hardworking, blue-collar type of man?"

I hold his gaze and keep my smile in place as I tell him, "I know who you are, Sebastian Black."

My taunting doesn't get me the reaction I'm after. Instead, he slips his mask back into place, hiding from me.

My next breath is accompanied by a long stretch and then I take another drink. A coldness sets in between us. I can feel it coming. It used to come so often when we were forced to be together. The moment he knew he'd let me in, he'd shut it down.

I should have known better than to think it would last. Maybe I didn't think it would, but I sure as fuck want it to.

"Something is truly wrong with me," I speak the thought without conscious consent.

"You're a product of your environment," Sebastian answers me. He sinks back against the booth and stares at me long and hard. The fake, thin leather protests as he watches the front door.

"I should get home," I tell him, so we can end whatever this moment has been. "I'm sorry I came and…. decided to be crazy and vent to you."

"I'm not." He answers me the same way he did with paying for lunch. No nonsense, no bullshit. And the same response flows through my body. For years, in school and up till the day my uncle died, I wanted him to be like this with me. To just talk to me.

"Be careful what you say at the shop though," he tells me and then adds, "people listen." The tone in which he says it brings an uneasy feeling over me and with a tightness in my throat, I start to tell him I'm sorry, but he cuts me off.

"Just so you know for next time." The softness to him, it does something to me I can't explain. *Next time.* As if I could have this moment again with him.

"You're different," I marvel at the revelation out loud.

"I'm not the one who's different."

"What do you mean?" I search his eyes for answers, wanting to know how he meant me to take that statement. *Needing* to know.

"Does it matter?"

"I don't know what matters anymore."

"What do you know, Chloe Rose?"

The way he asks it, or maybe it's just my own thoughts, but it feels like the way he asks it is so much dirtier than what he actually asked.

"I know I should go to work or go home." Neither of those options sounds appealing, but both are true.

"It'll already be two by the time you get to work," he says and shakes his head, "don't bother."

"Home it is then," I say, easily conceding, and reaching for my purse as I scoot out of the booth to stand. "Thank you for lunch," I tell him and then add, "I can walk since it's--"

"Let me take you home." He doesn't look me in the eyes when he gives the command, he doesn't even look at me. It's clearly non-negotiable, so I don't bother objecting.

The drive back to my place is even worse than the drive to the diner. Thankfully, it only takes about four minutes. And two of those were spent at a red light.

"I really could have walked," I tell him as I slip out of his car. He opened his door first, intent on getting out rather than just dropping me off, so I walk a little quicker, eager to get to my front door first and cut him off there. I just want to be alone for a while. I want to hide away if I can. I need to process everything, but Sebastian has a way of bringing me out of my hiding place and showing me more of this world that makes me want to risk living.

"Should I come in and look around?" he asks as his car keys dangle from his hand. He stands in front of me expectantly, but I can't give him that.

"I'd prefer it if you didn't." The moment I unlock the door and turn around, I block the doorway and put a hand on the doorknob. It's only open wide enough for me to stand in the gap comfortably. "I think I need to decompress; today's been a lot to handle."

He cocks a brow at me in that way I like. "You wouldn't lock me out, would you?"

The way he asks makes me smirk, which slowly shifts into a genuine smile as I consider him. He's so tall, so much taller than how he is in my thoughts. And his shoulders, so wide. He could protect me from anything. That pull to him is so strong it's scary. But Sebastian himself doesn't scare me, not in the least. He never has. It's the power he has over me that's terrifying. "I would... but if you asked to come in, I'd let you."

My answer puts a smile on his face that matches mine. "See? I told you, you're different."

I huff a laugh, shaking my head. I'm not so sure that I'm different. It's more like I'm letting him see more of me. That's not the same thing.

He leans in close as I fail to summon a response, so close that I know exactly what he would want if I didn't lock him out tonight. I'm in over my head with him, hot and bothered and wanting the same thing he does.

I need to get away from this city more than ever.

"Get some sleep then," he says softly, in a deep, rugged tone when my eyes meet his. The carnal need that burns in his gaze sets my body on fire. I'm still standing there, watching him walk away when I can finally breathe again.

What is he doing to me?

The feeling deep in my gut, the one that used to be constantly present, still lingers as I walk up the stairs. Something is telling me it's not all right, it's not a coincidence. But that something is quieted by the thoughts of Sebastian and the idea that if it's not all right, I can run to him. It brings out a strength in me I desperately need. He does that to me. And I find it hard not to be drawn to him even more because of it, my stupid heart especially. He's been good at hurting it in the past, but it still wants more of him.

SEBASTIAN

The second her door closed, I felt eyes on the back of my head. I could feel someone watching. But when I turned around, there wasn't a single soul in sight. No neighbors on their porch, no kids playing in the street.

Fuck, I'm just as paranoid as she is. The sound of my boots slapping on the cement stairs pounds as hard as my pulse does in my ears.

When I get in my car, I lock the doors but don't turn the key in the ignition. Not just yet. The light in her bedroom isn't on and I wait, staring at the curtains until the soft yellow glow floods the window. Even though dusk hasn't hinted at its arrival, I can still see she's turned on the light.

I'm tired as fuck. I couldn't sleep last night, and I don't have a clue when I'll finally be able to rest easy again. The image of Chloe in my bed soothes the beast inside me. The caged animal that needs to be released. If she was next to me, in my arms and in my bed, I'd sleep then.

I pick up my phone and call Carter, needing some relief tonight and wondering if he'd drive by and keep a lookout for me. I don't like the way she's thinking and worse, the way she's acting. I can't risk her doing anything stupid, like telling anyone else about that list.

The phone rings. And rings. An unsettling feeling in my gut churns until he picks up. I'm reminded that his mom's doing worse and worse. One day he'll answer and tell me she's gone. I fucking dread that day. The cancer's been eating at her for two years now; she doesn't look like herself anymore with all the weight she's lost. She can't go anywhere without getting winded. It's only a matter of time at this point.

"Hey man, I'm having a rough time. I was just about to call you."

"What's going on?" I ask him, feeling guilty that I forgot the shit he's going through.

There's silence for a long time before he tells me, "It's just getting harder."

"You all right?"

I can hear him swallow before he replies, "As all right as I can be." I forget what it's like to have a family, let alone what it would be like to watch someone you love to slowly die in front of you. "You need me to do anything?" I ask him.

Again, there's only silence.

"Nah," he says. "What is it you needed?"

With his question, comes a beep signaling I've received a text and instantly I think it's Chloe. Looking up and watching as the light goes off and the window loses its light, I answer him, "It was just a passing thought, it doesn't matter."

"You sure?"

"Yeah," I answer him. "But if you need anything, let me know. I got you."

I don't rush getting off the phone with Carter, but he does, ending the call right then with the sound of his father yelling in the background. My heart goes out to the kid.

More than a time or two I've thought about showing his dad what it's like to have someone take out their anger and fear on a man, but I don't know if Carter would forgive me for stepping in. Or whether it would just make things worse on him. His family is his. It's what he told me when I suggested it once. I never want to get between him and his family. Never. No matter how fucked up they are.

The second the line goes dead, I check my text messages, but the message isn't from her.

Are you going back on your word?

I read the text from the unknown number with a mix of anger and fear coloring my consciousness as I stare at the words.

I turn the key in the ignition, although I know I'll be back tonight once the sun has set. I'm dead set on staying right here tonight. Right in front of her house until the early morning's passed. I don't need to sleep. I can sleep when I'm dead.

I answer, *No, I understand what I have to do. She's staying out of it. She doesn't know.*

The unknown number replies, *Good. I'd hate for you to find out what would happen if you go back on your word.*

CHLOE

*"Y*ou didn't come visit me on my birthday."

I hear my mom's voice in the pitch black of my dream. The darkness spreads all around me. I can't see.

"I missed you," she says but her voice sounds closer this time and it echoes all around me. The only other sounds are my chaotic breathing and the pounding of my heart as fear filters into my blood. Every pulse feels harder and forces the desperation to get out of here to climb high into my throat.

Run.

I try to run; I try to scream. But I can't.

Open your eyes. Wake up!

I wish I could obey my own pleas.

Slowly my eyes open, but I'm not in my bed. I'm in the alley on Park Street. I swear I feel tears on my face. My throat is raw from hours of screaming. My nails are broken and there's blood everywhere. The metallic scent of it, the feel of it dried but still sticky and wet in other places over my skin, it's all I can smell and feel.

My body is so heavy.

"Why didn't you come visit me?" My mother's voice taunts me as I try

to lift my head.

My body's heavy, lying on the ground. My cheek is flat against the cold, hard asphalt.

"I wanted to sing you a lullaby, baby girl. I miss being your mama." I feel fresh tears start.

"Please don't," I whimper where I am. The pain flows as freely as the fear of seeing her again. I wish I could run.

"So, did I, baby girl," my mother responds to my unspoken thoughts. "Or for someone to help me," she adds.

I hear footsteps behind me and my heart pounds harder and faster. The adrenaline in my body is useless.

On instinct, I scream for help, but my voice is so quiet.

"No one can hear you, baby girl." She's closer. My body trembles and I try so hard to move, but not a single limb obeys. I try my fingers. One by one, please. Please move, but nothing moves. I'm cemented where I am.

"Well, maybe they can, but they don't listen."

The chill from the night air gets colder as a darker shadow covers my body. She's behind me now. I try to swallow, so I can clear my throat and beg her, but it's pointless.

"It's time for your lullaby," she threatens.

"I promise I'll sleep." My words come out as a strangled plea. I remember the way the heavy base of the glass vodka bottle landed against my temple. She didn't sing it like this, so calmly. It started out this way though. And once she started, she never stopped. Not until I was unconscious. She knew when I was pretending. She always knew.

"Go to sleep," she sings to me in a gravelly voice, dry and slurred from drinking, "go to sleep, lit-tle Chlo-e."

Tears stream down my cheeks.

"Close your eyes, rest your head."

Remembering how she beat me furiously with the bottle.

She drags her finger across my skin, trailing along the curve where my neck meets my shoulders. Her nail is jagged and slick with fresh blood. Pulling my hair behind my neck so she can whisper in my ear, she finishes the lullaby, "It's time for bed."

SEBASTIAN

I debate on sending the text. I'm staring at the phone in my hand like I'm back in high school.

You didn't go to work today either?

The words stay right where they are, waiting for me to send them. I know she's all right; no one's approached her, no one's messaged her. Although, she hasn't left the house since I walked her to her door. Not two nights ago, not last night and she called out from work again this morning.

I know she's in there. I've been watching every inch of that place.

"Mr. Black." A man's deep voice disrupts me from my thoughts. Sitting at the lone desk in the back room of the shop, I can see him through the open door. He's standing in the front of the butcher shop, peeking behind the counter, and trying to get a look into the kitchen.

"Officer Harold," I answer him in a monotone and slip the phone into my pocket. I just got in and didn't see his car in the lot. But I didn't check for it either. I didn't do anything except worry about leaving Chloe Rose alone in that house. She's getting to me even worse than she did back in high school.

All I can do is think about her, and that's a mistake. For both of us.

"What can I do for you?" I ask him as I walk out of the back and head straight toward him. As I cross my arms, I make a mental note of who all's in here. Eddie's behind the front counter and watching everything, although he's pretending to go through the weekly invoices. I don't know why he bothers putting up a front. Officer Harold is in Romano's back pocket and Eddie knows that. As does everyone else who's working in the back.

So that means Romano sent him, or this is a test.

Either way, I don't care for it. Other than Eddie, I don't think anyone else is here yet. Which could be bad news for Eddie if this goes south.

"Have you heard about the recent killing spree?" he asks me and gestures to one of the two small tables in this place. They're circular with peeling, flaking vinyl on the top and thin metal legs that match the rickety chairs. They're dated and not meant to keep people wanting to stay. Most of the people who come in here pick up their packages and leave. Those who decide they want to hang around often change their minds as quickly as they can sit their asses down in these spindly seats.

"Killings?" I question him like I haven't thought much about it. The sound of the metal feet of the chair dragging across the floor makes Eddie cringe as he peeks up from scratching his pencil on the notepad. "I know Tamra Stetson was shot and killed, I heard about that the other day."

"Tamra and before her, Barry Jones, a few days before him a girl named Amber Talbott was found dead." Officer Harold doesn't sit like I do. Instead, he remains standing. Fucking prick.

I push back the chair and spread my legs wide as I sit back and shrug. "I only know what you know," I offer him, and he gives me a smug smirk.

"And what is it that you think I know?" he taunts me, sucking his teeth and keeping his back to Eddie. Eddie doesn't hide the fact he's watching.

Again, I shrug and say, "Whatever's in the paper and on the news."

It's quiet for a moment. Not a sound from anything. Not the air conditioner, not the cars outside. Nothing as he watches me, looking over my expression. I keep it easy and relaxed. It's something I worked hard to accomplish. You never let them see a damn thing from you. Carter said his dad taught him that once. That you don't give anyone anything. It's the one thing Carter taught me that's helped me survive longer than I would have otherwise.

"And what about your girl, Chloe?" Officer Harold asks me, and Eddie stops jotting on his pad. The scratching of the pencil halts and my heart pounds heaviy. I can feel my lips twitching on my face to pull down into a scowl and the need for my forehead to show a sharp crease.

I want to rip out his throat for even mentioning her name. I wish I could see her right now. That I could see she's safe and ensure they'll leave her out of this. Adrenaline pumps hard in my blood knowing she's involved now, but she did that to herself when she came here. Fuck, I wish I could take it back.

I can protect her though. I *will* protect her; I'll make this right.

"Chloe Rose?" I say her name and force my face to soften, to stay casual wondering how the best way to play this would be. I rub the stubble on my chin and look past him. "What about her?"

"Why did you go to see her?" he asks me. Anxiety races through me. She's always flown under the radar. Gorgeous and tempting, but no one's paid her any mind. No one wants to deal with the sad girl who's stuck here with no one and nothing. Now she's a person of interest, all because of me.

"She came to see me," I correct him.

"That's not what I heard." My pulse pounds at my temples. And again, I struggle to keep my composure. I feel my throat get tight as I swallow.

Letting out a low sigh, I exaggerate. "A few nights ago, she was walking home." I meet his eyes to add, "Alone. And the streetlight went out. Spooked her some."

His eyes stay hard as I sniff and shrug my shoulders. "She wanted some company. I checked out her place. I don't know if you know this, officer, but someone broke into her house a while back."

His eyes narrow; I know damn well that he knows what I did. I had to tell Romano, who tells Officer Harold when he doesn't have to go searching for a killer. Problem is, Romano doesn't know who's doing these killings. Romano should know if I had something to do with it, I'd tell him. The fact that Officer Harold is here is telling. The uneasiness flows through me the more I think about it.

I shrug. "I guess she liked that I was willing to give her some company." I tilt my hips up some, implying a little more happened. "I liked it too."

"So, this has nothing to do with Tamra Stetson or the killing spree?" he asks me and sucks his teeth again, but his demeanor has changed. No longer on the attack, instead he's desperate for a lead.

"It's freaking Chloe out some, being alone and watching these girls turning up dead... which is only helping me get laid. But I don't know shit that could help you."

"Just to clarify." The good officer puts both hands on the table and leans forward, getting so close I can see where he nicked his chin when he was shaving. "For everyone," he adds, although the heavy implication is that Romano will hear about whatever I say. I already know that though. This little visit was obviously triggered by Chloe running in here the other day. I know damn well that Romano doesn't know shit, and neither does this prick.

"Whatever you want to know," I say and stare him dead in his eyes, feeling the tension rise.

"You don't know anything?" His eyes search mine as I answer him, "Not a damn thing."

My heart beats chaotically and I swear if he could hear, he'd know I'm lying.

Sniffing and standing straight, Harold fixes his shirt, tucking it back in. "If you hear anything…" he says even though he's already walking out. With his back to me, he doesn't bother to give any parting words. Only the sound of the bells bids him farewell.

"What's up his ass?" I ask Eddie even though my eyes are on the glass door as it closes behind him.

After a moment with no response, I look over at Eddie, but he's already gone. The notepad remains on the counter, the top piece ripped off.

There are enemies everywhere. Every step of the way.

The deeper I get with Romano, the less likely it is I'll ever have a chance to leave.

CHLOE

*T*hey feel so real. That's why I can't shake them.

The nightmares are something I was used to when I hadn't come to terms with the reality.

My mother's gone.

She died years ago.

I remind myself once again and blow across the top of the full cup of tea in my hands, but it's no longer hot, it's barely lukewarm. I've only just now realized I must have been holding it for a while without even taking a single sip. I'm slow to set the cup down on the end table and then reach for the blanket. My fingers grip on to the soft woven fabric like it can save me. Just as I used to think when I was a child.

My mother's gone.

She died years ago.

It was hard to say the words back then, but I have to keep saying them now.

Not because I don't believe them, but because every time I fall asleep now, she's there, haunting me and saying things that scare me. Things she knows would put true fear into my heart. She's reminding me of memories I've long buried.

She's angry and wants revenge for what happened. I can feel it. Her killer joining her six feet in the dirt isn't enough justice. She's starved for more. A taste of his blood wasn't enough.

When I wake up breathless and terrified by how realistic the dreams are, I can feel the weight of her hand gripping my arm, but no sane person would believe me. I would just sound crazy.

I'm going crazy. I know that's what they'd say and as I pull my knees into my chest on the sofa, I struggle to deny it. I'm fucking insane.

All I can think, is that whatever Sebastian gave me is fucking with my head. I can't sleep without seeing her, without *feeling* her. I swear the scratch on the back of my neck is from her.

I don't want to go to sleep. I only took the sweets, as Sebastian calls it, that one time, but I've been so fucked up since then. Although, so much more has happened since then too.

My fingers press into my tired eyes, feeling the burning need to sleep and I remember how I woke up last night, sweating, crying, my throat raw as if I'd been screaming. I prayed like I'd never prayed before and when I whispered for someone to help me, I felt the coldness of her presence. As the chill traveled up my spine, I swear I heard my mother whisper, "I am."

A sudden knock at the door has my heart galloping in my chest. Two days of not sleeping but also not knowing what to do has left me jolting at every sudden sound.

"Chlo," I hear Sebastian's voice call out through the front door and he knocks again as he says, "Open up."

Just hearing his voice is calming, and I easily swing my legs down and listen to my bare feet pad across the floor as I go to unlock the door and let him in.

I swing open the door without even looking in the small mirror in the hall to see if I look presentable. I'm sure I look like hell, and I wouldn't keep him waiting, so it doesn't matter anyway.

With his hand still raised to knock again, we both stand there for a moment, waiting for the other to say something. I swallow thickly, feeling the nervousness rise up again. He's never taken so long to say anything before.

"You look like you're ready for me to drag you to bed," he finally tells me and then steps inside, not waiting for me to invite him in.

"If you're lucky, I'd let you." I try to make it sound like a joke, but at this point, I would. "I feel like I'm going to fall over," I tell him groggily and turn my back on him to saunter back to the living room, but he grabs my wrist as he kicks the door shut behind him.

It closes with a click.

"What?" I ask him, staring pointedly where his fingers are wrapped possessively around my wrist. "I wasn't serious. You aren't dragging me anywhere."

Keeping my face deadpan, he cracks a smile and then I mirror his, a small simper of a smile, but it doesn't reflect anything that I feel.

"You okay?" he asks me.

Blowing a lock of hair away from my face and straightening the strap of the tank top on my shoulder I nod and ask, "What's going on?" No matter how much I want to tell someone about my nightmares, I refuse to speak the words out loud. It would only make me sound unhinged.

"The cops wanted to know why I came to see you."

Cops. That was the last thing I wanted to hear. My stomach drops, as does my gaze and I pick under my nails to distract myself.

"How would they even know?" I ask him without thinking, but if I'd just let it sink in for one second, I'd know better. *Everyone here is crooked, everyone knows everything.* It was the only good advice my mother ever gave me. *If you keep that in mind, you'll be all right.*

"Ignore me," I tell him absently and rub the tiredness from my eyes as I walk to the sofa. I plunk back down into my cozy seat and pull the throw blanket around me again.

When I peek up at Sebastian, he's eyeing me with a look I can't place. "What did you tell them?" I ask him to get the attention away from me.

"Well, I had to tell a white lie."

"What did you say?" I whisper and fight off the yawn that threatens.

"I told them you meant something to me and I was just checking in on you."

It's quiet for a moment as I take in his words. I have to remind myself of what he said. Me meaning anything to him is a white lie. The thought makes my fingers ball into a fist under the blanket.

"Okay," is all I give him as I sit there, with my neck craned so I can stare up at him as he stands in front of me.

"And now they think we may be a thing." His eyes assess me, and if I wasn't so tired, I would blush, practically ignite like I've done before. But right now, all I can think is how he said it was a white lie.

I almost ask him what a white lie means, so he can tell me to my face in blunt terms that I don't mean anything to him. Instead, I just ignore it all and focus on a pounding ache that grows in my temple.

"What's in that stuff you gave me?" I ask him a question that's been nagging at the back of my head.

"Nothing serious." His forehead creases as he answers me. "Why?"

"It feels serious to me," I tell him. although my heart beats rapidly, begging me not to push him away with my insanity.

The moment passes, and with the silence, the tension grows.

"What happened?" he asks me. "Are you sick?" The concern in his voice is so genuine that I nearly tell him to be careful, that everyone will see that I mean something to him. But the spite and jabs from his white lie comment mean nothing to me right now.

He's here. He's listening to me. Whether he realizes it or not, I know I mean something to him. So, I couldn't care less if that's what the cops think. I couldn't care less about people running their mouths or any of that right now.

There's only one thing haunting me at this moment.

"I'm just..." I trail off and swallow thickly, burying the words in my throat.

"When's the last time you took it?" he pushes for more information as he takes the seat next to me, making the old sofa groan with his weight. He sits closer to me than I sat to him last time. He's so close, I can still feel that heat that lingers on his shirt from the summer sun.

"I only took it the one night." I look up into his steely blue eyes and watch the grey flecks mesmerize me as I add, "The night I texted you."

"You're supposed to take it every night, Chlo. It doesn't stay in your system for long."

"Are you sure?" I ask him quickly. "Because it feels like it's still in my system."

The sofa protests as I readjust in my seat to face him more and he asks, "Have you been sleeping?"

I only nod with a small frown gracing my lips as my chest tightens with worry. "I don't want to though," I whisper the confession.

"Chlo," he scolds me, immediately running the middle finger and thumb of his right hand down his temples. His large hand covers his eyes as he does it.

"Don't do that," I bite back, not hiding the sadness and disappointment at his reaction. "I'm not a child and I'm not okay." Although my voice wavers, I say the words as strongly as I can.

He lets out a heavy breath as his hand drops to his side and my eyes plead with him to understand.

516

"I'm afraid. I'm dreaming these things..." I gulp down the confession and settle on a simple truth as I conclude, "and it's not okay. I think it's what you gave me."

"You think the sweets has something to do with what you're dreaming about?" he asks me, and I can only nod with a tension in my stomach that threatens to make me sick. "Tell me," he says, and his command is soft and comforting. As if confiding in him will make it all go away. "Tell me what's got you worked up like this."

"It's my mother," I tell him and struggle to confess to him that every time I drift to sleep, I relive the hell that existed before she died. Every memory I've shut away and buried with her is back. "I feel crazy because the nightmares are so real." I can feel myself breaking down and the moment Sebastian notices, both of his hands are on me. One on my thigh, rubbing back and forth and the other on my shoulder. I'm in a sleep shirt that comes down to my knees, my legs covered by the blanket. His right hand though is touching my bare skin. The rough pad of his thumb rubs soothing circles against my collarbone and I lean into it. I've never felt the need to be touched so gently before. The need to be held.

If I had even a hint that he'd still respect me after, I'd climb into his lap right now.

"It's all right." His voice is strong, but also frustrated and it reminds me of that day back in high school. He's barely keeping it together as he takes me in.

"I'm sorry." I don't know what else to do other than apologize. "I don't want to be this way," I plead with him to understand. "I think when I drank the--"

"It's not the sweets. It's what's going on around us. This shit is bringing up old memories. The drug is just a knockoff pharmaceutical. Most people don't even know about it. It's like any other sleep med, Chlo. A friend gave it to me to sell, but no one buys sleep meds off the street."

"You don't understand," I tell him.

"Make me understand."

I think long and hard about exactly how to explain it. It's not an old memory. These terrors are so real and lifelike, they don't leave me when I wake up. "I'm scared," is all I can say, and the confession comes out as a whisper.

"I want you to come spend the night with me," Sebastian speaks like it's a request, but it's not. I can hear it in his voice and along with the shock is something else.

Desperation.

I can't move, thinking I've misheard him. All I can do is stare into his eyes and listen to every single beat of my heart.

"It's in my best interest to keep an eye on you," he tells me slowly and then licks his lower lip. It's slow and sensual but there's something else there like he can't quite figure something out. "You look like you could use some company. It'll do us both good."

He gives me five minutes to gather a few things. It hardly takes me that long as I toss my toiletries on top of a stack of folded clean clothes and grab my purse. That's it. I don't bother with anything else.

We're not driving far, but even so, the car ride is quiet in a way that absorbs my every thought. Sebastian Black... and me. Maybe one day I'll wake up and all of this will be a dream. Or maybe one day, he'll come with me and we can run away from this nightmare.

"Haven't you ever thought about leaving?" I let the internal thought wander to my lips as I rest my cheek against the car window. The hum of the engine and the gentle vibrations threaten to lure me to sleep, but I fight it.

"You don't think I want to leave too?" he asks me, taking his eyes from the road to look at me. I don't answer, I just take him in, right here at this moment. The strength that is Sebastian Black, veiled with the secret that he'd rather run away. My heart hurts for him in this instant; I always thought he ran this city and that he thrived because of it. How foolish I was. I realize that now as he tells me, "When you figure out where you're going to run to, let me know."

SEBASTIAN

I didn't even think to be embarrassed or ashamed until Chloe stopped in the foyer. All I was thinking was that I was done leaving her alone. I don't have a good feeling about any of this shit and I just want to keep her close. I never considered what she'd think of my place though. Or what she'd think of me.

"Welcome home," I tell her as I toss my keys onto the skinny kitchen counter next to the pile of unopened mail I got yesterday.

There's a sofa, a coffee table, and a TV. Nothing else in this room. It's never looked bare before, until now. It's never felt like it was lacking in any way until I see Chloe not moving from where she is.

The sofa came with throw pillows I didn't like, so I tossed them out, but there's a standard bed pillow and an old blanket in a heap on the far end of the sofa. That's where Carter sleeps when he needs a place to crash.

This house is small, with only one bedroom and the kitchen is the size of a freaking dime, directly across from the living room. But I paid with cash and I own it. That's the only thing I was looking for when I knew I needed to leave my ma's old place.

There was too much shit there. Too much of the past cluttering and smothering my every thought.

"Not what you expected?" I ask her dully and keep walking to the sofa to take off my shoes.

I have a nice car and nice threads for when I need them. All my cash is hidden in the floorboard under my cabinet sink. I don't spend anything I don't have to. You never know when you may need to run, and I'll have the cash for that, make no mistake about it.

"You're such a man. You could at least grab a candle at the corner store or something. Maybe hang a picture?" she suggests, and her lips pull up into a teasing smile.

She finally walks into the room, kicking off her shoes next to mine and slipping into the side of the sofa Carter usually takes. She goes to grab his blanket, but I stop her. It's weird seeing her gravitate to his things. And to want his things.

"You can have the bed," I offer her and then add, "That's Carter's stuff."

"Oh." A shyness spreads through her expression as she gently pushes it away. "Sorry," she adds and then clears her throat. "Do you have a throw for out here?" she asks.

"You like being under the covers, don't you?" I ask teasingly, and it makes her smile as she nods. I like that. I like how I can make her smile. I like that even when she's worked up and upset. When her mind is wandering to disturbing things, I can make her smile and give her something to take away the pain.

"Let me grab you the other blanket," I say as I stand up. There's a small linen closet outside of the bathroom, and I have my old blanket in there.

"I don't know that the Cross boys like me much," she tells me from the living room even though I can barely hear her in here.

I just washed the blanket the other night and I can still smell the laundry detergent as I bring it out to her. "Why would you think that?" I ask her and play dumb even though I know why she would.

"My mom was kind of into their dad once, and couldn't take a hint," she says softly, but cheers up when she sees my blanket. "Ninja Turtles?"

A huff of comforting humor leaves me as I nod.

"You aren't your mom. They know that," I say to try to ease her worries.

"Yeah, but..." she starts to say, but I shake my head and she trails off, waiting patiently to hear what I'm going to tell her. She brushes a lock of hair behind her ear and snuggles into the sofa, resting her head on the back cushion.

"I know Carter, and he likes you just fine. More than he likes most people." I focus on Carter, not his family. It wouldn't be fair to blame Chloe for her mother's mistakes. That'd be like her judging Carter for his father's actions.

"I think he's all right, too," she says softly with her eyes closed, nestling deeper into the sofa.

"I said you could sleep in the bed, Chlo," I remind her and watch as her eyes slowly open, giving me more of that soft blue mix of pale hues that look through me.

"I don't want to sleep," she tells me just above a murmur.

A sickness spreads through my chest and down to my gut, settling into a heavy pit there. "You need to sleep."

Even though my words are hard and non-negotiable, she gives me a sad smile. "No shit. I can't stay awake forever, but it feels like I'm trying."

"You don't like the sweets?" I ask her, remembering what she said about it fucking with her and making her remember shit she didn't want to. "It's just supposed to relax you. I think everything that's going on is messing with your head."

"I don't want it to happen again." Sadness slowly seeps into her eyes, but she doesn't elaborate.

"Don't want what exactly?" I ask her, and her expression falls completely as she searches my gaze.

"They're just nightmares," she whispers, and I don't know if it's more to convince herself or me.

"They come and go; you can't stop them by running yourself into the ground like this," I tell her and run my hand over the back of my head. As I do, I feel the weight of my own exhaustion taking over.

"I have Benadryl. I could go get Nyquil?" I give her some options, just hoping she'll take something. The person who gave me the sweets made it sound like it was the best thing to take to relax and sleep easy. That's the only reason I gave it to her. It worked for me and I thought it might help her. "You gotta sleep, Chlo."

"I know I do," she tells me and then readjusts her head on the cushion until she's more comfortable, but still looking at me. The look of exhaustion drives a primal need inside me to help her sleep however I can. Even if that means fucking her into my bed. The thought is only a flash in my vision of her legs wrapped around my hips, her heels digging into my ass as I pound into her. A split second of that thought has me rock hard instantly.

I want to kiss her again, but that would just complicate everything. It feels good to have someone needing you like this though. Wanting you and letting you get close.

Word is already going around. As long as I do what I'm supposed to, maybe I can have her...

"Let's go to bed," I suggest, readjusting and trying to ignore the aching need that's pressing against the zipper of my jeans. I've wanted her for so fucking long. With a quick glance at her curves hidden beneath the covers, I start wondering if she'd let me. If she needs me like I need her.

"Sebastian, tell me you didn't bring me here just so you could fuck me." Her voice is breathy, but there's a tinge of fear there. She hasn't moved from where she's sitting, but she's still as she waits for my answer.

"Why do I keep finding myself telling you that you should know better?" I expect her to flinch at my tone, or to drop the subject altogether. I don't expect her to press me, which is exactly what she does.

"So, you don't want to sleep with me?" she asks, and I don't hesitate to tell her, "I want to fuck you more than I want to breathe right now."

Chloe Rose's eyes widen and her breath hitches as my blood heats.

"But it's not why I brought you here, and you know it," I add.

I can hear her swallow as she glances at my throbbing cock. "We can just go to sleep. I'm tired too," I offer her.

I hadn't realized I was holding my breath until she nods her head. "Okay," she says, already pushing off the sofa and standing up with a yawn. "Should I bring this one too?" she asks, holding up the corner of my blanket.

"Leave it there," I answer her and start walking down the hall. I walk slowly so she knows to follow, and she does. Her footsteps are soft and hesitant.

Pulling back the sheets for her, I look over my shoulder and then nod to the left side of the bed, the farthest from the doorway where she's still standing.

She has one hand on each side of it, and in her sleep shirt, her legs are on full display. Smooth and lush. She rubs one calf against the other as she nervously waits in the doorway. "No funny business?" she asks.

"Not unless you want," I tell her, feeling the disappointment overwhelm me. I've thought about having her here for years. Literally, years. I have to stare at my nightstand as I strip out of my shirt. When I unzip my pants, I see her walk around the bed, but more importantly, I feel her eyes on me. Her lust-filled gaze doesn't see mine on hers as she nearly walks into the bed in her rush to get under the sheets. She doesn't notice how I watch her lick the seam of her lips as her gaze travels down my body.

And I'll never forget how her eyes widen and her bottom lip drops slightly for her to take a deep inhale when I kick off my pants and she sees what I have for her.

Every fucking inch of it will slide into that tight cunt of hers.

Maybe not tonight, but knowing how much she wants me, how much she's desperate for what she sees, brings a cocky smirk to my face that I can't hide.

When the sheets stop rustling and Chloe's nestled under the comforter, I ask her, "You want to be the big spoon or little spoon?"

And I'm rewarded with the sweet, sarcastic laugh I knew she'd give me.

"No spooning," she answers with the smile still firmly on her face.

"You sure?" I ask as I slip into bed beside her. "It can get a little cold, you may find yourself wanting some warmth." I cock a brow, but she's not having it. "I'm practically a heater myself. My body temperature is just a little hotter than normal."

When she laughs this time, I smile wider and set my head down on the other pillow in the bed. She rubs her eyes and then rolls over to lie on her side, facing me with both of her hands tucked under her pillow.

"You're the different one," she whispers, reminding me of the night I dropped her off at her house when she said I was different and I said it right back to her. "This wouldn't be so easy if you were still the way you were before."

I have to lick my lower lip to keep from saying anything. She has no idea. "I guess we're both a little different, but can I tell you a secret?"

She only nods, her hair ruffling against the pillow as she does. "I've always wanted you."

With her teeth sinking into her bottom lip, she tries to stifle her smile, but she can't.

"Aw, aren't you cute when you blush?" I tease her, and I'm rewarded with a little more of a smile.

"What if we did do something?" she asks after a moment. Her breathing picks up and I can feel her nervousness.

I nearly groan from my cock leaking precum at the thought of doing *something* with her.

"What kind of something?" I ask her, doing my best to tread lightly. I get the feeling that she'd run from me and put those walls back up if I made a single misstep. I'm so eager to be inside of her, I could stumble and fall my way down a flight of stairs into fucking this up.

She shrugs and waits for me to say something.

"Is there anything you wouldn't do?" I ask her out of pure curiosity. With her hips, the image of her face down on my bed with her ass up is everything I want right now. My cock stiffens again at the thought and this time I let out a small groan.

Her eyes travel away from my gaze and downward.

"I'm sure there's a lot I wouldn't do... or maybe not," she says absently. "My friend said she liked being choked." The mention of choking catches me off guard. Of all the things for my innocent Chloe Rose to say, that wasn't one I couldn't have guessed.

"You want me to choke you?" I ask her, not hiding my surprise.

"No!" Pushing her hand against my chest, she backpedals real quick. "You were just asking what I wouldn't want to do but I don't know what that list would be." She nestles back down as I try to think of what she needs to hear next.

I know what I want to say. I want to go through my list of all the dirty shit I want to do to her and then have her tell me where her limits are. But I'm pretty sure that'll have her jumping out of bed faster than I can finish my laundry list of how to make Chloe Rose cum harder than she ever has before.

Confusion mars my face; I can feel it in the deep crease on my forehead. "I'm getting some mixed signals here, and I don't want to fuck this up." It's such a simple thing to admit that, but as I swallow, I feel more vulnerable than I have in a long time. Probably since the day she ran from me in school, when she ran out the door and I followed her.

"I don't want to fuck it up either," she whispers and then leans in closer, pressing a small, quick kiss to my lips. Before I can deepen it, she's already pulling away. My hand was already half up, ready to spear through her hair and keep her pressed to me, but I'm too slow, too shocked that she'd make the first move.

"If we did do something, it would only be because I think I would sleep really well after," she tells me softly, watching my expression and judging my reaction.

"You love lying to me, don't you?" I ask her with a cocked brow as I stretch out, putting one arm behind her head. She lets out a small laugh but also inches closer and rests her cheek on my arm.

With her thumbnail between her teeth, she keeps her arm up between us and I don't miss how the bottom half of her body is still farther away from me.

I glance at the clock and see how late it is before taking a look back at her, nestled in my arm with her eyes closed.

"What if tonight you take from me, whatever you want?" I offer her and then say the second half of my suggestion when her eyes flutter open. "And tomorrow night, I take from you. Whatever I want." My blood pressure rises instantly at the thought of her agreeing. I'm hot and wound up and ready to make a deal with her. "Whatever you want," I add.

Her lips part and there's a sudden movement of the bed along with the comforter. "You have to squeeze your thighs together like that?" I tease her even though the very thought of her scissoring her legs right now is killing me.

"We can do that," she agrees in a single breath. Again, she inches closer, so close, but her ass is still pointed the wrong way.

"How do you want me?" I ask her and then add, "Tomorrow

night when you're ready, that's how I want you to ask me too." I'm so damn hard at the thought of her asking me that I nearly lose it when she nods her head in agreement.

"So, how do I want you?" she asks, her wide doe eyes shining with a desire that must reflect my own.

With my body coursing with adrenaline at the thought of fucking her tonight, I nod my head and say, "Tell me what you want."

She turns away from me, and for a split second I think she's going to say she doesn't want to do anything, but then she brings her ass closer to mine and all that desire rises inside of me again.

She peeks over her shoulder and grabs my hand, kissing the tip of my fingers one by one as my heart beats faster and faster. "I want your hand here," she whispers and pulls down her panties while telling me, "I've never been fingered; I want you to get me off with your hand."

I don't believe her for one second, but I don't argue. I don't even consider arguing.

All I can focus on is that she's in my bed, taking off her panties and telling me she wants me to finger fuck her. I'm content getting to third base from Chloe tonight because tomorrow night I'm getting everything I want.

Planting a small kiss on her jawline, I let her move my fingers between her legs. She's hot and already slick with arousal. Fuck, I don't know how I don't immediately cum just from grazing my fingers across her clit.

"You're so fucking wet," I tell her the second my fingertips touch her hot entrance. I force back a groan as I push my fingers inside of her. "And so tight," I comment out loud, but the next thought is whether or not I can even fit my cock inside of her. I have to work my fingers in slowly, pressing against her front wall and holding her body down as she bucks out of instinct.

Her hips tilt up and I press my thumb against her clit. Slowly she adjusts, letting me push my fingers in deeper and deeper and stroking her front wall to get those sweet sounds to spill from her lips in a strangled moan.

Her cry of pleasure is accompanied with her pushing her head back into my shoulder as her neck arches and her body begs to do the same.

I'm barely inside of her and she's already so responsive. So easy to pleasure. As her hand moves to the back of my head, her fingernails scratching as they go down my scalp, I lean forward to kiss her neck. I'm teasing and slow with each calculated kiss, nipping and biting from the sensitive part just below her ear down to the crook of her neck.

My eyes stay open the entire time as I push my fingers deeper and deeper inside of her, working her and desperate to warm her up so she can take me.

"Fuck," she moans a muted sigh of the word. My fingers press against her front wall, rubbing hard and forcing her pleasure from her, all while keeping my thumb pressed to her clit.

Her body writhes against me as she tries to turn over, to move away, but I wrap one leg around hers and move my arm around her chest, pinning her body to mine and holding her in place. Strangled moans are all she gives me as I pump my fingers in and out of her cunt.

My touch turns ruthless as her heels slam into the bed and she frantically grabs at the sheets. She's so fucking close. "Give it to me," I command her through clenched teeth. I can't even breathe, knowing how close she is.

"Bastian," she's moaning my name as her body trembles with my relentless touch.

I've never heard anything sound so fucking perfect as Chloe Rose moaning my name.

"Say it again," I command her, and she gasps while yelling it at the same time, "Bastian, Bastian!"

I can't help rocking my hips against her, loving how she does the same, grinding her ass against me.

"I want you," I beg her, pressing my cock against her, the only shield being the thin fabric of my boxers.

I've never wanted a girl this much. I've never felt the need to be inside of a woman like this before. I need her. I need to feel her pussy wrapped this tight around my dick. My heart races with hers as she gets closer.

"I want you," I moan again against the shell of her ear as I press my dick against her ass, searching for relief. Instantly her pussy clamps down on my fingers, tightening and spasming as she cums.

I cum violently with her. If she wasn't so preoccupied with her own climax, I'd be embarrassed that I just came in my boxers, dry humping her.

I take my hand away from her slowly, letting her sag on her side as she tries to catch her breath. I have to hide that I'm doing the same as I flip my fingers in my mouth and make sure she's watching as I suck.

"You taste sweet too," I tell her and smile wide when she blushes that much harder.

"How did that feel, Chloe Rose?" I breathe against the shell of her ear before nipping her lobe. Pride and the heat of my own orgasm roll through my chest.

"Bastian," she whispers my name as sleep finally claims her. Her body's still trembling next to mine.

"Answer the question," I say before getting up to wash my hands and get her a washcloth, but she shakes her head slightly before I leave the room, ignoring my question as she passes out in my bed.

CHLOE

*I*t's amazing what a good night of sleep can do to a person. And a good fuck for that matter.

Sebastian was right, I was just tired and needed to sleep. It all feels so stupid now, even though the uneasiness still lingers whenever I hear whispers about the recent murders.

I can still feel Sebastian inside of me. Even as Marc, my boss, gave me a ridiculous lecture about how many sick days I have left, all I could think about was how Sebastian touched me last night.

Not just touched me. There isn't a suitable word for what he did to me. How he dragged the pleasure from me in a way I didn't know could exist.

And that was just foreplay.

The memory of how his lips felt, how his hard body felt, how his hard cock felt…

My nipples harden as a shudder rolls through my body at the thought of tonight. Sebastian is handsome, classically so with a darkness that hints at danger, but last night, everything about him resembled a sex god. The way the dim light caressed his stubble, the way his lips seemed to pout and then glisten when he licked them. And his eyes swirled with a desire I imagine could never be tamed. It's more than just lust though. The more I'm around Sebastian, the more I let myself believe there's something *more* between us.

The click of the air conditioner in the office brings my gaze up to it and then to Angie, sitting in the desk chair cross-legged and on her phone. While I'm on the floor with six piles of paper as I try to organize these documents alphabetically by last name.

"Oh, my God," Ang drags out the last word as she throws her head back and stares at the ceiling in exasperation. "Can it just be five already?" She drops her gaze to me and I have to crack a smile.

"Hard day?" I taunt her, knowing she didn't do shit. We had four clients come in today. So, she checked in four people. And that's all she's done. For eight hours.

I sit upright, stretching my back. "We could switch on Monday?" I offer her, and she tilts her head.

"I don't know why you even agreed to that shit," she tells me while making a circle with her pointer finger to encompass the papers on the floor, right before going back to her phone.

Agreed? It's my job. I bite my inner cheek to keep from responding. I need my paycheck. I need to add it to my meager savings.

The thought of why I'm so desperate to save up makes my heart squeeze in my chest.

It's so I can leave and get out of here. But things have changed. That would mean leaving Sebastian and whatever it is that we have going on now.

It's odd to feel so much, so quickly. To feel that raw loss at the thought of one day getting out of here. I'm so used to feeling lonely that it didn't take much for me to feel some sort of attachment to him. Although that feeling has come and gone for years and yet every time, I know there's something between us I'd never have with anyone else.

It only took that single kiss years ago to know that.

"I say we just get out of here," Angie suggests, interrupting my thoughts.

I shrug at her suggestion. "Marc won't notice, that's for sure."

I'm not leaving this city any time soon. And whatever I have with Sebastian will more than likely be short-lived. I'm still shocked it's happening at all.

I'll be counting the days until it ends.

Even knowing that, so confidently certain it will end, I'm still going to give myself to him tonight. I didn't question it for a moment.

I was always his to take. And that's exactly what I want. For him to be my first.

My breathing comes out shaky as I realize the clock is ticking down to that moment and I still haven't decided if I'm going to tell him or not.

"Okay, let's just get out of here." Angie hops down from her seat, letting it roll backward and carelessly slam into her desk as she slips her ridiculously high heels back on.

"Why do you even work here?" I feel the sarcastic question slip out before I can stop myself. I feel like half a bitch, but with the nerves of what I'm going to do tonight, I'm not as careful with my words as I should be.

Angie pauses for a second and then laughs, loud and unrestrained. She shrugs, slipping on the first heel and then the second. "The perv wanted to hire me," she says and looks up at me as she continues, "and I had to pay my rent."

One point for honesty, I suppose. "Fair enough." I can't argue with that. Pushing on my thighs, I force myself to stand up and stack the piles, so I can get back to filing tomorrow and not lose my place. As I'm setting a generic glass paperweight on the stack, Angie asks me if I want a ride.

My heart does a somersault, the weirdest movement as the jitters set through me. It's been like this on and off all day.

I'm going to go to Sebastian.

Sebastian Black is going to fuck me tonight. All the anxiety and nerves mix in the pit of my stomach. Maybe if I keep telling myself it's just sex, my heart will start believing it.

"I'm good; I'm going to walk." I think I do a good job at keeping the nerves out of my voice, but I have to stare at the stack instead of looking at her.

I can feel her eyes on me though, and when I peek up, looking as innocently as I can at the only woman I've ever met who owns her sexuality like she does, she asks, "You sure?"

That little place between her eyebrows is scrunched and I'm sure she can tell something's off, but I'm not telling her shit. Not. One. Word. I don't want advice; I don't want to hear stories. Worse, I don't want her to tell me the list of women he's screwed. She has a habit of doing that whenever a man's name comes up. She's a walking encyclopedia of all things sexual and provocative.

"Yeah, I'm good," I tell her nonchalantly, and her expression tells me that she isn't buying any of it, but she doesn't ask again. She grips the doorway once, looking between the pile of papers I refuse to take my eyes from and then back up to my face.

"See you tomorrow then?" she asks and then adds, "You're not going to take another mini vacay, right?"

The smile she gets from me is genuine. "Your concern is adorable," I tell her and roll my eyes before adding, "but no, I'll see you tomorrow."

"All right, sweet cheeks," she says while tapping the doorway, "See you in the morning."

"Have a good night, Buttercup," I tell her and then scrunch my nose at Buttercup. I could have come up with something better, but the more I let it sit, the more I like it.

I listen to her heels as she walks out and then immediately grab my bag and head out the back, rather than the front. The stairwell is all concrete steps down the back, which is why no one ever leaves this way, but it heads to the north part of the city, where the butcher shop is.

My fingers feel sweaty as I pull my purse onto my shoulder, the nerves kicking into high gear.

Every step I get closer to him, I get more nervous about each detail.

I don't have sexy lingerie, but I can wait for him naked.

I didn't pack all of my makeup yesterday when he brought me back to his place, only my mascara, so that's all I have to work with.

I have to clear my throat to get the knot out of it as I get closer. I know he's working, and he told me to come to him when I was done, so I am.

Part of me recognizes how... docile I'm being. The only thing that keeps me moving forward and only mildly second-guessing all of this, is how easy Bastian is making it for me. He's not giving me hard glares until I look away. He isn't pretending I don't exist. He isn't ignoring me.

Something changed and I don't know what, but he still makes me feel safe. He always has. I may be crazy in other ways. But I know what I've felt for Sebastian for years has merit. There's something real between us, and that's not a white lie. And I wish one of us would have the courage to say it out loud because deep down I know that neither of us can deny it.

* * *

I DON'T KNOW *if they'll let me stay here now that my uncle's dead. He died last week and right before my eighteenth birthday. The lawyer said he willed everything to me, but with the debt he left behind, they may have to take the house from me to put into the estate.*

And then I'll have no one and nowhere to go.

Those are the thoughts that keep me up tonight even though I know school will come tomorrow. I can't keep skipping class, so I need to sleep, but I can't.

I'm so fucking angry. That's what I feel most guilty about. I had one person who barely even spoke to me, but he let me stay here, and occasionally it felt like we were family. Uncle Travis was a good man, a trucker his whole life, but he didn't much like other people. A lot of the time, I wondered if that meant me too. Being alone for so long will do that to you.

He came home two weeks ago, and we talked about what was coming after high school. Tears flood my eyes again at the thought and I angrily brush them away.

Even if he wasn't physically here for me, or even if he never showed me much of anything other than a place to stay, I knew without a doubt last week that he loved me.

And now he's gone. It's not fair.

I take in a staggered breath and try to calm down as I cling to my pillow. I've never felt as selfish as I do now, being filled with anger when I should be mourning him.

What's wrong with me?

Just as I think the question, I hear the floorboards creak behind me, toward the open door to the hall.

A shiver runs down my spine as my eyes open wider and then narrow. Swallowing thickly, I know it wasn't just the chill in the air that made the old boards bend in the night. I can hear whoever it is walking closer.

It better be him, *I think bitterly as I reach slowly into the nightstand. My uncle left everything to me, and that means his gun too.*

"You don't need it," the deep voice calls out from the doorway just as my fingertips brush the cold metal. Slowly shutting the drawer, I let my eyes close and try to calm the adrenaline racing through my body.

"Why are you here?" I ask him without turning to face him. My chest aches with a pain I can't describe. Sebastian used to come all the time at night when I first moved in here.

"It's been a while," I tell him and hate the nostalgia in my tone.

He's quiet; he always is.

He kissed me, he followed me, and then he left me alone.

"I'm fine," I tell him and then turn in bed, slowly bringing myself up to sit cross-legged under the covers. "As fine as I can be." Years ago, when

he'd come, he wouldn't leave until he believed me when I said those words.

And I loved him for it. Truly and deeply, I loved him for it. If it had been anyone else, I'd have been terrified, angry and a mix of everything hateful, but it's not just anyone. It's Sebastian.

Tears cloud my vision of his dark shadowy frame in the doorway.

"You don't look fine."

"Well gee," I say sarcastically, bitterly even as I wipe my eyes. "So kind of you to point out the obvious." It's been years since he's visited me and I'm not the same person I was back then. I've stopped praying for him to come and wishing he'd slip into bed with me and hold me.

I don't want to be held by anyone anymore. Even as I think it, I know it's not true.

"Just go," I tell him and then lie down, turning my back to him and pulling the covers up closer to my face so I can use the soft bedding to wipe at my eyes. "You're good at leaving," I add and hate myself for even bothering to speak with him when he merely chuckles. It's a deep low rumble that fills the bedroom and sends a shiver of want across my skin, igniting something I thought was long forgotten. It seems the hate I have for him leaving me, ignoring me day in and day out isn't enough to drown out the desire to be held by him after all.

"Someone told me you might be leaving."

"Who said that?" I barely speak the question. My heart does a stupid pitter-patter at the thought of leaving him. My heart is stupid. I listen as he walks into the bedroom. He stops somewhere far from the bed, but I don't know where and I don't turn to look at him.

"Are you leaving?" he asks me.

"I hope not," I answer him, and the truth of that answer makes me close my eyes tightly. I couldn't wait to get out of here, but I need a place to stay. Everyone needs a home, somewhere they can run to.

"Is it money? Or are you moving somewhere else to be with other family?" he asks me.

"There is no other family," I admit, feeling lonelier by the second.

"So, it's money?"

Time ticks by slowly until I answer him, "Yeah."

He's quiet and doesn't say anything for a long time. So long, I think maybe he's left me until he says, "It'll be okay. Go to sleep, Chloe Rose."

I REMEMBER THINKING how much I wish I didn't want him to be here as I drifted to sleep, feeling his eyes on me. But I did. I had no one. And of everyone in this place, he was the only one I wanted. So, if that was the way I could have him, I'd take it.

I don't know if he heard me later that night when I woke up and started to cry out of nowhere. I confessed how much I missed him and how lonely I was as I wiped the tears away, still huddled in my spot, gripping the pillow. Or maybe that part was a dream. It's hard to know anymore.

SEBASTIAN

"*W*ell, you only have one more year," I tell Carter.

"I don't have time for it," he answers me as he bounces the old tennis ball against the worn brick of the building.

"You don't have time for school?" I ask him in a tone that's as filled with disbelief as my expression is. "Remind me again, where is it that you make your money?"

Carter's being a dipshit. "You don't need to start working for Romano. You need to graduate, and you can make that extra cash from the schoolyard."

He's a dealer at Crescent Hills High, only pot but he makes some good cash since he's the only one with good shit in this area. The only other dealers are past Walnut Street and the highway that runs behind it, but those are claimed territories, one of them being Romano's.

"Romano's never going to hire you anyway since you're Irish."

I feel like a prick reminding him that he'll never be trusted, but it's for his own damn good. He should be focused on finishing school and then he can figure out a way to go down south and make some good cash at the fishery on the docks or some other shit. Something better than this.

"You don't get it." His voice is tight and his teeth are clenched. "We have bills."

He throws the ball harder at the wall and catches it after it ricochets with a force that sounds like it hurt. "You forget there's more than one person I have to look after."

It fucking hurts every time he brings it up. To me, he's my kid brother. To him, he's the older brother taking care of his family. A family I'm not a part of.

"It's good money," I remind him. "Both the fishery and the pot. Romano's not going to pay you shit."

I'm still shaking my head when he looks back at me. "Because I'm fucking Irish?"

"Because he doesn't have a need for you." I'm blunt and harsh and my stomach twists. There's no room for him in Romano's territory, but even if there was, I'd lie. He doesn't have the stomach for this shit. He should be better than me. He *is* better than me. I get paid to fuck up people who owe money to the wrong guys, assholes who think they can steal from establishments who pay for protection. I get paid to be a villain, a thug, and a version of myself I hate. It used to help with the anger; it made me feel like there was a purpose to it all. But that's bullshit. I fucking hate who I am, and I don't want this life for him. I don't want it for anyone.

It's quiet other than the thud of the ball hitting the brick as he considers everything.

"It's just one more year, Carter."

"A lot can change in a year." His voice is muted, low and defeated. I know he wants a change because of his mom, but I can't help him there. I can't keep her from dying. The rubble beneath my feet kicks up as I walk to the cement steps and face the parking lot.

"Is that Chloe?" Carter asks me, and I have to get up to look down the street.

Just the sight of her pulls my lips up into an asymmetric grin. "Yeah, that's her."

"So much for picking her up," he tells me with a glint in his eyes. I check my watch and see she's early, then peek back up at her.

With her jeans hugging her curves, I watch as she walks up the street, not taking my eyes off her.

"Real quick," Carter tries to get my attention, so I give him a short hum of an answer to let him know I heard him, but I refuse to look away from her as she walks to me.

"Can you come with me to give my dad that money?" His question is enough to break the stare I have on her. He adds, "Tomorrow night?"

"Yeah, of course," I answer him with a shrug like it's no big deal. His mom's bills are adding up, so I'm loaning him some cash to keep them afloat. But the last time I did that, Carter's dad laid into him, thinking he stole it and wanting to know from where.

It's not really a loan, as I never want to be paid back, but Carter insists I call it that. For only being sixteen with not much to be proud of, he's a proud kid.

"How is she doing with everything?" Carter asks to change the subject. I know that's why he did it. "Is she still freaking out?"

My gaze is brought back to her as he asks. Nice timing on his part, as she's just walking up the parking lot.

"She slept at my place last night," I tell him. She slept easily and deep like she hadn't slept in years, waking up with a yawn and a stretch that was so relaxed and at ease. Although the second she saw me, she blushed violently and tried to hide under the covers. "Good morning," were the first words she greeted me with as she covered her mouth and hid under the sheets.

Carter's chuckle cuts off any thoughts of sharing particulars. "So that's how you deal with it," he says and nods his head in approval with a wide grin.

If I had that ball in my hands, I'd throw it at him. But damn if the pride in my chest won't go away at him thinking I fucked her worries away.

"Hey." Chloe gives a hello while she's still a good ten feet away, walking through the parking lot and to the back behind the shop where we're standing.

Thump, Carter tosses the ball at the wall, but I don't break my gaze from her. She's already blushing. Her skin is so beautiful like that, with that rosy tinge creeping up her cheeks and growing hotter every second I keep my eyes on her.

"I don't get a hello?" Carter asks jokingly, and for the first time since she's walked up here, her attention goes to him.

"What makes you think I wasn't waiting for you to say hello first?" she asks him, quipping back without missing a beat and with the trace of a friendly smile on her lips. I can see she's a little tense; it's the way she is around people. Tense at first, quiet too, but if she wants, Chloe opens up easily and what's inside is raw and beautiful.

Carter grins back at her as he says, "Hello." He pronounces the word carefully, enunciating each syllable and it makes her laugh although that shyness is still there.

"Are you working here too?" she asks him and the hair raise on the back of my neck. Everyone here works for Romano, but Carter needs something better than this. I keep my thoughts to myself and wait for him to reply.

"Still in school," he answers and she's quick to add, "I always forget you're younger than us."

It's odd how she says it. Like she knows him or maybe she's just paired us together like other people have.

"Were your ears burning?" Carter asks her with his brow raised. "We were just talking about you."

Chloe hums a small laugh with her lips closed tight although she can't hide her smile. "I hope good things," she adds after a moment of the two of us staring at her and waiting for her reply.

"Mostly," Carter jokes with her, but I can tell he makes her nervous by the way her smile slips.

"Yeah," she says honestly. "I kind of figured you might be..." her voice trails off and she offers me a small smile although I can see how nervous she is. She picks at the hem of her shirt while she talks. "I might have been talking about you too," she tells me, biting down on her lip after and looking me up and down.

"Is that right?" I ask her and she's quick to shake her head. "No, I'm just playing."

Carter barks out a laugh while I stand there looking like an asshole.

"I didn't give you anything good to talk about?" I joke with her, but she just clears her throat, slowly letting those walls come back up.

She didn't talk about me because she has no one to talk to. I feel like a prick when the realization hits me.

"I'll make that up to you tonight then," I add before she has to say anything. Her cheeks must be on fire to be that red.

I let my hand travel to the small of her back to lead her away and I nod a goodbye to Carter. He's waiting for the bus to go to the hospital, but it'll be here in minutes. It's almost 5:15.

"See you later, Carter," Chloe says sweetly, giving him a small wave as I walk her to my car.

I open the door for her, but before she can slip in, I wrap my hand around her hip and bring her closer to me. I have one hand on the door, with the other on her hip and her stance mirrors mine. It's as if she's waiting for what my next move will be, so she can determine hers.

Her lips are parted and her eyes dart between my gaze and where Carter's standing behind me.

All I wanted was to give her a small kiss. So, I do, just a short one on her lips. Pressing my mouth to hers and making sure to run the tip of my nose over hers. The cops already know; people are already talking. Might as well give them a show.

That shy smile I love plays on her lips and she can barely look me in the eyes.

"You nervous?" I whisper against her cheek before pulling away. Her wide eyes stay on mine as she settles into the seat and answers honestly in a single breath, "Yeah."

CHLOE

My heart's being stupid. It keeps fluttering and flipping all sorts of ways like it's trying to escape or run away. I try to swallow again, but I can't. Instead, I snuggle closer to Sebastian on the sofa, although every inch of his side is covered with mine right now.

It's just sex.

I keep reminding myself. Every time the nerves work their way up from my heart to my brain, I have to remind myself. It's just sex.

Not just that, but every part of me feels like it was supposed to be this way. Like Sebastian was meant to have me. Even the little bits of me hidden away in the pages of my books, all the way down to the marrow in my bones; it was supposed to happen like this.

I haven't told him, although I almost did earlier. We were sitting on the sofa, but not cuddling like this, sitting cross-legged, and eating Chinese food from the cartons. He's been good at keeping the conversation going and giving me those cocky smiles. I think he's drawing it out on purpose.

First dinner and now a movie, although it's almost over.

And thus, my heart is doing that stupid thing knowing the movie will be over soon. I swallow it all down as best I can and nestle my head into Sebastian's chest.

"You comfortable?" he asks me although it sounds like he's picking on me. I only hum a response.

"You can't go to sleep," he tells me, and instantly my eyelids fall shut just to fuck with him. He shrugs his shoulder and I give him a look.

"Stop moving," I complain in as flirtatious of a voice as I can and feel pride rise when he rewards me with that charming smile of his that drives me wild.

He smells like fresh woods, the kind you want to get lost in; his body is hard and dominating. Every piece of him chiseled like Adonis. I splay my hand on his chest and revel in the fact that he's letting me.

Back in school, I thought that he was avoiding me because he was older. At least at first. Then when I realized who he was and why everyone else avoided him, I wondered how a boy like him could be interested in a girl like me. The more he avoided me, the stupider I felt.

When the only piece of reality you crave is revealed to be all in your head, it does something awful to you.

"I like you coming to me after work, but I could have picked you up." Sebastian starts up a conversation as the credits to the comedy scroll on the screen. If someone asked me to repeat a line from what we just watched, I'd come up with nothing. All I'm thinking about is how Sebastian is going to fuck me.

I've masturbated but I don't know if I have a hymen or not. I've used a few toys I've read about in books although I don't often feel the need to do that. Not unless I read a steamier romance. Or one where the hero reminds me of Sebastian.

"I wanted to leave work early. It was a short walk." I answer him with a shrug and try to keep my train of thought on the fact that he hasn't made a move yet. He hasn't done anything other than to put his arm around my shoulder and pull me to close to him under the covers on the sofa.

"You sure like to walk everywhere," he remarks like he doesn't like it.

"I don't mind it." It's one of the things that took me a long time to do alone. I don't know if it's because I was old enough to understand what happened to my mother, or if I was always afraid of walking alone, but learning to accept the fear and proving it wrong is one way to cope. "Sometimes it's nice," I add, swallowing down the memories that beg to ruin this moment.

Sebastian shifts on the sofa and it dips, making me fall slightly.

"You ready for bed?" he asks me, pulling me back up by my waist and shifting me into his lap. His warm breath tickles my shoulder as he kisses me for the first time since we came back to his place. Right on the crook of my neck, sending shivers down my body and hardening my nipples.

My body feels alive with need. Every nerve ending is waiting to go off and sitting on an edge that feels so close.

With both of my eyes closed, I hum a response. "I was wondering what was taking you so long," I tell him as he stands, leaving me with the chill of his immediate absence and forcing me to open my eyes.

He offers me a hand and I take it to stand but he only smirks at me, not giving me any words in the least.

Cue my stupid heart.

It's just sex.

That ball of nerves threatens to suffocate me as I walk in time with Sebastian to the bedroom. He doesn't waste any time stripping down to nothing. So, I follow suit. First my shirt and then my pants, but by the time I'm left in my bra and underwear, he's already naked and stroking his erection.

Oh, my God.

My pussy heats and clenches around nothing. Fire blazes inside of me. I can't take my stare away from him as he strokes himself.

He's cocky as he asks me, "Need a hand?"

A voice inside of me begs me to tell him I haven't done this before, but instead, I meet his gaze steadily and unhook my bra, letting it fall carelessly to the floor. Then I easily step out of my thong, even though I know he's let his own gaze wander to my body.

He doesn't say anything. No comment on my body at all as I walk to the bed and get under the covers. It's dark in his bedroom, but there's enough light enough to see. There's hardly any light from the windows with the curtains drawn even though there are streetlights close by. And he left the hall light on, which he didn't do yesterday, so that had to be on purpose. So, he could see.

Adrenaline races through my veins as the bed groans with his weight and dips.

Still, I feel like he can see everything. Even as I'm hiding under the covers.

"No covers," he says with a playfulness I wasn't expecting. "I get to have you my way tonight, Chloe Rose," he teases me.

"I'm cold." The excuse slips easily from my lips as my heart pounds furiously in my chest.

His lips find mine in a slow, languid kiss. His hot tongue dips into my mouth as he pulls back the covers.

Suddenly, I actually am cold. In every place, he isn't touching me, and I feel like I'll freeze to death if his hands don't find every inch of my body right this second.

He breaks the kiss, towering over me and climbing on top of me to tell me, "I'll warm you up." I expect another kiss, but his lips fall to the dip below my collar. One kiss there, then one an inch below. I can't breathe.

Goosebumps flow down my arms and the heat burrows itself in the pit of my stomach.

"I'm hot," I moan out into the air and then my eyes open wide, realizing what I said. Sebastian could tease me, taunt me for being hot and cold, but all he does is kiss lower and lower, fueling the fire that licks over my body.

By the time his stubble is tickling my inner thighs, my hands are on his shoulders, my blunt nails digging into his skin. I'm at war with myself, not knowing if I want to push him down that last inch or push him away for fear of being inadequate.

A single languid lick from my entrance to my clit has my back bowing.

Sebastian chuckles and the vibrations nearly send me over. My cheeks are hot with embarrassment, but the threat of pushing me over so soon is looming larger and more aggressively than anything else I could feel.

His tongue flicks my clit and again I buck my hips, but his hands are already there, pushing me down and keeping me in place. Panting, I struggle to breathe and to know where to put my hands. So, I grab the sheets and fist them as he sucks my clit and massages it with his tongue.

My toes curl and a strangled sound is forced from me. With my eyes closed, I don't see him, but I feel all of him. He shoves his fingers inside of me and a pool of desire ignites in my core when he does it, forcing my back to arch and sending waves of heat through my body that feel uncontained.

With his mouth on my clit and his fingers inside me, I scream out his name from the pleasure that rolls through me. I push myself into his face shamelessly.

He finger fucks me brutally and doesn't let up on either ministration until I'm biting down on my lip hard enough to hurt and cumming on his hand.

The paralyzing pleasure rolls through me in waves like a vengeful tide, taking from me ruthlessly. I can't breathe or even move as he leaves kisses along my curves and guides the head of his dick to my entrance.

The battering ram in my chest is at it again and I force my head to turn, to look him in the eyes and nearly tell him.

But his eyes are filled with shades of blue so bright, so filled with the frenzy of passion, that even if I could stop him at this moment, I wouldn't. I won't take this from him. He was meant to have me. And this is how he wanted me.

"I want to feel you," he says, and his plea is a deep rumble of desire. He nudges the tip of his nose against mine. "No condom?" he asks.

No words come to me, so I simply nod my head and kiss him, eager to feel him too.

His large body is hot against mine and I shut my eyes as I'm inundated with emotion as he hovers over me, but without my eyes on him, he growls. It sounds like a growl. Deep and low in his chest, primal and threatening.

My eyes whip back to him and he crashes his lips to mine. With a gasp, I open for him and he uses that moment to spread my legs wider, nestling his hips between my legs and pushing himself inside of me just slightly.

I'm overwhelmed. Unable to come back from the high of my pleasure, from the high of knowing Sebastian wants me, and from the all-consuming kiss that he devours me with, I'm completely at his mercy.

I brace myself, ready for him to shove himself inside of me in one swift stroke. For him to tear through me and take me how I've always wanted him to, but as his heart slams against his chest and in tandem with mine, he pulls away from our kiss and nudges the tip of his nose against mine once again. My lashes flutter open and I stare into his gaze as he slowly pushes himself into me.

His lips are parted, and they widen just slightly as he lets out a deep breath and moves deeper inside of me.

I can't help that my lips part as well, that they form an O as he stretches me and the sharp pain of it mixes with the sweet, lingering pleasure. As he rocks out of me and then back in, he mutters with his eyes closed, "You're so tight," and I don't know what to say.

I should tell him, but I don't. I don't want to change anything.

"Take me," I beg him in a whispered plea and reach up to grab his shoulders while wrapping my legs around his hips.

I wasn't prepared for him to slam inside of me. For him to lower his lips to the crook of my neck as he fills me completely and stretches me beyond what I can handle. He groans a deep masculine sound of satisfaction as he tears through me, breathing me in and taking my virginity in a single movement. The pain makes me close my eyes tightly, it makes me tense and dig my heels into his ass. I feel hot and full, and it's too much. It hurts. Fuck, it hurts. It's more than I can handle.

But with my teeth clenched and no words spoken, Sebastian moves out of me slowly, giving me slight relief. It only lasts for a split second before he savagely slams back into me. My eyes close tight and I bite down on my lip to keep from screaming.

Again, and again, he thrusts, each time picking up his pace and each time the pain mixes with pleasure.

Each time I think it's too much, but every time he pulls away, no matter how briefly, it feels like a loss. I want this, I want him. I want more.

The bliss that thrills every nerve ending is caught in a vise. I can't control how my body begs for more, but it simultaneously wants to push him away.

It hurts.

It fucking hurts.

But it feels so good, it feels like everything I've ever wanted.

As he picks up his pace, my head thrashes, but Sebastian's hands stay on my hips, pushing me down and keeping me right where he wants me. His lips roam my body, sending kisses down my neck and shoulder, over my collarbone and everywhere. It feels like he's everywhere. And it's almost too much—almost, but it's not. I know it's not because my body wants to focus on how viciously he's fucking me.

My body focuses on the intense pain and equally intense pleasure.

Tears leak from the corner of my eyes, and I struggle to breathe, but somehow, I cry out his name. "Bastian." It's a single strangled breath. It's not from the pain, not all of it anyway. It's from everything. I'm losing myself to him and it's everything. I wish I could stop the well of emotion pouring up from me, but with every thrust, every sound, every touch from him... I can't stop it.

My nails rake down his back as he shoves himself deep inside of me, past the brink of pain and toward something blinding, numbing yet igniting. My head falls back limply as the pleasure rips through me, tearing every bit of me apart into a million pieces.

And then he stops, and the world is motionless with the orgasm still racing through me.

"Chlo?" Sebastian's voice is full of worry as the rough pad of his thumb wipes at the tears still falling down my face.

"Don't stop," I beg him but even my voice sounds pained, and he pulls himself out of me.

"Fuck, are you okay?" he asks me and reaches across me to the nightstand, turning on the bright light. I can only close my eyes as the pleasure still rages through me. The dull pain turns to a vibrant ache as I try to close my legs and involuntarily let out a pained moan as I curl over on my side.

"No, fuck," Sebastian's voice, full of worry and regret sends embarrassment and shame through me, and the tears come on harder and I can't stop them. My body is confused and the emotions inside of me are welling up and I can't stop them.

"I'm fine," I barely manage to say as I wipe at the embarrassing tears.

"Don't lie to me, what did I do?" He sounds angry as he tries to push my legs apart. "Fuck," is the last word he says before climbing off the bed and running to the bathroom. As my eyes adjust to the light, I peer down my body to see bright red staining the sheets. Both of my hands cover my face with the regret, and dread overwhelms me to the point where I wish I could disappear.

"I'm sorry." I hear Sebastian before I see him, but even as I register his words, he's already on the bed. He rubs a damp, warm washcloth soothingly on my inner thigh to clean me up.

The shock from the concern on his expression and how carefully he's cleaning me without worrying about the sheets keeps me from being able to speak.

He kisses my outer thigh with his eyes still open, gives me another kiss and gets closer. "I'm sorry," he whispers against my skin. "I knew you were tight, but fuck... I didn't mean to hurt you." I can't stand the look in his eyes like this was his fault. Like he has anything to be sorry for at all.

"I'm a virgin." The words leave an awful feeling in my throat as they come up like I'm suffocating. "I was... before... I should have told you," I whisper with my eyes closed.

And there's nothing but silence. He doesn't move or speak for what feels like forever. But finally, he asks, "Does it hurt?" I shake my head no as quickly as I can, refusing to cry anymore.

"You're crying, Chlo, please don't lie to me. I'll never forgive myself."

"Please, just pretend I'm not," I try to plead with him, my eyes still closed tightly and my hands reaching up to cover my face.

"Fuck that," he tells me, grabbing my hands and pulling them away. "Tell me the truth," his sternly spoken words force my eyes open. Through the haze of tears, I stare into his demanding gaze. "Did I hurt you?"

I shake my head, searching for the words to explain. "It's a mix, but the more you..." I have to pause and swallow before continuing, "the more you're inside of me, the better..." I struggle to calm

553

myself and my racing heart, which doesn't seem so stupid now for wanting to escape earlier. If I could vanish now, I would.

His hand cups my jaw, his thumb running along my bottom lip before he asks me, "Would you tell me to stop if it was too much?" Before he can even finish his question, I'm shaking my head.

"I need you to," he demands. His voice is laced with concern plus a plea I don't expect. "I need you to tell me." His eyes search mine, glancing over my face as he brushes the tears away. With him maneuvering himself back to where he was, my body calms and the heat lingers in my core.

"I want you," I beg him. "Please, I need this to be--"

"I want you too." His words calm every bit of anxiety and I reach up to kiss him, but it's shortened as he pulls away.

"You can have me," he whispers before giving me a chaste kiss I try to deepen, "but you need to tell me if it hurts too much." He says the last part with his eyes closed and then opens them, piercing me with his gaze. "Don't do that again," he warns me. "Don't let me hurt you."

His words are so full of certainty and a darkness I can't deny, so I speak immediately. "I won't. I'm sorry," I quickly add and feel the weight of regret bury the embarrassment.

"I'm afraid if you never tell me, I'll never know." His confession makes me repeat myself, "I'm sorry."

"Look at me, Chlo," he says then grabs my chin between his thumb and forefinger. Without hesitating he kisses me once, then again and a third time, silencing the doubt and regret. A kiss from Sebastian Black soothes everything. He is the healing balm to my soul. As long as he kisses me, as long as he wants my lips to brush against his, I'm safe and cherished in a way I can't describe. Even if it's all in my head, it's all I need.

With his eyes closed, his forehead resting against mine, he whispers between us, "If you don't tell me, I will hurt you. I know I will. I know it. And I don't want to."

I nudge him with my nose to get him to look at me. "It hurt, but it was going too regardless," I tell him and try to make him understand. "I thought I could hide the pain and when I couldn't, it didn't matter anyway because it felt... like everything." I cling to his shoulders and make him look me in the eyes. "I promise you, I want this." I breathe once, just once, waiting for him to say anything. "I want you and I want you to have me how you want."

"We have time for me to... to," he swallows thickly, "Chlo, I wanted to fucking destroy you." His words make me blush furiously. I watch the way he swallows, mesmerized by his confession as he adds, "I wanted to make sure you still felt me tomorrow, so whoever had gotten to you before me, didn't stand a chance at being remembered as a good lay."

"It's okay," I say but can barely get the words out. The idea of still feeling him inside of me tomorrow and what his intentions were does nothing but fill me with lust and make me wish I hadn't cried. I wish I could have hidden the pain like I've read about before. "You can have me, however--"

"Knock it off, Chlo," Sebastian reprimands, but he says it with a smile that calms my nerves. "I want you to remember this for other reasons. Now that I know..."

I'm hot all over and still trying to gain control of my body and my emotions when he tells me, "Don't hide this shit from me, Chloe Rose. I'll find out." His command comes out more teasing than anything else as he nudges his nose against mine. He reaches between his legs, his arm brushing my clit as he does, and it makes my head fall back against the pillow.

"I'll tell you everything," I promise him with the sweet feeling of pleasure building. He's stroking himself and moving back to where he was, but every small movement brushes against me too, burning hotter than before.

"Then tell me you want me."

The rhythm of my heart skips a beat. "I want you, Sebastian."

It races as he tells me, "Spread your legs for me." I obey him instantly. With him guiding himself back inside of me, I try to hide the wince from the lingering, stinging pain, but he sees. "I'll make it feel good." His words are soothing as he pushes himself inside of me and captures my scream with his kiss.

He rocks his hips steadily, each time brushing his pubic bone to my clit and he never takes his lips from mine. So long as I can kiss him back, he keeps his pace and massages his tongue along mine in swift strokes. A warmth floods through me as the pain morphs into divine pleasure.

I gasp for breath the second he parts his lips from mine, but then immediately he seeks them again. My eyes are closed and every touch of is his gentle, save the ruthless way he fucks me.

"Harder," I beg him while gasping for air, but instead of harder, he moves his hand between us and pushes his thumb to my clit.

Fireworks go off along my skin and deep in the pit of my stomach and lower.

With every thrust from him, I gasp. The sounds of our breathing, of him fucking me and the bed protesting, only fuel me to want more. I don't dare rip my eyes from his gaze as I cum, feeling him cum with me. I can feel everything, the way he pulses and puts more pressure against my walls, the way he fills me.

And then when he pulls away, I feel everything. Every sensation and tingling need to curl onto my side and recover from what he's done to me. My body's trembling, literally shaking.

I hear him go to the bathroom, but I can't open my eyes to see him. It feels like he's still there. I'm swollen and the ache is still raw.

But so is this feeling that takes over every inch of me. The rolling tide of pleasure that refuses to leave.

When he comes back to the bed, I want to ask him if it's always like that, but I don't.

Instead, I ask him if he wants me to take off the sheets, in a voice still breathless, but he shushes me, getting in behind me and scooting me to the other side of the bed. Even with fatigue weighing me down and the overwhelming sensation of pleasure still racing through me, I want to do something for him, anything.

Theres's a crushing need to make things right with him, to show him that it's okay and even better than okay. And that I'm sorry. I feel so fucking sorry.

But he hushes me again and plants a kiss on the side of my jaw, wrapping his heavy arm around me and pulling me close.

"Thank you," I whisper although I feel foolish doing it. Sebastian doesn't say anything; he just holds me tighter. I don't know if I've ruined everything and part of me starts to wonder if I have. It was intense and emotional and I'm still riding the high, but the nagging feeling that I'm alone, and that I destroyed whatever we had creeps into my thoughts.

"How did that feel, Chloe Rose?" The deep rumble of his chest accompanies his question.

It felt like he owned me. Body and soul.

"You can do that to me whenever you want," I answer him with sweet sorrow mixing in my chest. I don't know what tomorrow will bring, but tonight, I'll have forever.

He arranges me so I'm nestled perfectly against his chest on my side, his hand splayed on my belly as he kisses my hair and then my shoulder. Nothing but warmth and comfort flow through me. I've never felt so loved. Never in my life have I felt like this. So wholly wanted and cherished. It's the way he's brutal, but gentle just the same. I want to believe it's because of me, because of us. That it isn't like this with other girls. That he isn't treating me differently because he found out I'm a virgin. And although the doubt and worry are there, tonight it feels real.

I swear I hear him whisper, "I love you, Chloe Rose," as my eyes become heavier. He whispered it at the back of my neck. But as quickly as I thought I heard the words, I start to think I imagined it. It's something I've always wanted to hear from him, and I need to hear it now. I desperately need to hear it.

I don't know if it's a dream, maybe one I once had long ago and wish to remember, or if it's real. But as I feel sleep pull me under, I hold on to those words. Deep down inside of my soul, I know they'll keep me safe.

I only wish I had the strength to say them to him.

SEBASTIAN

How could I not have known?

I can't get the nagging thought to go the fuck away. I was so eager to have Chloe, to ruin her, to make sure she'd remember me forever, that I didn't stop to consider the possibility I'd be her first.

If I had known, I would have done it differently. She'd have a better memory of her first time.

I should have fucking known.

Drew dated her for a month when I was away, up north with Romano. He told me he was lying about the rumors of her sucking him off behind the school, but at the time, I wasn't sure if he was telling me the truth or not because I was slamming his face into the cement. I thought he took her first. The day I heard what he was telling other people, I thought he'd taken her V-card.

Her only other boyfriend was Jared Santack.

They went to semi formals together and I saw him kiss her. I know they went home together that night. It was the night I came home from my first stint in jail. I remember thinking for a split second how she deserved someone like Jared, then I planned how

I'd fuck up his car the next day, just because he needed to have something of his broken too.

"What the hell is wrong with you?" Carter asks me from across the dining room.

My gaze shifts to him and I try to fix the pissed off look I know is on my face, but I can't. Last night fucked me up in a way I can't explain. I run my hand down my face and try to shrug it all off. The chair legs scratch on the floor as I get up from the table and go to the window. Carter's family's house is on the outskirts of the city and backs up to the woods. It's dark and there's not much to look at out there, but I stare outside anyway, trying to get my shit together.

My knuckles rap on the worn-out buffet table in front of the window as he asks me, "She getting to you?"

Is Chloe Rose getting to me?

She's *always* gotten to me.

I don't answer him, instead, I try to make up a lie, but it doesn't occur to me that the lie is a truth until the words are spoken. "Being here just reminds me of family," I tell him. My spine stiffens and a chill runs through me.

"Shit, man," Carter tells me, "I'm sorry." As if it's his fault. As if he has anything at all to be sorry about.

I shake it off, hating that tonight of all nights I'm making this about me. That I can't focus and be there for my only friend.

"How did the treatment go?" I ask him. And the look on his face instantly changes. The sympathy morphs into anguish.

He doesn't say anything, although he tries. Instead, he looks me in the eyes and shakes his head.

My heart drops down to the pit of my stomach. "Fuck." It's all I can give him and then we're both looking out the window.

"Tell me something good."

His request catches me off guard and I consider him for a moment.

Something good. It takes me longer than it should to think of something. All thoughts lead back to Chloe Rose.

"I fucked Chlo last night," I tell him. "I was her first."

"Shit, really?" he asks. "She's twenty?" I nod, waiting for him to say something else. For him to understand what it meant to me. But I don't think he will. No one will. They don't get it. I don't even understand it.

Ever since I laid eyes on her, she was mine. It didn't matter that I didn't want anyone, because I didn't have a choice. She was mine. Fate picked her for me, and vice versa. Last night was meant to happen. I know it.

The sound of the door opening distracts us both, drawing our attention to the front door we can't see.

Carter grabs the edge of the buffet tighter at the sound of his dad calling out for him. "Back here," he replies and steels himself, staring straight ahead and trying to relax his posture.

I fucking hate it. I hate how he's scared of his own father. He tells me it's the way it is and that it's no different from how his father was raised, but that doesn't make it right.

I expect his father to be drunk and angry, like the last few times I've seen him. He pissed himself the one night he was so hammered, we had to drag him home.

His steps get louder and then the old man is right in front of us, his hands slipping into his pockets as he leans against the doorway. "You two eat already?" he asks us and gives me a short nod before pulling out a smoke.

He lights up as we answer him. I can feel the aggression rolling off of me, my expression getting tighter, but I know that's no good for Carter. He doesn't want a war, he just wants to do what's right by his mom.

Mr. Cross walks to the dining room table, sifting through the bills and puffing on his cigarette.

"How is she?" Carter asks him, and I glance between the two of them. His father's expression falters for a split second before he changes it to something else, something stronger than the weak man who's withering away just as his wife is.

He nods at Carter and tells him, "She had a good day." With his lips pressed in a thin line, he tells us he's going to bed. Carter told me the days he doesn't drink are different, but I haven't seen him like this in a long time. A long damn time. It's been two years of hell, with my hate growing for this man, but seeing him sober is different.

Carter nudges me as his father starts to walk away and I reach in my back pocket for the cash. "Mr. Cross," I call out to him and take the three steps forward to pass him the bundle. "I just wanted to help out if you'll take it," I offer. "I won it on a bet and I don't need it."

"I wish I had the decency not to," he answers me. "This isn't charity."

"Call it a loan then," I answer him quickly as he tries to give it back. Taking a step away from him, I tell him, "I don't care either way." He nods his head in agreement, but the old man's eyes turn paler and glossy.

It's quiet for a long time as I watch the man do his best not to break down in front of me, tapping the wad of cash against his palm.

"I don't know how to tell your brothers." He talks to Carter without looking at me, staring down at the cash before slapping it down on the dining room table. The strength he had diminishes, and his face crumples with hopelessness.

"She's not going to be here for much longer," he starts to cry and it fucking hurts watching a grown man lose it. "I can't lose your mother." He covers his face with one hand, his other bracing him on the table to keep himself upright.

"They know, Dad," Carter tells him, although he doesn't go to his dad, he doesn't try to comfort him. He stands strong and his father only seems to respect the decision as he rights himself, brushing away the tears and sniffling hard to be done with it.

"They don't know," he says in a single breath, his face going stony. "They can't know until it happens. Nothing can prepare you for it."

Carter looks down and stares at his mud-covered boots; I know he wants to object.

His father's right though. Even knowing the end is coming can't help. Nothing can prepare you for the type of destruction death brings.

"We'll be all right," his father sniffs and grabs Carter's shoulder, squeezing it and waiting for Carter to look him in the eye. "All boys," his father says and huffs a humorless laugh although a faint smile is on his lips. He looks at me as he asks, "Can you believe that?"

I offer him a weak laugh, feeling awkward and out of place.

"Their mother wanted a little girl and instead I gave her five sons. All Irish; the Irish boys have to be tough." He nods his head as he talks to neither of us in particular. "The men have to be tough," he repeats and then gives his son's shoulder one more squeeze.

"Carter will do good," he says and then sniffles again, giving me a glance before walking toward the worn doorway. "Carter will take care of them," he says softly.

"You're talking like you're already dead," Carter comments. "You're still here." The tension between them changes to something else, and for the first time, I see why Carter doesn't blame his father. He would never go against his father. It's the fear of losing him that keeps him loyal. Between the alcohol and his hopelessness, he's already close to losing him.

"I won't live much longer after she goes. That's how it works." His father doesn't say anything else in the awkward silence that follows and neither does Carter.

It's only when the stairs creak with the weight of his father going to bed, that Carter says anything.

"He's a different man when he isn't drinking. You see it, right?"

Carter asks me, his voice more hopeful than I thought it'd be. "He's not all bad."

I can only nod, not wanting to fight with Carter. Carter's told me his father treats him differently from Daniel, who's the second oldest. He's told me some days he doesn't even know if his father loves him. I can't forgive a man for treating his son like that. I won't.

"Thanks for the loan, man," he tells me, even though I'm aware he doesn't like that he had to take it.

"Yeah, no problem. It's nothing," I say and try to brush it off like it doesn't matter. "I have to go home to Chlo."

"Look at you," Carter jokes and I can feel the tension leave him, grateful to move on to a different subject. "Don't fuck it up."

I almost joke back and tell him that I know I'm going to ruin it somehow. But it's too close to the truth and I don't want to speak life into the words.

It wasn't supposed to be this way in my head, not like this.

"She has no one," I tell Carter, just wanting him to understand her the way I do. "The worst thing I can imagine is having no one." It's only when the words are spoken that I realize how alone I've really been. I wait for Carter to say something, but his mind is elsewhere.

Maybe there is something worse though. Like having someone, but knowing you're bound to lose them.

CHLOE

*I*t's weird being alone in this place without Sebastian. I'm surprised he let me stay here at all. I'd planned on sneaking out in the morning and being weird on my own rather than weird with him.

The biggest fucking lie I've ever told myself is that this is just sex. Last night was more than sex for me.

I woke up a few hours after I'd passed out, and I couldn't get back to sleep. I was wide awake and so very aware of everything that happened. With his arm still around me, I wanted so badly to stay in that moment. The moment where it felt like he still wanted me.

I knew it would hurt down there, and at 4 a.m. every tiny shift in my body seemed to be connected to the ache between my legs. It still hurts now in the evening after. I knew it would. But I didn't expect the emotional change, the emotional pain that comes with it.

Not able to sleep, and knowing I'd made a fool of myself, I thought I'd sneak out, leave him a note, and let him decide if he still wanted me. If I was worth still being around or with, or whatever it is that we have going on. I wanted to make it easy for him because I knew what I was doing, and it wasn't fair to him not to tell him.

That was the conclusion I came to at four in the morning as I breathed in his masculine scent one last time and felt the warmth of his hard chest at my back. I closed my eyes and savored that moment, memorizing it, just in case it would be the only moment I had like that with him. Of all the things that have happened between us, that's the one I wanted to hold on to.

Where he took from me what he needed, and I took from him what I needed.

With a deep and slow breath, I carefully crawled out of bed, taking my time and being as quiet and gentle as I could so I wouldn't wake him. It wasn't until my first foot hit the floor that I winced and seethed. It hurt more than I realized.

He woke up instantly, reaching behind him to turn on the lamp. He's so fucking beautiful. It's an odd word for a man, but it's true. With sleep still in his eyes and his stubble longer than usual, he looked groggy but sexy as fuck. Maybe it's the way the light hit him, or maybe it's the hormones and lack of sleep, but I've never been more attracted to a man before. I don't think I ever will be either.

"You all right?" His voice was laced with sleep and accompanied by the bed groaning as he sat up.

"Lie back down, I'm fine," I whispered as if he was being ridiculous, although my heart pounded knowing I was trying to sneak out and failed.

I thought it through right then. He'd turn out the light and lie down, I'd go to the bathroom to clean up. After a while, when I thought he'd fallen asleep again, I'd sneak out and let him text me. I didn't want to risk taking the time to leave a note and making it more awkward than it already was if he caught me.

I could walk to my house from here and at this time of day, no one would be up. There would be no one to bother me on the short walk home.

"You aren't sneaking out, right?" Bastian questioned. "'Cause I want to wake up with you in the morning." He said it so definitively, so sincerely.

If there was ever a moment where I knew I was his completely, it was then.

And that was over twelve hours ago.

Now I'm alone in his house wondering what to do with myself, other than snoop through his shit. Which has been a rather disappointing endeavor.

My phone pings as I close the last drawer in his dresser, finding nothing but a pair of his pajama pants. They're flannel and smell like him, so I slip them on and with my baggy t-shirt, I couldn't be more comfortable.

Sprawled out on his bed, I check my texts and bust out laughing. I'd texted Angie, *Sex is better than masturbation.*

And she finally responded. *Tell me who, you whore!*

I feel the blush rise to my cheeks, but the butterflies in my chest and belly are more prominent.

I consider telling her, but I'm not ready to share him, so instead, I tell her it has to wait till Monday. I assume the slew of texts afterward are from her, but I lie on the bed, staring up at his ceiling and wondering about how Bastian got to be the way that he is rather than answering them.

Every thought that comes only makes my heart hurt more for him.

The texts don't stop coming and as I remember every detail I know about Bastian and the way he was in high school, they annoy me more and more.

Grabbing my phone off the bed where I tossed it, I'm ready to silence it until I see the most recent text.

Did you hear about Mr. Adler? They found him dead.

My blood runs cold and I swear I feel it all drain from my face. Angie's still messaging me and threatening to do all sorts of stupid shit if I don't confide in her right this second. But I couldn't give two shits about her right now. Mr. Adler was next on the list. I feel fucking sick.

The message is from an unknown number. My fingers shake as I text the person back with the obvious question. *Who is this?*

Breathe, just breathe. I have to keep myself calm even as I start to shake from the adrenaline coursing through me. The fourth person on the list. Right in a row. One. Two. Three. Four. All found dead.

My phone pings and I look down to see a new text from the unknown number. All it reads is: *That doesn't answer my question.*

I can't stop trembling as I stare down at my phone.

Who else would text me? No one. No one else. The only other person who has my number is Marc because I had to give it to him.

I didn't mean to frighten you.

Another message comes through and my heart beats faster. The front door is locked, I know it is, but still, I climb out of bed and check it. It's hard to even swallow with my heart in my fucking throat.

Who is this? I text back and then add, *I'm not frightened. It's fine, I just hadn't heard that Mr. Adler had died.*

I almost write more. All lies though. Lies meant to deceive. Something to make it feel casual, normal even. Something that would prove I'm not terrified. But all that's running through my mind is that the person on the other end is a killer. The killer the cops have been looking for and failing to find.

I repeat over and over that I'm not crazy, I'm not paranoid. I remind myself what Sebastian said, that I'm scared and looking for answers. Which I am. Four in a row. It's a fucking hit list.

"Fuck," I grip my hair and clench my teeth before calling Sebastian. My throat's tight as I stand in the middle of the living room, vaguely aware that I'm on the brink of a panic attack.

I'm not crazy. I'm not crazy.

I don't know what to think. Other than someone has a copy of that list, or made the same list, but how?

Voicemail. It goes to voicemail. An hour ago, I felt untouchable here; now I feel like I'm in a cage, unable to go anywhere and so easily seen by anyone who could be watching.

Please call me. I text Sebastian as another text comes through.

I shouldn't have texted you.

Who is this? I ask again, but no reply comes. Not then and not thirty minutes later when I'm huddled in a ball on the sofa, wondering if calling the cops is even an option. There's no news at all that Jeff Adler was found dead. Not on the news online and not a hint of it on any social media.

Is he even dead? And if he is, and the person who texted me knew, but no one else...

The number is still silent an hour later when I leave a voicemail on Sebastian's phone. I wish it wasn't real. I wish I could blink and the messages would be gone. I would rather know I truly am crazy than to be living this nightmare. I don't mention any of it in the voicemail to Sebastian, I just beg him to please come back or return my call. The second I hang up, I lose it.

It's a slow spiral of a breakdown, and maybe that's what the person wanted.

I text the unknown number again and beg them to tell me who they are. And I get nothing. For hours, I have nothing but my own fear and a random text that was designed to inflict it.

Someone wanted to hurt me.

There's only one person I think of over and over again who could be behind this and it proves I'm insane.

It can't be my mother, but when I dig through my purse and find the list, a list no one else knows about, I can't think of anything other than her and the nightmares.

My mother is dead. *It's not her*, I tell myself over and over, resting my cheek against the flannel fabric on my knees and rocking back and forth. It takes everything in me to calm myself down, telling myself that I'm safe here with Sebastian. Whoever it was is an asshole. Someone who overheard me at the butcher shop maybe. Someone playing a cruel trick on me.

Whoever it is can go fuck themselves.

The anger and hopeful explanation are all that keeps me together. Just barely. I'm holding on by a thread and watching the clock tick by, wondering where Sebastian is and why he hasn't messaged me back.

For hours.

SEBASTIAN

"Where were you?" Chlo asks before the front door is even closed. Her voice is filled with accusations that make my body freeze.

Her eyes are bloodshot as she peeks up at me above her knees on the sofa. It's not too late yet. Past dinnertime, but it's not so late that she should be coming at me like this. Unless she knew something.

What the fuck happened? It's all I can think. My movements are slow as I toss the keys on the table and kick off my boots, taking her in as she watches me. My heart's hammering and I'm fucking confused. This isn't my Chloe.

"I was with Carter, they don't get good reception out there," I tell her and hope she accepts it as the truth. "What's wrong?" She can't be mad that I left her alone all day. There's no fucking way that's it when I know for a fact she was going to leave me last night.

"Someone texted me," she says in a quick breath and then closes her eyes to swallow. "I'm being stupid," she says while shaking her head, her eyes closed tightly.

"What'd they say?" I ask her, trying to hide the adrenaline and rage that mixes in a deadly concoction. I walk carefully to her, watching as she rubs her eyes. Sitting close to her and pulling her into me, I try to calm her down so she'll just talk to me. And she lets me, which is already a relief. "Just tell me what happened," I say, and the words come out even and calm. Deadly calm.

"I feel like... Bastian." Her words are choked as she buries her head in her knees, pulling away from me.

The only thing I focus on is keeping my hands on her. She's here with me. My Chloe Rose is right here, and I've got her.

"Whoever it was just wanted to freak me out, but I don't know how they know about the list unless they overheard at the butcher shop. But I didn't say the names out loud, did I?" Her words come one after the other, stumbling over each other, but the second she's done, she breathes in deep and rubs her eyes. "I know I didn't." She answers her own question before I can say anything. My blood is hot with rage, wanting to know exactly who messaged her and why the fuck they'd get in my way.

Still not looking at me, she apologizes. "I'm sorry."

Frozen and struggling to push the command through clenched teeth, I repeat my question, "Who texted you?" If they're fucking with her, they're fucking with me.

"They said Jeff Adler's dead. I don't know who it is. I don't..." She doesn't finish. Instead, she shakes out her hands and grabs onto her knees, burying her head so she doesn't have to look at me.

My blood runs cold. He's next on the list. She knows it. I know it. Only two left.

With a deep exhalation, she finally looks up at me and she apologizes again. "I'm sorry," she says, and her voice is soft. "I feel like I'm being crazy, but I'm scared."

She has no idea how ridiculous those words are coming from her mouth.

"I saw," I tell her, knowing she needs to be told enough so she thinks it's okay. That everything is okay. "On my way back from Carter's, there's a bunch of people around the site. Looks like a car hit him." Her mouth drops slowly as I give her the partial truth.

"What? No." Her first reaction is denial and she reaches for her phone, but I take it from her, hellbent on finding the number and who it belongs to. "I looked, no one was saying anything."

I don't respond to her and she stays stiff at my side as I look up the number and put it in my own phone. Nothing. Reading the texts, I know who sent it. I just don't know why and every thought that comes up makes my knuckles turn white as I try not to break the fucking phone in my hand.

Anger is a deadly thing.

"He's dead." Her voice shakes with fear and it's that sound that pulls me back to her.

"It was an accident." I'm firm with her, pulling her in closer to me. "Word gets around." I start coming up with an explanation. "I think people know you're freaked is all, Chlo." I feel her eyes on me, but I can't look down at her. If she looks into my eyes, she'll know I'm lying.

I have to stand up and start walking to the bedroom, stripping down and making it look like I'm anything but on the brink of tearing this place apart.

"People know what?" she calls out and I hear her get off the sofa to come after me, her footsteps echoing down the hall.

I need to calm the fuck down. If for no other reason than to calm her down, so she stops thinking about it all. She can't do anything to fuck this up.

With my jaw hard and my back stiff, I turn to her slowly, seeing her prettily framed in the doorway. I force a small smile to my lips. "It's no one, Chlo, but it's okay. I'd be freaked out too. Whoever it was, wasn't thinking."

I have to hide my shock at how well I just lied. How easy it came out. Desperation is an ugly thing.

Her distraught expression slowly fades, replaced with hesitant relief. Her lips stay parted as she lets my words sink in, slowly believing the little lies I'm feeding her.

And it fucking kills me. What I'm doing to her destroys everything in me.

"Come here," I tell her as I tear my shirt off over my head and toss it carelessly on the floor. My three steps take up the entire space of the room as I go to her, wrapping her in my arms and kissing her temple. Her fingers wrap around my forearm and she looks up at me, eyes wide and wanting so badly to believe what I'm telling her.

"I'm sorry you got spooked, but it's nothing. An accident."

"Another coincidence?" she questions me, but her tone isn't a question. My heart thrums and a chill spread over my body.

"It was an accident," I repeat, making my tone a little harder and staring into her eyes until she believes me.

"I don't know... that text and--"

I huff, cutting her off and staring past her. She squirms in my periphery and I'm a fucking asshole. I'm an asshole for making her think this is all in her head.

"This isn't how I wanted tonight to go," I say softly, thinking about last night and how easy it was to get lost in her. If I could live in that moment, I would.

"I'm sorry," she mumbles and her warm breath flows over my skin.

Glancing down at her, I feel like the prick I am. "It's not your fault," I whisper in her hair and then plant a small kiss on her crown. She's so warm in my arms, so small and fragile in so many ways. "I get it, Chlo, but I promise you it's nothing."

She stares deeply into my eyes for what feels like forever and I whisper against her lips, "It's all right, just have faith in me."

She kisses me tenderly, softly, and slowly, even though the pain and worry are still etched in her eyes.

"Come on, let me tell you a story." My hand splays on her back as I lean out into the hallway to turn off the light and then take her to bed.

She crawls in slowly, climbing on top of the sheets before pulling them back and sitting cross-legged where she slept last night.

"My grandmom used to do this thing late at night when she'd come home from work." I latch onto the first story I can think of, so I can occupy her thoughts with something else.

She leans forward slightly, waiting for more and eager to hear what I have to tell her. The way she looks at me with her beautiful blue eyes does something to me and I have to look away.

"Back when I was real little," I say and swallow the lump growing in my throat, "I still remember it."

I settle into the sheets next to her, kicking off my jeans first and flicking on the lamp to cast some light onto her face. When I get into bed, I slip off my watch and it clinks as I set it on the nightstand.

"I never met her," Chloe Rose whispers as she lies down like I'm doing, getting closer to me, and letting me put my arm around her so she can rest her cheek on my chest. Just knowing I have her like this, knowing I can ease her fears and she trusts me... it's everything.

"She worked real late, at least it was late for me."

"Where'd she work?" Chlo asks as I remember how I used to wait up every night for her, but sometimes I couldn't do it.

"At the diner past Walnut. She was a waitress up till the day she died."

Chloe nods and her hair tickles against my chest when she does, but I love it. It brings a comfort that rolls through my chest and I reach up to let my fingers slip through her hair.

"So, I'd wait up every night I could and if I did, she always had something for me. She always had a little gift." My words make Chloe perk up to look at me.

"Like what kind of gift?" She seems far too interested in that detail and it makes me smirk down at her with a huff of humor slipping through my lips.

That bright blush I love to see colors her expression and she finally looks like she might be getting over the text messages, thank fuck. "Sorry, I was just thinking you know how I'd like to get you something for being so nice to me," she confesses and then lets her finger trace up my chest. "I don't know what you like though."

My chest rises as I shrug and say, "You don't have to get me anything."

"I'm fully aware that I don't have to. That doesn't change the fact I *want* to get you something." She gives me a soft smile as she adds, "Thank you, by the way."

"For what?"

"For this," she tells me with that sadness and fear returning to her eyes. I can't respond, knowing what I'm doing, but I don't have to. She kisses my jaw and tells me, "Ignore me, keep going. I like hearing stories. Especially if they're about you."

"You sure you're not going to interrupt as soon as I get going again?" I tease her and instantly feel her smile against my chest. That makes it all right. It makes it all right because she's smiling now and that's what matters.

"Time will tell," is all she says, and I love it. I love all of her.

"So, my grandmom, she'd come home and put her purse down, and I'd get all excited." I glance down at Chlo and get back to running my hand in her hair as I remember what it used to feel like. "I never slept in my room, always the living room so I could hear her when she got in.

"Every time she'd smile down at me, like me waiting up for her made her the happiest person in the world. And I really believed it too. She'd set everything down and come sit in the recliner, letting me sit on her lap and tell her everything that happened that day at school."

It fucking hurts remembering the small pieces of it that come to me. Things I didn't even know I remembered.

"She'd always have a candy for me. Always. Sometimes there'd be a toy too, something small. Like things you'd get in a piñata."

Chloe hums a small acknowledgment and lifts her leg to lay over mine as she peeks up at me. I pull her in closer, loving that she's letting me tell her this.

"I always thought that she would go get something for me before coming home, you know?" I clear my throat, remembering how some nights if I wasn't able to stay up, I actually felt bad. She'd gone through that trouble of getting me something, and I couldn't even stay up for her. I remember wondering if that was why mom left. Because I didn't stay up for her.

"I was six, I think when she died. And after the funeral, everyone came back to the house." The depth of emotions that play in the soft blues of Chloe's eyes force me to look at the ceiling rather than at her.

"And I didn't know any of the people. I hardly recognized my own mother, because she'd been gone for years, but this one guy, an older guy with glasses, sat down in my grandmom's recliner. And when he did, he pulled up a Zip-loc bag, and it had all the treats in it."

I can feel Chloe's eyes on me, but I can't look down at her. It's so stupid, but I can feel tears pricking my eyes.

"Grandmom had a stash I didn't know about. She didn't pick one out every night. It was right there all along." I clear my throat and tell her, "I kicked him, Chlo. I kicked him hard and grabbed the bag from him. I grabbed it so hard that it tore, and the candy and little toys fell everywhere. They weren't his though. They were Grandmom's. It was her stash to give to me."

I feel the tears on my chest at the same time as I hear Chloe sniffle.

"I'm sorry," she whispers, and I hold her closer to me.

"It's all right, Chlo. Just a story I remembered." I don't tell her the rest. How my mom beat my ass in front of everyone and made me throw away all the candy. She struck me so hard I fell to the

577

floor. I don't tell her how I cried uncontrollably and my mother, who I hadn't seen in years, held my face up for everyone to see that she was punishing her brat of a child who didn't deserve any candy. And that was why she left. That's what she told them. That she was cursed with a bad kid.

She was so proud that everyone got to see her being the mother she never was. And the only thing I had to hold on to, was that those tears weren't for her. They were never for her.

"Your grandmother sounds like a wonderful person."

"She was," I tell her and we're both quiet for a long time.

"Hey, if you could up and leave, where would you go?" I ask her even though I can see sleep taking her already. She's going to pass out soon and then I need to take care of some shit. I'll be careful; I won't wake her up.

"Anywhere that would take me," she says playfully.

"I'm serious. What would you do?" I ask her, wondering if she's really thought about it. If she'd really run away one day. She props herself up on her elbow, still lying on her stomach and considers me.

"I think I could be a writer. Not like a reporter… but like my books. Fiction."

"If you could do anything at all, you'd write?" It takes me a minute to visualize it. Her bundled up on a sofa, with a mug of tea beside her, jotting down notes or typing away. I could see it. She'd be good at it.

"I feel like that's where I belong, you know? I can kind of be a little weird in person, but when I read or write, it's so freeing."

"I get that," I tell her, feeling a knot growing in my throat. "You could do it, Chlo. You know?" I ask her even though everything in me is telling me not to put those thoughts in her head. I don't want her to run away, I don't want her to leave me.

She gives me a weak smile that mixes with her shyness as she tucks a lock of hair behind her ear before settling back down and yawning.

"And what would you do?" she asks as she nudges me, peeking up at me to add, "If you could do anything."

I think about her question for a long time, long after I shrug and tell her to go to bed. Long after she nuzzles up next to me and falls asleep in my arms. The only answer I can think of is if I could do anything in the world, I'd run away with her.

The only place I want to be is with her.

"Chlo," I whisper her name not long after sleep's taken her from me. Her brow is pinched and the sweet expression on her beautiful face has been replaced by something else. Something that lingers in the place between fear and worry. A small whimper is all I get from her as her nails dig into my arm, holding on to me for dear life. Whatever's got her mind now isn't what I want her thinking about.

The only thing on her mind should be thoughts of us together. It would only be fair since she's the only thing I can think about anymore.

With one hand on her shoulder, I give her a gentle shake to wake her, hard enough to know I'll snap her out of her sleep. "Chloe Rose." I keep my voice gentle and soothing as her wide doe eyes peer up at me, the traces of fear still dancing in her gaze.

Her chest rises and falls with a slow and steadying breath as she looks past me, at the room and then back to my gaze. "You're with me, Chloe Rose." My words are meant to be soothing, but the reaction I get from her is more powerful than I could ever imagine. She pulls herself closer to me, molding every inch of her soft body to mine, kissing my neck, my collar, my chest. Her hands roam down my stomach and then she slips her hand up my chest, letting her fingers play with the small smattering of hair that trails down to my lower half.

The next time I say her name, it's merely a stifled groan. "Chlo." My dick is harder than it's ever been before.

She wants me. She fucking wants me.

"Sebastian," she whispers my name with desperation, brushing her lips against my neck again and letting her kisses trail everywhere they can.

She's in need and so am I.

I roll her over onto her back, and she lets out a small squeal of surprise. It's short-lived as I climb on top of her, kicking off my pants while her fingers spear through my hair and her lips hungrily find mine.

Her tongue brushes against the seam of my lips as I push my fingers inside of her. I have to pull away from the kiss, groaning deep and low in my chest from how hot and wet she is for me already.

"I need you," she whispers and rocks her cunt against my dick.

I don't make her wait, I push myself inside of her, getting harder from the sweet, tortured sounds she gives me in return. She's still so tight, so fucking hot and wet too. It takes me far too long to be buried deep inside of her and when I finally am, giving her a moment to acclimate to my size, her heels dig into my ass, her nails at my back and she begs, fucking begs me, to take her hard.

I give her everything she wants. With one slam of my hips, she screams out my name. Another thrust and she's biting her lip and muffling her cries, but her gaze stays on mine. Those beautiful hues of baby blue swirling with desire, and something else. Something deeper. Something that stirs the beast inside of me to do anything for her, give her anything she ever needs. And to make her mine.

All mine.

Rutting between her legs, I piston my hips, feeling the cold sweat spread along my skin as I hold back my need to cum.

"Bastian," she moans my name as her pussy tightens and her back bows under me.

"Cum for me," I command her in a voice I don't recognize. One desperate and breathless. One that's just for her.

And she does. She obeys me, instantly spasming on my cock.

Her head falls back and her lips part as her orgasm rocks through her.

I don't stop. The second her gaze is off mine, I fuck her harder, ruthlessly, riding through her orgasm and prolonging every bit of it that I can. Dragging it out of her.

She writhes under me and her head thrashes.

My heart beats hard against my chest, feeling hers in time with me.

She's mine. All of her is mine. For always.

Fuck Romano; fuck this city.

I pound into her harder, wanting her to feel every emotion that's raging through me. I'm staying with her.

Her gasp is followed with a strangled moan that fuels me to grip her hips harder, giving her every bit of me.

Nothing's going to keep me from her.

Nothing.

CHLOE

Sebastian's phone keeps going off. I thought it was in my dream at first.

My mother was hissing something. I still hear her words as my eyes flutter open. She said, *He's lying to you.* Her voice keeps me frozen under the warm sheets as the bed dips and Sebastian sits up to grab his phone.

I'm motionless as he moves. She was right here. I can still feel her. She was here.

His voice is groggy as I try to breathe and shake off the eerie feeling that my mother still haunts me in my sleep, even if I can't remember what the dream was.

He's lying to you.

"Yeah, what is it?" Sebastian's voice sounds off. The worry that lingers in his tone grabs my full attention, leaving the thoughts of my mother and whatever had come to me in my sleep where it belongs, in the past. In my unconscious.

"No, no..." He rubs his brow and turns away from me as whoever it is who's called him talks loud enough that I can almost hear the replies on the other end. "I'm sorry," he says with a pained voice, "Yeah, yeah. Are you okay?"

The dread grows as I watch him, how he looks so hurt sitting on the edge of the bed and listening to whoever it is on the other line.

He swallows thickly before saying goodbye and tossing the phone on his nightstand. With his head hung low, I can hear him swallow.

"Who was it?" I dare to ask in a whisper as if speaking too loudly would cause the pain he's feeling to cut even deeper.

I scoot closer to him, but slowly as he lifts his head to answer, "Carter."

My stomach twists into a knot, just like the one in my heart as Bastian adds, "His mom died."

My throat is tight as the swell of sadness rises. I didn't know her at all, but I knew the end had to be closer after she was moved into their house for hospice.

It's devastating to lose your mother, whether you know it's coming or not.

"So much death." The words escape me slowly as I tally up the number of gravestones.

"I care more about him than any of those assholes." Bastian's tone is harsh and unforgiving. I peek over at him as he rubs the sleep from his eyes angrily, his feet on the floor while he still sits on the bed. I've never seen him look so tired, so ragged from everything and the pain of it all forces me to move closer to him, pushing the sheets and covers away to just hold him. I rest my cheek to his back and wrap my arms around him from behind.

"I'm sorry," I whisper against his back and then lift myself up, so I can plant a small kiss on his neck. "I'm so sorry," I tell him again.

I don't know how close he was with Carter's mom, but it doesn't matter. He's hurting. Lacing his fingers through mine, he kisses my inner wrist. "Are you okay?" he asks me, turning his head so he can look me in the eyes. Of all the things to ask, he wants to know if I'm all right.

His eyes are red with lack of sleep, his stubble is too long, and there are dark bags under his eyes as well. I have to slip my hand from his to cup his cheek and sit up to kiss him on his lips. A chaste, sweet kiss. My heart flutters every time I kiss him. It's an odd feeling, like a magnetic pull to him.

I brush his lips with the pad of my thumb and whisper to him, "It's not always about me, Bastian." With his name on my lips, I look him in the eyes and say, "I'll be okay."

"You're wrong," he tells me, shifting to sit so he's facing me. "It is always about you."

His answer steals my breath, numbing me as he kisses my wrist again.

"You shouldn't say things like that." I can't help but tell him as the words come to me.

His steely blue eyes catch me off guard; they pierce into me and hold me hostage as he asks, "And why is that?"

"You make me feel like I'm more to you than I am." The words come unbidden, his simple question enough to draw the raw truth from me. I lick my lips as I blink away the haze of the spell he casts over me. Bringing my knees into my chest, I scoot away from him and wish I could take those words back.

"You're wrong again," he tells me, and I feel foolish.

"I know I'm an easy lay," I tell him dully, feeling my heart squeeze in my chest. I would let him have me whenever he wanted.

"I didn't say you were. I don't do this; I don't sleep around. I don't have girls stay over, so we're even there. So, whatever you're thinking right now, stop it."

Guilt rises inside of me and makes me feel sick to my stomach. This is not the time, nor the place. I can feel his gaze on me, I know he's waiting for me to simply agree and so I swallow the spiked knot and nod, but I can't look him in the eyes.

"You know you mean more to me than that. You're more than

that." His conviction is unmistakable, but I don't know that. I only know what he's told me, which is nothing.

He never tells me anything and I let him into my life because that's where I want him. It's as simple as that.

Taking a steadying breath, I turn to him.

"Tell me you know that," he commands me, and my eyes are drawn to his throat as he swallows. "Tell me you know you're more than just a lay for me."

"I do," I tell him. Things have always been *more* between us, but why? I don't know. And tomorrow holds no promises for me.

"I want to have someone, Bastian," I confess to him. "Even if I may lose them one day. I don't want to be alone anymore." I don't know where the words come from. Maybe it's the fatigue that still lingers. The sadness from hearing of Carter's mom passing. Or maybe it's because I feel a crack in Sebastian's armor, he's giving me a way in to tell him exactly how I feel.

It's too quiet as I stare straight ahead at nothing in particular, rather than at Sebastian.

He cups the side of my face and forces me to look at him. His touch is hot and his gaze even hotter as he tells me, "Then let me be that someone."

My heart beats in slow motion.

"What am I to you?" I whisper. Because deep in my soul, I already know Sebastian is that person for me. What I don't know is whether or not I'm that person for him.

"You were just the sad girl who looked at me like you couldn't wait to run from me. So, I refused to chase you, Chloe. Now that I have you, I'm begging you, don't run from me."

I love you is on the tip of my tongue, but the strength to let the words be heard is nowhere to be found.

"People know you're with me now, anyway," he tells me when I don't say anything. "There's nowhere to run."

"I want to run away from here. I don't know that I can stay

here, Bastian." I don't know why that's what comes out of me, but it's all I can say.

His answer is simple and unexpected. "When you figure out where, tell me."

His hand falls from my cheek and he gets off the bed, making my body sway where it is. My gaze drifts to him, watching him stand at the dresser and open a drawer, and then to the faint light of early morning filtering in through the window.

"Where are you going?" I ask him and then add, "To Carter's?" He only nods solemnly. Of course, he'd want to be with him. I'm sure Carter needs him there too.

"Do you want me to go with you?" I offer. I'd do anything for him.

"You keep looking for a way to run from me, Chloe Rose," he says and although he isn't facing me as he slips on a white cotton t-shirt, I can hear the smile that must be gracing his lips, "but I need you this time. You're not allowed to leave now."

"So, that's a yes?" I push him for more, feeling a warmth spread through my body and cloaking the sadness still buried within.

"It's a, 'you should have known you're coming with me.'"

SEBASTIAN

I knew it was coming. We all did. But we're dying every day, coming closer to the end of our time here on earth, and it's never easy to accept.

It's been four days since she passed. And four days of Carter not calling. I keep texting him, but he just gives me one-word answers. His dad was right, nothing can prepare you; I didn't think Carter would push me away though, not when he needs someone there for him. Even if it's just to sit around and do nothing, I don't care what, I just want to be there for him.

But he has his brothers.

Let me know when I can come over, I text him. And it takes a few minutes with only the sound of the paper bags rustling from Chlo getting the Chinese food out before Carter replies that he will.

I think he's lying though. I don't think he's going to ask for help or for anyone to come around. He's not okay.

"You should go to him," Chloe speaks up, dishing out the lo mein on both of the paper plates with the white plastic forks they threw in the bag. "I think he'd like that," she adds. She's on her knees in front of the coffee table in nothing but a shirt of mine.

587

Tossing my phone on the sofa, I get down on the floor with her. It's awkward and I have to push the coffee table away a foot, so I can fit between it and the sofa.

The sound of her small laugh soothes a piece of me that's hurting for Carter. I peer up at her with a smirk on my lips. "Not everyone's a tiny little thing like you," I tell her and watch that soft blush creep up in her cheeks.

"I love making you smile," I say and it only makes her blush harder. She bites down on her lip, reaching for another carton. She dishes out the General Tso's quietly until both plates have more than enough on them.

"I love it when you make me smile too," she says sheepishly, sitting back on her heels. "But seriously," she tells me, "I think he'd be happy if you stopped by."

"Yeah," I agree with her, remembering how she was at Carter's house and then at the funeral. She was quiet and polite, but the moment someone was ready to break down, she was right there. For Carter, but for Daniel too, his younger brother. All she wanted to do was be there to take away the pain as much as she could.

I love her for it.

I love her for being her.

She peeks up at me as the thought occurs to me, but she quickly looks away and repositions herself. She's barely eating, just pushing the food around on her plate.

"What's wrong?" I ask her, a nagging feeling inside of me that what we have is going to go away. It's all going to slip through my fingers and I'm going to lose her.

She clears her throat and glances at me, her gaze shifting between the untouched plate and then back to me. I have to put my fork down and push the plate away to face her. "Tell me what's wrong."

"I think I love you." Her answer is immediate, although each word feels hesitant like it was afraid to be spoken. "I think I'm weird and needy... and that I have problems," she says then swallows thickly, and the blush that was on her face turns a darker shade of red before she looks up at me again with those blue eyes shining with vulnerability. "But I think I love you, and I don't know if... if it's okay that I tell you." She bites down on her bottom lip and then nods once like she's said her piece. "But I wanted to tell you," she adds quickly before I can answer her.

She'll never know how she breaks something inside of me with her confession. With how genuine and sincere those words come out. I know she means it. She feels that she loves me, and she loves the part of me she knows. It shatters something deep down inside of me. The part of me that's hiding from her sight, the part of me I hate, that part of me falls to my knees for her, praying I could atone for all my sins and be worthy of that love.

"Lie down, Chloe Rose," I give her the command, feeling my heart slamming against my chest, begging me to tell her how I feel. I'm not ready though. I love seeing her squirm, and a part of me thinks if she knew how much she meant to me, she'd run.

She glances at me warily before setting her fork down and scooting out from between the coffee table and the sofa to lie down on her side only to ask, "On my back?"

Letting out a single huff of a laugh, I grin at her and say, "Yeah."

With her heels on the floor and her knees bent, she lies on her back, the t-shirt riding up and she lets it, so I can see her underwear.

"Take them off," I tell her from where I'm sitting, feeling my cock get harder for her. Pulling her hair behind her first, she obeys me. Shimmying out of her underwear and setting it next to her, she daintily readjusts so her legs are flat and I can't see her cunt.

"Like you were before, Chloe Rose. I want to see you."

Slowly, she picks up each of her heels, her pussy on full display, her center a dark, bright pink and glistening from arousal.

"Tell me you love me again."

She brings her gaze to meet mine and licks her lips. "I love you," she tells me like it's obvious. Like it doesn't change anything at all.

I have to practically crawl to her from where I'm sitting, but I don't give a fuck.

I don't need food; I don't need sleep. I don't need a damn thing, so long as she loves me.

With a single finger, I push on her inner knees and she instantly moves her legs farther apart for me. I trace her pussy, sending shivers through her body.

"So, does that mean you're my girlfriend?" I ask her the question I wanted to so many years ago. If I hadn't already been involved with Romano, heading down a path I knew she was too good for, I'd have asked her then. Shit, I'd have begged her to be mine.

The corners of her lips turn up as she smiles wide and beautifully. "Yeah," she answers me in a single breath and I reward her by brushing the rough pad of my thumb over her swollen clit. Her sweet, soft moan makes precum leak from the slit of my cock and I can't take it anymore.

She watches as I undress fast and recklessly, kicking the coffee table and almost spilling the food, but it doesn't matter. None of that shit matters.

She spreads her legs farther as I climb on top of her, bracing my forearms on either side of her head and kissing her softly, gently and giving her every ounce of goodness, I have, even if it is so little.

"You still sore, Chlo?" I ask her as I push into her slick folds just enough to feel her tight cunt gripping my cock before pulling out.

With her neck arched back, her lips parted, and her eyes closed, she whimpers, "No."

"Good," I tell her, "'Cause tomorrow you're going to be." I slam into her all the way to the hilt in a swift, merciless stroke. Her sweet gasps fuel me to fuck her on the thin carpet until she doesn't have a scream left in her.

CHLOE

"*I loved coming here." My mother's voice is calm and sober, which is at odds with the noise of the bottles clinking and everyone talking in the bar. It sounds like everyone's talking at once and over each other. The billiard balls collide on the break and the sound of a new game starting draws my attention briefly. The television's on with a football game and some of the guys cheer a player on, but he the whole bar voices its dismay as he's quickly tackled.*

I recognize a few faces, one of them Carter's dad as he orders a drink.

"That man's going soon." My mother's voice catches my attention. Goosebumps flow over my skin; she's so close to me. A thin, sickly smile is on her lips. She nods, not taking her gaze away from the far end of the bar as we sit on two stools next to each other.

I look back to the man I recognize and ask, "Mr. Cross?"

"No, no, baby girl," my mother tsks me, "the bartender."

Dave.

Ice flows over my skin as my mom laughs at my reaction. Fifth on the list.

The billiard balls clack noisily, and the bar carries on like nothing's happening. Like they can't even see us.

591

Sharp nails dig into my shoulder as my mom comes closer to me, whispering in my ear and making my body stiffen.

"I used to fuck him at the end of the night," she tells me with her smile growing. "He'd clear my tab in return, although sometimes he just wanted me to suck him off like a whore."

My words fail me and I struggle to breathe or to know what to say. It's only a dream.

"Yeah, yeah, baby girl. But that doesn't make it any less true," my mom tells me before letting go and sitting upright in her seat.

I swallow the tight knot in my throat and peek up at her.

"Just because you're dreaming doesn't mean shit." The smile fades and she stares at the bartender as he pours a glass of some clear liquor for Mr. Cross.

The music seems to die down, everything except my mother's voice turning to white noise.

"At one point, I thought he loved me," my mom tells me, staring down at the drink on the bar.

It takes me a moment to realize the smudge on the glass is blood. My gaze darts to her hand, to the broken nails and the bruises on her wrist.

My heart pounds, the anxiety and fear rising as her voice hardens and she picks up the drink. "Men don't love, Chloe." She sets the glass against her lips, but she doesn't drink. Instead, she stares at the man behind the bar. She stares down the bartender who doesn't see either of us. "Don't you ever believe that shit."

I grip the barstool tighter, feeling the blood draining from me as she looks me in the eyes, her own pale and lifeless. "Don't believe him, Chloe Rose."

I WAKE up drenched in sweat and alone. Trembling, I can hear the faint sounds of someone outside. I can't help getting out of bed, my heart still racing as I check to see who it is.

Peeking through the blinds, it's just two guys walking down the street. Guys I've seen before on the porch of a house down the street. They look like they're on their way back from the liquor store, carrying bags full of large glass bottles. That would explain the noises I heard in my sleep.

I'm still shaking as I turn from the window and slowly walk back to the bed, my mind racing with the memory of the dream. Of the bar. Of Dave.

I reach out to Bastian's side of the bed, but the sheets are cold.

Blinking the sleep from my eyes, I walk to the bathroom, my bare feet padding against the cold floor. The door's partially open and it's dark inside, but still, I push it open wide and flick on the light.

The brightness makes me wince, and I find it empty.

"Bastian?" I call out for him even though I know he's not here. His place is empty.

Where the hell is he? The clock on the stove reads 3:46. "Where the fuck is he?" I mutter, still breathless from the fear that woke me. I'd rather focus on Bastian than on the night terror, but when I get to my phone that I'd left on the coffee table, my blood runs cold.

Dave now too. They're going one by one.

I stare at the text message, reading it over and over.

Dave is dead.

I dreamed of it. And he's dead. I'm so cold. I can't feel anything but the horror I felt from the nightmare.

I don't know how I'm still standing. The scream of fear is silent in my throat, but it's there.

Tears prick my eyes and I can't control the shaking. Adrenaline and the need to run kick in before I can do anything. It all happens so slowly, each level of despair falling on its own. Like dominoes. And between each blow, I reread the text.

Dave now too. They're going one by one.

My knees collapse, and I drop the phone, pressing my hands together and begging them to stop shaking.

It was a dream. She's not real.

It's not real. Tell me the text isn't real. It's not true.

It's just some asshole fucking with me. There's no truth to it.

I swallow each of the thoughts, pushing my head into the carpet and trying to steady my head from spinning with the fear racing through me.

But how can it be a coincidence? It can't. It can't be.

It's not real.

"Bastian," I cry out for him like the crutch he is. The panic is slow to set in.

I know he'll make it better. He's a balm each and every time. He can make it go away.

But he can't explain this. Nothing can explain this.

I reach for my phone and miss it, but then I grab it again, my nails digging into the carpet as I drag it closer to me. "Pull your shit together," I mutter under my breath. I lift my gaze to the front door as I scroll for Sebastian's number.

My body is hot, and tense and the fear threatens to consume me.

It's locked. The door is locked.

Ring, ring, ring.

No answer.

I stare at the screen as if it's lying to me. I don't know how long I sit there on my knees, my ass on my heels as I stare at the fucking phone, hating it and hating this place and freezing. I'm so cold. I'm so fucking cold.

It was a nightmare, it's not real.

I try again and get the same result, voicemail.

Swallowing thickly, I brave looking at the text message again.

I could ask who it is, but they won't tell me.

I could ask for proof, but I don't want to see.

Instead, I try Sebastian again because he's all I have. And still, I get nothing. My heart races and the anxiety grows inside me, burning me from the inside out and nearly shoving me over the brink of insanity.

It's okay, I tell myself as I rock on the floor. *It's okay.*

It's just a nightmare. Just a text.

Just another coincidence.

"Bastian," I cry out for him and feel so unworthy. So unhinged. Where is he?

He has to be with Carter, out on the edge of the city where there's no reception. It's my fault. I told him to go there. It's my fault, I repeat to myself.

Finally, my body moves. I need to get dressed and go to him. I can't stay here. I won't do it. I need to tell him; I need to tell someone. I'm breaking down and I don't know what to do. I don't know what's real.

I'm not crazy.

A scream tears through me as the phone rings in my hand. I drop it, the vibrations feeling like fire against my skin.

It rings again, and I see it's Sebastian.

My fingers shake as I answer it and wait for his voice.

"Chlo?" he asks, and I struggle to put what's going on into words.

"I need you," is all I manage. I can barely breathe.

"Chloe, it's okay." I hear the tone of his voice morph from curious to concerned. "What's wrong?" he asks me.

"I had a nightmare," I cover my mouth with my wrist, remembering my mom and her words.

"Chlo, it's just a dream," he tells me as tears prick my eyes.

"I dreamed about Dave and then I got a text," I push the words out and take in a deep breath. Shaking out my other hand, and staring straight ahead at the stark white wall, I wait for him to say something that makes sense, something that will make me feel better.

"I'll be there soon," he tells me, and I nod my head, my throat raw with emotion.

"I'm not okay," I tell him in strangled words.

"It'll be all right," is his only answer before the line goes dead.

But it's not all right. It's not going to be all right. I wanted them all to die for having done nothing while my mother cried out for help. I wanted them to feel the pain and regret that I felt every damn day for years when I cried myself to sleep. They felt nothing, and it wasn't fair. That was years ago though and I don't want this. I would never ask for this now.

I'm living in my own hell.

SEBASTIAN

I hang up the call and stare at the dirt and blood on my hand that's holding the phone.

"I need to shower at your place before I go home," I call out to Carter who's still leaning against his father's beat-up truck.

My hands are numb and yet they still burn from the blisters that'll come tomorrow. I don't know what I'll tell Chlo if she notices them. The shovel did a number on me and it all proved for shit.

"You hear me?" I ask him, my voice barely carrying into the early morning darkness.

"Yeah." Carter's answer is weak. He looks like shit. He looks like he just lost it and that makes sense. 'Cause that's exactly what happened.

The river babbles in the night along with the sound of the crickets. It's all I can hear as the sun starts to peek over the horizon.

Another night with no sleep and another night with Chloe falling apart. She knows too much.

"You ready?" he asks me before pounding his fist so hard into the truck I swear he's going to dent it. He's losing it. He can't hold himself together.

The dew on the grass soaks into my jeans as I walk through the tall grass to the truck.

I grab his shoulder, shaking him. "It's over with; it's done." I'm firm with him even though my heart is pounding recklessly.

Carter nods his head but immediately throws up. He vomits off the side of the truck with both hands on his upper thighs. The smell is rancid, and I can't stand to be around it.

I feel fucking sick to my stomach too. I hate this. I hate this life.

I lay a hand on his back, patting him hard once before walking away from him and climbing into the driver's side. The truck rocks as I do, and I can't shake the eerie feeling that I'm being fucked over.

He texted her again. I'm blocking that fucking number. He crossed a line doing that shit, and I don't give a fuck who he is. I won't let him get to her. My Chloe is off-limits. There's no exception to that.

It wasn't supposed to happen this way, but it doesn't matter. He knows. I know he knows.

Laying my head back against the leather headrest, I wait for Carter, looking over my shoulder and watching him wipe his mouth with the sleeve of his shirt. He takes it off, leaving on his t-shirt underneath and throws it into the back of the truck before getting in.

The rusty door closes with a protest, right before slamming shut with finality.

"I'm sorry," he tells me as he looks out the window. I feel bad for him; more than anything, I feel fucking awful for the kid. I can handle Chloe. I'll figure it out for her, but this fucked him up.

"You're all right," I tell him and then swallow the rest of the thought. "It's fine."

It's this place. How many times have I said that recently? Crescent Hills is a living – waking – nightmare for everyone in it. Only the devil himself could live here and feel at peace.

"I have to tell Marcus he's here, but I won't tell anyone else, all right?" The truck rumbles as I start it up. Carter looks like he's going to lose his shit again; he's still shaking.

"It's just the adrenaline," I tell him, to try to calm him down.

He peeks up at me, the early morning light making his worn expression look that much more ragged. "I killed him," he tells me again. I can't count how many times he's told me that tonight.

Nodding at him, I look in the rearview at the river where I ditched Dave's body before putting the truck into drive.

"He was going to die anyway," I tell Carter although I stare straight ahead at the dirt road rather than looking at him again. "His name was on the list."

CHLOE

*I*f Dave is dead, Andrea is next.

And then me.

There are no coincidences like this, and I can't just wait around to be a sitting duck. I can't ignore it any longer. I can't pretend to be okay and walk through this life as if I'm only a ghost. It's what I've done for as long as I can remember, and maybe weeks ago, I would have prayed for the end to come quickly and peacefully.

But I'm not ready to go. I don't want to die.

I want to run away from all of this.

I want to be free of it all.

I want more than this shit life.

More than anything, I want Sebastian to come with me.

The front door to his house opens, and I don't wait for him to speak. "There's something wrong with me," I tell him, feeling every inch of my throat go dry and the pit in my stomach growing heavier and heavier. I heave the words up my throat. "Someone is killing them and if you don't believe me, that's fine." The last word cracks as I feel myself unraveling.

Sebastian stays by the door, completely still and watching me, watching as I transform into a lunatic in front of him. I don't know what he thinks of all this, of how often I'm nothing but an emotional mess. The nightmares, the list. I can't imagine what he thinks, he always brushes it aside, but I can't do it any longer.

"I can't pretend it's a coincidence."

He finally speaks, low and with a note of apprehension, "What brought this on? The text?"

My body is ice cold as I sit on the sofa, pulling my knees into my chest and refusing to look him in the eyes. "I don't think it's someone messing with me." I dare to peek up at him, willing him to feel the very real fear that keeps me on the edge of sanity.

"I wish I could kill him. Whoever it is that's fucking with you."

It shreds me inside to hear the pain in his voice. "I'm not crazy," I beg him to understand.

"I wrote that list, Bastian. I wrote it." The confession is so close, it's begging to come out and be brought to life. With each word scarring its way through my chest, I give in to the weight of it. "And my name was on that list. I wanted them dead and I wanted to die," I tell him as the tears prick at the back of my eyes and I hold myself closer.

Tears leak down my cheek as I rest my heated face against my knee. "I don't want to die," I repeat the one thing I know to be true right now, even if that hasn't always been the case.

"Shh," Bastian shushes me, coming closer and sitting next to me on his sofa. I'll never know how he so easily comforts me, how he doesn't hesitate to wipe my tears away and pull me into his arms. When I'm like this, on the brink of insanity.

"I'm not crazy," I whisper and wonder if it's true.

He rocks me as I gasp for air and try to force the crying to stop. "It's my fault they died," I whisper the harsh truth and his rocking stops, but then continues. My heart races, needing him to tell me something. Anything. To tell me I'm not crazy and that he'd run away with me. That's what I want more than anything.

"Please," I beg him, but I don't have the strength to voice the only thing I've ever wanted.

"There's nothing on the news about Dave," he tells me after a long moment. My head shakes, wanting him to listen to me and believe me. I don't care what's on the news; I know what I feel in my gut.

"I need you to believe me." I try to convince him as I say, "I can feel it. I know it. Whoever it is, they aren't lying."

I'm holding him so tightly; my knuckles turn white. "I can't go to the cops, and I can't run from whoever it is. I feel helpless, Bastian." I've felt helpless for so long and there's only so much a person can take before it turns to hopelessness. "I don't know what to do." The last words are barely spoken. All that lives inside of me now is true fear.

"You need to relax," he tells me softly, but his steely eyes aren't cold. They hold so much sympathy that it nearly makes me break. As if there was any piece of me still whole.

"I can't explain this without sounding crazy," I tell him, although I can't look him in the eyes when I say it. I wipe at my face, hating how weak I am. I would give anything to be strong. "I could wait for the night to come. I have my gun--"

"Chlo, stop it," he warns me, his tone threatening.

"I could try to--"

"Stop it!" he yells at me, so loudly, it shakes me. My body's trembling as I try to get a grip. I have no one and no idea when it's coming. There's one more person before me if Dave is really dead. That's all I know.

"I don't want to live here anymore."

"Then what do you want to do?" he asks me with a hard look that would force me to be silent if it were on anyone else's face.

"I want to run away... for good." My body is numb as I hold my breath, waiting for him to say anything at all, but my chest squeezes with a new kind of pain when he says nothing.

"Please say something," I beg him.

"You have no idea what lengths I would go for you. But you need to stop this, please. Don't do this. Please, Chlo, for me." His words are a plea that rubs salt in the sharpest and deepest wounds I have.

"You don't understand." I take in a quick breath and then another, feeling lightheaded as I confess, "I heard my mom screaming for help and did nothing. I did nothing." I search his eyes for understanding, but also for the hate I felt for myself so long ago. "Whoever is killing them... if it has to do with her... they're going to come for me."

"Chloe, please," he tries to silence me, to brush it off again and I push his arm away instead of accepting the comfort that comes with his touch.

"I don't feel safe here," I tell him while backing away. "I won't stay here any longer." The words themselves are both freeing and suffocating.

I've never belonged here; I've always wanted a way out.

But I've always belonged to Sebastian. In every way. And the idea of running, to never see him again, is the most painful thing I could ever feel.

"Please," I beg him, not just to understand but to come with me.

"If you can't come with me," I try to be strong, to force the words out, but instead I turn into a blubbering fool. Covering my heated face with both of my hands, I feel the tears burn into my flesh.

"I'll never let you leave me," he tells me, and it only makes me cry harder. Because I don't want him to let me go, I want him to come with me. I need him to come with me. "I don't want to leave you." I gasp for air and give him a singular truth in a despite whisper, "I can't leave you."

He pulls me in close to him, even though I'm no help at all, covering my face and ashamed of what I've become.

"I just need time," he answers me and my head shakes of its own accord.

"I can't... I can't stay here anymore." The last words come out strangled as tears prick my eyes. I can't stay, but I can't leave without him either.

I swear I could be a better person. I could be happy and sane. But not here. All I am here is a name on a list. Waiting for my death.

"I love you, Chloe. I love you." Sebastian's voice is soothing as he wraps both of his arms around me. I crave his touch so much that I bury my head into his chest. He whispers, "I can take you away. We can leave tomorrow."

My body stills, my heart beating far too loud to be sure of what I heard. *Please, let me have heard right.* I can barely manage to swallow as I look into his steely blue eyes, praying he's telling me the truth and not just saying what he knows I want to hear.

He kisses my hair and then brushes it away from my face as he repeats himself, "I can run away with you."

"I love you, Bastian. I love you." The words tumble from my lips. "Please tell me you're telling the truth." I interlock my fingers with his, needing to feel him and know that he means it. "I want to run away with you."

"I love you," he tells me, his gaze never straying from mine, "we can't stay here. I can't stay here anymore."

SEBASTIAN

I did this to her.

But I wouldn't take it back.

I wouldn't take it back because I have her now. I'll run away with her, as far as she wants. I'll hold her every night and watch her fall asleep in my arms.

Always.

She'll never be without me again.

"Is there anyone you still want to talk to?" I ask her as I figure out every detail. Every single thing that has to be done before we leave. She's nestled in the crook of my arm in my bed, her small frame curved around my side. Her hair brushes my arm while she shakes her head. "No," she whispers. Clearing her throat, she adds, "I just want to leave."

I know she does. She's always wanted to leave. Ever since the first day I met her, I knew I'd run away with her if I could.

"I want you to leave your phone," I tell her, and she asks quickly, "Because of the person who texted about Dave?"

"Partly," I tell her honestly, feeling the anxiety spike inside of me. I don't want her to know the truth. I'll never tell her all of the truth. Never. "I don't know who it is. And I don't like that." I play the possessive card, although I'm sure she can see right through it. "If there's no one you want to call, I'd rather you just leave it behind."

She's quiet for a moment, but instead of asking questions, she concedes. "I can leave it behind. I can leave everything behind." I release a breath I didn't know I was holding and stroke her hair.

"There are a few things I have to do tomorrow. I'll run into work, come back, pack and then we leave." Adrenaline is coursing through me, knowing this is a decision I can't go back on. Once I leave, that's it. There's no coming back and I have no idea where we'll run to.

"Just like that?" she asks with slight disbelief, peeking up at me through her lashes.

"Just like that," I tell her and bend down to kiss her, listening to the bed groan in time with a faint siren from outside. No more streetlights drifting through the window, no more yelling down the street. No more of this city and the people in it. Wherever we go, I want it to be quiet and far, far away from here. I need somewhere we can escape to where no one will find us and where it'll feel like home.

"It's all going to be okay," I whisper against her hair before planting a small kiss on her forehead. She holds me tightly, like she'll never let me go. "It's all going to be all right."

"Promise me you'll run with me?" she asks me again like I'll back out of it.

"Tomorrow we pack up everything in one car," I tell her firmly, "and we leave." I'll do it. I'll leave it all behind to be with her and keep her safe.

"And we leave forever, promise me?" her voice begs me, and I swear I'd give her anything I could. Anything and everything I ever have will be hers.

She's tense at my side, waiting for my answer. I know there's no going back, but I choose her. It's always been her.

"As long as you love me forever," I give her my one condition, feeling the tension in my heart, needing her to agree and say she's mine forever.

"I can make that promise," she breathes, "I'll love you forever."

"I've always loved you," I whisper against her cheek. And it's true. There have never been truer words spoken.

* * *

I TURN NINE TOMORROW. I think, anyway. I want to ask the guy behind the counter, so I'll know for sure. I don't know why I care; I just want to know, I guess.

Peeking over my shoulder, I make sure Jim and my mom are occupied so I can go ask what day it is.

We just moved here. Mom took me with her, although part of me wishes she'd left me at Grandmom's, even if there's no one there anymore. At least I have the memories there. This city is different, everyone's always watching me. Looking at me like I'm going to do something so they can pick a fight.

They say I'm a bad kid. They say I'm angry.

I used to think they were wrong, but I don't anymore.

Boys like me are trouble. Too tall for my age, too smart for my own good. I'm not worth the air I breathe. That's Jim's new saying. He likes to remind me every chance he gets, even though he's the one giving my mom that shit that makes her go numb. He's the one who isn't worth the air he breathes but saying that only gets me punched in the face until I go numb too and black out.

I pull out the candy from my pocket. I only have two pieces left and as I pull out my hand, both of them drop to the floor and one rolls faster than I can catch it.

The candy stops rolling when it hits the edge of the counter and bounces off, only to stop in front of a small pair of shoes. They're white but scuffed up and I slowly lift my gaze to the owner of the shoes. To the short girl who's bending down to pick up my candy.

She can't have it!

My jaw's hard, and I clench my teeth even though the bruise there makes it hurt. My hands turn to fists. All I have left of my grandmom are these two pieces.

She can't have it!

She picks it up so delicately and carefully, then smooths out her dress. It's then that I notice how dirty it is like she's been sitting on the ground all day. It's wrinkled too. When she stands up her big doe eyes are filled with worry and she turns to look at a woman by the fridge doors. The woman's skinny, skinny like my mom. That's what I think as the bottles she's picking up clink together.

The girl looks like she wants to say something, but she's scared, so she says nothing. Her gaze drops to the ground, then she lifts her head back up to look around.

She's looking for me; I know she is.

The instant she sees me, the worry goes away and she smiles. A genuine smile that's just for me.

"Is this yours?" she offers in a soft voice that makes the anger go away. Only for a second though, because the moment she asks me, she peeks over at the woman and looks nervous to even be talking to me.

Because I'm a bad kid. That's why. Everyone knows it. Even her.

Her knees nearly buckle as she stands there, holding the candy out to me even though I'm feet away from her.

She's afraid to move. "My mom told me to stay here," she explains.

I nod and swallow the lump in my throat. She looks sad like me until she smiles at me, then it changes everything.

She's strange. Like she doesn't want to be here.

I may not belong here, but she doesn't either.

"Thanks," I tell her as I walk to her and she nervously looks between me and the woman again, her mom.

She's shy as she talks to me. "I haven't met you before." And then she smiles again, even sweeter this time. She smiles at me like her happiness was meant to belong to me. Like I could take that happiness from her. Like I could be happy too. "I'm Chloe Rose."

CHLOE

*M*aybe if I leave, the nightmares will go away.

Places hold memories. They can't help it. The image of a dented brass doorknob comes to mind. I'll never forget the memory of what put that dent into the hard metal. The sound of a click against a window, the window he crept through late at night. It can't help but exist, yet it carries so much heaviness with it. So much more than just an object, so much more than just a place.

I'm done crying; I'm done remembering.

I think I've been ready to leave for a long time. Longer than the time that first light went out on the street and I had the urge to run in such a primitive way. I think I was ready to run the first time Bastian's lips pressed against mine. My heart knew it, but it would only beat if he came with me.

There's a method to the way I place each item in the old duffle bag. I was given the bag in gym class one year in high school. It was a promotion for some sports drink and I think it could carry at least two weeks' worth of clothes. That's all I need.

Each piece fits in easily. My books I can put in a cardboard box and place in the back. I'll always need my books.

Other than my clothes, I don't know what I'll take. Toiletries, obviously. But these photographs aren't mine and the ones I have, I don't want.

The light catches the glass of a photo on the far right of the wall. A photo of my mother when she was young, and I was in her arms. I don't remember that far back, but my uncle said she loved me deeply. That she bundled me up in that picture because it was so cold out and she was worried about taking me outside for the photos.

She loved me once.

But she loved the alcohol more.

I'm okay with it. I'm okay with it all. Because I survived, and I still know how to love. A piece of me will always love her. I'll love the woman in this photo because she's not the woman in my nightmares.

My fingertips brush along the edges of the frame as my throat tightens and I wish I could go back to that time to tell her. I wish I could go back to so much.

You can only move forward, a voice tells me, and I close my eyes, letting the last tears fall. They linger on my lashes as I open my eyes again and say goodbye to her, leaving the photo where it is.

I carelessly brush them away, gazing at the full duffle bag as my phone pings. It's only one of two people. I already know that.

Please tell me you're okay. I read the text message from Angie and my heart sinks. I think I would have been good friends with her. Even though neither of us ever belonged here. I'm grateful to leave, but I don't know how much this place will take from her before she walks away, if she can even walk away.

I don't know why she'd stay here any longer than she has to. But it's her choice, and she knows what she's doing. Maybe me leaving will push her to run; I try to justify leaving her in the dark with the thought of her being warned to stay away with my disappearance. I can only hope that's what she does.

There's not a damn thing good that lives in Crescent Hills.

Answer me, she texts me, but I don't text her back. The next time it pings, I turn off the phone without looking.

Bastian said it's better to just disappear and for no one to know where we've gone. He's right, and I don't want anyone to come looking for me. If I could disappear and be lost in the wind with Bastian forever, I would. Tonight, I'm going to try to do just that.

I leave the phone on the bed, on the sheets that never belonged to me. It can stay there and when the men come and take everything inside because the bills go unpaid, they can have it.

They can have every piece of what's here.

It never belonged to me and I'm done belonging to it.

SEBASTIAN

I can't stop staring at the note on the counter. It's only a Post-it with the words, "Leaving for the weekend – Seb" written on the yellow square. Eddie will get it on Monday, or maybe this weekend if anyone comes in. The shop is supposed to be empty, with most of the guys going down to the docks for Romano this weekend. There's a large order of coke coming in. And the butcher shop isn't needed for that.

I'll leave a note and I'll ghost. He can try to find me all he wants, but I'm done with Romano and this place. Just as the thought hits me, I hear the bells chime at the front door and a chill seeps into my veins.

"Eddie," I greet him with a grin, hiding the fact that I didn't want anyone to know I was leaving until I was gone. I didn't want anyone to ask questions. "What are you doing here?" I ask and casually lean against the counter. The spool of butcher's cord is right below me. All of us who work in the shop are familiar with it; we use it to secure packages and orders.

I don't reach for it yet, but with the pounding of my blood, I know it's going to end like this. The desire to get it over with forces a numbness through my fingers and I shake it off, smiling as he answers me.

"What am I doing? How about, what the fuck are you doing here?" He shoots me a twisted grin as if he's being friendly, but the look in his eyes is filled with the psychotic glee he's known for. "I heard Romano wants to talk to you," he adds as he walks to the counter, the sound of his boots slapping against the floor in time with the pounding of my heart. He tosses the keys to the shop down on the counter and leans closer to me just as I reach for the cord.

I wind it over my fingers under the counter. The dumb fuck is so hellbent on letting me know my days are numbered in the darkened butcher shop that he doesn't realize his own imminent demise is only a moment away.

"Seems he thinks you have something to do with those assholes coming up dead," he tells me, eyeing me and then glancing out the window as the headlights of a passing car shine through the glass.

Dread rips through me, thinking it's someone else and I won't have time to finish Eddie off, but it's not. The lights flash and keep on going, heading down to the mechanic shop behind us.

"Why would he think that?" I ask him, wrapping the rope around once more and then starting on the other hand. I leave less than a foot of cord between the two. Enough to get the thin rope over his head, but not so much that it'll be too loose when I choke him out.

"Someone said Marcus came looking for information and was directed to you."

My lungs halt and a harsh thud slams in my chest. I ask him quietly, knowing the smirk on my face is dimming and finding it hard to swallow, "And who would that be?"

"Yours truly," he gives me the answer with his grin widening. "It was kind of a test," he tells me as I take in a single deep breath and grip the rope tightly with both hands, my thumbs running along the rough bundles that are fastened around both my hands. "And you failed, Sebastian." For the first time, his smile fades and he shrugs. "I'm sure there's a reason though," he says, feigning sympathy.

I nod once, making it look like I'm full of regret. And I am. I regret not killing this fucker sooner.

In one swift moment, my arms are up and around his head. He tries to turn and get out of my reach, but all that does is spin him around, so his back is to my chest as I get the rope right where I want it.

His feet come back first, trying to kick me as his hands reach up and try to grab the rope before it tightens. He gets the tip of two fingers in the loop, but I don't give a fuck. I'm squeezing so tight I can't breathe, I can't move. My muscles are on fire and my teeth grind together as I grunt out the pain. His large body slams into me, shoving me against the back wall. I grit my teeth as his boots squeak against the floor as he throws his head back into my shoulder.

He throws his body to the left, knocking us both into the tables and I almost lose my grip as I fall hard, smacking the side of my head against the edge of one chair as we tumble to the floor, but I hold on with everything I have, feeling the thin rope dig in deeper.

I watch his face closely, seeing how red his eyes are getting and how pale his face is.

His cheeks puff out as his strength wanes. Another kick, but this one's weaker. A few more seconds and his head lolls. I still can't breathe, and I pull back harder, feeling the rope nearly cut into his fingers, giving it more slack as the bones break. I hold on tight for another moment, and he doesn't react. He's limp and heavy, his dead eyes bloodshot and staring ahead at nothing.

When I finally release him, I have to slowly unwind the rope and bring the circulation back to my numb fingers. It's still dark as I pick up the chairs and tables, grabbing Eddie's corpse by the ankles to move him out of the way. There's no blood, no sign of a struggle. I check the wall we crashed into, feeling the burn and sting of my muscles. I'll bruise, but there's no dents or any sign of what happened. And that's what matters.

My shoulders burn as I drag his heavy ass to the back, kicking the swinging door open and pulling him through the kitchen to get to where the freezers are. He isn't the first and he won't be the last dead body to be stored here.

I shut the door hard, giving it the last of my anger and locking it with a loud click that resonates through every inch of me. My body is still on fire, my pulse hammering in my ears.

Shipments come on Mondays. I'll be long gone by then. I lock the freezer and look down at my hands. They're red and the skin is ripped from the rough rope digging into them. Swallowing thickly and breathing in deeply to calm the adrenaline still racing through me, I let a moment pass.

* * *

SITTING IN THE CAR, I'm still making sure I've thought through every bit of this.

Romano will send people to watch out for me to return, and he'll send people out looking for me, I know he will. He'll never find us though and I'm never coming back. I already know that.

Marcus will let me go, so long as everything happens the way it's supposed to tomorrow.

Carter though. I can't stop thinking about leaving him behind. Ever since we got in the car, I haven't let go of Chloe Rose's hand. She gives me the strength I've never had, but nothing can help me with this. With saying goodbye to him.

The keys jingle as I turn off the ignition after pulling up in front of Carter's house.

"Stay in the car," I tell her, turning off the headlights and passing the keys to her hand. Her fingers against mine still ignite something primitive and deep inside of me.

It stirs a warmth in my heart I never thought existed.

Her baby blue eyes plead with me not to stop, to just keep going and never look back. I lean forward, spearing my fingers in her hair and resting my forehead against hers. "I won't be long, I promise," I whisper against her lips.

She's quick to take a kiss, pressing her lips against mine and then pulling away to nuzzle the tip of her nose against mine.

"Kiss me first," she demands softly, with her eyes closed and her hands on my thigh. Her fingers lay across my jeans and when she tries to scoot closer to me, the sound of her nails against the denim is all I can hear along with my heart beating faster.

It beats fast and steady for her.

"I can tell that you love me when you kiss me," she whispers, her eyes looking deep into mine as the moonlight caresses her face. "Part of me can. Even if my mind can't keep up," she adds.

"Your mind can't keep up?" I ask her with a hint of a smile on my lip as I cup her chin. My gaze leaves her as I see a shadow on the sidewalk. Carter's outside and waiting for me.

Chloe shrugs, although it's a sad movement. "There's just something about the way you kiss me," she tells me.

"I love you, Chloe Rose," I tell her and as she parts her lips to tell me the same, I press my own against hers, slipping my tongue through the seam she gives me. She deepens the kiss, but for only a moment. My heart races and my blood heats.

She was always meant to be mine.

The second our lips part, both of us breathing heavier, she whispers, "I love you too."

I know she does, and with the parting thought, I open my door and close it as quietly as I can, so I can go to Carter.

My best friend. Only friend. And the only family I ever had.

"I was wondering if you'd come tonight," Carter says while I'm still a few feet away.

"Is that right?" I ask him as I walk up. Out here is more in the sticks than Dixon Street. All I can hear are grasshoppers and some kids playing ball in the street a block down.

Carter only nods in response and I can't fucking stand what I'm about to do.

"I have something to ask you," I start out and then backtrack. "How's it going? You guys doing all right?"

Carter gives me a weak smile and a half-assed laugh before kicking the ground. "Get on with it, man." His eyes reflect the way I feel. Like he already knows it's coming.

"Maybe we should settle the other thing first," I tell him, more willing to put an end to that shit than I am to say my final goodbye to him.

"Is it done?" Carter asks me the second I hesitate to speak. Standing outside of his house on the cracked sidewalk, he shoves both of his hands in his leather jacket pockets. He looks anxious as his eyes dart between the car and me. "I've got this feeling," he starts to tell me and then swallows visibly, before shaking his head.

I grip both of his shoulders and look him in the eyes. "It's done," I tell him with a strength that's undeniable. "Marcus left the cash yesterday."

"Cash?"

"I didn't know either. I thought it was, do what he said or die. I didn't expect the money."

Peeking over my shoulder, I take a look back at Chloe, my sweet innocent girl who will never know any of this shit. I'll protect her from it and from the man I was before her until my last breath. With the stack of cash in my pocket, I reach for it as I watch Chloe stare straight ahead at the dead-end street we'll never drive down again.

"Here it is," I say and hand it over to Carter, opening up his jacket and shoving it in before he can tell me he doesn't want it.

I'm the one who was told to kill them, all the names on the photocopy of the list that Marcus gave me. Marcus told me in the alley behind the butcher shop that he wanted information.

He gave me a list, and I was to get information for him and not say shit to Romano. I wasn't supposed to ask questions. There are whispers of Marcus, but no one ever sees him. He stays in shadows and they say if you ever see him, you're dead.

I was scared shitless that he chose me, and I was ready to do whatever he said to stay off his radar.

But her name was there.

It was right fucking there at the bottom of the list. I had to tell him whatever he wanted with this list, it couldn't be her. I had to beg for her life. He wanted them all dead. Every one of them.

Not her was all I could tell him.

However, he got a hold of Chloe's list, for whatever reason, she hadn't erased her name yet. The photocopy had her name there, written clearly at the bottom. And he'd added the last names in his own handwriting. At the time, I thought it was odd that two people had each written half of the names, but I never guessed it was her that wrote the list, I would never have known.

She'd made a list of who she blamed, or hated, I don't know which is more true. But Marcus decided it would be a hit list and now was the time for all of them to die.

I've never known fear like I did when I told Marcus it couldn't be her. I told him she couldn't die. Anyone but her.

He said he would spare her, but that he didn't want information anymore. He wanted them all dead in the span of three weeks and he didn't care how.

I bartered for her life, and then I killed them all. Each and every one. I set their deaths in motion. I paid off a thug with a pack of heroin to take care of Amber. Tamra was a bullet in her head. I can still hear the ringing in my ears. I'm a murderer.

But I did it to spare Chlo. I had to do it. I'd do it again if kept her safe. I don't care what kind of man that makes me, so long as she's still breathing.

Tomorrow is day twenty, leaving a single day to spare of his morbid deadline.

"Andrea picks up her package tomorrow. Can you just make sure she gets it?" I ask Carter. Andrea gets an eightball of coke on the regular. I knew that's how she needed to go when she came to the shop two weeks ago, but Marcus wanted them done in order. So, she had to wait until tomorrow.

Now I wonder if he requested that on purpose. If somehow, he knew it'd freak Chlo out and that's why he texted her the way he did.

He's a sick fuck, but I lived up to my end of the bargain.

"She's done, and it's done," I tell him. It's laced with so much shit, it'll be quick and easy. Marcus won't come looking for us. It'll all be over with.

We'll run away, and this nightmare will be over.

Dave was an accident, Carter's accident. He didn't know he was on the list, but Dave had it coming to him regardless, for what he did to Carter and his family. I could never blame Carter for what he did. It's his story to tell, even if it did fuck him up more than it should have. The fucker was going to die anyway. I told him that.

Carter's not a killer; he's not meant for this life.

"The money's yours. I can at least give you that," I tell him, knowing that money won't go far with the debt they have. But it's better than nothing.

"Take it back," Carter tells me angrily. "I don't want it."

"Maybe not, but you need it," I tell him, putting my hands up to refuse the money and then looking back to make sure Chloe can't see.

She can never know.

"I know you're leaving." Carter's voice breaks. I don't know how he knew. Word spreads fast, but if that's going around, Romano is going to hear it before long and that means I need to get the fuck out of here as fast as I can. I don't need him looking for me, or worse, finding the body I left in his shop before the weekly deliveries on Monday.

"Who told you?" I ask him, my pulse beating harder in my temples. My jaw stiffens with the fear of a fight coming.

"No one," he answers, "but I know when goodbyes are coming."

Time passes slowly, and I feel myself breaking down. My first reaction is to go to Chloe Rose. I forget it all with her. I forget who I am and all the pain that comes with it. With her, I'm not alone.

"You need it. You can't run far without cash." He gives me a look of complete sincerity as he pushes it back into my hand. "It's not for me, and I don't want it." His voice is clear like he knew I'd give it to him.

"I have enough cash," I tell him. "Take it for your brothers then." My heart squeezes harder in my chest knowing how fucked they all are. It's two grand, and two grand more than he'll get selling dope on the street corner like he thinks he can do. I worked for Romano, but Carter doesn't. And it's not safe.

Carter gives me a weak smile and shakes his head. "We'll be all right. I'm heading up to the north side. I'll take care of us." I know that means he's dealing something. Although what and for who, I don't know.

His eyes are so serious. He seems so much older to me now.

"You can come with me," I tell him. "I don't want to leave you here. Come with us."

The weak smile is pulled into a smirk, one cloaked with sadness. Goodbyes are never easy, but they shouldn't hurt this much. "Don't stay here," I beg him. "I want more for you than this."

"I can't leave my brothers," he tells me and then licks his lips before handing the money back to me. "Take it." The bills brush against my knuckles and I'm reluctant to take it, but I do. "Find a better place than here." The money weighs heavy in my hand as he pulls his away. I won't take it. If anything, I'll leave it in the mailbox and pray one of them finds it.

"It's good you're skipping out," Carter tells me in a tone that lets me know something's up.

"What's going on?" I ask him, feeling my nerves ramp up.

"I heard Eddie say Romano wants to talk to you on Monday. I think they know you're involved and they're pissed they didn't know."

"Good thing I won't be around Monday." I start thinking about all the possible outcomes of that meeting and I don't like a single one of them. I could never rat Marcus out, he'd kill me. And even if I did, Romano would kill me for following someone else's orders. I have protection from no one and enemies everywhere.

"Did you tell her?" Carter changes the subject abruptly. "Does she know you killed them?"

I shake my head, wishing all of this was a nightmare I could wake from. All of it but Chloe. "I had to lie to her, but it's never felt like that," I tell him, confiding in my best friend one last time.

"Felt like what?" he asks me.

"Felt like I was hurting her by lying to her. I've never wanted so much from someone and to give her so much in return."

He smiles a genuine but sad smile that reaches his dark eyes. "I knew you loved her," he says lightheartedly. Brushing his thumb against his nose, he peeks behind him. It's darker now than it was before, not a single star in the sky to cast light down on us.

"I think it is love," I tell him and kick the rubble on the broken concrete.

"It's all right to say it," he jokes, "I won't make fun of you."

"I only just got her. I can't lose her, Carter," I confess to him. If it wasn't for her need to run away from here, I'd stay for him.

"Go ahead, I'll be all right," he tells me, and I want to believe him. "Hey, do you have that stuff though? Before you go?"

It takes me a minute to realize he's talking about the sweets. I have the last vial in my pocket and I know Chlo is never going to want to take it again, so I hand it over to him.

He's quick to slip the vial into his pocket. "Thanks, man. It's been rough sleeping."

Giving him a nod of understanding, I wonder if I should tell him that Chlo thinks some of her paranoia is from the drug, but I think she's wrong. She was right the entire time. Call it fear and intuition maybe.

"I hope it helps you sleep," I tell him and then glance back at the car.

"Get out of here, man. Get out while you still can," Carter tells me and it fucking hurts that I'm leaving him, but I have to. I have to get the hell out of here and take Chloe far away.

I have to reach out and hug him, pulling him hard into my chest. And he's quick to give me a hard pat on the back, followed by a grip I'll never forget.

There's no way I'd have made it out alive without him. I know that much.

Before the tears can show, I pull away from him, the only family I've ever had. "She can't stay here," I tell him as if I'm begging him to understand, but he already knows.

She's never belonged here.

"Come with us," I plead with him one last time even though I already know his answer.

"I have to stay." His voice is calm this time like he's resigned to his fate.

EPILOGUE

Two weeks later
Chloe

The cool wind flows through my fingers as I rest my hand against the window. We've been off the highway for a little while now, still venturing into the unknown.

It's odd how the unfamiliar can offer so much comfort. How easy it is to leave everything behind and start a new life.

Countless times I've felt the fear of what could be waiting for us if we ever went back. And almost as if Bastian can read my mind, he asks me every time we stop somewhere new, "How about this place?"

"I can be a butcher anywhere. Or anything. We can be anything," he keeps telling me. "Just don't leave me." He says that a lot. As if I'd ever want to. One day, I think he'll know in every way that I'll never do that.

In every beat of my heart, I know I was supposed to run away with him. And he was supposed to run away with me.

We should have left when we were only children. We shouldn't have stayed in that place as long as we did. When the lights around you flicker and dim, it's a sign to run. To run far away and toward light and hope. It's an innate feeling I knew deep in my gut, but I swallowed it down and nearly let the darkness choke out what little life I had left in me.

It's only taken days of being away with Bastian at my side, holding my hand as we drive farther and farther away to know that's true.

I can smell the salty ocean air as the sun kisses my skin through the window. We're close to the ocean.

A line springs to mind and I jot it down in my notebook. It's half-full already, with ideas for a book so close to what I've been through. Some changes here and there because it's hard to write about the truth. It's hard to imagine what people would think of me if I told them my story. It's even harder for me to write it all down and to be okay with everything that happened. Because of what happened in my life, the things that were done to me and the things I did... well, it will never be okay, but maybe it would make a memorable tale.

"Do you want to stop here?" Bastian asks, pointing to the left at a sign for a burger place.

My shoulders lift easily in a contented shrug. With my cheek resting against the headrest, I ask him for the tenth time since we left, "Where do you think we're going?" I need answers to what we'll become. I know I love him and I only want to be with him, but the stirring in my stomach that this is too good to be true hasn't let up.

Bastian's large hand wraps around mine as he pulls my knuckles to his lips to kiss them one by one. The car idles at the stop sign and he looks me deep in my eyes.

"We're going where we're supposed to go. Together." His words are a balm to my broken soul. It's the only word that matters. It's the only word that's ever mattered. *Together*.

With tears pricking my eyes, the tears I wish would go away, even if they are from a happiness I never thought I'd feel, I whisper, "I love you."

He braces his hands on either side of my head, stealing a ravenous kiss from me, taking my pain away like he did so many years ago. But the pain now is minuscule and it's because of him. He's taken it all away. And I'll spend my life making sure I do the same for him.

With a bruising kiss, I can hardly breathe until he pulls away from me, letting the tip of his nose brush against mine. His eyes are still closed, his hands still tangled in my hair as he tells me, "I've always loved you. And I'll never stop loving you. I'll always choose you."

* * *

Sebastian
Years later

ABOUT TWO WEEKS after we got in the car and sped away as fast as we could, I got a call from Carter's brother, Daniel. I didn't let her see as I broke down against the bathroom door of the motel we'd stayed in for the night. We'd move from one place to the next, constantly on the go until we found a spot on the West Coast, far away from Crescent Hills. A local bed and breakfast was looking to hire a butcher for their farm and also in need of a bookkeeper for the inn. Fate gave us our opportunity to stay, to find a new home, and we did. We grabbed it with both hands and didn't let go.

That night in the motel though, it almost didn't happen. The first few days we were on the road, everything changed with a single phone call. I almost got into the car and drove back to that hellhole when Daniel told me what happened. I would never have brought Chloe, but she wouldn't have let me leave her behind either.

The Talvery crew almost beat him to death the night we left. Carter nearly died for selling on the wrong turf. Daniel told me not to come back, that my name had been marked now, and I knew what that meant. If I went back, I was dead.

When I talked to Carter, I knew I'd made a mistake letting him stay. He had no one anymore, and everyone to provide for.

If I could go back, I would.

I'd never leave him behind.

It took over a decade before I dared show my face in that city again. Years of the phone calls coming less and less often. Years of building a life with the girl I always loved, while the memories of my past faded to bad dreams.

Life is a compromise. I left behind a friend, destined to stay, and be held captive to a city that had no mercy.

It would force him to become a brutal man I didn't recognize.

The Carter I abandoned in Crescent Hills, died that night I ran, and I'll never forgive myself for it.

The End.

Carter's story is available now!
Keep reading for a sneak peek ...

Click here to sign up to my mailing list, where you'll get *exclusive* giveaways, free books and new release alerts!

Follow me on BOOKBUB to be the first to know about my sales!

Sign up for Text Alerts:
US residents: Text WILLOW to 797979
UK residents: Text WWINTERS to 82228

And if you're on Facebook, join my reader group, Willow Winters' Wildflowers for special updates and lots of fun!

SNEAK PEEK AT ALL HE'LL EVER BE

From *USA Today* bestselling author W Winters comes a heart-wrenching, edge-of-your-seat gripping, romantic suspense.

I should've known she would ruin me the moment I saw her.
    Women like her are made to destroy men like me.
    I couldn't resist her though.
    Given to me to start a war; I was too eager to accept.

But I didn't know what she'd do to me. That she would change everything.
    She sees through me in a way no one else ever has.
    Her innocence and vulnerability make me weak for her and I hate it.
    I know better than to give in to temptation.

· · ·

A ruthless man doesn't let a soul close to him.

A cold-hearted man doesn't risk anything for anyone.

A powerful man with a beautiful woman at his mercy … he doesn't fall for her.

CHAPTER 1

CARTER

*W*ar is coming.

It's something I've known for over two years.

Tick. Tock. Tick. Tock.

My jaw ticks in time with the skin over my knuckles turning white as my fist clenches tighter. The tension in my stiff shoulders rises and I have to remind myself to breathe in deep and let the strain of it all go away.

Tick. Tock. It's the only sound echoing off the walls of my office and with each passing of the pendulum the anger grows.

It's always like this before I go to a meet. This one in particular sends a thrill through my blood, the adrenaline pumping harder with each passing minute.

My gaze moves from the grandfather clock in my office to the shelves next to it and then beneath them to the box made of mahogany and steel. It's only three feet deep and tall and six feet long. It blends into the right wall of my office, surrounded by polished bookshelves that carry an aroma of old books.

I paid more than I should have simply to put on display. All any of this is a façade. People's perceptions are their reality. And so I paint the picture they need to see so I can use them as I see fit. The expensive books and paintings, polished furniture made of rare wood... All of it is bullshit.

Except for the box. The story that came with it will stay with me forever. In all of the years, it's the one of the few memories that I can pin point as a defining moment. The box never leaves me.

The words from the man who gave it to me are still as clear as is the memory of his pale green eyes, glassed over as he told me his story.

About how it kept him safe when he was a child. He told me how his mother had shoved him in it to protect him.

I swallow thickly, feeling my throat tighten and the cord in my neck strain with the memory. He painted the picture so well.

He told me how he clung to his mother seeing how panicked she was. But he did as he was told, he stayed quiet in the safe box and could only listen while the men murdered his mother.

It was the story he gave me with the box he offered to barter for his life. And it reminded me of my own mother telling me goodbye before she passed.

Yes, his story was touching, but the defining moment is when I put the gun to his head and pulled the trigger regardless.

He tried to steal from me and then pay me with a box as if the money he laundered was a debt or a loan. William was good at stealing, at telling stories, but the fucker was a dumb prick.

I didn't get to where I am by playing nicely and being weak. That day I took the box that saved him as a reminder of who I was. Who I needed to be.

I made sure that box has been within my sight for every meeting I've had in this office. It's a reminder for me so I can stare at it in this god forsaken room as I make deal after deal with crim-inal after criminal and collect wealth and power like the dusty old books on these shelves.

It cost me a fortune to get this office exactly how I wanted. But if it were to burn down, I could buy it all over again.

Everything except for that box.

"You really think they're going through with it?" I hear Daniel, my brother, before I see him. The memories fade in an instant and my heart beat races faster than the tick tock of that fucking clock.

It takes a second for me to be conscious of my facial expression, to relax it and let go of the anger before I can raise my gaze to his.

"With the war and the deal? You think he'll go through with it?" he clarifies.

A small huff leaves me, accompanied by a smirk, "He wants this more than anything else," I answer him.

Daniel stalks into the room slowly, the heavy door to my office closing with a soft kick of his heel before he comes to stand across from me.

"And you're sure you want to be right in the middle of it?"

I lick my lower lip and stand from my desk, stretching as I do and turning my gaze to the window in my office. I can hear Daniel walking around the desk as I lean against it and cross my arms.

"We won't be in the middle of it. It'll be the two of them, our territory is close, but we can stay back."

"Bullshit. He wants you to fight with him and he's going to start this war tonight and you know it."

I nod slowly, the smell of Romano's cigars filling my lungs at the memory of him.

"There's still time to call it off," Daniel says and it makes my brow pinch and place a crease on my forehead. He can't be that naïve.

It's the first time I've really looked at him since he's been back. He spent years away. And every fucking day I fought for what we have. He's gone soft. Or maybe it's Addison that's turned him into the man standing in front of me.

"This war has to happen." My words are final and the tone is one not to be questioned. I may have grown this business on fear and anger. Each step forward followed by the hollow sound of a body dropping behind me, but that's not how it started. Y can't build an empire with blood stained hands and not expect death to follow you.

His dark eyes narrow as he pushes off the desk and moves closer to the window, his gaze flickering between me and the meticulously maintained garden stories below us.

"Are you sure you want to do this?" his voice is low and I barely hear it. He doesn't look back at me and a chill flows down my arms and the back of my neck as I take in his stern expression.

It takes me back years ago. Back to when we had a choice and chose wrong.

When whether or not we wanted to go through with it meant something.

"There are men to the left of us," I tell him as I step forward and close the distance between us. "There are men to the right. There is no possible outcome where we don't pick a side."

He nods once and slides his thumb across the stubble on his chin before looking back at me. "And the girl?" he asks me, his eyes piercing into mine and reminding me that both of us survived, both of us fought, and each of us has a tragic path that led us to where we are today.

"Aria?" I dare to speak her name and the sound of my smooth voice seems to linger in the space between us. I don't wait for him to acknowledge me, or her rather.

"She has no choice." My voice tightens as I say the words.

Clearing my throat, I lean my palms against the window, feeling the frigid fall beneath my hands and leaning forward to see Addison beneath us, Daniel's Addison. "What do you think they would have done to Addison if they'd succeeded in taking her?"

His jaw hardens but he doesn't answer my question. Instead he replies, "We don't know who it was who tried to take her from me."

I shrug as if it's semantics and not at all relevant. "Still. Women aren't meant to be touched, but they went for Addison first."

"That doesn't make it right," Daniel says with indignation in his tone.

"Isn't it better she come to us?" My head tilts as I question him and this time he takes a moment to respond.

"She's not one of us. Not like Addison and you know what Romano expects you to do with her."

"Yes, the daughter of the enemy..." My heart beats hard in my chest, and the steady rhythm reminds me of the ticking of the clock. "I know exactly what he wants me to do with her."

Click here to keep reading All He'll Ever Be (Merciless Series Collection of all 4 novels)

ALSO BY W. WINTERS

Read Willow's sexiest and most talked about romances in the
Merciless World

This Love Hurts Trilogy
This Love Hurts
But I Need You
And I Love You the Most

An epic tale of both betrayal and all-consuming love...
Marcus, the villain.
Cody Walsh, the FBI agent who knows too much.
And Delilah, the lawyer caught in between.

What I Would do for You (This Love Hurts Trilogy Collection)

A Kiss to Tell (a standalone novel)
They lived on the same street and went to the same school,
although he was a year ahead. Even so close, he was untouchable.

Sebastian was bad news and Chloe was the sad girl who didn't belong.
Then one night changed everything.

Possessive (a standalone novel)
It was never love with **Daniel Cross** and she never thought it would be. It was only lust from a distance. Unrequited love maybe.
He's a man Addison could never have, for so many reasons.

Merciless Saga
Merciless
Heartless
Breathless
Endless

Ruthless, crime family leader **Carter Cross** should've known Aria would ruin him the moment he saw her. Given to Carter to start a war; he was too eager to accept. But what he didn't know was what Aria would do to him. He didn't know that she would change everything.

All He'll Ever Be (Merciless Series Collection of all 4 novels)

Irresistible Attraction Trilogy
A Single Glance
A Single Kiss
A Single Touch

Bethany is looking for answers and to find them she needs one of the brothers of an infamous crime family, **Jase Cross**.
Even a sizzling love affair won't stop her from getting what she needs.

But Bethany soon comes to realise Jase will be her downfall, and she's determined to be his just the same.

Irresistible Attraction (A Single Glance Trilogy Collection)

Hard to Love Series
Hard to Love
Desperate to Touch
Tempted to Kiss
Easy to Fall

Eight years ago she ran from him.
Laura should have known he'd come for her. Men like **Seth King** always get what they want.
Laura knows what Seth wants from her, and she knows it comes with a steep price.
However it's a risk both of them will take.

Not My Heart to Break (Hard to Love Series Collection)

Tease Me Once
I'll Kiss You Twice
Tease me once... I'll kiss you twice.
Declan Cross' story from the Merciless World.

Spin off of the Merciless World

Love the Way Duet
Kiss Me
Hold Me
Love Me

With everything I've been through, and the unfortunate way we met, the last thing I thought I'd be focused on is the fact that I love the way you kiss me.

Extended epilogues to the Merciless World Novels
A Kiss To Keep (more of Sebastian and Chloe)
Seductive (more of Daniel and Addison)
Effortless (more of Carter and Aria)
Never to End (more of Seth and Laura)

Sexy, thrilling with a touch of dark Standalone Novels

Broken (Standalone)
Kade is ruthless and cold hearted in the criminal world.
They gave Olivia to him. To break. To do as he'd like.
All because she was in the wrong place at the wrong time. But there are secrets that change everything. And once he has her, he's never letting her go.

Forget Me Not (Standalone novel)
She loved a boy a long time ago. He helped her escape and she left him behind. Regret followed her every day after.
Jay, the boy she used to know, came back, a man. With a grip strong enough to keep her close and a look in his eyes that warned her to never dare leave him again.
It's dark and twisted.
But that doesn't make it any less of what it is.
A love story. Our love story.

It's Our Secret (Standalone novel)
It was only a little lie. That's how stories like these get started.
But with every lie Allison tells, **Dean** sees through it.
She didn't know what would happen. But with all the secrets and lies, she never thought she'd fall for him.

You Are Mine Series of Duets

You Are My Reason (You Are Mine Duet book 1)
You Are My Hope (You Are Mine Duet book 2)
Mason and Jules emotionally gripping romantic suspense duet.
One look and Jules was tempted; one taste, addicted.
No one is perfect, but that's how it felt to be in Mason's arms.
But will the sins of his past tear them apart?

You Know I Love You
You Know I Need You
Kat says goodbye to the one man she ever loved even though **Evan**
begs her to trust him.
With secrets she couldn't have possibly imagined, Kat is torn
between what's right and what was right for them.

Tell Me You Want Me
A sexy office romance with a brooding hero, **Adrian Bradford**,
who you can't help but fall head over heels for... in and out of the
boardroom.

Small Town Romance

Tequila Rose Book 1
Autumn Night Whiskey Book 2
He tasted like tequila and the fake name I gave him was Rose.
Four years ago, I decided to get over one man, by getting under
another. A single night and nothing more.
Now, with a three-year-old in tow, the man I still dream about is
staring at me from across the street in the town I grew up in. I
don't miss the flash of recognition, or the heat in his gaze.
The chemistry is still there, even after all these years.
I just hope the secrets and regrets don't destroy our second chance
before it's even begun.

A Little Bit Dirty

Contemporary Romance Standalones

Knocking Boots (A Novel)

They were never meant to be together.
Charlie is a bartender with noncommittal tendencies.
Grace is looking for the opposite. Commitment. Marriage. A baby.

Promise Me (A Novel)

She gave him her heart. Back when she thought they'd always be together.
Now **Hunter** is home and he wants Violet back.

Tell Me To Stay (A Novella)

He devoured her, and she did the same to him.
Until it all fell apart and Sophie ran as far away from **Madox** as she could.
After all, the two of them were never meant to be together?

Second Chance (A Novella)

No one knows what happened the night that forced them apart.
No one can ever know.
But the moment **Nathan** locks his light blue eyes on Harlow again, she is ruined.
She never stood a chance.

Burned Promises (A Novella)

Derek made her a promise. And then he broke it. That's what happens with your first love.
But Emma didn't expect for Derek to fall back into her life and for her to fall back into his bed.

Valetti Crime Family Series:
A HOT mafia series to sink your teeth into.

Dirty Dom
Becca came to pay off a debt, but **Dominic Valetti** wanted more.
So he did what he's always done, and took what he wanted.

His Hostage
Elle finds herself in the wrong place at the wrong time. The mafia
doesn't let witnesses simply walk away.
Regret has a name, and it's **Vincent Valetti**.

Rough Touch
Ava is looking for revenge at any cost so long as she can remember
the girl she used to be.
But she doesn't expect **Kane** to show up and show her kindness
that will break her.

Cuffed Kiss
Tommy Valetti is a thug, a mistake, and everything Tonya needs;
the answers to numb the pain of her past.

Bad Boy
Anthony is the hitman for the Valetti familia, and damn good at
what he does. They want men to talk, he makes them talk. They
want men gone, bang - it's done. It's as simple as that.
Until Catherine.

Those Boys Are Trouble (Valetti Crime Family Collection)

To Be Claimed Saga
A hot tempting series of fated love, lust-filled secrets and the
beginnings of an epic war.

643

Wounded Kiss
Gentle Scars

Collections of shorts and novellas

Don't Let Go
A collection of stories including:
Infatuation
Desires in the Night and Keeping Secrets
Bad Boy Next Door

Kisses and Wishes
A collection of holiday stories including:
One Holiday Wish
Collared for Christmas
Stolen Mistletoe Kisses

All I Want is a Kiss (A Holiday short)
Olivia thought fleeting weekends would be enough and it always
was, until the distance threatened to tear her and **Nicholas** apart
for good.

Highest Bidder Series:

Bought
Sold
Owned
Given
From USA Today best selling authors, Willow Winters and Lauren
Landish, comes a sexy and forbidden series of standalone
romances.

Highest Bidder Collection (All four Highest Bidder Novels)

Bad Boy Standalones, cowritten with Lauren Landish:

Inked
Tempted
Mr. CEO
Three novels featuring sexy powerful heroes.
Three romances that are just as swoon-worthy as they are
tempting.

Simply Irresistible (A Bad Boy Collection)

Forsaken, (A Dark Romance cowritten with B. B. Hamel)
Grace is stolen and gifted to him; Geo a dominating, brutal and a
cold hearted killer.
However, with each gentle touch and act of kindness that lures her
closer to him, Grace is finding it impossible to remember why she
should fight him.

View Willow's entire collection and full reading order at
willowwinterswrites.com/reading-order

Happy reading and best wishes,
Willow xx

ABOUT WILLOW WINTERS

Thank you so much for reading my romances. I'm just a stay at home mom and avid reader turned author and I couldn't be happier.
I hope you love my books as much as I do!

More by W Winters
www.willowwinterswrites.com/books/

Sign up for my Newsletter to get all my romance releases, sales, sneak peeks and a **FREE** Romance, **Burned Promises**

If you prefer *text alerts* so you don't miss any of my new releases, text
US residents: Text WILLOW to 797979
UK residents: Text WWINTERS to 82228

Contact W Winters

BOOKBUB | TWITTER | GOODREADS | TIKTOK
INSTAGRAM | FACEBOOK PAGE | WEBSITE

Check out Willow Winters Wildflowers on Facebook.